Marc Elsberg is a for   debut novel, *Blackout*, a high-concept disast   er and one of the most successful thrillers of its kind   as also given a TEDx talk on the subject of the horror   cal grid failure. *Blackout* and his follow-up, *Zero*, were   Scientific Book of the Year in Germany. *Blackout* was named 1 ller of the Month by *The Times*. His latest bestselling thriller, *Greed*, contains cutting-edge research on the economy. He lives in Vienna, Austria.

Also by Marc Elsberg

Blackout

Zero

GREED

MARC ELSBERG

Translated from the German by Simon Pare

BLACK SWAN

TRANSWORLD PUBLISHERS
61–63 Uxbridge Road, London W5 5SA
www.penguin.co.uk

Transworld is part of the Penguin Random House group of companies
whose addresses can be found at global.penguinrandomhouse.com

Penguin
Random House
UK

First published in Great Britain in 2020 by Black Swan
an imprint of Transworld Publishers

Published by arrangement with Literary Agency Michael Gaeb

A CIP catalogue record for this book
is available from the British Library.

ISBN
9781784163471

Typeset in 11/14 pt Sabon LT Std by Jouve (UK), Milton Keynes
Printed and bound in Great Britain by Clays Ltd, Elcograf S.p.A.

Penguin Random House is committed to a sustainable
future for our business, our readers and our planet. This book
is made from Forest Stewardship Council® certified paper.

1 3 5 7 9 10 8 6 4 2

*For Alma, Alois, Anna, Elisa, Erik, Georg(s),
Itta, Kick, Lina, Matthias, Moritz, Nadine, Noah,
Paul, Phillip, Sebastian, Theo, Tibbe, Ursula,
Valerie and every other young person*

Weighing Day

Dana wiped the sweat from her brow. She leaned on her scythe and surveyed the golden fields. The air was quivering in the midsummer heat. The bodies of the other mowers all around Dana swayed and twisted to the rhythmic swoosh of their scythes over the sea of waving heads of grain. *It's like a dance*, Dana thought, *a slow, contemplative dance of life and death – the infinite cycle of nature*. Every swipe sent another swathe of grain toppling to the ground, the stalks collapsing like men in front of a firing squad. The reaping made a series of shifting steps in the landscape, and by the end of the day all that remained were dry spears poking randomly out of the soil like stubble on an old man's wrinkled face. Scattered across the fields like tiny volcanoes stood stacks of sheaves, bundles of the precious grain that would feed Dana and her family through the winter and well into the following year. Until next spring, when the future would sprout from it again, just as it had year after year for generations.

It had been a good year for Dana and her family. The weather had been kind, and the cold winter had blanketed the seeds in the soil and frozen all the pests. The warm spring had then tempted the young shoots forth into the air, and the generous early summer rains had driven them upwards from the fertile soil. Storms, hail and fungal diseases had spared them, and there had been sufficient rain at the right times over the hot summer to endow them with the life force they would pass on to Dana and all the other villagers in the form of porridge and bread and maybe the occasional slice of cake.

She gazed over at Bill's field in the distance where the heads of grain were dancing too. Dana wondered how he'd fared this year.

Weighing day was here. Once the sheaves had dried in the fields, Dana and her family gathered them together and carried them back to the farm. There, over hours of back-breaking toil, they threshed the grain from the chaff, then put the usual share in their granaries as food for the winter and seed for the following year. The remainder was poured into sacks and driven by ox-cart to the market in the local town. Dana was looking forward to the hive of activity there. She, Ann, Bill, Carl and the other farmers in the village would each sell their crop to the highest bidder and when they returned home that evening they would celebrate as they did every year.

Bill greeted them with a broad grin at the merchant's scales. A stocky man with blue eyes and thick black hair, he was heaving his own sacks on to the scales under the trader's beady eye.

'Bet I brought in more than you this year,' he said. 'More than any of you.'

Dana shrugged. She didn't care if she'd harvested more or less than Bill. She'd be satisfied if they could all make it through the winter and if her crop earned her enough money to send her children to school and make some urgent repairs to the house. She might even be able to afford a new cow.

The merchant weighed her produce too.

'You had a good year,' he said with an appreciative nod to Dana. 'Your yields are much higher than Bill's.'

'We both had a good year,' she answered. 'No pests, no drought, no hail and no floods.'

She could tell Bill was disappointed and angry though. He'd always been desperate to be the best, even as a child. He would always measure himself against others, issuing challenges, preferring competition to play. He was determined to win every race and stand at the top of the podium. He farmed the same rich soils as Dana and grew the same grain. They had the same amount of land; they lived under the same sky with the same weather conditions. Bill worked just as hard as Dana and was equally good at what he did. He was a nice guy, in fact, and good-looking to boot. Dana was quite attracted to him, but she found his belligerent approach to life tedious, especially because she was more successful than he was.

'There's something fishy going on!' Bill cried. 'I slaved away all year, I did everything properly, but you still had a better harvest than I did – three years in a row now! How does this keep happening?'

These idiot men and their thin skins! Any minute now, he'll be accusing me of witchcraft! Might be time to let him know my little secret, Dana thought.

FIRST DECISION

'At the beginning of all life, a few self-copying chemical structures obey a mathematical principle that gives them an advantage.'

Will Cantor

FIRST DECISION.

I

The streets were on fire. Thick clouds of smoke drifted over the asphalt. Molotov cocktails exploded like falling meteorites in balls of flame and acrid smog. Occasional black ghosts darted through the fog, vanishing from one place only to reappear in another.

'It's full-scale war out here!' roared Melanie Amado, ducking.

A dark mass of people emerged from the haze behind her. Heads, shoulders, placards and banners.

'What do those say?' Ed Silverstein asked, zooming in on the banners the demonstrators were holding up.

End greed! Homes for people, not property for speculators! Yes to universal basic income! I can't afford a lobbyist! Peace now! Death to capitalism! Climate action now!

Amado clutched her microphone more tightly. 'With the bursting of the corporate debt bubble, the risk of a financial crisis has reached a similar level to that of 2008. The climate crisis is escalating. Hundreds of thousands of people have poured into the streets of Berlin to merge with climate activists and protest against a new era of austerity designed to save banks and companies from bankruptcy. Who would've imagined a few short months ago that something like this could happen here? Suddenly, Greece is everywhere!'

The camera panned round to show a second force emerging from the smoke.

'Skinheads in bomber jackets!' Silverstein yelled into the camera. Some of them were wielding lengths of two-by-four and baseball bats. *Foreigners out! Germany first! We are the people!* Shaved heads and enraged faces filled the screen.

Alongside the action, Jeanne's eyes glowed green as she applied mascara to her lower lashes. Parts of the enormous bathroom mirror doubled as a TV screen. The novelty fittings these luxury hotels dreamed up . . .

Meanwhile, Amado continued her report. 'We're receiving reports of similar scenes in cities in the United States . . .'

As Jeanne redid her upper eyelashes, Bloomberg TV switched to two excitable journalists in New York City. Alongside Jeanne's reflection, police officers were chasing and beating protesters through billowing waves of smoke. Flares bathed this running battle in a demonic red light.

'Whole neighbourhoods of a dozen American cities are ablaze after an alt-right sympathizer ploughed his car into a demonstration, killing three African Americans.'

Jeanne reached for her highlighter as Bloomberg TV showed images of warships, missiles being fired and smirking Asian politicians hurrying into meetings.

'And there may be worse to come,' explained the newsreader. 'Manoeuvres by the Chinese fleet around Asia are riling China's neighbours to the point of conflict. Saudi Arabia, Iran and Israel are escalating their proxy wars on the Arabian Peninsula, and we've heard the first threatening noises about deployment of nuclear weapons. Russia is stoking resentment in Eastern Europe. The global situation is at its most explosive since the end of the Second World War.'

Footage of dust-caked children bleeding among ruined

buildings after a bombing raid somewhere in the Middle East.

Jeanne refreshed her lipstick.

Pictures of European and US politicians at lecterns, in wood-panelled rooms or around conference tables. 'In this febrile climate, a long-planned meeting of foreign ministers in Berlin has been hastily upgraded to a crisis summit, and prominent politicians, central bankers and business leaders are converging on Germany from around the globe.'

Jeanne drew herself up to her full height, checked her hair and smoothed her silk evening dress, which had been tailor-made for her by Sook Dwala's studio in Los Angeles. She could easily have passed for a model.

Ted Holden appeared in the mirror. Wearing a tuxedo, he was only a little taller than her and a few years older. Jeanne was momentarily confused. Was Ted on the news or genuinely standing behind her?

'Ready?' he asked. He was real.

She nodded as he ran his eyes almost imperceptibly over her body.

'And now back to Mel and Ed in Berlin . . .' Flames licked at the gutted carcass of a car.

2

In spite of the air conditioning, the stench of burnt material mingled with the aroma of the limousine's leather upholstery. Will Cantor nearly retched. The car windows muffled the sound of smashing bottles, thunderous detonations and roared slogans outside. *But how would they stand up to someone chucking a cobblestone?* he wondered, clinging to the safety handle.

The car had slowed to walking pace. A short distance ahead of them a car was blazing at the side of the road. Will's chauffeur, a stocky moustachioed German man in his mid-fifties, cursed.

Next to Will Cantor on the back seat, Herbert Thompson was holding his phone tightly in one bony old hand. 'We're driving through hell on earth, dammit!' he rasped. 'We'll talk again later.'

Like so many elderly people, he seemed to have shrunk until his suit no longer fitted him. The shoulders were too broad and the sleeves hung from his arms in folds. He might have looked altogether lost on the luxurious leather seat were it not for the sense of coiled energy contained in his small frame.

Scraps of what the person on the other end of the line was saying filtered from the phone. '. . . most influential economists of the modern era . . . sabotaging your own scientific career . . .'

'Rubbish!' snapped Thompson. 'This is the most important work I've ever done.'

The response was lost amid the noise of the demo.

'My life's work?' cried Thompson. 'This'll be my first real achievement. These ideas will end the madness out there by creating greater equality and prosperity for everyone. They'll listen to a Nobel Prize winner.'

'. . . laughing stock!' the voice screamed down the line.

Thompson pressed hard on the button to end the call and slid the notes for his speech back into the briefcase on his lap. 'What an idiot!' he barked. 'He's scared we're going to tread on the toes of people like him.' He squinted through the car window at the banners. 'What do those say?'

' "End greed! Death to capitalism!" ' Will said.

'They've no idea what capitalism is, and yet they still blame it for everything that's gone wrong with the world,' Thompson said, then continued with a dry laugh, 'Ha! We're in just the car for a situation like this. If only they knew who was driving towards them right now . . .'

Will found the thought rather less amusing. If they had only known, the next Molotov cocktail would be landing right on the roof of their shiny limousine.

Thompson revelled in this kind of disturbance. He'd never been one to shy away from confrontation. Competition, the survival of the fittest as the basis of success, growth and wealth: his economic models illustrating these concepts had earned him the Nobel Prize twelve years previously. He was a living legend and VIPs, the powerful and the rich of this world sat up and took notice when he spoke.

Thompson's phone display lit up. With an exasperated

snort he took the call. 'What now?' he yelled. 'I explained in detail that we have proof. *Mathematical* proof!'

Will pricked up his ears.

'. . . save you from this stupidity . . .'

Thompson's face was flushed with rage. 'A paradigm shift is on its way. You won't stop me making my speech – no one will.' He switched off his mobile abruptly and put it in his pocket.

The chauffeur glanced round for guidance. A few cars were stuck in line behind them, the hindmost one swallowed up in an advancing wall of smoke. More figures emerged from the gloom.

Too stiff to turn around in his seat, Thompson asked, 'Who is it now?'

Will peered out of the back window. 'The banners say "Foreigners out" and "Germany first".' Some of the figures were making the Nazi salute. 'Nazis!' he cried.

Thomas shook his head slowly. 'These neo-nationalist movements shouldn't really come as any surprise. Dismantle the nation state over decades and soon all you have left is nationalism, and now it's primed to blow up in our faces – national, international . . .'

His words were interrupted by something crashing into the rear window. Will recoiled in shock. Shards of glass, held together by the paper label, slid down the window. Not a petrol bomb, just a beer bottle.

Thompson had also flinched, but now he addressed the driver. 'I'm on my way to make an important speech with the potential to end all this.' He patted the man's shoulder. 'What was it Churchill said? "If you're going through hell, keep going." So keep driving, my good man.'

3

He was sitting in a hotel room in front of a screen full of lines of code when the message flashed up on the display of the sixth of eight old-fashioned-looking keypad mobiles arranged in two neat rows of four to the left of the computer. He'd drawn the semi-transparent orange-brown Venetian blinds and could therefore see very little of the city below. It could have been a metropolis anywhere in the world, but in this case it was Singapore.

He opened the message and immediately recognized who'd sent it. As usual, he didn't know the sender's real name – he was writing under a standard pseudonym. They had met on a regular Darknet platform where all kinds of specialists offered their anonymous services for hire. He was a hacker.

The message consisted of a single word: *Icarus*.

He booted up a second laptop. His fingers darted over the keys and within seconds he'd dispatched the order. Seven windows popped up on the screen so he could verify that his instructions were being executed correctly. The pop-ups showed folders with documents from a variety of email programs and servers via which his software had monitored every update in the months since his client had first made contact. It had also installed little time bombs in all the files in expectation of a simple command that would delete every single one, should that prove necessary.

He'd just given that order.

In a flash, individual files began to vanish from all the folders as if by magic. He reviewed the folders one last time and then broke off the mobile connection. The windows melted from the screen. He closed the laptop before typing a single word into his own mobile: *Done*.

He removed the SIM card, snapped it in half – a nonsensical ritual he nevertheless followed out of superstition – and went into the bathroom where he wrapped the pieces in toilet paper and flushed the little parcel away. He hurled the phone several times against the stone floor of the bathroom until it shattered. A few stamps of his foot reduced the larger fragments to a size that would also fit down the toilet. This too was an excessive precaution, but he preferred to play it safe and do things the old-fashioned way.

He returned to his desk and resumed work on the code on the other screen.

4

Through the windscreen of the Range Rover, Eldridge had a direct view of the rear of Thompson and Cantor's Mercedes. The demonstrations outside the castle must have spilled over from their authorized route. The police barriers meant to contain them were obviously leaking like an old garden hose, and here they were, trapped in the overflow. The first tattooed skinheads and bearded rockers caught up with the vehicles behind them. They didn't scare Eldridge – he and the other four men in the car were accustomed to far worse.

Next to Eldridge, Jack sat at the wheel, awaiting instructions. His dark green combat trousers moulded around his powerful thighs, his massive arms and shoulders taut under the grey shirt, and his eyes narrowed to slits in his broad, scarred face. His head almost touched the car ceiling, and had his crew cut not been so short, his hair would have brushed the headliner.

Eldridge's earpiece announced an incoming call. There was only one person it could be. 'Accept.'

'Plan Icarus,' said the voice in his ear.

'Copy that,' Eldridge said. 'Plan Icarus.'

'Roger that.' The caller hung up.

Eldridge – El to his crew – tapped the tablet on his lap and it lit up. The outline of a car viewed from above appeared on the screen, its interior and all of its systems made visible: seats, dashboard, engine ... The power and steering systems – engine, steering wheel, gears and pedals – were illuminated in blue. Above the engine a speedometer read 2 mph. In the top right-hand corner of the screen was a red box marked 'Enter'. One tap and 'Enter' changed from red to green.

El again laid the tip of his long, notched index finger with its clipped nail on the tablet, right over the blue accelerator on the picture of the transparent car. He looked up at the back of the limousine ahead of them with the remains of a beer bottle dribbling down its rear window and gently began to press the button.

5

Will was forced back in his seat by the car's sudden acceleration. The vehicle was heading straight for the crowd. Demonstrators were screaming, some diving headlong out of the way while others along the route shook their fists in rage.

'Be careful, man!' barked Thompson. 'I said *going through* hell, not *raising* it.'

'Something wrong,' the chauffeur shouted in broken English. Will detected disbelief in the man's voice.

'What's going on?'

'The car drives itself.' The chauffeur stamped desperately on the brake while his hand jabbed at the horn. The blaring Mercedes ploughed through the smoke and the scattering shadows, gaining speed all the time.

'The brakes don't work!' cried the driver in panic as he waggled the gearstick. 'No gears, nothing.' He took his hands off the wheel. 'Look!'

'Put your hands back on that wheel!' Thompson ordered. The driver obeyed.

Will glimpsed wide-eyed, open-mouthed faces through the windows of the car. A banner slapped against the windscreen, momentarily blocking their view before being whisked away again.

The driver spun the steering wheel in vain.

'My God,' Will stammered. 'Our car's been hacked.' He fumbled for his phone in his jacket pocket, but despite his desperate tapping the display stayed black.

Outside, the smoke was thinning. People were fleeing in all directions, conscious that their skin, flesh and bones, indeed their lives, could not withstand the impact of a hunk of metal travelling at thirty miles per hour.

'Have you got a phone?' Will asked the driver.

'Here.'

Will turned on the phone as the man rattled the steering wheel and the gearstick. No response from this device either. He glanced at Thompson, who was cowering on his seat, shoulders hunched, clutching his briefcase to his chest, his face as pale as a ghost as he observed Will's frantic efforts.

As the limousine continued to accelerate, the street grew emptier, with fewer and fewer demonstrators and no traffic as yet. Will had to blink twice before he could believe his eyes – the road ahead of them looked completely normal. He glanced back. The scene receding into the distance still looked as though it had been hit by a tornado. Only a dark SUV had followed them through the breach they had opened.

They crossed a junction and turned past a no entry sign on to a multi-lane highway. Will spotted the Victory Column up ahead. They were driving through the Tiergarten!

'Give me your phone,' he said, stretching out his hand, palm up, to Thompson.

The Nobel laureate searched his jacket pockets for what felt like an age. They were now heading along a broad, empty avenue through the park.

'Where is everyone?' Will cried.

'They've blocked the road already for tomorrow's march,'

18

the chauffeur explained. Drops of sweat stood out on his forehead.

Will finally got hold of Thompson's phone, but it was as dead as the other two. He tossed it on to the seat in frustration.

'We're being kidnapped,' he cried. 'We have to attract someone's attention!'

'Who?' roared the chauffeur. 'There's no one out there!'

The car was flung to the left before swerving back to the right with a squeal of tyres. Too far, though – it was heading straight for the woods. The front right wheel hit the kerb. The passenger side of the limousine reared up and twisted over as the vehicle soared through the air towards the trees.

6

Jan saw only a huge shadow before a ton of metal thundered over the cycle path from the road. He instinctively ducked as the vehicle flew over his head before deflecting off one tree trunk, slamming into a second and crashing to the ground. He jammed on his brakes and nearly lost control of the bike.

The vehicle was resting on its roof eight or nine yards into the woods. Smoke was beginning to rise from the bodywork near the front wheels.

Jan dropped his bike. It was one of those moments when all thought ceases and the body becomes pure muscle and movement. He started to run, dug his phone out of the front pocket of his jeans, made an emergency call. Sprinted towards the battered heap of scrap.

A black luxury car in a sea of broken glass. The driver's seat was closest to him. It was the place where the roof had best withstood the crash. A middle-aged man was hanging there motionless. Dark suit. Moustache. Deflated airbags around him. Jan heard a voice in his ear.

'My name's Jan Wutte,' he said. 'There's been a serious car accident in the Tiergarten between the Victory Column and the Brandenburg Gate.'

He pushed the phone back in his pocket. *Jan, you're a nurse. You know the human body.* He put his hand on the man's neck. No pulse. He tugged at the car door without success. Behind the driver an old man in a dark suit lay upside down, strangely slumped, on the ceiling of the car. No seat belt. Soaked in blood. His arm was dangling through the car window. No pulse either. Beside the old man, another figure was hanging from the back seat by his strap. A young man. His lips were moving. Jan rushed to the opposite side of the car and tried to push his head through the narrow gap that had recently been a window.

'Are you all right?' he heard himself shout. 'An ambulance is on its way.'

Eyes shut. Whispering. The expression on an upside-down face is impossible to read because all its features are the wrong way around.

'Are you in pain?'

Beside the man's head lay an open briefcase on what was really the ceiling of the vehicle, a sheaf of unbound sheets of paper spilling out of it. A mobile and other items lay scattered near by.

The man was whispering too quietly. Jan wriggled a little closer to his lips and tried to calm him. His eyelids were fluttering, but he now looked straight at Jan. His eyes gleamed white at their lower – now upper – edges.

'Elemen . . .' he groaned. 'Shan . . . dal . . .'

Elements? Chantal? It didn't make any sense.

'Sorry, I don't understand. But keep calm – help is on its way.'

The man didn't seem to hear Jan. 'Fitzroi piel . . . a . . . gold . . . bar . . .'

'Fitzroi what?'

Jan couldn't do much on his own. Even if he managed to unbuckle the guy's seat belt, he'd fall and possibly injure himself even more.

'Fitz . . . roi piel,' he wheezed. 'Shan . . . dal . . . ee . . .'

'Chantal E.? Is that someone's name?' He peered at the man out of the corner of his eye. No sign of life. 'Fitzroi – is that a name too?' He'd never heard it before.

The man closed his eyes – did that mean yes? – and whispered, 'Golden . . . bar . . .'

Jack had pulled the Range Rover to a halt a few yards from the scene of the accident. The Mercedes had literally used the kerb as a take-off ramp. Eldridge and Sam had leaped out and were staring at the wreckage among the trees. At this time of the night, there wasn't a soul on the path that ran parallel to the closed road. There was a bike lying there though. El soon caught sight of the man – or rather his backside poking out of the rear passenger window.

'Come on!' El shouted to the others. 'We've got to get to the car. Jack, get ours out of the exclusion zone.'

Rob and Bell jumped out of the SUV. Athletic hulks like El and Sam, they too were decked out in dark jeans and jackets.

The guy had now retracted his upper body from inside the limousine and was straining to open the door. A tall, gawky kid, dark brown hair with an undercut, dark hoodie, faded jeans. He almost fell over backwards when the door suddenly came unstuck and flew open. He arched his upper body inside again, rummaged around and reappeared. They had almost reached him.

A second later he spotted them. 'Thank God!' the Samaritan cried. 'At least one of them's alive. He can talk. We've got to get them out before the whole thing goes sky-high.' He pointed to the swirls of smoke rising from the car's engine.

But it wasn't going to explode. Not on its own, anyway.

*

The four men advanced towards Jan and the wreck like a SWAT team. Tall, muscular guys in dark casual wear. Practised movements. So much the better: some strong pairs of hands would come in useful right now.

The newcomers split up, two heading for the far side of the car where the lifeless bodies were hanging, and two towards Jan. Why were they wearing gloves on a summer evening? They crouched down beside him and peered into the car.

'What happened?' asked a man with a chin like an anvil. Jan didn't recognize his accent. American maybe? He was wearing an earpiece on the right-hand side.

'He said something just now,' Jan said. 'Maybe together we can drag him free.'

Anvil Chin grabbed the back of Jan's neck and smashed his head against the side of the car. Jan's vision went black. Dazed, he toppled to one side and banged his head hard on the ground. *What the . . .?*

The earth was lurching to and fro before him. His head was pounding and his eyes watered. The man who'd attacked him squeezed his powerful torso through the car window. Behind the front wheel on the other side, one of the men was attending to the spot from which smoke was rising. Jan tried to scramble to his feet, but crumpled helplessly back to the ground. Someone issued curt orders in a foreign language. English. Another guy was also scouring the inside of the vehicle, while a third fiddled around at the rear of the car. He was opening the fuel cap . . . Petrol gushed out. Sirens started to blare somewhere in the middle distance and Jan tried for a second time to push himself upright.

Anvil Chin re-emerged from the car, holding the briefcase. He turned to Jan, grabbed his ankle and dragged him towards a pool of petrol that had formed on the ground. Jan tried to shake him off, but the man's anvil chin was matched by a vice-like grip. Jan's hands flailed around, searching desperately for a hold until they came across part of the car that felt sharp and pointed. Mustering all his strength, he rammed this makeshift skewer into the hand clutching his ankle. The man grunted and let go. Jan scrambled to his feet. Petrol was now seeping all around the car. The man beside the fuel cap screwed it shut again. The two guys on the far side stepped back from the car. Anvil Chin jumped up, glaring at the deep stab wound in his gloved hand, which was dripping blood.

Jan heard the hiss of a match, and at the same time spotted the sudden uppercut out of the corner of his eye. Evading it by a whisker, he threw himself into a desperate sprint just as the petrol caught light, the resulting blast of heat adding impetus to his flight. With the flames licking at his heels, he risked a glance over his shoulder. Two onrushing hulks were silhouetted against the ball of flame. His legs had never carried him so fast . . . Jan heard his pursuers' pounding feet, then sirens, but drowning out everything else was the sound of his own breathing. His head felt as though it was about to explode.

There were people in that car! One was still alive, and they went and set him on fire!

Two men were running towards him from the Victory Column in the fading light. Dark trousers and shirts. Were they with the other lot? One of them was fiddling with his waistband. Did he have a gun?

Jan looked around. Fire, no one pursuing him, but the two men ahead were still running towards him.

'Stop! Police! Where are you going? Stay right where you are!'

Jan's breathing was even faster than his pulse. Through

the flames and thick smoke he could now make out flashing blue lights at the accident scene. Several cars. The men in dark clothing had vanished. Something inside the burning wreck exploded, sending a shower of sparks into the night sky. Nearby trees caught fire. There was nothing more Jan could do. The thought of the three men in the car made his stomach churn, and nausea spread to the tips of his fingers and toes, the roots of his hair, and his loins, convulsing his whole body with spasms.

'Why are you running away?' one of the police officers asked.

There's no way you'll believe me . . .

Jan's lips were unable to form a single word.

'You're coming with us.'

7

The noise of rotor blades in Jeanne's head. Silk on her skin. The thrum of the helicopter's engine coursing through her body. Sitting to her left was Ted and to her right was Ted's security chief, Mitch McConnell. His head lobbyist, George Lamarck, had taken a seat on the other side of Ted, and opposite them were the United States Secretary of the Treasury in a tuxedo and his wife in an evening gown, flanked by their minders.

The secretary was gesticulating furiously. 'What? Again?'

They were forced to raise their voices despite the sound-proof cabin.

'I have it from a reliable source,' Ted said, 'that General Motors can no longer service all its debt and BLA is on the brink of collapse.'

'The Chinese conglomerate?' George Lamarck asked in disbelief.

'The very same.' Ted looked the secretary straight in the eye. 'You do realize what this means?' He probably didn't, but this was Ted's way of making people feel his equals. 'If the markets start to doubt GM's ability to pay, Volkswagen and other car manufacturers will be next in line. And within a matter of hours so will every single company that has run up exorbitant levels of cheap debt to finance costly takeovers or drive up their share prices via buybacks. That's one hell of a lot of companies, not to mention millions of jobs in many different countries.'

Ted knew how to get a politician's attention.

'Wow, look at that!' cried George, his face pressed to the glass. 'What is it?'

The wavering lights of night-time Berlin rose towards them. On one side of the dark park stood the brightly illuminated Charlottenburg Palace, with a glittering web of street lamps on the other.

'Demonstrators?' asked the treasury secretary.

'Six hundred thousand of them, or so the organizers claim,' noted Mitch. 'Four hundred thousand according to the police.'

'And we're supposed to land down there?' George cried, his voice anxious.

'What's that glow?' the secretary's wife asked.

'Smartphone screens,' Jeanne said. 'The modern equivalent of waving your lighter.'

'Like at pop concerts?'

'Demos are parties too.'

On a square next to the Berlin Palace, the fairy lights coalesced into a single gigantic glowing image of a round golden cake. A small slice had been carved out at the bottom. The figure on it – '99%' – didn't stand for a birthday though. Written on the larger upper piece was '1%'.

'Tidy design,' Jeanne said with a sideways glance at Ted. 'The vast majority have to share one tiny piece of the cake.'

'Soon they won't get anything at all,' Ted retorted. 'BLA will sell off its stakes in foreign companies. Their market price will fall, putting their bonds and share values under even greater stress. Other Chinese firms will follow in getting

27

rid of their Western stocks. Without investment, those companies will go bust and fire all their employees.'

The lines on either side of the piece of cake began to move upwards like the hands of a crazed clock, highlighting two new narrow slices to the left and right of the 1%.

An illuminated slogan appeared below the cake in alternating languages: *We want our share! Wir wollen unseren Anteil! Nous . . .*

'These pictures will be shown around the world,' Jeanne muttered as the chopper slowly descended.

The helicopter landed in a circle of light on the lawn behind the palace. Attendants in livery put up umbrellas to shield the ladies' hair from the turbulence, and electric lanterns flanked the path to the orangery's picturesquely illuminated baroque arches. Jeanne noted a large number of dinner jackets and evening dresses, both inside and outside the building. The noise and blast from the rotor blades diminished with increasing distance. Some first strains of classical music drifted towards them – Bach, if Jeanne's ears didn't deceive her. Conversation was possible once more.

'If the story about GM and BLA gets out,' Ted said quietly, 'then the global corporate bond market will collapse tomorrow morning, taking the CLO market with it.'

Jeanne knew this stood for collateralized loan obligations, similarly opaque investment vehicles to the CDOs that had narrowly failed to destroy the global economy during the 2008 subprime crisis. The famous billionaire investor Warren Buffett had called these assets 'financial weapons of mass destruction'.

'The same goes for the stock markets, followed by virtually every major bank, insurance company, asset management firm, shadow bank . . .' Ted continued.

'Who else knows about this?' asked the treasury secretary.

How come he didn't know about this before Ted? Jeanne wondered.

'A few of the people here, I expect,' said Ted, running an eye over the gathering, 'but let's keep the circle as small as possible.'

More guests appeared beside them, heading for the reception in the orangery. The fading buzz of the helicopter grew increasingly inaudible over the roar of the demonstrators on the other side of the staterooms and police barricades. Jeanne's gaze alighted on the welcome banner in a dozen languages and, alongside it, the small posters announcing the evening's speakers.

Herbert Thompson, winner of the 2007 Nobel Prize in Economics
Ofalu Nkebi, Secretary-General of the United Nations
Leymah Gbowee, winner of the 2011 Nobel Peace Prize

Thompson would be at their table. How uninspiring – an old man who'd been presenting the same ideas for the past fifty years, his sole claim to fame being that he'd once won a Nobel Prize for them.

They had almost now reached the orangery where the other guests were already assembled. The 2015 Paris Climate Agreement negotiations had ushered in a new era in the international community's discussions of issues of global importance. Summits were no longer restricted to politicians and diplomats but had been opened up to representatives from NGOs, the business world and other stakeholders. It was still debatable how representative this collection of lobbyists really was though.

Here they all were, meeting and parading. An air kiss

here, a handshake there, a photo alone or in a group. The gentlemen wore dark suits, tuxedos or traditional costume, the ladies evening attire and jewellery. Only the occasional small cluster of guests was engaged in anxious whispered conversation.

Some of them had noticed Jeanne's group arrive and came towards them. Jeanne recognized the CEO of a large French bank, the German minister for economic affairs and the white-haired billionaire investor Kemp Gellund.

'You've heard the news?' Gellund asked.

Jeanne had a flashback. She'd first noticed this tone in people's voices back in 2008. She'd experienced the financial crisis first-hand as an intern for a New York investment bank. Days of agitation had eventually given way to naked panic among people she'd imagined had nothing to fear due to their eight-figure salaries and far larger nest eggs. They had barely managed to conceal their terror behind a polished veneer. Dread in their voices, their eyes, their every movement.

'You mustn't let this happen,' Gellund said to the politicians. 'You have to do something before the public finds out.'

'If it's true, then the state bailouts are going to be even larger than in 2008,' the senior banker said, his face pale.

'Except that no state can afford it this time,' was Ted's response.

'Exactly!' Gellund interjected. 'That's why it'll be followed by a collapse in government bonds.' His tone was shrill now. 'The emerging economies are already broke. It would be the sovereign debt crisis all over again, only worse.'

'Oh God!' the German minister groaned. 'Italy wants to leave the euro as it is.'

'It would be forced to,' Ted said. 'So would Spain, Greece and maybe others too.'

'The low interest rates mean the central banks wouldn't

have any effective instruments to curb the losses either,' the German minister said.

Opinions flew back and forth.

'The euro and the EU will implode.'

'Many people would welcome that.'

'They haven't considered the consequences though.'

'It'll just pour more fuel on the fire.'

'2008 will look like a cakewalk in comparison.'

'A hellish spiral.'

'The plebs will finally take up their pitchforks and come after us!'

'You've got to speak to the others quick!'

'The Chinese first. The Asian markets open in a few hours.'

Ted leaned towards Jeanne and whispered in her ear, 'Take note: fortunes will be made tonight.'

8

Jörn Schesta looked on as firemen in breathing equipment inspected the smoking carcass of the car and the charred remains of its occupants. Behind him his colleagues were making sure that the sixty or so bystanders stayed outside the police tape.

Not far away, an emergency doctor was closing his bag. The gawping onlookers were holding their smartphones as high in the air as they could as if they were at a pop concert. *Bastards!*

A column of twelve different emergency vehicles stretched back along the road. It included two fire tenders, a smaller fire engine, three ambulances and patrol cars of varying sizes from units around the city.

'We could have done without this, eh?' Jörn said to the head of the fire crew. The man's face and his impressive moustache were black with soot. He looked like Super Mario, which endeared him to Jörn, but instead of blue dungarees, this guy was wearing thick red overalls. 'As if we didn't have enough on our plate already.'

Fireman Mario pushed his helmet back on his head. 'Always a fire to put out somewhere,' he said laconically.

'Did you have to deal with the demos?' asked Jörn in an attempt to strike up a rapport between the emergency services.

The fire service incident commander nodded. 'Nothing too bad so far.'

Jörn cast an eye over the man's shoulder at the wreckage. It looked nasty. 'Any idea what happened here?'

'Looks pretty run of the mill. Driver loses control, crashes into trees, game over.'

Jörn could barely see the corpses among the twisted metal coated with patches of filthy foam. 'Did they die on impact?'

'Only the coroner's report will tell us.'

'That car was the latest model. They really burn that easily?'

Fireman Mario shrugged. 'Not usually, but this one flew quite a distance. It must have been travelling at quite a lick for the city. Particular forces come into play. The tank can burst, the metal of the vehicle's bodywork strikes a few sparks on landing, and boom . . . It can happen if you're out of luck.' He turned to look at the wreck and contemplated it in silence, as if it were a work of art. 'Now you mention it . . . The burnt area would look a bit different if it had exploded on impact. Less regular. Unless . . .'

Jörn controlled his curiosity and said nothing, allowing Fireman Mario to study the scene, reflect and draw his conclusions.

'Unless it lay there for a while first and the petrol leaked out of the tank before the whole thing went up. And this,' he said, taking a few steps forward and pointing to bits of glass, 'isn't from a car, it's from a bottle.'

'A Molotov cocktail, you mean?'

'Were there any demonstrators around when the accident happened?'

'A few hundred yards away,' Jörn said.

'Then the glass must just be litter.'

'What could've ignited the petrol if it wasn't sparks? What

if the car was already at a standstill?' His eyes wandered to the alleged witness making his statement to Jörn's fellow police officers.

'We'll soon find out,' Fireman Mario said.

'When?'

'Today? Tomorrow? In a week? Anyway, as you said, we should probably be somewhere else right now.'

'As always.'

'Too true.'

Jörn heard hurried steps behind him. Two police officers were walking over quickly, one of them holding up a glowing smartphone. 'They've traced the number plate,' he told Jörn.

'See you later then,' Jörn said to the incident commander, turning to his colleagues.

'The car belonged to a limousine service,' the policeman explained.

They all groaned.

'I do hope it's no one important,' Jörn said.

'Someone called Herbert Thompson,' his colleague said. 'Nobel Prize winner for economics.'

Oh shit!

Jack had driven off in the Range Rover and was waiting in a side road near the Brandenburg Gate. El and Sam were keeping a low profile at the scene of the accident, making absolutely certain they weren't inadvertently caught in some bystander's snapshot. Just in case, they had pulled the peaks of their baseball caps right down over their eyes.

El was keeping a careful watch on the Samaritan, who'd picked up his bike and wheeled it away. For the past few minutes, it had been propped up on its stand beside him as he talked to two police officers, pointing and gesticulating to illustrate his descriptions. His movements were very expressive. His arm was currently tracing an arc through the air from the street to the trees. *The car flew like that.* El could imagine every single word. He must be describing how he'd tried to help, how the bad guys had arrived to deal with him and then set fire to the car. El saw the police officers nodding, their facial expressions telling him more than the Samaritan realized in his agitation. Suspicious looks. Furrowed brows.

Good.

'The briefcase?' asked El.

Bell was carrying it as though it belonged to him. Wedged under his vast muscly bicep, it looked like a little toy. He'd provisionally patched up his wounded hand with a couple of heavy-duty plasters.

Bell opened the bag and El hunted through the contents. He found a slim wallet, two pens, Thompson's hotel key card and a notepad, which he flicked through. It was empty. There was also a folder containing a loose bunch of A5 filing cards, each pasted on to thin cardboard. The topmost one said in English, 'Ladies and gentlemen, your excellencies . . .' followed by further titles. A greeting. This had to be it. He rifled through a few more cards. Yup, it was. A glance at the Samaritan. He was still busy chatting to the police. Back to the briefcase. A fat pile of bound A4 sheets and a cover with the title *'Wealth Economics' by Herbert Thompson and Will Cantor.* A memory stick. What kind of dinosaur still used these things? A loose A4 sheet, filled from top to bottom with tiny scrawled handwriting that El had trouble deciphering.

Quickly checking the Samaritan's whereabouts, he held out a hand to Bell like a surgeon in the middle of an operation.

'Envelope.'

Bell passed him a prepared envelope. El stuffed the folder containing the filing cards into it, along with the bound papers, the scribbled sheet of paper and the memory stick, pulled off the protective strip and stuck the tab down. He handed the package to Sam. 'You know what to do.'

Sam walked away.

'Ring A-G,' El ordered via his headset, his eyes once more on the Samaritan.

His client's voice came on to the other end of the line. El could hear a jumble of voices in the background.

'Targets disabled,' El reported. 'Package on its way.'

'Everything go to plan?'

'Pretty much. One small matter still to take care of.'

'Anything for me to worry about?'

'Nope.'

El ended the call and focused all his attention on the scene with the police officers again. They appeared to be asking the Samaritan something.

What did the men look like? they would want to know. Eloquent gestures in response. A palm held up horizontally about a head above the Samaritan's own. *This tall.* Elbows out, arms bent like a gorilla's, to suggest *big, muscular.* The police officers conscientiously took everything down, exchanged glances, asked more questions. The Samaritan looked around, pointed in the direction in which he'd been running and shrugged. *No idea where they went.*

We're over here. Closer than you'd like to think. Extremely close. We've got you in our sights.

The firemen were retrieving the three charred corpses from the limousine behind Jan. The ozone smell from the metal-cutting torch joined the odour of burnt flesh and a whiff of rubbish from the woods. Insects were swarming around the street lamps. He could hardly bring himself to look round.

Dazzling spotlights made the scene look inappropriately

garish. Jan barely recognized the smashed-up car around which the firemen were milling. He once again felt an urge to retch, but couldn't take his eyes off the grotesquely blackened bodies.

'Jan Wutte?'

The policeman was wiry, the kind of man who works out at the local boxing gym – or at least tries to. He was accompanied by five colleagues, including the two who'd apprehended Jan.

'I'm Jörn Schesta,' the new man said. The head of this lot, apparently. He squinted at Jan, then looked down at his mobile. 'So, eighteen years old, a trainee nurse, first offence at fourteen, several arrests for disturbing the peace . . .'

'A couple of parties . . .'

'Repeated arrests for illegal drug-taking . . .'

'Oh come on, man, it was only a few joints . . .'

'Suspicion of causing actual bodily harm . . .'

'That's not true!' Jan objected. 'It was exactly the opposite: I was keeping out of that brawl in the pub when I got hit by a flying chair. Witnesses confirmed my account. Why's it still on my record?'

'And now three people are dead.'

What do you mean, 'And now'?

'What is this? I made a full statement to your colleagues.'

'Sounds pretty far-fetched to me,' the policeman remarked. 'Why were you running away?'

'I've already explained that! Because those guys knocked me down and tried to burn me. Look – here!' Jan tapped his forehead, the right side of which was still smarting from its involuntary encounter with the bodywork of the car.

The police officer's eyes didn't linger on it for long. He sniffed. 'You smell of petrol.'

'Of course I do.'

'Because you were fooling around with it?'

'No! Listen . . .' *Keep calm.*

'Where were you coming from? The demos? Or is that where you were heading?'

'I've got better things to do. I'd just come off a twelve-hour shift at the hospital. Check if you like. All I want is to go home, shower, eat and get some sleep.'

The policeman nodded. 'Know who was in the car?'

'How would I know that?'

'You told my colleague you'd managed to speak to one of the men.'

'He stammered something. Names, perhaps. I couldn't understand him very well. I told all this to your colleague.'

'If those other men were there, as you claim—'

'I'm not *claiming* anything . . .' Jan retorted.

'Then why were you the only one my colleagues came across?' the police officer continued impassively. 'More likely, you were on the run . . .'

'I . . .'

'. . . and the others don't exist.'

'I don't know. Maybe they didn't look properly.'

Wrong answer. Jan knew it straight away. This guy was a real arsehole, that put-on smile on his face and ruefully shaking his head. The police officer walked away. His colleagues followed and gave him their views. Jan pricked up his ears.

'As soon as . . . find out who might have died . . . on our backs,' the policeman hissed. 'The mayor, politicians, the media . . . a nightmare.'

'On the other hand,' another man said, 'the summit will be a distraction . . .'

'Not if rumours . . . triple murder . . . victims . . . Nobel Prize winner Herbert Thompson.'

Was he talking about the smoking heap behind them? A

Nobel Prize winner? As inconspicuously as possible, Jan took a few steps closer.

'. . . only witness . . .'

'*If* he's a . . .'

If? What was that *supposed to mean? Were they talking about him? What else might he be?*

'Radical . . .'

'Molotov cocktail . . .'

'Cover-up . . .'

'Set fire . . .'

They surely didn't think . . . They must be discussing something other than the wild fantasies he was piecing together from the fragments of their conversation – they had to be. He'd called the emergency services. He . . .

The police chief tapped on his phone and raised it to his ear.

'. . . murder, why run away? . . . need results . . . suspects . . .'

'Bring him in . . . tell him it's as a witness . . .'

'What the hell's that?'

A policeman was staring up, mesmerized, into the now dark sky. The others followed his example and, one after the other, they moved towards the road to get a better view, their eyes glued to the heavens. The focus of the bystanders' attention had shifted too. They were no longer pointing their phones at the wreckage but off into the distance.

Jan looked round. Further west, beyond the Victory Column, sparks were soaring into the blue-black sky. Hundreds of them. Thousands. As if there were a fire, a gigantic conflagration, over Berlin-Charlottenburg.

9

The champagne glasses in people's hands and the cheerful smiles on their faces were not enough to hide the tense atmosphere in the orangery from Jeanne's perceptive eye. Waiters wended their way through the crowd, balancing trays of hors d'oeuvres on their fingertips, but hardly anyone helped themselves to the food. Jeanne's small group made its way unobtrusively towards the Chinese trade minister and his entourage.

'Whatever you do, don't mention the BLA affair directly,' Kemp Gellund warned them. 'The Chinese would take it as an affront and immediately clam up. Approach the subject cautiously, allude to it obliquely and let them take the initiative.'

'How do we solve the problem of the Western investments they're going to sell off?' the treasury secretary asked.

Jeanne allowed herself to be swept along by the others. She was now the only woman, as the treasury secretary's wife had stopped to talk with a different group. No one paid any attention to Jeanne – she was invisible among the political leaders and billionaires. Although she'd completed her studies in record time with top grades, enjoyed a successful career as an investment banker and worked for a hedge fund, right now, in the inner circle around the man to whom she might perhaps mean more if she was inclined to be, for a brief moment in the centre of the parquet floor she was – or at least felt like – Cinderella.

She pulled back her shoulders to cover up this hairline crack in her ego and noticed that the tone of the conversation around her had changed. More and more pairs of eyes peered out through the glassed-in arches of the orangery.

'What's that?'

'Looks like Loi Krathong.'

'The Thai festival of light?'

Glowing dots were rising into the air like giant fireflies over the heads of the demonstrators. Hundreds of them, maybe more.

'Someone will have to take on the investments without it leaking to the public,' Ted explained, ignoring the spectacle outside.

'National governments won't be able to cover it this time,' the German minister for economic affairs shot back. 'Not the full amount, anyway.' Naturally, he was well aware that BLA and other Chinese corporations had bought stakes in dozens of German companies in recent years or taken them over completely. A Chinese withdrawal now would mean hundreds of thousands of job losses.

'I could, though,' Ted said. 'So could Kemp here, and Wilbur over there.' He nodded in the direction of another elderly man around whom a cluster of more or less famous faces had gathered. 'I bet he's already considering it . . . and he's not the only one.'

'Does he know?'

'You can assume he does. Of course, it would be better if we coordinated the operation.'

So that's what Ted had meant when he said that fortunes would be made tonight. Just as some financiers had done during the 2008/09 crisis. The legendary Warren Buffett, for example, had put five billion dollars into the investment bank Goldman Sachs when the markets hit rock bottom to secure options on shares. Five years later, the five billion had become eight – a return on investment mere mortals could only dream of.

'Obviously, we could only do it under certain conditions,' Ted said.

'And what conditions would those be?' the minister enquired.

'Drones!' someone shouted. 'Those are illuminated drones out there.'

There must have been thousands of them by now, and they had captured the attention of Jeanne's group too. From where she was standing the flying objects seemed to be converging to form suspicious-looking swarms.

'Someone's coordinating them,' she announced with simultaneous fascination and concern. 'That's the only explanation.'

More and more guests were raising their phones to film the display through the orangery windows.

'The price would have to be right,' Ted said, returning coolly to the matter at hand, 'but the Chinese are under pressure so they'll make us a decent offer. It's still risky, mind you. We'd need government guarantees and tax breaks or even tax exemptions for the first few years.'

The dots of light began to arrange themselves into a huge circle the height of a skyscraper. A vertical line divided it in half, and two diagonal lines appeared.

'The peace sign!'

It must have been three hundred feet in diameter.

The first guests rushed outside to get a better view. More than half the people at the reception were now using their phones as cameras, even billionaires and first ladies.

'You intend to make a killing, and we're supposed to underwrite the whole operation, with bonds and tax breaks to boot?' the German minister snapped.

'We merely want to help,' Gellund said, coming to Ted's aid. 'We're quite willing to risk billions ... but not our necks.'

'That wouldn't be in anyone's interest,' Ted said. 'We have to minimize the risk to protect our investors and we need to act quickly. We require binding commitments before the Asian markets open.' He shrugged. 'We described earlier what the alternative would be' – he pointed outside – 'and if that came to pass, not even light shows would help the people out there.'

The bright peace sign began to rotate on its axis like an alien spaceship hovering over the city. The murmur of voices in the hall grew louder and gave way to terrified shrieks.

'It's heading our way!'

10

'Get it out of the sky!' thundered Deputy Superintendent Eduard Köstritz, head of operations, as he studied the screens at the Berlin-Mitte command and coordination centre. 'What is this? Have they gone completely mad?'

Maya Paritta was spellbound by the pictures of the peace UFO on the central monitors. Other screens showed a crazy, flickering patchwork of scenes filmed from helicopters hovering over Charlottenburg and a sea of demonstrators.

'Why are our colleagues impeding peaceful demonstrators,' Maya had asked Köstritz, 'and not those hooligans over there?' Footage from an area north-east of the main demo showed masked individuals emerging from clouds of smoke, hurling objects and engaging in running battles. Burning cars. No police.

'My funding depends on images of uncontrolled violence, not pictures of sweetness and light,' was Köstritz's response.

His cynicism had left Maya speechless for a moment – a rare occurrence. She was actually part of one of Berlin's nine homicide squads, but like all her colleagues who weren't looking into crimes committed in the preceding forty-eight hours, she had been placed on standby for special assignments. She'd drawn the short straw: operational headquarters.

'Those bastards!' Köstritz raged. 'Fucking arseholes – they're going to pay for this.'

Some of the monitors were playing breaking news channels and live streams. Without exception they were broadcasting the images of the peace UFO around the world.

'Get it out of the sky!' Köstritz roared again in a tone verging on panic. 'Use a jammer or whatever it takes.'

'Too late,' said another officer who was staring at the screens. 'They would all crash down on the orangery.'

The symbol continued to rotate slowly where it was, then it tilted as if in slow motion until it was hanging horizontally in the air. The guests at the official reception would be able to see it better now.

'What a nightmare,' Köstritz groaned. Obviously he'd be hauled in for an explanation. How could it have come to this? What if it was something more than a glowing peace symbol? What if the drones had other intentions? They might be toys, but then again, who could be sure they weren't armed?

His assistant was hurrying towards him with a mobile phone in his hand.

'Let me guess,' Köstritz grunted. 'The chief of police? The interior minister? The—'

'Something else entirely,' the other man said.

Köstritz shot his assistant a quizzical look as the latter pressed the mobile into his boss's palm.

The glowing sign was slowly returning to its vertical position.

'It must be over the demo outside Charlottenburg Palace,' speculated a policeman next to Jörn.

'Who's responsible and how did they do it?' another man was asking.

'Drones,' Jörn said, just as his neighbour tapped him on the shoulder and gestured towards the wreckage of the car where Jan Wutte had been standing.

'Where did he go?' asked Jörn. 'He was here a second ago.'

'His bike's gone too.'

Jörn frantically surveyed the exclusion zone. 'The bastard's run away! That's our proof. OK, call out a manhunt!'

11

The Samaritan had been standing near the wrecked car, listening to the police officers. El could almost see his ears growing. Then, while everyone else was occupied by the light display over Charlottenburg, the kid had given the police squad the slip, ever so slowly, casually picking up his bike as he tiptoed away. *OK, I'll be off now*, he seemed to say. El had to admit the youngster was good. No hurried movements, no signs of nervousness; El wouldn't have thought him capable of it. The kid had pushed his bike past the scene of the crash without anyone noticing and strolled away from the uproar like a ghost. The police had been so caught up in their own affairs and what was going on overhead that they didn't see him manoeuvre his boneshaker under the tape, unchallenged by any of the nearby officers. Their task was to prevent anyone from entering; no one had told them not to let anyone leave. As soon as the Samaritan had got on his bike on the other side of the crowd of bystanders, he had pedalled away like a maniac – not along the road, but through the pitch-black park. Seconds later, the police officers who'd been questioning him realized that the Samaritan had vanished, triggering much agitated searching and lots of barked orders. Not very professional.

By then, though, El and Sam were already in hot pursuit

through the woods leading to the Brandenburg Gate. Rob had been told to stay put for the time being. Maybe he could find out why the Samaritan had run away. El could think of only one possible reason: the police didn't believe his story, whatever it might have been. Or, even worse for him, they thought he'd been involved in the fire. Presumably he'd told them the truth. Or what he thought was the truth. But people don't always want to believe it, especially when it doesn't fit the picture they've already formed in their minds. One of the police officers must have done precisely that – got it into his head that the Samaritan best fitted the profile of the likely culprit. Classic confirmation bias: you only take into account information that confirms your own views. After all, who needs facts if you have an opinion!

The Samaritan was cycling towards the Brandenburg Gate. El and Sam were in good shape and although they were losing ground on him, he was still in sight. El relayed this news via his headset to Jack in the Range Rover. The only question was who would get to him first – the police or them.

Jan was pedalling like mad. The police needed a suspect, a scapegoat; he needed a plan. Maybe running away hadn't been the best idea, but he didn't fancy being framed and he couldn't face it. They were trying to twist a few minor offences into a noose for his neck! And that pub brawl: he'd been a witness, nothing more. He'd tried to avoid the flying chairs, bottles and fists by flattening himself against the wall, but even so, a bottle had hit him on the temple and a chair in the stomach. He'd had the bruises for weeks. Three of the fighters and two innocent bystanders had been critically injured, and four other louts had escaped. Like the guy just now, the cop at the police station had immediately suspected Jan. It was a shitty feeling being treated like a criminal even though he was innocent. Had a doctor examined him? You had to be kidding. They had eventually been forced to release him because enough people had testified to his innocence, and yet apparently it was still on his police record!

There had been no other witnesses tonight, and if one of the dead really was a global celebrity, then the police were in big trouble. They would be under severe pressure to come up with quick results. Jan didn't want to be a quick result. Running away, though, might have made him precisely that.

He couldn't go home for now. He looked around. Had the killers left, or had they been watching the whole thing? The park was gradually filling up. There was a small demo in front of the Brandenburg Gate where the big one would be held the next day.

The gate itself and the Pariser Platz beyond were already blocked off by huge police barricades. Jan headed north instead and then swung right below the Reichstag towards Friedrichstrasse. There were lots of people here, and he felt a little bit safer.

What had the man tried to say to him? Chantal. In any case, that's how Jan had interpreted the word he had whispered. A second name too perhaps: Fitzroi Piel. 'What kind of a name is *that*?' the police officers had asked. Jan didn't know either.

He stopped and scanned his surroundings. The coast looked clear.

'Hold on!' El ordered via his headset. 'He's stopped.' The Range Rover was about two hundred yards behind the Samaritan, with four other vehicles in between. 'Pull over, Jack.'

Jack steered the car into a driveway. El saw the Samaritan take out his phone.

'OK,' El said, 'move closer, but slowly. Don't attract his attention. As soon as we're level, we'll drag him into the car.'

Jack spun the steering wheel hard and waited until there was a gap in the traffic to make his approach.

Did you mean Fitzroy Peel?

I've no idea what I meant, Jan thought.

2,307 hits. The first few images all showed the same lanky guy. In his mid-thirties, Jan guessed. Not much hair. The man was always at a gambling table with cards in his hand and a pile of chips in front of him. Jan scrolled through the results. The internet did indeed list a guy by this name. He appeared to be a professional poker player. An Englishman. Jan skipped a few pages. More pictures of the same card sharp. There was no one else.

Jan could find no information online as to where Fitzroy Peel lived, or why a dying man might breathe his last words about this guy of all people – if, of course, that was what he'd said. Maybe the man in the car had been attempting to tell Jan the identity of his murderer!

Jan tried to recall the faces of the four killers. Anvil Chin wasn't Fitzroy Peel, nor was Petrol Cap Man. He hadn't had such a good view of the other two, but neither of them was particularly tall.

There was no point looking for Chantal. Which left Goldenbar. Or Golden Bar. Or something else entirely? Jan typed the second option.

The Samaritan was standing about a hundred yards away, hunched over his phone. Ahead of El and his men, a tiny Fiat 500 was trundling along behind a cyclist. The nearest headlights were another two hundred yards back. There were very few pedestrians around and none in the immediate vicinity, but someone might be watching from a window somewhere. Not that it mattered: no one would be able to identify their number plate.

'Pull up right alongside him, Jack,' El said, 'and I'll trap him with my door.' With a glance at the two men on the back seat, he added, 'Sam and Bell, you pull him inside.'

The search engine brought up its first suggestions while Jan was typing. The third one down was 'Golden Bar, Berlin'.

So there was a bar of this name in Berlin-Mitte, about three-quarters of a mile away. There were millions and millions of other hits, but none of them any good in this context.

Then again, nothing was any good about this situation. Jan needed a plan, and only one came to mind. He put his phone away and jumped back on his bike.

Most of the eyes trained on the screens at the command and coordination centre were still captivated by the gigantic glowing peace sign. Some of the lights broke off from its upper edge as if blown away by the wind and made off towards the demonstration. Others soon followed.

'Now what's happening?' shouted Deputy Superintendent Köstritz, clutching his assistant's phone in his distraction.

'Are they attacking?'

The symbol dissolved from the top down like a crumbling jigsaw puzzle as one by one the lights were extinguished. Within thirty seconds the haunting sight was no more.

'Bastards!' Köstritz hissed again, but this time there was relief in his voice.

'The batteries must have gone dead,' one of the technicians speculated.

'Mission accomplished,' said another man. 'The pictures have gone global.'

'I've got a job for you, Paritta,' Köstritz said, turning to Maya.

About time, Maya thought. She could finally get out of here.

Köstritz lowered his voice. 'There's been a car accident. The vehicle caught fire, killing the three people inside, none of them identified yet. A witness has suspiciously vanished.'

'Suspicious or vanished? Or both?'

'Check it out, but make sure you keep this very, very quiet!'

'Very, very quiet?' she asked. 'Someone important?'

'The limousine was hired for one of the speakers at the summit – Nobel Prize winner Herbert Thompson.'

12

'We'll meet again later this evening,' announced the Chinese trade minister, his expression inscrutable.

'Of course,' the US treasury secretary replied. 'We're likely to be here for some time.'

Jeanne's group nodded goodbye and walked away with the French business minister and a British diplomat they had met while talking to the Chinese delegation. They needed to get to their tables because the German chancellor was about to give her welcome address.

'That went reasonably well,' the treasury secretary said.

'A little too well, if you ask me,' muttered Gellund.

Jeanne didn't hear what he said next. A good-looking man in his mid-forties was striding towards Ted with a big smile on his face.

'Ted!'

'Maurizio!'

Jeanne knew this was the Italian minister of economy and finance, Maurizio Trittone, the leader of a right-wing nationalist party and a key proponent of Italy's leaving the European Union. She'd seen him on the news in the bathroom mirror only an hour ago. He flashed her a charming smile. Ted deftly took half a step back and guided the minister's already outstretched hand towards Jeanne.

'Jeanne Dalli,' Ted said without further explanation.

Jeanne Dalli. His colleague? A presentable companion for the evening? Her official unveiling as something more? Ted's other assistants didn't suspect a thing, at least she hoped they didn't. In any case, they had shown no surprise when he'd invited her to accompany him to this dinner. One member of his team always had to stick close to Ted at this kind of event, while the others stayed in the background.

'Come with us, Maurizio,' Ted suggested, placing his fingers gently on the Italian's forearm. The minister looked flattered. They caught up with the rest of their group.

'. . . sacrifice GM this time,' the US treasury secretary was saying. 'We mustn't reward poor management.'

'Now is not the time to discuss moral hazard,' his colleague from the trade department retorted. 'We've already been through the potential consequences. Remember Lehman Brothers in 2008.'

Jeanne did. There had been much debate back in 2008 about letting firms go bust to punish managers for their recklessness. It would have hit the employees hardest, though – the executives had already stashed their fortunes safely away. Virtually none of the culprits was ever sent to jail.

'The survival of the fittest . . .'

'The survival of the best adapted,' the British diplomat said. 'A good theory . . .'

'The survival of the strongest, you mean,' the treasury secretary corrected him.

'When Darwin wrote "the fittest", he wasn't talking about the physically or psychologically strongest,' the diplomat explained. ' "Fittest" comes from "fitting in", by which Darwin meant those who adapted best to the circumstances.

So "the survival of the fittest" refers not to the strongest, but to those who adapt the best.'

Jeanne had never considered the famous phrase in those terms.

'So you're saying there's been a huge misunderstanding?' she asked. 'All the alpha males in this room think they've reached the top of their companies because they're the best, the strongest, the most exceptional, when in fact they're the most conventional?'

Not very diplomatic. There was an embarrassed silence. The only reaction she got was a broad grin from the Brit, a stocky man in his early sixties with a halo of white hair. Ambrose Peel, if she remembered correctly.

'She's right,' Ted said with a loud guffaw. 'Look at what we're wearing.'

Every man in the group was wearing a tuxedo. They laughed and in a flash their irritation was gone.

Ted winked at Jeanne as if to say, *Very witty!*

'It means,' the US treasury secretary said, turning serious again, 'that businesses have not adapted well enough to present conditions. It comes down to the same thing.'

'As poorly adapted as the dinosaurs were to the impact of a giant meteorite,' the German business minister suggested. 'No one's prepared for what we're about to go through.'

'What you've *caused*,' Peel shot back. 'Unlike a meteorite, a financial and economic crisis is not a natural disaster – it's entirely manmade.'

'But companies and individuals still have to face up to the situation and change,' the US treasury secretary insisted.

'It obviously confronts a conservative social Darwinist like yourself with an impossible dilemma,' Peel said. 'In a constantly changing world, adaptation implies constant change, which is the complete opposite of conserving and being conservative. You have to decide: survival of the fittest or of the conservative? You can't have your cake and eat it.'

'This is why I love coming to these events,' quipped George Lamarck, the lobbyist, who'd noticed his treasury secretary's growing irritation and was trying diplomatically to head off an outburst. 'You always learn something new.'

'Ms Dalli put her finger on it,' Peel stated, stubborn but smiling. *Oh, thanks for endearing me to the treasury secretary!* 'If everyone here accepted they're not the strongest but simply the most conventional, then there'd be no need for them to strut about trying to prove their supposed strength and they could all get on together just fine in harmonious uniformity.'

Funny guy, Jeanne thought, *but he can kiss goodbye to any career ambition he might have had.*

'Fantastic!' the Frenchman said laughing, patting the British man on the shoulder. 'Well, that solves all our problems.'

Yeah, apart from the fact that the global financial system's about to go into meltdown again, Jeanne mused, *even though everyone assured us it was much more resilient than last time. Only a few hours left to prevent it as well.*

The slightly muffled sound of hundreds of thousands of awestruck spectators reached them inside the orangery. An unbidden memory popped into Jeanne's head. Following the mass shooting at Virginia Tech in 2007, she and countless other school pupils across America had gone out on to the streets to hold vigils and call for stricter gun laws. It was the first and last time she'd done anything like that. She'd felt such togetherness, such motivation, such change and urgency, and experienced several days of inner turmoil. Her father had been furious, but that had simply spurred her on. Teenage provocation. They hadn't got anywhere though. In 2011 when she passed the Occupy Wall Street campaigners in Zuccotti Park on her way to work at an investment bank, all she could do was smile, pity them and think, *You'll never change anything out here.*

13

Golden Bar, Tucholskystrasse, right in the centre of Berlin's trendy Mitte neighbourhood. Jan checked the address against the details on his phone. This had to be it. A few hardy people and some smokers were sitting around the outside tables with half-full glasses of beer. Jan locked his bike to the traffic sign on the other side of the road. The place was heaving with demonstrators and partygoers. Regular people. Pretty tame by Mitte standards. A group spilled out of the pub, laughing.

Jan stared at the front door of the bar. *What are you doing here?* He checked Fitzroy Peel's face on his phone one last time and screwed up his courage.

It took him a couple of seconds to get used to the murky orange light inside the pub. It was packed. A clamour of excited voices over upbeat background music. There were shouts from cheery groups here and there. Dark wooden panelling from floor to ceiling, a dozen tables and beyond them a long horseshoe-shaped bar with a huge number of bottles on display behind it. On either side of it, more tables stretched away into the gloom. Waiters fought their way through the crowd. Going by the trays, people were ordering just about every drink imaginable, although mainly beer.

How was he supposed to find a total stranger in this

place? The guy probably wasn't even here. The memory of the man in the car suddenly came to his mind, whispering words he couldn't understand. He might have made it through until the ambulance arrived.

Frustrated, Jan drifted around the room, scanning people's faces. Conversations about overseas holidays, girlfriends, enemies, colleagues, cars. Flirting. Talk of barbecues, laughter, bored expressions. He pushed his way to the bar and waited his turn behind two women. Pounding music. Next to the women he spied a group of young people and couples chatting. Some of them were clearly on Tinder dates – it was obvious from their body language. Trying hard to act cool, so hard in some cases that they ended up looking inhibited. The other person would seem interested but holding back or too tense. Jan knew the feeling only too well. He ordered a small beer and as the barman drew it, Jan searched the crowd. At the very back of the pub he spotted a particularly animated group of people gesturing and talking loudly. In the middle was a tall guy with a shaved head.

Jan got out his phone and retrieved the webpage of photos of Fitzroy Peel. He felt butterflies in his stomach. It might just be him.

The barman put the beer on the counter. Jan paid hurriedly without taking his eyes off the bald guy. His features looked more angular than in the photos he'd seen, his nose bigger. He grabbed his glass and elbowed his way towards the man.

SECOND DECISION

'As evolution proceeds, certain chemical entities
obey the same beneficial principle and form
compounds known as cells.'

Will Cantor

14

'I'm going to win,' roared a tall man whose T-shirt had a quote stretched taut over his impressive paunch. At least a dozen people were clustered around a table dotted with half-empty glasses. None of them was sitting down.

'Tell me the rules again,' demanded a shorter man with a wispy moustache. He reminded Jan of a Gaul in one of the Asterix comics. The guy's brown leather jacket was a couple of sizes too big for him.

'Fine. One last time for all you smart-arses,' the man who looked like Fitzroy Peel said in an English accent. 'The game goes like this . . . You start with one hundred points. We toss a coin. One hundred times. If it's heads, you win fifty per cent of your points; tails, you lose forty per cent of them. If after a hundred coin tosses you have more than the one hundred points you started with, I double your money. Let's set a maximum stake of a hundred euros. If you win, you get two hundred back. So . . . are you in or out?'

'I'm in, obviously!' Mr T-Shirt cried. 'It's a dead cert. Let's get this show on the road.'

Jan wondered whether he should play. One hundred tosses would come out roughly fifty-fifty, heads and tails. For half of the tosses he'd be up fifty per cent, for the other half, down forty, leaving him ten per cent in the black overall. So he was bound to end up with over a hundred points and win. Sounded like a dead cert all right. Maths wasn't his strong suit, though. When did it ever come in useful in real life? His mind wandered back to the wrecked car, and he clutched his beer more tightly.

'What do you mean, a dead cert?' asked a woman with orange hair and fiery red lipstick. She was wearing a black denim jacket over a close-fitting top with a glittery design on it.

'It's very simple,' Mr T-Shirt explained confidently. 'You only have to work out the average – every possible result divided by the number of results. In this case, it's one hundred and fifty per cent of your hundred points, or sixty per cent. Add them together and you get two hundred and ten, divided by two for the average equals one hundred and five per cent of the original points. You're up five points every round. On average, of course.'

Aha, that wasn't how Jan had calculated it. Better odds, greater winnings every round. He hadn't considered that.

Mr T-Shirt gazed smugly at the faces around him. The others thought about it for a while before one of them shouted, 'I'm in!' A second person soon joined him.

'Hold on a sec,' a third interjected. It was the Gaul. 'It's not as straightforward as you think. You have to calculate the average differently to reflect the probability.'

Jan had guessed it wasn't so easy. Maths – not his strong suit.

'Oh yeah, wise guy? Let's hear you then,' Mr T-Shirt challenged the third guy.

'If the coin lands on heads, you win one and a half times your stake,' the Gaul said to clarify. 'Tails and you're left with sixty per cent of your money. Times 0.6. The probability of either outcome is fifty-fifty – times 0.5 in each case.'

He took a paper napkin, produced a pen from his jacket and began scribbling on the napkin. 'So by this means of calculation, the game's expected outcome is 1.5 times 0.5 plus 0.6 times 0.5, which comes out as 1.05 times your stake. Five per cent per round.'

Jan stared at the napkin. The sums made his head spin. He took a long swig of beer.

Mr T-Shirt burst out laughing. 'Five per cent. Just like I said, you bloody know-it-all!'

'Yeah, but calculated using the correct method,' the Gaul insisted, somewhat offended.

'Whichever way, it means average winnings of five per cent per toss. And over a hundred rounds that comes to . . . a hell of a lot,' declared Mr T-Shirt.

'131.5 times as much,' the Gaul explained.

'I'm in,' Mr T-Shirt said, waving a one-hundred euro note. 'If you can turn one hundred points into 13,150, then you can bet your life I'm going to double this.'

Were they really going to gamble? Toss a coin one hundred times? They were in for a long evening.

The shaven-headed man, Possibly Peel, sat down and pushed the beer glasses aside. He placed a paper napkin on the table and fished a pen from his jacket. Why was he so willing to take their bets if they were nailed-on winners? 'I'll take your stakes first. Each of you will need a coin.'

Another seven men and two women joined in, and a crowd of curious spectators gathered around them. The players slapped down banknotes on the wooden table. One hundred euros or fifties and, next to each note, a one- or two-euro coin.

'OK, pass your coin to the person on your right to prevent any cheating and we'll get started. Toss your coin, catch it, put it on the back of your hand and show everyone. I'll keep score.'

He drew nine columns on the napkin and wrote the letters A to I across the top, followed by the person's stake and the one hundred starting points.

Jan was sure there was something fishy about this whole thing. Why else would Possibly Peel accept these bets? But he didn't yet know what role Peel might have played in the murders. He couldn't speak to him directly in front of all these people. He had to find a less conspicuous approach.

'Count me in too,' he announced.

Possibly Peel glanced up. 'Your stake,' he said.

Jan dug out a fifty. He didn't have much more than that. A coin, sure. He sat down next to the man with the shaved head and pushed his coin across the table. The man passed it to the person on his right and added a tenth column to his napkin. J for Jan – a coincidence. One hundred points.

'I'm Jan, by the way,' Jan said, offering his hand.

The man looked at him in surprise, then shook his hand. 'Nice to meet you, Jan,' he said. 'I'm Fitzroy.'

'What's he doing?'

El was lingering near the front room of the pub where the Samaritan was unlikely to spot him. Jack had followed him inside. The driver was the only one of El's team the Samaritan hadn't seen near the burning vehicle.

'You won't believe this,' El heard Jack say via his earpiece. 'He's playing a game.'

'What?'

'Gambling. I've no idea why.'

Someone bumped into El from behind as he tried to get past. El stepped aside and scanned the room. There was a deal going on by the entrance. Easy to spot if you were observant and knew what you were looking for. Did the staff know? El couldn't identify the drug. Just weed, to judge by the customer. That matched the feel of the place.

'What are they playing?' Sam asked via his mike. 'Cards? Poker? Blackjack?'

'Can't see any cards, just money.'

'How are we doing for escape routes? Back and side emergency exits?' El wanted to know.

'Two emergency exits,' Sam reported, 'one on each side. And a third one out the back through the toilets. That's also the route to the kitchens.'

'Stay where you are,' El ordered him.

The Samaritan was gambling. Either he was cooler than he looked or he'd lost his mind. Another person shoved El and again he gave way.

'This is nuts.' Jack wasn't easily surprised, but it did occasionally happen. 'They're tossing coins.'

'Ha, I win!' Mr T-Shirt roared, showing the coin on his wrist. Heads.

Jan had thrown tails. He could scarcely keep up with Fitzroy's pen as it noted down the scores on the napkin. Jan had only sixty of his original hundred points left. Mr T-Shirt's one hundred had swollen to one hundred and fifty. Four of the ten players were down, while six were winning. The first round had taken less than a minute. Fitzroy was a pro.

'Next round!' cried Fitzroy.

Coins whooshed through the air. Catch, hand, uncover.

Heads. Plus fifty per cent for a win. Jan's account went back up from sixty to ninety.

Hang on a sec. Fifty per cent of Jan's starting score of one hundred was fifty, so where had the other ten gone?

Fitzroy was about to announce the next toss when one of

67

the women objected. Like Jan, she'd lost the first round and won the second.

'I only got thirty points,' she said. The same as Jan.

'Of course,' Fitzroy hastened to explain. 'After the first toss you had sixty points. If you throw heads, you get fifty per cent of that, and fifty per cent of sixty is thirty.'

'Oh yeah,' she groaned, taken aback. 'Of course.'

Oh yeah. Of course.

Jan needed to fashion an opportunity to have a quiet word with Fitzroy. He waited until after the next round.

Mr T-Shirt was gloating after another win. His one hundred and fifty had already ballooned to two hundred and twenty-five. Jan, on the other hand, had less than he'd started with after one victory and one loss – ninety instead of a hundred. How was he supposed to accumulate over thirteen thousand points after a hundred throws?

'Toss!' Fitzroy called. Jan wasn't the only one who'd needed a little time to check his score.

Whoosh.

Heads.

'They're tossing coins,' Jack reported. 'One guy's the croupier. He's playing against everyone else. Looks like a pro to me. I'm curious to see how long the staff let him carry on. I can't imagine this is permitted in here.'

El had forced his way closer to the table but was careful to make sure he stayed out of the Samaritan's line of sight and could duck behind someone at any moment. By now the pub was so full that the barkeepers were only serving those who clamoured for their attention.

'That could come in handy, but first I'd like to know why the Samaritan's here. I can't believe he ran away from the police simply to come and gamble.'

'Maybe he wanted to lie low.'

'I can think of less attention-grabbing ways than illegal gambling. You followed him into the pub. How exactly did he behave?'

'He went to the bar and ordered a beer, then waited. As soon as he'd been served, he went over to the group at the back where's he's sitting now.'

'Sounds purposeful. Do you think he was coming here all along?'

'It's possible.'

'Friends, maybe.'

El rubbed the back of his neck. 'You reckon he's cool enough to come and meet friends after all he's been through? I'm not so sure. He's a witness and we have to deal with him. We need to check all the people he's been in contact with to be safe. Take photos of the people with your phone but don't let anyone see you doing it, then run them through facial recognition and databases.'

15

At first glance one might have mistaken it for a building site. The arm of the crane swung away from the blinding lights and into the night sky. The only things visible in the darkness were the ropes hanging down to lift the misshapen grey, black and white sculpture into the air. But the sculpture was in fact the battered wreck of a limousine, while at the side of the road a guy from forensics was just closing the rear doors of a grey van on its cargo of three coffins. The thrum of a helicopter could be heard in the distance where it was hovering over the demonstration. Even further away came a clap of thunder.

Maya fitted the scene perfectly with her short, muscular physique, jeans, sturdy boots and waterproof jacket over a long-sleeved T-shirt. The ponytail poking through the gap at the back of her baseball cap swung to and fro as she moved her head. She popped a mint in her mouth. It couldn't mask the taste of alcohol nor did it alleviate her growing headache. She'd overdone it the night before. Again. She really should know better by now. She was well past the age where a good night's sleep could repair the damage.

She watched as the hearse drove away and disappeared into the night. She couldn't quite shake off saying farewell in her head. She wandered over to the spot where the limousine must have taken off. Someone had been in a hurry and taken a wrong turn. There was no other explanation for the height of the impacts on the trees or the distance the car had flown. It would be some time before forensics were in a position to give her any further details.

Maya turned to the uniformed officers who'd received her: Oskar and Jörn. They sounded like cartoon characters.

'So the only witness got away?' she said.

'Maybe because he was more than just a witness.'

Jörn held up his phone so Maya could see the portrait of a young man on the screen. Average-looking, seemingly harmless, dark brown hair with an undercut.

'Jan Wutte,' Jörn said. 'Eighteen, training to be a nurse. A few minor offences – disturbing the peace, weed. He ran straight into a couple of officers as he was fleeing the scene of the accident. Told them some absurd story. Said he'd just finished his shift, that one of the victims in the car had stammered something to him before some killers turned up, took a briefcase and set fire to everything. Then he ran away.'

You let him get away, Maya thought but kept her mouth shut. Remarks like that didn't win you any friends, and she'd need some tonight.

'Doesn't look innocent to me,' Jörn concluded.

'Well, let's get the facts straight first,' Maya said. 'What have we found out from the limousine service?'

'They've confirmed that the car was hired for Herbert Thompson.'

'The Nobel Prize winner?'

'Correct.' Jörn swiped his phone screen. 'We have his schedule. Here it is. Thompson was staying at the Hotel Podium, near Alexanderplatz. He was heading to Charlottenburg Palace, where there's a reception this evening for—'

'I know. Carry on.'

'The driver rang the office immediately after the pickup. There was another passenger with Thompson.'

'Who?'

'The driver didn't say. Thompson asked the driver to take his guest back to Mitte after dropping him off in Charlottenburg. The guest would give him the destination. The driver was calling to get clearance for the extra trip.'

'And he got it?'

'Yes. The car had to return to Mitte, in any case.'

'Do we know where the passenger wanted to go?'

'No.'

'So this mystery passenger, who may be one of the victims, wanted to drive to Charlottenburg with Thompson and then back to Mitte on his own. Why?'

Jörn shrugged his shoulders. 'Maybe they needed to discuss something urgently.'

'And Thompson's fellow passenger didn't have an invitation to the Charlottenburg reception. That might explain it. Any traffic cameras near by? There must be. Check it out, will you?'

Jörn pulled a face.

'Has anyone looked into Wutte's details?'

'You know how mad things are out there,' he replied with a non-committal flick of his wrist. 'Every available officer is already in the field.'

'You and I are clearly available,' she said, 'otherwise we wouldn't be here.'

Heads.

'I've never seen you here before,' Jan said to Fitzroy, as if he'd been here before himself. 'First time?'

Once more, Fitzroy Peel had recorded the scores at

lightning speed. Jan was happy to rely on the fact that the pro's calculations were correct and merely kept a rough count for himself. It wasn't looking good.

'Yes.'

'What brings you here?'

'The summit.'

The man's pen moved incredibly fast. He'd jotted down all the results as they talked.

'Coins at the ready,' he ordered, and all the competitors tossed.

It was nowhere near as glamorous as James Bond playing poker, but on the plus side, Jan wouldn't get tortured afterwards. He hoped.

Tails.

'I guessed as much,' Jan continued. 'Your accent. You don't sound local.'

Jan's score shrank even further.

'I'm English.'

Jan had won three and lost four. His hundred points had dwindled to forty-three and a couple of decimals. Fitzroy rounded the number up. If Mr T-Shirt's and the Gaul's admittedly differing explanations were to be believed, Jan simply had to hang in there for long enough.

'Your German's good.'

Heads.

'I lived here for a few years.'

Heads.

That's better.

Tails.

Jan's score went up and down. The speed of Fitzroy's calculations made flipping the coin into an almost meditative activity. Now and then Jan even forgot what had happened in the Tiergarten.

Tails.
How luck can change on the flip of a coin.

It took Bell a few minutes to walk to the nearest subway station, from where he caught the next train to Alexander-platz and came up under the TV tower. It was another few minutes' walk to Rosa-Luxemburg-Strasse. He kept his face well hidden beneath his baseball cap from the CCTV cameras along the way, his disguise make-up doing the rest.

The streets were teeming with the usual evening crowd, or at least that's how it seemed. Only the occasional small group held up banners, talking earnestly as they made their way to a demo or back home from one.

He'd concealed the envelope diagonally across his chest inside his shirt, the bulge barely noticeable beneath his bulging pecs.

In the arched doorway of an old house a young man was smoking a cigarette. He was wearing a pair of chinos and a polo shirt and barely came up to the tip of Bell's nose.

'Nice evening, isn't it?' Bell said.

'Depends if you're spending it with friends.'

'I am,' Bell said, continuing the exchange as agreed.

'In that case, it is a nice evening.'

All right then. Bell undid three buttons of his shirt, extracted the envelope and handed it to the other man. He weighed it briefly in one hand, and took a last drag on his cigarette before grinding it out with his shoe, then tucked the package under his arm and sauntered off without another word.

'Parcel delivered,' Bell reported to El via his headset.

'Good. Meet us at Golden Bar in Tucholskystrasse. In a couple of minutes we strike.'

16

The chancellor and the UN Secretary-General had talked before the entrée, which was *mousse de foie gras* on a lavender and port *jus* – a surprising choice for a German summit. The dining rooms of the orangery could accommodate forty round tables with twelve people at each. The seating order was subtly graded according to rank and importance. The closer a table was to the speaker's lectern, the more important the guests. As Ted's companion, Jeanne was seated at the very front. Dining with her were Ted to her left, a female politician, three male politicians, one of them accompanied, the head of a central bank, a bishop, and a Chinese billionaire and his wife. The seat of the Nobel Prize winner remained empty, like a missing tooth. The guests didn't appear to have heard the news. They chatted about the crises of yesteryear – which had been dramatic enough – as well as swapping recent holiday stories or tips on where to shop locally and showing off snaps of their children's graduations on their phones. The chanting of the demonstrators and the noise of circling police helicopters were almost inaudible. The situation felt increasingly surreal to Jeanne.

'Why don't we stretch our legs for a moment?' Ted suggested, getting up. Although this was unconventional behaviour for such a prestigious sit-down reception, many other people seemed to have had the same idea. The situation was simply too tense, and people had too much to discuss with guests placed on other tables to remain in their seats between courses. A whisper of fabric and a hubbub of voices ran through the room. George Lamarck appeared behind Ted. His table was at the very back of the room.

'I need to speak to a few people,' Ted said. 'George, will you take care of Maurizio, please.'

'Nothing would give me more pleasure,' gushed George, who had a soft spot for right-wing populists. 'Italy is sorted.'

'Jeanne, I need to borrow a phone for a minute.'

Caught off guard, Jeanne handed Ted one of her two work phones. Normally he would give her quick instructions in this kind of situation or use one of his own many mobiles.

'Cary,' he said, turning his back on the table, 'short GM and the other selected car manufacturers.' Jeanne caught only snatches of the rest of the conversation due to the background noise. Ted reeled off the names of about twenty other famous or less well-known companies, but after that she could no longer hear what he said. He was obviously betting on a fall in the markets – a risky strategy that could leave him open to charges of illegal insider trading or front running, given that he knew about the problems facing these firms before the information had been made public. He generally knew what he was doing though. The deals were probably being made via remote and sufficiently anonymous subsidiaries, registered in some tax haven or other and part of his complex web of companies. Jeanne was more surprised that he was doing it at all. Markets couldn't fail to notice large amounts of money being staked on a collapse in the shares of a company, and it would only drive their price down even further. That might lead to speculation about the very difficulties that were supposed to remain secret until this gathering of politicians and businessmen had come up with a solution. It would set in motion the very chain reaction people feared. To Jeanne's mind, there was only one possible explanation, but her train of thought was interrupted when an elderly man with gold-framed glasses stepped up to the lectern. He cleared his throat and tapped the microphone.

'Ladies and gentlemen, our first scheduled speaker, Herbert Thompson, has not arrived yet, and I am therefore inviting the winner of the 2011 Nobel Peace Prize to address us. Please welcome Leymah Gbowee.'

There was a round of applause, and those still seated rose until everyone was on their feet. Ted returned Jeanne's phone and then walked round to the Chinese billionaire at their table. Jeanne couldn't make out what Ted was saying to him. The Chinese man nodded and, deep in conversation, the two of them wended their way through the applauding crowd to the back of the room as most of the other guests began to retake their seats. Jeanne saw them whisper to three other people as they passed their tables. She recognized a Swedish billionaire investor and the CEO of one of the world's largest asset management firms. The third was another Chinese man.

Ted hadn't invited Jeanne along this time. She sat down and turned to face the podium, where the Nobel laureate was commencing her speech. Ted, the Chinese man and the head of the central bank were missing from her table. Finding herself abandoned like this, she felt a fresh outbreak of the Cinderella complex. How she hated this role of passive companion! She glanced around the room again to see if she could spot Ted. Now that most people were seated again, she realized that all the heads of state had disappeared.

17

The sixties residential block in the Beusselstrasse looked as
though it should have been renovated long ago. A Chinese restaurant on the ground floor had posters up advertising an 'all
you can eat' bargain for seven euros, while the dry-cleaner's
shop next door had a 'two suits for €18' offer. The window of
the third store showcased nothing but grime, wonky shelves
and a few dead insects lying dried-out on the windowsill.

'Nice,' Jörn remarked with a disparaging sneer.

Maya rang the doorbell marked 'Wutte'.

'Yes?' a shrill voice asked over the intercom.

'Maya Paritta from the police. Is your son Jan at home?'

'No. What's he gone and done this time?'

'May we come up for a minute?'

Incomprehensible muttering, a buzz as the door was
unlocked, and Jörn went inside.

There was a smell of dust and old age, and a whiff of
recent cleaning in the stairwell. The Wuttes lived on the
first floor.

Jan's mother was Maya's age. Half a head taller, dyed
blonde hair, a tight sequinned jumper and jeans. *A good-
looking woman*, Maya thought, even if life and cigarettes
had rather hollowed out her features.

'I don't know where he is.'

78

'Do you mind if we come in quickly?'

'If you want.'

The woman went ahead, leaving it to Jörn to shut the door behind them. The flat was clean and tidy, even if the furnishings weren't really to Maya's taste.

'The twat's got himself arrested again, has he?' crowed a voice from the living room. A teenage girl was lounging on the couch with her mobile. She was a younger version of her mother and hadn't yet grown out of her puppy fat, judging by the gap between her crop top and denim shorts.

'Shut your mouth, Regina!' her mother snarled. 'Make yourself useful and take that washing down instead.'

The doors to the other rooms were open. A rack festooned with drying laundry stood in one corner. Frau Wutte returned to her place at the ironing board and picked up where she'd left off.

'You're welcome to take a look around,' she told them.

'Sure,' Maya said. 'We're looking for him in relation to an accident he witnessed.'

'Or . . .' Jörn began, but Maya dug her elbow into him. *Be quiet!*

Frau Wutte seemed to age before their eyes. Her voice quavering, she asked, 'An accident? Is he all right?'

'Don't worry, he's fine,' Maya said.

'What happened?'

'That's what we'd dearly love to find out.'

Frau Wutte went over to the coffee table to get her phone. 'I'll give him a ring.' She dialled a number, swiped the screen and waited. 'No answer.'

'Might he have gone somewhere else? To a friend's? His girlfriend's? A relative's?'

'Not to his dad's, that's for sure,' Regina bleated from the sofa.

Her mother rolled her eyes. 'I told you to take down the washing!'

'Mine's no better,' the daughter shot back without moving.

'Will you shut up, I said!' Turning to Maya, the mother said, 'She's right, I'm afraid. I don't have much luck with men.'

'You can say that again,' Regina chipped in from the sidelines.

'Nor do I,' Maya said. 'Any friends?'

'A bunch of dossers and losers,' Regina said.

'Do you have any names, phone numbers, addresses?'

'Nope,' the teenager said without looking up. 'For that lot? Gimme a break.'

'I can give you two or three,' the mother said. She scrolled through the contacts on her phone.

Maya took a shot of them on her own phone, then gave the woman her card. 'Ask Jan to call us as soon as you see him, will you?'

'He'd chuck his phone in the River Spree before he called the cops,' Regina muttered from the sofa.

Heads.

It was something like round fifty-five. Jan's score was now in single figures, as were those of another six of the ten players including the Gaul. Mr T-Shirt's account was still in the twenties but he too was on the slide.

'And what do you get up to at the summit when you're not gambling?' Jan said, trying again to draw Fitzroy out.

'I gamble,' he replied.

Heads.

That took Jan up from two point something to a fraction over three.

'There's something wrong here,' another player complained. He'd thrown tails, and his score was also in the low single digits. 'I'm never going to make it to thirteen thousand points like this.'

Heads.

'Be patient,' Mr T-Shirt suggested, no longer sounding quite so confident.

'We just have to stick it out for long enough,' the Gaul seconded him, but his expression was uncertain and he was now deep in the red.

'You gamble?' Jan attempted to revive his conversation with Fitzroy.

Tails.

One woman only had amassed more than a thousand points. Her next toss came up heads, whereas Jan landed on tails again.

The game went on, Fitzroy keeping score. The way things were going, he'd only need to double one stake; he could keep the rest. He was doing all the maths in his head, quick as a flash. On the other hand, no one could really predict what the outcome would be.

By now only the decimals were changing in Jan's score and each one of them could toss a coin like a pro. Jan was about to flip again when Fitzroy sat up with a jolt.

'Take a look at this, will you?'

Jan gave a start and the coin slipped off his thumb.

'There are ten people playing, four of you as good as broke. Three still have a tiny bit in the bank. Two are hovering around their starting score, and only one person has made any real gains.'

That was a good summary of the situation. Jan belonged to the first group, unfortunately.

'Interesting, isn't it?' Fitzroy said. 'That spread of points is fairly representative of the actual distribution of wealth among the population. Forty per cent have no cake at all, another thirty to forty per cent have a tiny slice. The upshot is that a small number have a great deal without having worked any harder for it than the others. A toss-up. Pure chance.'

Where was this leading? To a lecture on economics?

'And if it continues, you'll rake in every one of our bets,' the Gaul said. 'So what are you in your comparison? The banks? Marie-Antoinette?'

Fitzroy laughed.

'This can't be right,' another person mumbled. 'In a random distribution, there ought to be a relatively normal range of scores. So why are most of us in the red while one person has all the points?'

'Let's carry on,' Fitz said, grinning. 'We haven't finished yet.'

But Jan had – with this particular game, anyway. His head was throbbing. From the gambling or from his unwanted encounter with the side of the car? It was time for him to talk to Mr Peel in private.

'I've got their faces,' Jack's voice announced via the earpiece. El had shifted his position in the room several times and treated himself to some lemonade. They had been tossing coins for half an hour now. 'You can find them in the team folder.'

Top facial recognition software, professional IT skills, access to a few decent databases and a few people who knew how to use all these things: it wasn't rocket science.

'The Samaritan is a nurse called Jan Wutte. He's eighteen and from Berlin. A few minor misdemeanours like noisy parties and joints, but nothing serious.'

El checked his phone. He scrolled through the pictures Sam had taken and the accompanying captions. Two women, seven men and the Samaritan.

What the hell are you doing here?

Something had bothered El on his first flick-through. He swiped back and spotted what it was – the guy with the shaved head. If he'd understood Sam correctly, and his own eyesight was to be trusted, he was the croupier. All the others were locals and had German names, but the croupier was British. Fitzroy Peel. A peculiar name. A professional gambler. El was about to read on when the voice in his ear said, 'One of them's flashing dark red. He's the only Brit in the group.'

'Fitzroy Peel.'

'There's more though. Have you read up on him yet?'

'I was about to.'

'Look at the pictures at the end of the report.'

El scrolled down. Two pictures of two young men beaming at the camera. In one they were wearing black graduation gowns and mortarboards, in the second they wore expensive suits, looking like young investment bankers.

The two of them seemed about ten years younger and yet El immediately recognized the men's faces.

One was gambling at the table over there with the Samaritan. The other had been hanging upside down in a crumpled limousine a mile from here an hour ago, hoping the Samaritan might save his life.

18

'So you've come to the summit to gamble?'

Fitzroy studied the kid next to him from the corner of his eye. He was nosey. A good-looking beanpole – the word 'loose-jointed' popped into Fitzroy's head – despite his awful haircut, cropped short underneath and long on top, which reminded Fitzroy of the Hitler Youth.

'Same as here? Is that how you make your living?'

The kid had been the last to join the game.

Four heads, six tails. Fitzroy wrote down the scores, most of them in decimal figures now. With one exception: a woman.

'From gambling? Not really, no.'

The kid didn't seem remotely affected by his losses. Fitzroy had a nagging feeling he was after something else.

'Why not?' the kid asked, pointing to the pile of money in front of Fitzroy. 'A few hundred euros in less than an hour. I wouldn't say no to that kind of income.'

'Watch and learn.'

Eight heads, two tails. No great help to most of the players, including the two bigmouths who'd enlisted the others. Even the lady who'd had a couple of hot streaks had just seen her score drop from over two thousand points to around one thousand two hundred.

As far as Fitzroy was concerned, the only surprise was that the pub staff had left him alone for so long.

'There's something going on here. You're cheating!' the fatter of the two wise guys yelled at Fitzroy.

'Yeah!' a second man howled.

Other voices joined in with the recriminations. It was amazing it had taken them so long; he'd known rowdier groups.

'Your coins,' Fitzroy reminded them. 'You flipped them, you accepted the bet and you did the maths.'

'Exactly. That's why I should've earned more by now!' the fat wise guy said.

'Maybe you got your sums mixed up?' Fitzroy remarked. 'Maybe you calculated the wrong average?'

'The wrong . . . ?' the man murmured in bewilderment. 'No way!' He leaped to his feet and, reaching across the table, made to grab Fitzroy's collar. Fitzroy had seen him coming, though, and dodged him with ease. This only enraged the guy further, his neighbours also jumping to their feet, yelling accusations and starting to get physical.

Fitzroy sprang to his feet too so he wouldn't be caught on the defensive. He was definitely as tall as the fat guy and certainly in better shape.

'You're running an illegal gambling session!' the man roared. He struck out at Fitzroy again, but once more his fist met nothing but thin air.

'What about you, eh?' Fitzroy said with a chuckle. 'It takes two to tango.'

'Give me my money back, you cheat!' the fat man shouted. As expected, the other players backed up his demand.

Fitzroy pointed to the woman who was still in the black. 'So she doesn't get to keep her winnings?'

This brought them up short for a moment.

'We made a bet,' Fitzroy reminded them.

'I don't give a shit!' the fat man thundered, his face dark red. 'I'm reporting you to the police, you bloody con artist!' He thrust his hand into Fitzroy's pile of money.

'All right,' Fitzroy said with a nervous laugh, 'we'll break off and everyone gets their money back—'

But the fat man was no longer listening, far too aggrieved that his calculations had somehow turned out to be faulty, and too conceited to admit it. He leaned forward, one knee on the table, and took a swing at Fitzroy's head. The croupier ducked, but there was such a throng of people pressing against him from behind that he couldn't properly get out of the way and the punch grazed his lip. The other players were busy trying to retrieve their coins, grab some of Fitzroy's stash of cash or join in the assault. Nothing he wasn't used to.

Once again El scanned the ceiling of the room for surveillance cameras, as he'd done on entering the pub and several times since. There were none.

'This is our chance,' he told Jack and Sam over the headset. 'Our Samaritan Jan Wutte and Fitzroy Peel won't make it out of this punch-up alive, I'll make sure of that. But watch out for smartphone cameras.'

Fitzroy Peel was almost a head taller than the Samaritan and most of the other gamblers. Nevertheless, at least four of them were attacking him with others preparing to follow their lead. Peel raised his arms in self-defence, chuckled and cried out, 'Stop! Stop it!' as if it were all a joke.

His victims were no longer interested in what he had to say. Their ringleader, a tall guy with quite a beer belly, landed a hard punch flush on Fitzroy's nose. He staggered backwards into several other guests. Beer was spilled, people tripped over one another and screams of pains rang out. Within seconds a tangled mass of arms, legs, bodies and heads lay writhing on the floor. Previously uninvolved parties were also now starting to jostle because someone had shoved them or covered them in drink. A waiter cleared a path for himself, but even he could no longer prevent the kerfuffle from escalating into a full-scale brawl. More and more hands were jabbed into people's chests, and fists slammed into stomachs and faces. The Samaritan did his best to escape the pandemonium, but the crush of bodies was too great.

El gave the order. 'We're going in!'

Jan was trying his best to avoid the swinging fists and escape the fighting. The back of the pub where they had been playing moments earlier had descended into all-out war. Staff members had abandoned their attempts to calm the situation. Two were engaged in excited phone calls behind the bar, presumably with the police. *Not again!* Jan could really have done without any more hassle. The place was so jampacked still that non-combatants had little hope of getting out unscathed. He'd lost sight of Fitzroy Peel. Bottles and glasses flew through the air, followed soon afterwards by the first chair. Even people well away from the battle zone were being hit, extending it further out. Jan was closer to the exit to the toilets than he was to the more peaceful area at the front. To get there he'd have to pass at least twenty brawlers, a horde of anonymous faces in the half-darkness. He'd be running the gauntlet. He spied Fitzroy in the midst of the fray, defending himself against Mr T-Shirt and two other men.

It must have been instinctive. Images seared into his unconscious by the intensity of the moment allowed him to recognize one of the faces, as though it were picked out under a dazzling spotlight.

Anvil Chin. Standing behind an unsuspecting Fitzroy, brandishing a broken bottle which, any minute now, he would slash down on the Briton's head. A second assassin in dark grey clothing stood with his back to Jan, his silhouette also familiar. He was charging Fitzroy as well, a twinkling blade in his hand. Jan sprinted towards him and launched himself on to the man's back, shouting, 'Behind you, Fitz! Get down!'

The torso beneath Jan felt like a stone clad in fabric. The man didn't even seem to notice his presence.

Hearing Jan's warning, Fitzroy ducked. Anvil Chin's lunge with the broken bottle missed his neck by a hair's breadth and slashed open Mr T-Shirt's arm instead. The fat guy screamed, and his blood spattered over them all. Jan's mount brought up his arm to plunge the knife into Fitzroy's back. At least that's what Jan thought until the man twisted his wrist, swung back his arm and tried to stab Jan over his shoulder. He managed to swivel to the side at the last moment so the blade only nicked his jacket, but he was thrown to the floor.

Not content with this, the man now switched his attention from Fitzroy to Jan. He was much taller and weighed twice as much as him, a block of pure muscle and still with the knife in his hand. Jan was scrambling for the exit when a rabbit punch knocked the wind out of him. He crumpled to his knees. Something hard and cold smashed into his face and Jan toppled on to his side, caught against the legs of the brawlers surrounding him. The shouting all around him came to him as if filtered through cotton wool. The next second, a punch to his stomach like a wrecking ball forced the last remaining air from his lungs. Black spots danced in front of his eyes, blurring his vision. Vague shapes leaped at him.

Shadows darted in all directions. Steelfingers grabbed his hair and pulled his head back and now the cold edge of a metal blade pressed against his throat. His legs kicked out and his arms whirled but everything seemed to happen in slow motion. He'd seen hundreds of horror films and gory thrillers. He'd never watched any actual terrorist videos online, but had read enough about them. *What the bloody hell was happening?*

Jan's warning had saved Fitzroy's carotid artery from being severed by the broken bottle. Now the wound the madman had slashed in the fat guy's arm gave Fitzroy an opportunity to strike back. A well-aimed kick to the side of the man's knee and it buckled, before a chair to the skull sent him tumbling to the floor where he just about managed to cushion his landing. The reptilian part of his brain fighting for survival, Fitzroy had no time to think. His gambling had often got him into trouble, but he'd never experienced anything on this scale. These men in dark clothing weren't just here for a good old punch-up – they hadn't even been taking part in the game. Fitzroy had escaped bleeding to death by a fraction of an inch.

The fat guy's screaming and the shower of blood drew everyone's attention in their direction. The other attacker had thrown Jan off his back and, along with another beef-cake, was pounding the kid to a pulp. Then Fitzroy spotted the knife against Jan's throat. The chair Fitzroy was holding was only half broken, so he reduced it to matchsticks over the assailant's head. The second guy must have annoyed a few people in the crowd, or else someone was still desperate for a fight, because three other men immediately set upon him. Jan's would-be killer could swat them aside like flies, but had to let go of his victim for a moment.

Fitzroy grabbed Jan's wrist and dragged him to his feet. Jan's knees were like jelly. Fitzroy threw his new mate's arm around his shoulders and fought his way to the toilets. There was an emergency exit out the back; he'd checked before the game. They burrowed through the crowd that had gathered in the corridor to escape the fighting. Everyone recoiled, horror and disgust written on their faces. The pack closed behind them, shielding them from the prying eyes of potential pursuers. Fitzroy knew his height might give them away and so kept his head down. Gradually Jan began to support some of his own weight again.

The grey metal emergency exit door was open. It led out into an alleyway packed with people, some of them standing around in groups, staring at the pub, having presumably fled the mayhem inside. Others were the usual revellers or perhaps demonstrators. Leaning on Fitzroy still, Jan gulped and gasped for air before a coughing fit shook his frame. Eventually, he took one last deep breath, then stood up straight and looked Fitzroy in the eye.

'They were trying to kill me,' he croaked. He glanced around anxiously, then thanked his companion.

'Thank *you*,' Fitzroy replied. 'If you hadn't warned me, I'd be lying inside with half a bottle buried in my neck.'

Jan tugged Fitzroy along the alley by the arm. 'We've got to get out of here.'

He pushed the Brit into the entrance of an old building. The gate was ajar and led into a passageway that ran through the courtyards of a block of houses. There was no one in sight and the courtyards were only dimly lit.

Fitzroy let out a sigh of relief. 'What the hell was all that about?'

19

El and Sam chased their two targets along the corridor, past the toilets and through the emergency exit out into the open air. El didn't believe in bad luck, only bad preparation. Or hubris. They had underestimated the two men's will to survive. *Our mistake.* And the dynamics of the pub brawl – more violent and more participants than expected. Innocent parties had stumbled into the middle of their attack. Not good. Mistakes were part of their business. They only had to be rectified. Their client need not find out about this.

Escapees from the pub were mingling with night owls in the back street. There were no cars or bicycles to be seen. They couldn't have got far. It was at least seventy yards to the nearest junction. No one running. Were they street-smart or just fast? Sam and El zigzagged through the crowds until they reached the next crossroads.

A bigger road. More people. Even more opportunities to disappear.

El had a quick think. Jan Wutte wouldn't go home, given that he was on the run from the police. He would have to reckon with some unpleasantness if he did. He glanced through the data on Fitzroy Peel. One important detail was missing, so he contacted Jack, their man for online research.

'I need Fitzroy Peel's current address in Berlin.'

They were barely making any headway, even with the flashing blue light they had attached to the car roof – or maybe because of it. The people in the street made no particular effort to make room for the police car to pass. Jörn was driving right on the edge of the law. They listened to updates on the demos on the police radio. The main one had been peaceful so far. Only on the margins and in Kreuzberg were black blocs skirmishing with the police, while right-wing extremists were throwing stones and shouting Nazi slogans in Friedrichshain.

'I can't believe they authorized these demonstrations,' Jörg was ranting.

'You mean the rich should be free to assemble, but no one else?'

Radio news: heads of government and experts were conferring at the reception in Charlottenburg Castle. Groups of negotiators were going to work late into the night.

'How long will it take us to get to the Golden Bar?' asked Maya.

'Ten minutes or so,' Jörn muttered. 'I can't fathom why you'd take that story seriously.'

'We've been through this already. For the time being, "that story" is our only lead. Golden Bar. Fitzroy Peel. Chantal.'

'We'd probably have been quicker on foot,' Jörn grumbled to himself.

Maya turned off the radio and used her phone's voice-activation function.

'Herbert Thompson,' she said. 'Wikipedia.'

The phone dutifully read out the online encyclopaedia's

entry on the Nobel laureate. Born in 1937, he'd studied Economics in Chicago and Harvard, taught in Chicago, London, Stanford and at other top international universities, and made significant contributions to monetary theory, on unemployment and economic cycles. He'd advised the United States administrations of Gerald Ford and Ronald Reagan on economic policy, and counselled the World Bank and the governments of various post-Soviet states on large-scale privatizations in the 1990s. He had later come in for a great deal of criticism, as these reforms had essentially turned several oligarchs into billionaires while the vast majority of the population remained impoverished. He'd gone on to work for George W. Bush's administration, but had turned down the post of Secretary of Commerce. He was a free-market liberal who defended individual liberties and the invisible hand while seeking to keep the state as small as possible. He was still an adviser to a number of politicians as well as international institutions such as the International Monetary Fund and the United Nations, and had also written a number of bestselling books.

'Sounds important,' remarked Jörn.

'And he was due to give one of the opening addresses at this evening's gala dinner,' Maya said, 'as well as a keynote speech tomorrow.'

She turned up the police radio.

'*I repeat: fighting in Mitte, Tucholskystrasse. Golden Bar. Reinforcements needed.*'

One glance at Jörn and she knew what her colleague was thinking: *OK, this little 'story' has just taken an interesting turn.*

There were replies from officers in the vicinity of the fight, and some were already on their way.

'Time for the old blues and twos,' Maya said. Her final

word was almost inaudible, drowned out by the blare of the siren that Jörn had switched on. Startled pedestrians jumped aside. At long last they were getting somewhere. They might well catch Wutte sooner than expected.

Jan emerged from the passageway on the other side of the block, Fitz hard on his heels. These were familiar shortcuts for a local like Jan. They had thrown off their pursuers for the time being, but now they stuck to particularly busy streets where it was easier to hide. A pale violet bruise was blossoming around his right eye. Various areas of his head and torso were throbbing painfully. He hoped the blows hadn't caused any serious damage.

'The police must have reached the Golden Bar by now,' Fitz said. 'Someone needs to report those madmen to them.'

'Be my guest,' Jan said. 'I'm not going to. I wouldn't be surprised if they've staked out the pub.' He glanced around nervously. There was no sign of Anvil Chin and his posse.

He stopped and looked Fitz up and down. A sprinkling of blood on his shaved pate looked like freckles. Jan dragged him into a shadowy doorway.

'Listen, I've got something to tell you. I was witness to a triple murder this evening,' he said. 'The only witness—'

'Wow – stop! What?'

'As I was saying . . . The police wanted to take me in as a suspect. Thought I had something to do with the crime, but the real perpetrators were the guys who attacked us at the bar.'

'You should ring the police as soon as possible!'

'So they can take me in after all? No thanks. One of the victims was apparently a Nobel Prize winner.'

'That means the police are under pressure. They'll have to produce results and fast.'

94

'Correct. Me, for example.'

'But what do I have to do with any of this?'

'Before he died, one of the victims mentioned your name and the name of the bar. I went there on the off-chance and happened to run into you.'

Even in the dark, Jan could see Fitzroy's face go pale.

'I'd arranged to meet an old friend there,' he whispered, 'but he never turned up. Was he . . . Was he the victim who gave my name?'

'No idea. A guy of roughly your age.'

Fitzroy pulled out his mobile and tapped on it, his hands shaking. He showed Jan a picture of a man in his mid-thirties, good-looking in a fairly drab way with a neat side parting, glasses and a peculiar expression that was simultaneously arrogant and shy.

'Was it him?'

'He was upside down inside a flipped, wrecked car. Let me see.'

There was a name at the bottom of the screen: 'Will Cantor'.

Jan couldn't have said why, but second time around, Will Cantor's face looked like that of a small boy, marvelling, surprised at the world and at the people who lived in it. It made him look both inquisitive and wary. He turned the screen upside down. 'Was he an old friend of yours?'

Fitz gave an audible gulp. 'Yes.'

How should he break it to him? 'I'm so sorry,' Jan said softly.

20

Jeanne let the waiter take away her dessert – an arrangement of petits fours and mini-éclairs – almost untouched. The uniformed servers topped up people's glasses, but Jeanne stuck to water. For her figure. And for greater self-control. The first guests were starting to fidget and shift in their seats, eager to get back to their hotels and villas, or else they had been summoned to the late-night crisis meetings that had begun somewhere near Berliner Platz. People, however, were still hanging on for the evening's final speaker, when the compère, who'd already announced Thompson's delayed arrival, stepped up to the microphone.

'Ladies and gentlemen, it is with great regret that I must announce that our third speaker, Mr Herbert Thompson, will sadly no longer be able to attend this evening.'

The guests groaned and within minutes, the first chairs scraped on the wooden floor as people rose to their feet. No one was really terribly disappointed not to have to listen to another speech. There were gaps at many of the tables as it was.

At Ted's table too, the guests politely took their leave before melting, individually or in groups, out into the crowd.

'Did you get anywhere with the Chinese?' Jeanne asked Ted quietly.

'We'll see.'

Ambrose Peel's sonorous baritone interrupted their conversation. 'Ah, the charming Ms Dalli and her companion. I hear the Chinese are still acting coy.'

'Just a matter of time,' Ted retorted sharply.

His gaze shifted smartly to a tall, austere-looking man who was making his way towards them. Walter Ferguson, a lead executive at Solid State, one of the world's largest asset management firms, which had grown on the back of exchange-traded funds, ETFs, most of which were simple and inexpensive funds that tracked the market index. This had been one of the most popular forms of investment since the 2008 crisis and had transformed the company into a big beast of the financial system alongside companies like Black Rock and Vanguard.

'Walter,' Ted said in greeting, before introducing Jeanne and Peel.

'I hear people have been discussing special rescue operations?' Ferguson asked in a low voice.

Ted had sized him up in a second. Ferguson knew it would have been a cause for concern if such a major player had been in the dark. He was guarded in his response because he didn't know whether Peel was informed. Grasping this immediately, Ted cleared up Walter's unspoken question with his answer. 'Are you in? The more, the merrier.'

That wasn't altogether true. The more parties that showed an interest in potential offers, the higher the prices would rise and the less attractive the deal would become.

'We're in,' Walter said in a whisper.

'Good.'

'On the other hand . . .'

Peel's bushy eyebrows met in a frown.

'On the other hand . . .' Ted began, and then he realized.

Jeanne had never seen Ted turn pale before, but in a split second her boss had recovered his composure. She could tell from his eyes that his brain was whirring, as was hers.

'You always claimed those things were safe,' Peel said, glaring at Ferguson. 'That's how I understood it. You're basically buying stakes in a sort of investment fund, which itself owns stakes in the companies whose index it mirrors. Obviously, when those share prices fall, the ETF prices fall too. And when the shares go up again – and at some point they always do – then the ETFs go up with them. Now, I'm no financial expert . . .'

Jeanne stared at Ferguson. 'The synthetic ones, right?'

Alarmed, Peel said, 'What are those?'

'What you just described,' Jeanne said, 'are known as physical exchange-traded funds, but there are others called synthetic ETFs.'

'What does "synthetic" mean here?'

'They don't necessarily own any stocks of the index they're tracking.'

'How does that work?'

'They use different assets and a range of financial derivatives such as swaps to replicate the index. They often do a better job than physical ETFs, but they need partners in the financial industry with whom they can execute more complex deals. In return, those partners want guarantees, generally some kind of collateral.'

Ted was listening closely to her explanation and nodded encouragingly. This was her turn to make an impression.

'I can guess where this is heading,' Peel groaned. 'The whole thing runs smoothly in normal circumstances, but with the threats we're currently facing, the underlying securities may well suffer a dramatic drop in value. The ETF managers' trade partners want more guarantees, but because the market's at rock bottom, they can't get them.'

'In addition, those securities have often been borrowed, swapped and so forth, meaning that other segments are infected.'

'Synthetic positions only account for a portion of the ETF market,' Ferguson objected. 'And the maximum derivative share is only ten per cent . . .'

'The problem is that most clients, particularly small investors, won't distinguish between the two,' Ted replied, 'and will join the stampede to get rid of their ETFs. That's what Jeanne's driving at and she's right. It'll force the market into a downward spiral.'

'Oh God,' Peel gasped, 'so we're in for the same mess as in 2008? No one knows exactly where the risks are? So if the markets nosedive in the next couple of days, none of you lot will trust anyone else and global financial flows will dry up because the banks won't lend to one another?'

'A little simplistic,' Ferguson said stiffly, 'but fairly accurate, yes.'

Another domino falls.

'Fairly?' Peel hissed, his face now puce. 'And what are you going to do about it?'

'Pray,' Ted said. 'For bargains.'

21

Gangs of people were chatting outside the Golden Bar, making phone calls or staring at their mobiles. They were probably busy posting tales and short videos of their evening adventures on social media. Two patrol cars with flashing lights had drawn up beside the entrance, and two more were inching along the lane towards Maya and Jörn. A couple of police officers were pushing people out of the pub after taking their details. Jörn cleared a path for Maya to enter.

A few small groups remained inside the pub. Maya kept an eye out for Jan Wutte. Fallen tables, chairs and broken glasses were lying in a cocktail of beer, wine and other fluids at the front of the pub. The area at the back to the left of the bar looked as if someone had been splitting wood on an industrial scale. Splashes of red and skid marks where people had slipped were visible in the broth on the wooden floorboards. The place reeked of alcohol and sweat. A guy with a beer belly and a very pale face was sitting with his back against the wall. A waiter was kneeling beside him, pressing nervously on a blood-soaked bandage around the man's arm. Three other men were leaning against furniture or lying on the floor, attended by a police officer. A few women were still patching up their injuries at the bar or being comforted or scolded by their friends. Maya spotted a uniform there too and made straight for the bar.

'Hi, where's the landlord or landlady of this place?'

A man behind the bar held up his hand. 'I'm the duty manager.'

Maya introduced herself and asked a few questions. The man didn't know very much. A whole bunch of people at the back of the bar had suddenly started an argument.

'Do you have CCTV?'

'Only over the doors.'

'We need the recordings.' She wrestled with herself for a second before asking, 'I couldn't have a drink, could I? A Pisco Sour.'

'Aren't you on duty?' he asked in bemusement.

'That's my business.'

As he mixed the cocktail, Maya showed him a photo of Jan Wutte on her phone. 'Did you see this man here tonight?'

'I couldn't say. There were hundreds of people here, but I don't think so, no. Which isn't to say he wasn't here.'

'How about this one?'

Maya had searched for the name Fitzroy Peel online to see what happened. Most of the entries referred to a professional poker player.

The landlord handed her a glass containing a cloudy liquid.

'Nope.'

Maya drained half of the drink with one swig. The refreshing zing of the lime spread from her stomach to her whole body. She took her glass and wandered over to the injured man by the wall. Beerbelly didn't look too clever.

'Have you called an ambulance?' Maya asked the waiter next to him.

'Of course,' he replied in some agitation.

Maya saw now that blood was oozing through the gauze bandage between the waiter's fingers. The wound must have struck a major artery.

'You've got to press harder,' Maya said. 'Do you have any more bandages?'

The waiter shook his head.

Maya kneeled down and put her glass on the floor.

'Can you talk?' she asked the injured man.

'Who . . . you?' he moaned.

'Detective Inspector Maya Paritta. Do you know what happened here?'

She tore a strip from the bottom edge of the man's T-shirt.

'There was this cheat,' he groaned. 'Gambled with us . . . Ripped us off.'

'Gambling? What sort? Cards?'

'No. Tossing . . . coins.'

Maya folded the strip into a thick wad and pressed it on to the wound. Beerbelly winced.

'Keep pressing it hard,' she told the waiter.

Tossing coins? Maya picked up her glass. 'He cheated? And you wouldn't stand for it?'

His only response was a snort.

'Who did that to you?' Maya asked, pointing to his arm.

'No idea. This hulking guy in black, I think . . . Aargh!' He shut his eyes and rested his head against the wall.

Maya shook him gently by the shoulder of his good arm. 'Stay with me!' She whispered to the waiter, 'Go and see if the paramedics are here. This guy needs to be treated first.'

She put her fingers on the compress as he removed his and pressed down hard. The waiter was only too happy for her to take over and rushed away towards the exit. Beerbelly opened his eyes.

'You're going to be all right,' Maya said. She had to ensure he remained conscious, but that needn't stop her doing her job. She showed him Jan Wutte's photo with her free hand.

Beerbelly stared at the phone.

'Yep, he was playing with us,' he said eventually.

'But he wasn't the cheat?'

A weary shake of his head.

'And this guy?' Fitzroy Peel.

A gurgling sound rose from his chest as he sat up abruptly. 'That's him.' The movement hadn't done him any good. He slumped back against the wall, his head pitched to one side. Maya rushed to prop his body up and felt for his pulse.

'Thanks, you can step aside now,' said a warm but energetic female voice behind her. 'We'll take it from here.'

Paramedics – near the top of Maya's personal list of heroes.

'So you won't go to the police?' Fitzroy asked, striding through the narrow streets of Mitte, past the closed shops and open bars. His young companion continued to shoot wary glances in every direction. Fitzroy was also jumpy, checking constantly to see if there was anyone on their tail.

'Not yet, I won't,' Jan said. 'They reckon I'm a suspect, and there are no other witnesses to back me up.' He aimed a kick at the side of a building suddenly. 'Fucking hell! Shit! All I want is a quiet life. I do everything I'm supposed to – train to be a nurse, get a badly paid job. I can't even afford a decent flat in central Berlin and I won't get much of a pension either, but I take it all on the chin. I play by their shitty rules, and what happens? I'm suspected of murder. Fuck them!'

'Then you need to play by different rules,' said Fitzroy with a shrug.

'Which ones?' he shot back. 'The ones the arseholes set?'

It was hardly surprising the kid was freaking out after the events of the past few hours – if those events really had taken place. Why come up with a story like that? But what if he had?

Fitzroy suddenly felt a flicker of hope – maybe Will was still alive. Maybe this was all a trap. He'd keep his guard up, an old gambler's habit. People often bluffed. But what if Jan wasn't bluffing? What if Will really was dead? Murdered? He refused to follow that train of thought any further.

'*You* could go to the police, though,' Jan said when he'd calmed down a bit, 'and report the brawl.'

Fitzroy touched his face cautiously and gave an audible wince. 'I'll spend the whole night at the station, and that fat guy'll accuse me of illegal gambling. No way. I'm meeting someone later.'

'But your friend's dead . . .'

'And it's *your* statement that's key to finding out who's responsible, not mine,' Fitz retorted.

'Who's so important you have to meet them tonight? You're hardly at your most fetching, you know.'

'It's not a date. It's a serious game of poker with a pot of millions.'

Could he really go there now, after everything that had happened?

Jan was dumbstruck. 'Millions?'

'Around events like summits, you always find a few very, very wealthy people who aren't averse to a lucrative spot of poker and like to see how they measure up against a pro like me.'

'And that's legal?'

'Who cares?'

'Oh, I get it. You can't afford to be done for illegal gambling, because you want to go home a few million better off?'

'Sometimes I do, yes. I can still go to the police in the morning.'

'Hey, I'm walking the streets of Berlin with a millionaire!'

Fitzroy didn't reply.

'So why get yourself beaten up in an ordinary pub then?'

'It was fun! Well, until someone turned out to be a bad loser, that is.'

'I obviously have a very different idea of fun.'

Suddenly Jan grabbed Fitz by the arm and forced him into a doorway. He slowly poked his head out and peered back along the road, then relaxed. 'Sorry,' he said. 'I thought . . .'

They emerged from the safety of the shadows and hurried on. There were lots of people on the street round here. The illuminated cupola of the cathedral rose up ahead with the museums off to one side. In the foreground, a dishevelled figure was rummaging in a rubbish bin.

'Actually, I was just planning to kill time until Will turned up. I got chatting to a few people . . . and suddenly we were in the middle of a game. I need to go back to my hotel and freshen up.'

Jan walked alongside the tall Brit in silence for a few more yards. Lightning lit up the sky on the horizon.

'The police might be waiting for me at home,' Jan said. 'Could I use your bathroom quickly too?'

They had only known each other for about an hour, but the kid was no stranger any more. A distant roll of thunder. Fitzroy had been counting the seconds since the flash. The storm was at least six miles away. 'I'll tell you right now – I never have sex on a first date.'

'Don't worry, you're not my type. Where's your hotel?'

'A few minutes from here.'

They reached Unter den Linden almost at a jog. Fitzroy felt safer on the broad avenue packed with traffic and pedestrians. Demonstrators had set up a small protest camp outside a bank and stood chatting in a patch between a few tents by the light of their lanterns. On Unter den Linden!

'What are they doing?' asked Jan.

'Copying Occupy Wall Street?' Fitz said as a wild guess.

'What's that?'

'Oh, you're too young to have heard of it. In response to the great recession after the 2008 crash, protesters around the world occupied squares in all of the major financial districts. They didn't hold out for very long, though, because they were poorly organized radicals without any clear objectives.'

'What did they think they'd achieve?' Jan asked, with a last glance at the encampment. 'Why were you meeting Will at the Golden Bar anyway?'

'Why does anyone meet up with old friends? He knew I might be in town and got in touch. We hadn't seen each other in a long time.' *A very long time.*

Maya was holding her second Pisco Sour amid the stench and the blood, still trying to make sense of Beerbelly's statement. If Jan Wutte really had made up his story, then the question was why. And why come here after the incident in the Tiergarten when he might have anticipated that the police would track him down?

What was Fitzroy Peel's role in all this? He was real, in any case. There might well be some pre-existing link between the two of them. They could look into that if they had the time and the manpower.

If the story wasn't invented, however, Maya had a

problem, and a big one at that. She turned to her colleagues. They had begun taking witness statements.

'Make sure you ask if anyone filmed it on their phone. If anyone did, ask for the videos, if they're not on social media already. If they are, retrieve them.'

A number of patrons had come forward with videos of their own accord. Maya flicked through them, but most were either too dark or too blurred for her to identify anything at first glance. Someone would have to analyse them in more detail as soon as they had time. It might have to be her. She needed support. Jörn would be no real help while he continued to view Jan Wutte as a suspect rather than objectively, besides which, he wasn't trained to investigate murders. Everyone else was busy with the summit or on other cases. They were all up to their eyeballs in work.

Maya rang HQ. 'I need some information about hotel check-ins,' she said. Jan Wutte had run away from the scene of the accident, so there was little chance he'd make the mistake of turning up at his home. Which left the second person they had identified. 'A man called Fitzroy Peel,' she said, spelling out his name.

Waiting accounted for the rest of her Pisco Sour.

Fitzroy Peel was staying at The Dome Hotel. Wow, the man had splashed out on one of the most exclusive addresses in the city. He must play a mean game.

Maya looked around for Jörn.

22

They had hurried across Unter den Linden, but Fitzroy was now lost in reminiscences of Will. They'd become close friends over years of studying and working together, but since then had seen each other less and less. The odd phone call, an occasional email, a meet-up perhaps once a year.

'I understand why they're trying to get shot of you as a witness,' Fitzroy said, breaking the silence, 'but why me?'

'Because you're a cheat?'

'I'm not a cheat. People can't do maths, that's all. Or they can't think. Or both. That's not my fault.'

'Those two guys calculated it.'

'Incorrectly. They worked out the average of all the possible outcomes, what's known as the ensemble average, as if they were calculating the average height of the population. But what they didn't consider is that the odds change after every coin toss. They acted as if decisions and their consequences weren't a factor. As if dynamics that play out over time weren't a factor. As if time itself wasn't a factor!'

'So how should they have calculated it?'

'The *time* average. Every saver is familiar with the principle from compound interest. The basis of the calculation changes after every increase. You save one hundred euros at two per cent interest . . .'

'Yeah, right. Tell me where I can get two per cent interest!'

'It's just an example . . .'

'I don't earn enough to put any money aside in any case, and yet every upstart banker and politician is making a fortune!'

Ignoring this outburst, Fitzroy continued. 'At the end of one year you have one hundred and two euros. That's the new basis for the following year's two per cent, which comes to two euros and four cents. And so it goes on, year after year. With large sums of money, it adds up to quite a tidy amount over the years.'

He turned into a side street.

'So why did we have less and less money?'

'Oh, for goodness' sake. Because we were playing with different numbers! The time average is negative for the special bets we were running. Calculate just two rounds and it becomes clear. If you start out with one hundred points and lose the first toss, you're left with sixty points. If you then win the second toss, you get fifty per cent of sixty, which is . . . ?'

'Thirty points,' Jan answered. 'I can get that far.'

'Added together that makes . . .'

'Ninety.'

'After one loss and one win you're already ten per cent down,' Fitzroy summed up.

'So I have to win first,' Jan said. 'That turns my original score of one hundred points into one hundred and fifty. If I lose forty per cent on the next toss, that's . . .' – Fitzroy left him to do the maths; he needed to work it out for himself – 'minus sixty points,' Jan announced proudly. 'So . . . Hang on a second! That's ninety points too!'

'Exactly. With a special wager like this, in the long run you lose 5.1 per cent per round.'

'The – what was it called? – ensemble average is different from the time average? The same thing can have different averages?'

'Correct. Mathematicians call it "non-ergodic". Most people believe that the ensemble average and the time average always produce the same result. Or in mathematical parlance – that they're ergodic.'

There were fewer people on the streets in this part of town, Fitzroy noticed.

'A gambler needs to know these things.'

'Many people make that mistake. Which is one reason most people are bad at dealing with money and other things . . .'

'I'm the same.'

'. . . and don't understand that a share that loses ten per cent of its value has to gain more than ten per cent to reach its former level again.'

'Huh?'

Was this guy thick or something?

'A share worth a hundred euros loses ten per cent, meaning it's now worth ninety,' Fitzroy explained impatiently. 'Ten per cent of ninety is nine, so a rise of ten per cent makes . . .'

'Ninety-nine. Shit, not a hundred.'

'That's right. The share would have to go up not by ten per cent but 11.1 per cent to return to a hundred.'

'Do you work all this out in your head?'

'Yes, and so could you if you wanted to.'

Jan gazed at him quizzically. 'Still, that doesn't make it any clearer why those killers were out to get you.'

The thought of his attacker wielding that bottle made Fitzroy break out in a sweat again. 'No, it doesn't.'

My God, how must Will have felt in his final seconds when he realized what was coming? If Jan's story is true, of course.

The kid cast another anxious glance over his shoulder.

'I can think of only one explanation,' Fitzroy said. 'Those guys reckon that before he died Will told you something no one's allowed to know and that you've repeated it to me.'

'But he didn't.'

That's what you say.

'Are we nearly there?'

El's team fanned out into the roads around the Golden Bar. He wondered if the area was always so busy or if it was delegates to the summit and demo-tourists who were getting in their way. It was quieter at least in the side streets, but in the Samaritan's and the gambler's shoes, he too would have mingled with the masses. The needle in a haystack principle. They checked the other bars without much hope. He'd dispatched Rob to Jan Wutte's home address to be on the safe side. Bell had long since caught up with them again. Wutte was a local and if he was hiding out with friends who lived nearby, there was little prospect of their finding him.

Anyway, this was voluntary overtime. They'd fulfilled their primary mission. If some nutter were to publish conspiracy theories about the limousine accident, the worst scenario was that it would occupy the traditional media for a day and social media for a few hours, and then, apart from a few fans of fake news, it would vanish into the boundless expanses of the worldwide wasteland.

El could have settled for that, but that wasn't the problem. Their client was the problem. The instruction had been no witnesses, or else . . . He was conscious of a trickle of cold sweat running down between his shoulder blades when suddenly he heard Jack's voice in his earpiece.

'I've found out where Fitzroy Peel is staying.'

23

Jan was struggling to keep up with Fitz's long strides. They were hurrying towards Gendarmenmarkt. There were very few other pedestrians. The empty streets made him nervous, even though he didn't think Anvil Chin had followed them.

'The last time I saw Will was almost a year ago,' Fitz was saying, 'at a conference in Los Angeles. Similar to this. Only a few quick messages since – how you doing, that kind of thing. Until a week ago when he wrote that he was working on something big.'

'What was it?'

'He didn't say.'

'Something to do with your conversations in Los Angeles?'

'No idea. At the time he was obsessed with a particular formula called the Kelly criterion. He knew I was familiar with it from gambling.'

'The Kelly criterion?'

'You can use it to calculate whether a recurring bet is worth it or not – tonight's, for example. And what share of your winnings you should bet to maximize your winnings in the long-term.'

'So I could've won tonight?'

'Not really. Using the Kelly criterion would immediately

have demonstrated that no one wins in the long run in a special game like tonight's.'

'How do you know all this? Did you learn it from gambling?'

'From mathematics, and physics too. I studied both, including two years in Heidelberg.'

'So that's why you speak such good German.'

'I did my PhD in the States though.'

'A PhD in maths? Crikey!'

'Physics. I only have a Master's in maths.'

'Only . . .'

The bruises on Jan's face were stinging more than ever. Instinctively he looked back the way they had come. Still no one.

'Will and I studied together and then joined the same New York investment bank.'

'I thought you were a gambler?'

'Same thing,' Fitz said, laughing. 'The only difference being that I gamble at my own risk, not with other people's money. Whatever. I soon got bored at Goldman.'

'Why was Will interested in the Kelly criterion? Did he gamble too?'

'Will?' Fitz said with a smirk. 'No, he stayed at Goldman for a few years before switching to a boutique—'

'He went from being an investment banker to selling clothes?' Jan asked in disbelief.

'A smaller, classier finance company,' Fitz explained.

'Classy and finance are a contradiction in terms.'

'And from there he went to Ted Holden's hedge fund.'

'Who's Ted Holden?'

'Who's Ted Holden? One of the world's richest men!'

'Oh yeah! The kind of guy I see every day on the trolleys in the hospital corridor.'

'If Will really was in the car with a Nobel Prize winner,' Fitz said, thinking aloud, 'then they were obviously trying to terminate the other guy. Have the police announced his identity?'

'Habetomson or something.'

Fitz tapped and swiped on his smartphone as he walked. Jan made the most of the opportunity. He hadn't checked his mobile since the fight.

'Shit.'

'What?'

'My mum's tried to get through several times. She's left voicemail and sent texts, wanting me to get in touch. The police were there. Someone rang from an unknown number too.'

'Tell her everything's fine,' Fitz advised him, 'or she'll worry herself to death.'

'Not my mum.'

'All mothers. Well, almost.'

'But everything isn't fine.'

'Would it make her feel better to hear that you've been badly beaten up, suspected of murder and are on the run from a gang of lunatics?'

He has a point. Jan typed a short message: *I'm OK. Will call later.*

'Herbert Thompson,' Fitz finally announced, showing Jan a series of photos. 'Was he in the car?'

Jan stopped, enlarged the pictures and studied them. 'Well, I'm fucked,' he groaned. 'That's him all right.'

'You really didn't do it?'

'Of course I didn't!'

'So then the question is: why were they murdered today and here?'

Fitz looked at his phone again and after a short search

said, 'Thompson was scheduled to give a keynote speech at the summit tomorrow.'

'He won a Nobel Prize,' Jan said. 'That kind of person has an office, assistants, staff. Maybe one of them knows something.'

'Yeah, and they're bound to tell us,' Fitz said in a mocking tone, setting off again.

'Bluffing's your job.'

Fitz stopped again and searched for something on his phone.

'Can't that wait until we get to your hotel?' Jan asked impatiently.

'The hotel's not going anywhere.'

'Nor is the info about Herbert Thompson.'

'He teaches at Stanford, the London School of Economics and in Singapore.' An advanced search produced the phone numbers of all three universities.

'Forget Singapore,' Fitz said. 'They're six hours ahead of us, so it's the middle of the night. It's already evening in London too, but California's nine hours behind. It's morning there.'

Fitz tried Stanford. The line was busy. Again. Busy. There was someone there.

'I'll try again later,' he said, looking up. 'Here we are.' The hotel was a hundred yards further on.

Jan grabbed Fitz's arm. A police car was parked in the hotel driveway, and a tall man in uniform and a woman were getting out. She was in her mid-forties, small, athletic, strong-looking. Jeans and a similar hoodie to the one Jan was wearing. A ponytail poked out of the back of her baseball cap.

'I know that policeman,' Jan whispered. 'He wanted to haul me in!'

'What are they doing at my hotel?' Fitz asked.

The woman strode firmly up to the entrance and showed something to the doorman.

'There goes our plan to freshen up,' sighed Jan.

One of the same officers who'd questioned Jan Wutte at the scene of the crash turning up outside the hotel was no accident. Fitzroy Peel was yet to appear, and the German was still missing. El had no idea whether they'd split up after their joint escape. What bothered him most, though, was that the police had traced the British guy through Wutte. What did he have to do with any of this?

'Well, there's no chance Peel will put in an appearance with that police car in the drive,' reckoned Jack.

'Only if he's with Wutte,' El said. 'If not, then it'll probably scare him away even more. Whatever, it doesn't make our task any easier. Now think: where might we find them?'

'Maybe Wutte will go home after all.'

'No way. The police will be waiting there, and so will we. Will Cantor obviously handed him something. That's why he tracked Peel to the Golden Bar.'

'Dammit,' Jack said. 'But what I still don't understand is why Wutte got involved in Peel's game? If he simply wanted to talk to him, he could either have done it straight away or waited until the game was over.'

'That's what I've been wondering this whole time,' El admitted. 'I reckon Cantor sent Wutte to Peel because Peel knows something.'

'But then he'd have reacted more quickly to Wutte's arrival. My guess is that Peel doesn't know anything either. Which means they're going to want to find out why we're after them.'

'Yeah, unfortunately. That brawl will have told them we're serious.'

'So which way will they turn? Where would you go?'

Good question.

One place immediately sprang to El's mind.

24

Fitzroy stared up into the night sky. They'd retreated to a doorway a couple of blocks away. A gust of wind whipped dust across the pavement. The thunder and lightning had abated for now, but helicopters were again buzzing around overhead.

'I still need a wash,' Fitzroy said. He inspected Jan. 'They won't let you in anywhere looking like that.' He handed him a handkerchief. 'Give your face a wipe. How do I look?'

'A splash of water wouldn't do you any harm either.'

Fitzroy spat on his palms and ran them over his face and hair.

'At least all the spots of blood have gone,' Jan said.

The Brit stepped out into the street and spotted several bars a short walk away in either direction. A man was rummaging in a skip outside one of them. He had a boy with him.

'More homeless people,' Fitz observed. 'It's the same as London and New York here.'

'It's become normal,' Jan said. 'You should see other parts of the city.'

'OK, let's go.'

Jan wet the handkerchief with his tongue. 'What if they were in fact trying to kill Will?' he said, dabbing gently around his eye and grimacing with pain. 'Did he come up with something that cost him his life? Something linked to your last conversation?'

'With the Kelly criterion? It used to be derided by economists including Nobel laureates, but more and more fund managers are using it as the basis of their investment strategies because it generates the best return in the long run and also stops you from going bankrupt. Survival combined with maximum yield – not that that's a secret.'

They peered into the first bar they came to. It was packed and gloomy, and there was no bouncer outside. A normal-looking crowd, not too smartly dressed. They wouldn't immediately stand out.

'In here.'

They headed straight to the toilets. The weak light from the ceiling lamp softened their appearance in the mottled, cracked mirror. The wall above the single washbasin was plastered with layers of posters advertising a variety of events. Clumps of tattered wet paper towel dotted the floor. The dispenser was empty.

'Shit,' Fitzroy mumbled as he and Jan examined themselves in the mirror. A bump had appeared beside Jan's left eye, and blood was drying on an open wound on his fat lower lip. Like Fitz he'd managed to smear yet more blood all over his face.

'I look sunburnt,' remarked Fitz, splashing water on his face.

'Maybe Will discovered some amazing trick,' Jan said as he carefully pulled up his T-shirt. The left side of his ribs and chest resembled the spots on a giraffe.

'So what? That doesn't get you killed,' Fitzroy shot back, water dripping from his chin.

'Oh, people have been stabbed to death for less,' Jan said,

wincing as he touched his ribs. 'Fitzroy . . .' he said. 'What kind of a name is that?'

'My mother thought it was original,' Fitz replied. 'English aristocrats like to be a little eccentric.'

'Too complicated for me. I'm going to call you Fitz.'

'No, you're not.'

'Oh yes, I am.'

'What if Will had invented some new type of cash cow for Ted Holden?' Fitz suggested, thinking out loud as he straightened out his collar.

'A cash cow?'

'That's what Will and I used to call successful investment strategies.'

Fitz smoothed down his shirt. He could almost pass for normal now.

'Cash cows for the super-rich? Can't say I like the idea of that.'

'You may find this hard to believe, but Will loved the challenge. He was less interested in the money.'

'I'm sure he still took it though.'

'Oh, Will wasn't interested in the whole jet-set scene of million-dollar apartments, chalets, yachts, drugs, luxury trips and high-maintenance women. He was a classic quant,' Fitz said, dabbing at imaginary bloodstains on his dark jacket with some damp toilet paper. Jan's bewildered expression, reflected in the mirror, begged for an explanation. 'A quantitative analyst – very smart, maybe even slightly autistic, I don't know. People like him perceive patterns, order, processes and systems where others see only chaos or noise. They come up with formulas and algorithms in their sleep that hordes of less gifted individuals couldn't devise in a lifetime of trying. And the financial industry rewards them handsomely for their work, of course.'

Fitzroy paused and stared at Jan in the mirror as the latter washed his neck. They looked human again – at least on the outside.

'Something just occurred to me. During our last conversation, Will posed a number of questions I couldn't answer. For instance, which criteria should guide economic decision-making? I said he'd better ask some economists.'

'And did he?' Jan enquired.

'Well, there were enough of them at his firm. He even mentioned a name.' Fitz knitted his brow. 'Jean. Or maybe Jeanne. That's it – Jeanne Dalli.'

It was Jan's turn to stare at Fitz in the mirror.

'Shan-dall-ee – that's what Will Cantor whispered to me. I thought he was trying to say Chantal.'

Jeanne Dalli – Chantal. The dying man had barely pronounced the final 'i'.

The extravagant flower arrangements in the hotel entrance alone would have cost at least two months of Maya's salary. In the lobby and bar running along the back of it sat a sprinkling of mainly international guests whose devilishly expensive but rarely tasteful designer apparel could not distract from their villainous faces. Having plundered their countries and robbed their fellow citizens, they had moved to safer parts of the world to enjoy the proceeds. These were the migrants who really deserved to be chucked out.

Maya asked Jörn to stay near the entrance until she gave him the signal. She tried her luck at reception by taking the easiest option.

'Good evening, I'm Maya Paritta. I have an appointment with Fitzroy Peel. Could you please let him know I'm here?'

The receptionist consulted her computer and then picked

up the phone. After a few rings she hung up again. 'I'm sorry, there's no answer.'

'Is he here?' Maya tried. Modern key card systems should allow the receptionist to see whether the card had been used or not.

The woman hesitated for a second while deciding whether to give Maya the information, then said, 'He doesn't seem to be in.'

'That's strange,' Maya said. 'No problem, I'll try his mobile. Thanks.'

She was on the phone to headquarters before she'd even left the hotel. 'I need permission to locate a mobile.'

Jan and Fitz had fought their way through to a table by the wall at the back of the bar, along with a couple of beers. The bar was still full, but the other patrons weren't too noisy. It wouldn't be easy to be found in here. Fitz looked fighting fit again apart from a slight swelling below one eye. Jan's scrapes and slightly black eye might have been the result of a bike accident. Fitz was fiddling with his mobile again.

Holding it up for Jan to see, he said, 'This is Jeanne Dalli.'

Her look was that of a gorgeous actress playing the part of a successful rookie lawyer or a banker. Did such people really exist?

'She used to work for Syllabus Invest, the hedge fund Will worked for. Look, there's an announcement that she changed role within the empire.'

'What kind of empire are we talking about?'

'Ted Holden's. Jeanne Dalli joined Holden's PA team seven months ago. Poor her.'

'Why's that?' Jan could imagine the assistant of a multi-billionaire probably earning a tidy sum, and with her looks she might well end up marrying him.

'It's a nightmare,' Fitzroy said. 'Twenty-four-hour days, plus Holden's a notoriously quick-tempered bully.'

'I guess he can afford to be.'

'Maybe she and Will did discuss ideas. We have to try to get in touch with her.' He swiped on his phone again. 'Ted Holden's head office is in San Francisco. It's morning there.' He even seemed to have found a phone number.

'Hello, this is James Donahue from Templebridge Capital. I'd like to speak to Jeanne Dalli, please.' Fitz grinned at Jan, whose meagre English was nevertheless sufficient to follow the conversation.

'Oh, really? Fine. Thank you. How can I reach her?' He frowned. 'I understand. Maybe you could give me the name of her hotel so I can ring and leave her a message, then Jeanne can decide herself if she wants to talk to me.' He pulled a face. *Will she bite?* His expression changed. *Dammit.* 'Thanks all the same. Goodbye.'

He cut the connection, mumbling something Jan couldn't understand though it didn't sound too complimentary.

'The good news,' he told Jan, 'is that Ted Holden is here for the summit and Jeanne Dalli is with him.'

'That's the good news – so what's the bad news?'

'The lady on the other end of the line wouldn't give me the name of her hotel or a number to reach her on.'

'Now we've even more reason to find out what Will wanted to tell us,' Jan insisted. 'What did he know that killed him? A super investment strategy, or something else?'

'Or else he was just collateral damage when Thompson was assassinated?' Fitzroy said, his brow furrowed. 'I can't shake off the feeling that we're in too deep here.'

'I know I'm repeating myself, but why would he have sent me to you? What do you know?'

'I have no idea. Not the foggiest.'

'Did Will tell you where he was staying, by any chance?'

'Hotel Raal.'

'Then we need to go and look there. Maybe we'll find documents or something.'

'*I* definitely don't need to. There's no way I'm breaking into any hotel rooms, anyway. The only thing I really need to do is be at my poker game two hours from now, preferably after a shower and a change of shirt.'

'Don't you care who murdered your friend? Don't you even want to know who tried to kill you . . . and may well try a second time?'

Fitz sighed. 'That thought did cross my mind, yes . . .' he murmured.

'So where's the Hotel Raal?' Jan asked.

Fitzroy checked his phone. 'Not far from here.'

'There's time to do it before your game. Maybe we'll find something. You can wash there.'

THIRD DECISION

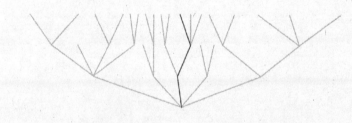

'In the next stage of evolution, the cells
form cooperatives according to this same
mathematical principle.'

Will Cantor

25

'And what might these gentlemen be discussing now?' Ambrose Peel remarked scornfully as he stood chatting with Jeanne next to one of the arches at the edge of the hall. 'How to present themselves once more as the saviours of the world, even though they're responsible for this whole mess?'

Ted had left her in the company of the slightly wacky British diplomat. His question was rhetorical. Ted and many of the people he'd conferred with that evening, from businessmen to politicians from a variety of countries, were engaged in heated discussion over at the most isolated table in the room. Minders and assistants were trying with varying degrees of tact to ensure that none of the remaining guests disturbed them.

Peel emptied his glass of champagne and plucked a new one from a passing tray. 'Would you like one too?'

Jeanne declined. She was sticking stoically to water.

Peel chuckled. 'It was really funny when you said that thing about these types fitting in best by being the most conventional,' he said. 'Not to mention daring in the circumstances. Whatever made a perceptive and witty person like you go into the financial industry?'

'Money?' Jeanne replied without hesitation, but not without noting that he'd made no allusion to her looks or gender, as many other people would have done in the same situation. *Whatever made a perceptive, witty and* pretty woman *like you go into the financial industry?*

'Oh, how boring,' Peel said ruefully.

'Only if you've always had enough of the stuff,' Jeanne retorted with a laugh. Unlike her, born in Arizona to a bus driver and a teacher.

'And with a quick tongue too!' he replied, grinning and raising his glass to her.

'Just following someone else's example,' she said, tilting her head to one side. His pronunciation, his attitude and his whole demeanour were so typically British upper class. Peel couldn't disguise his background – he clearly came from money – but he also probably chose not to.

'And why would an irate provocateur like yourself go into the diplomatic service?'

'Maybe it was the diplomatic service that made me into an irate provocateur?'

'Then at least they were useful for once,' Jeanne said, laughing.

'You remind me of my youngest son,' he interjected, and then his expression darkened. 'He's brilliant but he can't take anything seriously.' He looked pensive. 'On second thoughts, maybe it's *because* he's brilliant . . .'

'You'll have to ask him.'

'We don't see each other that often.' Peel stared into space for a moment, before adopting his usual inscrutable mask and winning smile. 'The world is saved,' he commented, nodding towards the table on the other side of the hall. The gathering was indeed disbanding. Hands were being shaken, shoulders patted. A lot of shoulders had been patted tonight.

'Oh well, cheers anyway!' he cried, draining his glass.

26

Will Cantor had been staying at the Berlin address of an international luxury hotel chain near Friedrichstrasse. A room here probably cost the equivalent of Jan's monthly salary. How did all the people hanging around the lobby and bar in their smart clothing even come by their money? They couldn't seriously work any harder than Jan did – after all, there were only twenty-four hours in a day, and they had to sleep and shit too. How come their time was so much more valuable than his?

Behind the thirty-foot-long lacquered red-brown wooden counter, six female and male receptionists in dark brown uniforms were waiting or attending to guests.

He and Fitz had a plan. The great thing was that, as a native English speaker, Fitz had to be the one to put it in action. Jan's English was good enough for watching films and TV series in the original language, but not for an operation like this. He'd have to keep a low profile, which was fine by him – his face was still a mess, whereas after his trip to the gents Fitz once more looked thoroughly presentable.

The Brit marched up to one of the unoccupied receptionists. Jan took up a position a few yards away next to a rack of tourist brochures and flyers for forthcoming events.

'*Gooden arrbend*,' Fitz said in his thickest American

accent. His willingness to speak German was rewarded with the friendliest of fake smiles. '*Ich haabe* a *groosse* request? *Ich* checked in *heute* afternoon and I've forgotten the key card to my room. *Kann ich bitte* have a new one?'

The woman switched to English to answer. 'Of course. What's your room number?'

'Oh, that's the other problem. I just arrived and I didn't write it down. Room 345, I think. The name's Cantor, Will Cantor.'

The Bond reference is a little over the top, thought Jan, *but otherwise it's a good act. I hope she thinks so too.*

The receptionist typed something into her computer and her smile grew warmer. 'Here you are, Mr Cantor. You're in Room 756 on the top floor.'

Fitz raised his hand theatrically to his forehead. 'Oh dear, my brain's not what it used to be. I knew there was a five in it. Thank you very much.'

'You're not far from the rooftop terrace and the pool.'

'Great!'

A jangle of keys and she produced a card from somewhere under the desk. She hadn't even asked Fitz to prove his identity.

'One or two?' she asked.

'Better make it two, just in case I lose one again.'

Don't lay it on too thick.

Fitz accepted the two black cards with a slight bow, thanked the receptionist and walked off into the lobby without so much as a glance in Jan's direction.

A good performance. Gamblers had to be actors too. Jan made his way slowly towards the lift, which was where the tall Brit was heading with long strides.

*

Jörn swore at the heavy traffic.

There was no way Maya was going to find Jan Wutte and Fitzroy Peel with only Jörn to assist her. All was not lost though. There was a wanted notice out for Wutte with his photo, and maybe Maya could speed up the search.

She phoned an old friend at the summit coordination centre.

'Maya! What can I do for you?'

'Who said I needed anything?'

'Maya,' he said, his voice dripping with sarcasm, 'why the hell else would you be ringing me?'

'Well . . . you lot have thousands of eyes out on the street at the moment, plus choppers and cameras and all the rest of it . . .' She desperately needed a drink, but managed to pull herself together.

'Tell me about it.'

'The police have put out a wanted notice – they must've sent it to you as well. Maybe you've been giving it special attention?'

'Like we don't have enough to do already . . . Come on, out with it. Name?'

'Two names. Jan Wutte, a local kid, and Fitzroy Peel, a British national who's staying at The Dome. You'll have the photos, or do you want me to send you some?'

'Who do you think we are?'

'Geniuses.'

'Precisely. I'll be in touch as soon as I hear something.'

'Thanks.'

Done. Next on the list – Herbert Thompson. What did you get up to today?

It shouldn't be so hard to find out in the age of social media. There were more than enough attention-seekers around who were only too happy to film themselves in front of incidents like this. A photo with the dictator of Something-istan here, another with a film star there – that 'there' often being a political summit, for some reason. One with a twenty-something tech billionaire, a second with a Nobel Prize winner perhaps?

She scanned the main social media outlets on her mobile: Instagram, YouTube and the others. She found a few clues about the planned speeches, but nothing to confirm Thompson's whereabouts during his final hours.

'Let's go to Herbert Thompson's hotel. Maybe we'll learn something there.'

Fitz had wangled the key cards, so Jan let him go first. The gambler held the card to the sensor and the door unlocked with a gentle click. He used his elbow to press down the door handle, and they went inside.

Jan looked around. A parquet floor stretched away from the door, with a space for hanging coats, a luggage rack and a wardrobe on the left. To the right was the bathroom, white marble with mock vintage fittings and a full-length mirror. The spacious bedroom had a glass wall at one end looking down on to a courtyard full of plants and trees. A staircase next to the window led down to the living area on the mezzanine below, which was furnished with sofas, a bar and a desk. The bedroom was big enough to accommodate two wingback chairs and a coffee table. It was the size of Jan's mother's entire flat and far more chic. *Had he really expected anything else from a hedge fund manager?*

'Modest,' noted Fitz. 'Typical Will.'

What does immodest look like? But suddenly Jan's mind was filled with the image of the burning man in the car.

Fitz used the tip of his shoe to open one of the low-level cupboards. He held out a small fabric bag to Jan. 'Put this on your hand,' he ordered, 'and don't touch anything without it.' Fitz stuck his own hand into an empty laundry bag emblazoned with the hotel logo. 'Fingerprints,' he said.

There were a few sheets of paper and a folder lying on the coffee table. Fitz got there first. Pinning them down with the knuckles of his free hand, he flicked through the papers awkwardly with his plastic-wrapped hand. Jan took a peek over his shoulder. It was all in English.

'Nothing special,' Fitz said. 'Tourist brochures.'

'I'll start with the wardrobe,' Jan said. 'You check the bedroom.'

'OK.'

Somehow Jan found his fingers still perfectly dextrous inside the little bag from the complimentary shoe-cleaning kit. Opening the doors of the wardrobe he found five suits in shades of dark blue or grey, along with shirts in white, blue, and some with pastel stripes. Several ties. A belt. Knee-length socks rather than ankle ones. Two pairs of expensive-looking shoes, classic in style, polished to a brilliant shine. Underwear.

All very tidy and neatly folded. The maid, Jan was guessing. A small safe, unlocked, its door ajar. Empty.

Every so often Jan would check what Fitz was up to. Right now he was inspecting the bedside table, which had an open packet of tissues on it, and then the neatly made bed. Fitz turned back the sheets and lifted up the pillows. He even lifted up the heavy mattress to look underneath.

They moved on to the living area downstairs. A large pad of the hotel's headed notepaper and a pencil sat on the desk, alongside it a file containing the hotel rules, the menu for room service and an unmarked folder whose colour didn't match that of the others.

Fitz opened it, and Jan saw that once more all the writing

was in English. This time, however, there were no glossy photos of tourist attractions. Forms, printouts. His fingers lingered on a small, high-quality, folded card. He examined it.

'It's a personal invitation to the official opening ceremony of the summit tomorrow morning,' Fitz announced with surprise in his voice. 'How on earth did Will get hold of this?'

'You told me he worked for one of the world's richest men. Maybe that's why.'

'Ted Holden has hundreds of thousands of employees worldwide in thousands of companies, if you count all his investments. No, there has to be some other reason.'

27

El and his team were careful not to enter the hotel all together, even if their clothing was designed to attract the least attention. The city wasn't home only to politicians and billionaires over these few days, but also to their security personnel. El and his men looked fairly smart in comparison with many other guards.

Who even invented the dark grey or black strongman uniform with sunglasses? The CIA? The Russians? Or was it TV? Looking at most of these guys, one would have guessed the latter because they all seemed to act as if they were auditioning for a part in the next special agent series. Shades, baseball caps and disguise make-up would at least make it hard for facial recognition software to identify El and his gang. He made straight for the lifts. Jack had just got in one to the seventh floor, Sam was staying in the lobby, and Bell was following El at a safe distance.

There was a group of senior citizens in El's lift – clearly Americans on a long-planned European trip. They were very upset about the summit, which had caused the closure of streets, museums and other sights. The higher the lift rose, the emptier it got.

El was the only person who got out on the seventh floor. An empty hallway, beige-striped wallpaper, deep-pile dark blue carpets with a yellow scrollwork pattern along the edges. Very plush on the surface, but underneath one would find the same plasterboard and reinforced concrete as anywhere else.

Jack was waiting for him, and Bell arrived in the next lift. They turned right towards Room 756.

They were still carrying the key cards they'd used on their previous visit, having removed anything relevant once Cantor had left to meet the old man. There hadn't been a lot to take.

They hadn't planned to be back quite so soon. They'd make themselves comfortable and then wait for the two fugitives to run straight into their arms.

El had already pulled out his card when he heard two voices inside. He raised a finger, and Jack and Bell froze. They all listened hard. Two men. El couldn't make out what they were saying, but their voices and the way they were talking ruled out room service. Intruders would have been more quiet about it. The police? There'd be more of them, accompanied by a hotel manager. Which left only one option.

El hadn't expected them to get here so fast. He gave another signal and the three of them retreated to the other side of the hallway for a quick confab.

Fitzroy and Jan searched the desk drawers with no success. His hands on his hips, Fitz looked around the room.

What the hell were you playing at, Will?

Jan bent over the desk. 'Fitz!' He held the notepad up to eye level, examined it and finally turned it until it was very flat and he was looking at it at an oblique angle. 'Someone wrote something on the last page, but it's gone.'

Fitzroy studied the top sheet. 'It could've been anything.'

Jan pulled out the small wastepaper bin from under the desk. They hadn't paid any attention to it so far, but now he picked out several balls of paper, unfolded them and smoothed them flat with his hand.

All three sheets had similar diagrams on them. Whoever had drawn these had corrected two of them to the point of illegibility, then crossed them out. The drawings on the third sheet were clearer. They showed two distinct groups of concentric circles with small dots on them.

Each of the groups of circles showed one particular dot ringed with small spikes. An arrow pointing to the right between the two groups clearly marked a progression from one state to another.

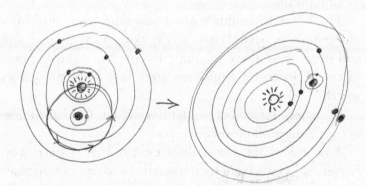

It was hard to make out the three words below the diagrams from the dreadful scrawl. *Dogma. Paradigm shift.*

'What's this supposed to mean?' asked Jan.

Good question.

'Stones tossed into a pool?' Jan ventured.

'Will was a mathematician and a physicist. It looks like atoms with electrons orbiting around them. And as if there were an evolution from stage one to stage two . . .'

'The right-hand picture looks a bit like the solar system,' Jan said, thinking out loud, 'but the other one?'

Fitz clapped Jan hard on the shoulder with excitement. 'That's right! Then the words make sense too. On the right is our solar system, and on the left is a sketch of the geocentric view of the universe that dominated until the early modern age, with the Sun and all the planets revolving around the Earth. This is an intermediary stage – Tycho Brahe's sixteenth-century epicyclical model. The Earth was still at the centre of the universe, but he thought the Sun went around the Earth and the other planets around the Sun, while some went around both.'

'Complicated.'

'The Church wouldn't allow anything else. Ptolemy's old geocentric worldview was ecclesiastical dogma and had to be obeyed, even though the simplicity and elegance of the heliocentric worldview had long since proved its worth.'

'I vaguely remember something about Galileo Galilei or . . . "And yet it moves." '

'And indeed the Earth does exactly that. Copernicus, Kepler and Galilei laid the foundations of one of the greatest paradigm changes of the last millennium – that is, the end of the Church's power and supremacy over society, and the beginning of the Enlightenment.'

'But why should Will be interested in that stuff?'

'He was interested in many things. Maybe there's something else on the pad,' Fitz said. He followed Jan's example and held up the paper almost flat. 'I can see something other than the diagrams – more writing.' He laid the pencil against the sheet and drew it rapidly back and forth until the top inch had turned grey except where the writing on the page above had left an imprint. White scribbles in a sea of grey.

Jan spun round. 'Someone's there.'

Fitz had obviously heard it too. Someone was trying to open the door.

28

El placed the master key card against the lock, and the green light immediately came on. He opened the door slowly and almost silently. Ahead of him lay the narrow hallway of the suite with the coat rack and wardrobe on the left and the bathroom door on the right. The door was shut. El advanced stealthily into the bedroom. There was no one there. A glance down into the living area: no one there either. He turned to see Jack pressing the bathroom door handle down gently. It wouldn't open. He nodded to El.

Neither room service nor a maid would shut the door behind them, let alone lock it.

Jack already had his penknife out. Bell had been waiting outside the room, but now he entered too, closing the door softly behind him.

Jack pushed the tip of his screwdriver tool into the slit on the door handle that was there for emergencies. El and Bell got into position behind him. All this had taken place with barely a sound. Unless someone had seen, they'd have no idea they were there. The result of years of training.

Jack turned the screwdriver slowly to avoid making any noise, although someone in the bathroom would have noticed the doorknob moving.

With a final jerk of his wrist Jack forced the door open.

Over his colleague's shoulder El caught sight of two wash-basins to the right, on the other side a bathtub with a full-length glass anti-splash screen and beyond that a shower cubicle.

The window straight ahead was wide open.

Bloody hell! Bloody fucking hell! Jan longed to be having a beer with friends or lounging on the couch at home watching a series. Or playing video games. But instead he was clinging to a ledge by his fingertips and shuffling along another ledge in search of the next toehold. Tom Cruise always made this kind of stunt look so easy.

'What if it was only room service?' he whispered to Fitz. They could turn back. Well, not now they couldn't. If they'd stayed in the room, they could have pretended to be guests, but now they'd clambered out of the bathroom window that was hardly credible. Fitz was a couple of steps further along the façade, papers and pad stashed safely under his shirt.

'Without knocking or asking? And extra quiet as well?'

Good point.

'Shit!' he heard Fitz murmur. No, he wasn't talking to Jan. He was peering past him. A figure was wriggling out of the same bathroom window they'd just struggled through. A large shadow, not five yards behind them.

'There, up ahead,' Jan hissed.

Some twenty feet in front of them the flat expanse of wall ended at a corner. From there, a series of decorative blocks of stone about a foot square led up into the sky with gaps in between wide enough for their fingers. The blocks stretched the entire height of the façade. Fifty feet down, seven feet up to the rooftop terrace of the hotel. They had to make it up there.

Jan was discovering a hidden talent for balancing on ledges.

When needs must ... The shadow that had appeared from the window was creeping along the front of the building faster than they had done. They were running out of time. If Jan's heart beat any harder, it would hurl him off the ledge and into the void below.

Fitz was first to the cornerstones. Without hesitation he wedged the tip of his shoe into the first gap, lunged around the corner and pulled himself upwards. He had to hurry because they could only get away one behind the other on this escape route. Jan could not even start his climb until Fitz was far enough ahead of him. He could hear the gurgle of a swimming pool and a hum of conversation, and in the distance helicopters were still keeping an eye on the demonstrators despite the darkness.

Their pursuer said something. To whom? Were there more of them? He was gaining on them. Jan's palms were sweaty. The guy was no more than six feet away from him by the time he was finally able to start his ascent. There was no time to think: he rammed his fingertips into the first gap, put his right foot on a stone and pulled himself up, belly tight to the wall. Next handhold, his fingers cramping, the other leg up. Jan was shaking and perspiring from head to toe, but his mind seemed to have broken free of his senses, and his senses from – from what? As his trembling body scaled the wall as if on autopilot, thoughts popped and whizzed around his brain one second while the next he was coolly observing himself from the outside, albeit a little surprised to find himself attempting this reckless feat, an actor in someone else's film.

The man below had almost caught up with him now. He was like all the others – fit, brawny, short hair, dark clothing. Jan knew his face from the Golden Bar. He hadn't been at the scene of the accident, though, which meant there were more of them – and they were hot on his heels. The guy made a swipe for Jan's leg.

'They're climbing up to the terrace,' Jack's voice gasped in El's earpiece. 'I've almost caught up with them.'

Bell and El were standing guard beside the lifts and the door to the stairwell.

'Sam, get yourself up to the roof terrace,' El ordered their colleague down in the lobby.

'I'm on my way. Fuck, I can see them! The only way they're going anywhere is in free fall.'

'That'd solve our problem,' El panted as he and Bell sprinted up the stairs to the top floor.

They walked sedately and unnoticed along a hallway, past the waitress at the bar and out on to the terrace where forty or so guests were sipping drinks by the pool while enjoying the view. More and more heads were turning towards the end of the terrace where Fitzroy Peel was leaning a long way out over the railing. With one quick movement he helped Jan Wutte on to the terrace.

All eyes were on the two men. A barman reached for a phone while two other hotel employees hurried towards the intruders. As excited guests wondered whether these men were robbers or maybe terrorists, El and Bell made their way discreetly and efficiently through the gawping crowd. The first glowing mobile screens appeared over people's heads.

Wutte was bent double with his hands on his knees, gasping for air as he recovered from his exertions. Peel had one hand on his friend's back, but his eyes were scanning the terrace. Pulling Wutte upright, he dragged him away towards the far side of the terrace. He'd spotted them.

Bell and El increased their pace without breaking into a

run. El didn't want to attract any unwelcome scrutiny. If it came to it, they'd pretend to be security guards. That was true, even if they didn't work for this hotel. Via his headset he instructed Jack to wait on the other side of the railing until people's attention was elsewhere.

Peel and Wutte were running away from them along the railing in search of an exit. More and more phone screens lit up as they filmed the action. The terrace ended in a six-foot wall belonging to the next building. There was a scattering of bistro tables and chairs under a metal structure that in the daytime supported an awning. Hurrying past it, Wutte grabbed a low table and a chair, and Peel picked up a second one. They pushed the table against the wall with one chair in front of it and the other on top.

Some of the guests, fearing for their safety, had left. Others had now decided that the two intruders posed no real threat and had moved closer to find the best possible angle with the cameras on their phones. Voices could be heard commenting on the events for future, or perhaps live, audiences. Now that no one was looking, Jack had straddled the railing and jumped on to the terrace.

Wutte was the first to use the chairs as steps and, as nimble as a mountain goat, hauled himself up on to the adjacent roof. The fight in the pub had demonstrated to El and his men that the Samaritan was no wimp. Peel, aided by his height, was almost as agile. These guys were starting to get on El's nerves.

'Create a diversion,' he ordered Jack over the headset.

'Watch out, he's got a gun!' came Jack's cry from behind them. Stunned faces with panic in their eyes. People swivelled their heads and cameras towards the pool again, ran this way and that, ducking and throwing themselves to the floor. Jack followed their example so no one knew who'd shouted the warning. Bell and El took advantage of the diversion and in a few short strides, El had leaped on to the roof from the higher of the two chairs, with Bell close behind.

This was totally surreal. Fitzroy should have gone straight to the police, but instead he now found himself sprinting across a rooftop in the dark. It was about thirty yards long and had a relatively shallow pitch for the first dozen feet or so before falling away more steeply. Chimneys obstructed their path, but they were able to dodge and swerve between them. The glare of a skylight blazed ahead, but it was impossible to tell what awaited them at the end of this roof. The only thing they could see was the pale glimmer of the city lights in the night sky. They had no choice but to keep going. Two shadows were chasing them now. At least two . . .

Fitzroy could forget his poker game.

Maybe they might have hidden among the crowd on the hotel terrace, but they'd have had to move towards their adversaries to do so, and every fibre of Fitzroy's being had opposed the idea. Who knew what these men were capable of, and how far they were prepared to go, even in public. *You can't think in moments like that. You just want to get out of danger. Run. Climb. Jump.*

The clamour of the helicopter patrolling the demonstration was growing louder. Jan and Fitz came to the end of the roof. The noise was deafening now. Were they that close to the protests?

Suddenly everything around Fitz turned white. He squinted skywards in disbelief, one hand raised to shield his eyes from the dazzling rays.

The helicopter had them in its sights! A blinding white

disc with a radius of about thirty feet was shimmering over the grey metal cladding of the roof. He could feel the blast from the rotor blades.

He almost laughed out loud. The police searchlight was illuminating the top of the building ahead, and only three feet below them lay a large expanse of bitumen, surrounded by a knee-high wall, from which tall chimneys reared up like a petrified forest.

Jan too had turned to stone beside him, but after their initial momentary shock had passed, they jumped and continued running, pursued by the disc of light, which created a weird pattern of shadows out of the chimneystacks.

They'd already made it halfway across the stretch of roof when Fitzroy glanced over his shoulder. The police searchlight had had another welcome effect beyond that of indicating their escape route. The assassins were obviously none too keen on sharing the limelight, as Fitzroy could see them ducking out of sight behind the chimneys, so as long as the police had their giant eye on them, he and Jan were safe from attack. Maybe they should stop running, signal to the helicopter that they'd like to surrender and wait for the police to come and arrest them? Put an end to this crazy chase. Fitzroy had been blissfully ignorant of this whole thing until Jan had turned up. The police could then clear up the circumstances surrounding Will's death – that was their job – and Fitzroy could still make it to his poker game.

His cheek was smarting. Something sharp must have hit it. Red splinters erupted from the chimney beside him.

'They're shooting at us!' roared Jan, pulling Fitzroy into cover behind the nearest stack.

29

As they drove towards the Nobel laureate's hotel in Mitte, Maya browsed the publicly available information about the dinner at the orangery. Among the guests were at least ten billionaires, over two dozen near-billionaires, various important and top-rank politicians, and senior officials from international institutions, as well as countless people she couldn't name at first glance. Some were described simply as 'businessmen', others as lobbyists, diplomats, PR executives, investors, financiers and so-called 'philanthropists'.

She stopped reading to answer her phone. It was her acquaintance from the coordination centre via video link, his face ghostly pale in the dim light of many computer screens.

'You probably want to see this,' he said.

Maya's display disintegrated into a mass of black and brown splodges, shot through with flashes and bursts of light, before once more turning a dazzling white. The man's camera then focused on an image. A screen. He was filming one of the centre's monitors and streaming it live to Maya's phone. Legal this was not.

A white disc was moving shakily over parts of a building. Maya could make out chimneys and skylights. The footage must be coming from a drone or a helicopter. Two figures were sprinting across the illuminated zone.

Maya heard voices from the coordination centre. The camera zoomed in, but the images remained out of focus.

'We have better footage than this,' her contact said, panning round to a different screen showing blurred, badly overexposed stills of two male faces, staring frantically up into the sky. She had no trouble recognizing Jan Wutte and Fitzroy Peel. She and Jörn could turn around.

'It's them, but what are they doing?'

'We're not really sure. We received a call from Hotel Raab in Mitte a few minutes ago. Two unidentified men had apparently scaled the building and run across the roof terrace before clambering on to the next roof, as if being pursued or escaping from something.'

'Or someone. Did the chopper spot anyone else?'

'Not that we know of.'

'Why was the helicopter even there?'

'It was heading away from the main demo towards Kreuzberg, so we sent it over to have a look. A number of summit guests, if only middle-ranking ones, are staying at the hotel. But those two men have nearly reached the other end of the block now.'

'I need the exact address. Can you keep an eye on them?'

'Depends what happens at the main hotspot. They won't have anywhere to go soon, in any case. This is their last remaining roof.'

Jan sprinted through the beam of the searchlight, leaped over ledges, struggled to keep his balance on sloping sections of roof and slalomed between chimneys to keep out of the killers' line of fire. The world beyond the disc of light was plunged into even deeper darkness. It was like being in a video game, except that the tiles and roofing felt beneath his feet were real – and so was the gaping void of the street to his right and the roar and rush of the rotor blades, which were driving dust into his eyes and overworked lungs.

The lanky silhouette of Fitz, his sidekick in this video game, was zigzagging between obstacles diagonally ahead of him. How many roofs had they crossed? He had no idea. What was certain, though, was that they'd soon reach the end of this one, and then what?

Then, out of the blue, there were people waving. Jan ran into the back of Fitz, who'd stopped dead. The searchlight beam expanded to reveal more and more people, all staring up at the helicopter. Some were shaking their fists, some were giving the pilot the finger, others were beckoning. To them, to him and Fitz? In invitation? What were these people doing up here all of a sudden? They were waving a banner at the helicopter. *This house has been liberated!*

Oh bollocks! First a hit squad and now a bunch of raving anarchists. Out of the frying pan into the fire. OK, there was a difference, at least for the moment.

More and more faces were crowding together in the search-light, shouting, 'Fuck the cops! Piss off, pigs! Get lost.'

There was a three-foot wall between them and the next roof, but a thicket of helping hands were reaching out to them.

'This way!'

'Come on!'

Two arms seized Jan. Fingers grabbed his hands firmly and pulled him over the edge of the wall.

'Why are they chasing you?'

'You're safe here.'

If only!

Crouching breathlessly on his haunches, Jan scanned the rooftops. Where were their pursuers? They were bound to be keeping out of the searchlight.

Fitz was panting beside him and gesturing in the direction from which they had come. 'More might be after us the same way.'

'Which way?'

'Over the roofs.'

Laughing, a voice said, 'They can try.'

Laughing? Someone was laughing? The guy didn't have a clue. And yet the laughter made Jan relax. Some genuine laughter always helps.

Jan and Fitz were sucked into the middle of the crowd. There must have been dozens of people there. Beer bottles. Sausages. What on earth was going on here?

The sound of the helicopter was getting fainter and its light less bright as it rose into the sky. There wasn't much more to report. Jan squinted at the rooftops they'd just sprinted across. Were those shadows he saw behind the chimneys?

'How do we get down from here?' he asked the nearest person. He could hear the panic in his own voice and tried to steady himself.

'Thanks,' Fitz said beside him to a bearded man with shoulder-length curly black hair who was almost as tall as the Brit.

'No worries, man.'

'I'm Fitzroy.'

'Hi, Fitzroy, I'm Christo. Why didn't you come in through the front door?'

'It's a long story,' Fitz said, glancing over his shoulder.

The helicopter banked away, and a murmur of voices replaced the clatter of rotor blades. They would have to make do with the light from the city and their phone displays now. Jan's eyes scoured the neighbouring roof for signs of the killers, but found none.

Christo noticed where Jan was looking. 'Don't worry, the

police won't intervene during the summit. Too tricky, and besides, it'd pin down too many men. And even if a few were to try' – here he grinned – 'we have ways of stopping them.'

The police maybe, but they're not the ones we're scared of. Jan didn't say this aloud though.

'The police have gone,' El said into his headset. 'How do things look down there, Sam?'

'Parties. Banners outside people's windows. No police in sight. Squatters.'

Illegal tenants shouldn't be a problem. Despite the fact that these left-wing anarchists found war a stupid, capitalist, imperialist enterprise, an amazing number of these after-work revolutionaries went around in combat trousers, army shirts and other war-appropriate clothing. Some of the guys were strutting around like gorillas or like the kind of moviegoer who assumes Jason Statham's rolling gait when they come out of an action-movie screening. Yet none of these blokes with their cross-training muscles would withstand El and his gang for long.

'We're going in,' he said, already sprinting forward.

30

'There! Over there!' Jan saw the orcs emerge from the shadows and run towards them over the nearest roof. However, before he could even move, two dozen squatters, men and women, closed ranks in front of him along the boundary with the next building, their mobiles held aloft, screens glowing in the dark.

'Who are you?'

'Police?'

'Got a search warrant?'

The killers stopped in their tracks, covered their faces with their arms and turned away.

'Hey, what's going on?' cried someone on Jan's side of the roof. The dark grey figures were caught in the cross-beams of several flashlights, and at least a dozen phones shone like fireflies as people used them to film the intruders. The killers darted back into the cover of the chimneys and vanished into the darkness.

'Who the hell were they?' Christo said with a chuckle. 'Vampires?'

Wow! was all Jan could think. *Phones take on guns . . . and win.*

Christo patted Jan and Fitz on the shoulder. 'See! No access for unauthorized people.'

*

'Listen to me!' Maya yelled into the telephone. 'We have an arrest warrant out for the guy, and he's just been spotted near Hotel Raal in Mitte.'

Jörn glanced at her from the driver's seat.

The man on the other end of the line said he was sorry but there was nothing to be done – the entire force was needed elsewhere right now. *Bullshit!* Most likely there was a flashing red light next to her name at headquarters to say: get rid of her!

Enraged, she ended the call and watched the city flash past outside the car.

Two panellists on the radio were discussing the possible consequences of Italy leaving the EU. Exit from the euro, massive devaluation of a new currency, the collapse of various banks and businesses, mass unemployment, then a domino effect that would ruin Spain, Portugal and Greece too. The coupon rates of those countries were already at record levels. The remaining euro would either implode or be hugely overvalued – a disaster for exporting countries like Germany which would be plunged into crisis in the event of a trade war. Who could have imagined this situation even a year ago when the economy was purring along like a cat having its tummy stroked? And now there was the threat of an even worse collapse in exports for Germany and the others. Banks and companies would go bust, unemployment would skyrocket; soon everyone would be feeling the effects of the recession.

Maya didn't want to think about how bad the demos and riots might get if more people lost their homes and couldn't earn enough even to cover their basic needs. The most recent polls showed the extreme-right and far-left parties in the lead. Irritated, she switched off the radio.

She still hadn't received the results of the interviews at the

Golden Bar. The summit would be over by the time her colleagues had written up their reports. Besides, who needed written reports in the age of technology in any case?

Maya typed in various search terms and checked YouTube, Instagram and other social media, starting with 'Golden Bar'. Aha! The first videos of the fight had already been uploaded. Maya fast-forwarded through them in search of Jan Wutte and Fitzroy Peel's faces. At the sixth attempt, Wutte appeared for a split second in the middle of the brawl, and then a second time. There were at least thirteen other fighters in the excerpt. Some were merely shoving, others were lashing out with clenched fists and even bottles. Wutte was struggling against two men who were almost a head taller than him and probably twice his weight. On closer inspection, they were actually beating the crap out of him. Maya stopped the film. Between the two attackers, Peel was in full swing. So the two of them really had been involved. She ran the film on. Subsequent events were obscured by shadows for a few seconds, followed by some shaky footage. The cameraman had focused on something else.

She watched the scene again. Wutte had taken some serious hits; she didn't like to think of the state of his face right now. But how had he and Peel made it from the Golden Bar to the roof in Reinhardtstrasse, and why?

'What's this?'

'Our headquarters for the next couple of days,' Christo explained. At his side was a wiry woman with a shock of brown curls and piercing eyes.

'Hi, I'm Kim,' she said.

Jan's throat went dry.

A little structure on the roof housed the lift motor. The spiral stairway leading down into the building was packed with people holding bottles of beer and plastic cups, chatting and flirting with one another. No one was remotely bothered by the off-putting garish light from industrial lamps mounted on the plain concrete walls.

Christo greeted people on all sides, asking where Fitz and Jan might stay.

'Oh, Christo, I'm glad I found you.' This was from a young woman of about Christo's age. Powerfully built, dark skin, jeans and a beige shirt. Jan was electrified all over again – *Wow!* – and could barely contain himself. 'I was about to get in touch.' Jan had seen her somewhere before. 'Who's this you've brought along?'

'They've taken refuge with us,' Christo said, introducing the woman as Amistad Salgado.

'Cool,' Fitz said, shaking her hand. 'Nice work.'

'Thanks.'

She drew Christo aside and said something to him in a whisper. He listened, nodded and gave her an answer.

Fitz rolled his eyes when he saw the enthralled look on Jan's face. 'Amistad is one of the most important international activists on human rights and justice,' he told Jan. 'An Argentinian farmer, worker and student leader.'

'What's she doing in Berlin?'

Fitz looked annoyed. 'Bringing about change?'

'Why isn't she doing that in Argentina?'

'Maybe because the Germans aren't managing by themselves? Anyway, she *is* doing the same thing over there.' He leaned closer to Jan and murmured, 'Her parents were poor farmers, murdered along with their entire village by a hit squad on behalf of local big landowners who wanted their land. Amistad was a little girl at the time and the only survivor.'

'Were the killers ever punished?' Jan asked.

'Not as far as I know, but you can ask her yourself.'

'Some other time maybe,' Jan mumbled.

Amistad glanced at them again, nodded, muttered a quick 'See you later' and disappeared into the next room.

On the first floor Jan saw several flats resembling IT start-up offices. People in hoodies were hunched over laptops, among racks of servers and computer towers, with lights blinking and cables snaking across the floor; the place looked like the inside of a spaceship from a film made long ago.

'One of our IT and communication hubs,' Christo said, noticing the confusion on Jan's face.

'What for?' Jan asked.

'We're not just some bunch of disorganized fanatics here, you know,' Kim said. The arrogance in her voice interested Jan . . . and attracted him. 'There are over a million people on the streets out there. They need to communicate, exchange information, coordinate their actions. Demos like these are being held in over thirty cities worldwide. We're talking to them, keeping track of what's going on where, harmonizing our message and deciding together which content and pictures we'd like to produce – and provoke – so we're not dependent on traditional media and networks.'

'A few centres like this one can do all those things?' asked Jan in disbelief.

'No. They're only one part of the technical infrastructure. Most of the information is transmitted via a blockchain app anyone can download and use for all kinds of purposes. Discussions, votes – anyone can participate.'

'Doesn't that lead to chaos?' Fitz asked.

' "We don't trust institutions, not even our own." That's a quote from the Arab Spring,' Christo said.

'It's the main reason so many protests have failed in the

long term,' Kim added. 'We need lasting institutions. A properly constructed blockchain app can more or less institutionalize trust between all involved by building it into the app itself. It's worked well so far.'

Christo winked at her. 'There are also some very smart people here who get hold of information that's not so easy to come by. Police and army operations planning, PR strategies and the like.'

Jan noted with fascination that the nerve centre of the demonstrations consisted of four rooms.

'*One* of the IT and communication centres, you said?'

'We have several of them, obviously,' Kim explained, 'in case one goes down, or is shut down. Who knows, you two might be undercover cops? If necessary, a team in another city will take over. And then there's the app – it uses a blockchain and meshes, so it's hard to turn off or manipulate.'

'Can they also get hold of information that's not so easy to come by?' Fitz asked.

'What do you need?'

'Not much. An address and/or a phone number.'

Christo had a quick word with one of the men in hoodies.

'The name?' he asked.

'Jeanne Dalli,' Fitz said, supplying a few extra details.

'It'll take a little while,' the guy announced. 'I'll come and find you.'

Fitz thanked him, but the young man was already focusing on his monitor again.

As they were leaving the IT centre, they bumped into a bike courier. Grabbing his arm, Fitz said, 'Would you mind doing an extra delivery?'

'That depends.'

Fitz pressed a fifty-euro note into the man's palm. *Fifty!*

Just like that. 'You wouldn't have an envelope, would you?' Fitz asked the messenger.

The guy searched his bag and produced a battered cardboard box.

Fitz stretched out his hand to Jan. 'Give me your phone.'

Jan pulled a face.

'The police could get a fix on you,' Fitz said.

The younger man hesitated.

'You'll get it back,' Fitz reassured him.

'I just need to check something.'

'Your mother?'

'Yeah. Man, is she pissed off!'

There were at least two dozen text and voicemail messages.

Fitz peeked at the display. 'She sounds worried to me. In some of her messages at least.'

Maybe.

'Send her a text and then hand it over.'

I'm fine. Will call soon.

Reluctantly Jan gave Fitz his mobile. Fitz put both their phones in the box and pressed down the sticky flap. 'Do you have a pen, please?' he asked the courier.

Impeccable manners. Must be his posh upbringing.

Fitz wrote the address of his hotel and his room number on the cardboard. 'Please deliver this tonight sometime. Thanks.'

'No problem,' the man said and left.

'Now neither of us can contact anyone,' Jan said.

Fitz produced two simple mobile phones from the inside pocket of his jacket. Ones with physical keypads. 'Yes, we can. In my line of business, you always have a couple of burners on you.'

'Burners? Sounds like a weird business to me.'

'Disposable phones not registered under your usual number. Pay as you go. You can still get hold of one when you need one. You only give the number to people who really need to know, like your fixers, for instance.'

'Is it legal?'

'Legal? Who cares?' Fitz said, handing him a phone. 'It's for emergencies. My number's on it, no one else's.'

31

Not everyone was tired when they reached The Estate. The chairman of the board of an international construction firm was telling the head of a major development agency based in Geneva with great enthusiasm about his motorbike tour of East Asia the previous year. He was illustrating his account with photos of himself clad in leathers, along with shots of his mud-caked machine. The two men were greatly amused at the contrast between that outfit and the tuxedos they were wearing now. The director of the aid agency, a Peruvian, held up his own phone to show a snap of a Harley-Davidson, saying, 'I treated myself for my fiftieth.' More swiping, more pictures, more laughter. Soulmates. The trivial pleasures of important men.

Jeanne wasn't remotely interested in cars or motorcycles. Her only question was: *What do these unhealthy-looking men do when their big bikes fall over?*

Ted was deep in conversation with Kemp Gellund and a high-ranking World Bank official, while a Spanish minister was chatting to a Chinese businesswoman – probably another billionaire; you never knew with the Chinese – and her husband. Jeanne was lumbered with a Lebanese entrepreneur and a Gambian conceptual artist touted as a future superstar of the art world. George meanwhile was buttering up the Italian minister, Maurizio Trittone. A dozen guards lingered more or less discreetly in the shadows. The Lebanese and the Gambian were competing hard for Jeanne's favours, but her attention was focused on any snippets of conversation between Trittone and George that reached her ears.

'. . . as a commission for advice,' she heard the Italian say. 'Paid to anonymous companies, belonging to certain firms, on an island somewhere.'

The Lebanese businessman served up more small talk. Jeanne smiled.

'We'll come up with a scheme,' George said, patting the Italian on the shoulder. 'A few lucrative directorships in associated industries when you leave the world of politics . . .'

A man in a black tailcoat and white gloves led them gracefully past the other patrons to a semi-private room from where they could enjoy the atmosphere of the bar without anyone seeing or bothering them.

'Maybe we can sell you a few pieces of real estate in Frankfurt, Paris or London at a knock-down price and you can resell them at the market rate.'

That was pretty unequivocal. Some would view it as a reward for favourable treatment by Trittone, others as bribery, corruption and money-laundering. What did George want from the Italian?

Jeanne felt Ted's hand on her back. A classic male gesture that was meant to show a combination of concern and support but was actually a sign of control, an intimation of ownership . . . until it reached the lower back, when it entered the grey area of harassment or intimacy, depending on the situation. Ted's hand was in this grey area right now.

'Or stocks . . .' George said.

'Not so profitable right now,' Trittone replied with a laugh, before the two men slipped out of earshot.

Jeanne was surprised not to feel harassed by Ted's touch. The nature of her relationship with Ted wasn't clear yet. They'd slept together a few times. There was nothing binding about it on Jeanne's side, while Ted seemed to find her manner both pleasant and provocative. He saw himself as a fantastic catch, one of the most eligible bachelors in the world. So what would he make of a woman who didn't entirely succumb to his charms? She'd wait and see. She let his hand rest where it was for a while to suggest what might be in store later. *Might*, not *would*.

Waiters hurried past, bearing trays laden with glasses of champagne. Ted removed his hand from her back to take a couple and handed her one with a grin. Ted's smile could be seriously disarming. He was by some distance her wealthiest admirer to date. 'A rich man is never ugly,' apparently, but Jeanne didn't subscribe to this Chinese proverb. She had no trouble admitting that looks were important to her, but they weren't the be-all and end-all. Ted wasn't bad-looking. He paid attention to her and was well groomed. She liked that. He could be amusing and thoughtful, and he was definitely interested in her. It was actually too good to be true. Then again another maxim stated, 'If something's too good to be true, it probably isn't – or it isn't good.'

Whatever.

Maurizio Trittone raised his glass. 'To a successful conference,' he toasted loudly.

Seems to have been a success for you already, Jeanne thought, recalling the snatches of conversation she'd just overheard.

32

Christo invited them to sit down at a kitchen table in a third-floor flat.

'I've got to go,' he explained. 'Kim here will look after you until you've either made yourselves at home or decided to leave.'

Gesturing at Jan's and Fitz's faces, Kim asked, 'Did the police do that?'

'Yes,' Fitz answered without a moment's hesitation.

'Juice, beer, sandwiches,' she said, pointing to the fridge, 'but please don't get drunk.'

Jan would have liked nothing better, but he had to keep a clear head. 'Don't worry, we won't. What's your role here exactly?' he asked, pouring himself a glass of water. He watched her out of the corner of his eye. She had a pretty upwardly curving nose.

'I help out with organization.'

'And when you're not organizing?'

'I study sociology in Heidelberg.'

He'd have liked to ask some follow-up questions, but unfortunately didn't have the first clue about sociology or even what it was. Not wishing to reveal his ignorance, he asked instead if she'd like some water.

She smiled at him. 'Yes, please.'

Fitz was meanwhile fiddling with his phone. 'There goes my poker game,' he sighed. 'It's almost midnight.'

'How about you?' Kim asked.

'I'm a trainee nurse,' Jan said, 'and Fitz . . .'

'Fitz-*roy*,' the man in question objected.

'. . . is a weirdo. A physics graduate, ex-investment banker and now a professional poker player.'

'Not just poker,' Fitz mumbled.

'Well, you make an odd couple,' Kim said, with one eye on what Fitz was doing. She drained her glass and got up. 'I need to do the rounds. See you later.'

Blink and you missed her. Slender figure, with that mop of curls on top, almost an Afro. An easy but determined gait. She was amazing.

'Mind looking this way for a moment?' Fitz mocked. He'd laid out in front of him the pad from Will's hotel room next to the sketches of the solar system.

Paradigm shift.

He began to shade in the top page of the pad.

'Is this really going to help?' Jan asked.

'Got a better idea? You were the one who found the pad so intriguing.'

'Yeah, well . . .' he grumbled. *A sheet of paper!* He turned Fitz's burner over in his hand. 'How do I go online with this thing?'

'The "at" symbol opens the browser,' Fitz replied without looking up. He was concentrating hard on shading the top inch or so of the sheet of paper with his pencil.

In the meantime, Jan was typing something into the search engine. 'Hey, get a load of this,' he said, plonking the device in front of Fitz.

BREAKING NEWS: NOBEL PRIZE
WINNER HERBERT THOMPSON KILLED
IN CAR ACCIDENT IN BERLIN

On the tiny screen was a picture of the burning car, probably grabbed from a bystander's video. There was a two-line summary of what was known so far. It was assumed to be an accident. The identity of the other casualties had not yet been established, but . . .

'Apparently you understood those policemen correctly,' Fitz remarked. Lost in thought, he stared down at the sheet with the diagrams of the solar system. 'So what's the link between this and a Nobel Prize winner?'

Two young men crossed through the kitchen and went into the next room without paying any attention to Jan and Fitz.

Jan slipped the burner into his pocket, and Fitz resumed his shading. Some scribbling appeared in the grey area in the top left-hand corner. More circular diagrams, this time five in a row.

The first was a simple circle. The second showed a circle with a vertical line through it. The third was divided into quarters by the addition of a horizontal line. An extra curved vertical stroke further subdivided the fourth diagram, reminding Jan of the lines on a boules ball. The fifth and final diagram looked like a blackberry – a rough ball made up of lots of smaller balls.

'Can you make out the scrawl alongside the drawings?' Fitz asked.

'*The*?' Jan said, guessing.

'The next word might be *formula*,' ventured Fitz.

'*Of life*,' Jan said, reading the last two words aloud. Even his English could stretch that far.

The house stood out among the other buildings on Reinhardtstrasse. It was a handsome, though slightly dilapidated nineteenth-century patrician residential block with banners and flags floating from the windows.

> *Leave them be & they'll leave us with nothing!*
> *We're not anti-system – the system's anti-us!*
> *This house has been liberated!*

Light still streamed from most of the windows, while bunches of people were standing around in the street outside. From somewhere in the building came the blare of loud music.

'Oh, great. This is going to be fun,' groaned Jörn.

'There's no way they'll let you inside in that get-up. Not tonight,' Maya said.

'I'm not going to let yobbos like them flout the law, not in this country. I'm the police!'

'You know exactly what would happen – even if they did let you in, we'd never find anything. I'm going in alone.'

'It'll take you for ever and while you're searching every flat, the criminal will leg it down the stairs.'

'*Criminal?* Mind your language. The guy's a witness at most. You're the one flouting the law.'

'Criminal, suspect, witness – it's all the same right now,' Jörn grouched. 'We have to catch him.'

Because you let him get away.

'So what do *you* suggest?' Maya asked, doing her utmost to keep her voice calm. God help her, she was having to de-escalate situations with her colleagues now.

'The report came in over half an hour ago,' Jörn said. 'They could be miles away by now.'

'If I were in their shoes, I'd take a breather here first, unless they need to get somewhere fast. Think about it. Here they don't have to worry about the police. No one's going to clear this building while hundreds of thousands of demonstrators are clamouring for affordable housing just a stone's throw away. Besides which, it'd take a whole brigade of officers to empty this place, and all available units are busy policing the protest. I bet you they're in there.'

'In which case, I'll just have to ditch the uniform,' he said. He stopped the car before they got to the building, did a U-turn and headed back the same way they'd come. 'I've got my sports kit in the boot.'

'You're going to pretend to be a personal trainer for squatters?'

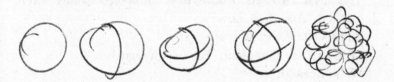

'Cell,' whispered Fitz. A new word had appeared alongside the five diagrams and the phrase 'The formula of life'.

'It's a fertilized egg starting to divide,' Kim said, bending down between them to study the drawings. Jan hadn't heard her coming. She smelled so good.

'During cleavage, the cell first splits down the middle, creating two cells. In the next stage, the two cells separate again horizontally, as shown in the diagram. Two cells become four. The following step is that four cells divide into eight. And so on and so forth until the so-called morula stage is reached.'

Once more, this was double Dutch to Jan.

Fitz stared at Kim in surprise. 'Hey, you could be right, you know.'

'What did you say you were studying – biology?' asked Jan.

'Sociology.'

'Morula?'

'Mulberry,' Kim explained. 'The cell cluster looks a bit like one.'

So blackberry hadn't been so wide of the mark.

'What is this game you're playing?' Kim wanted to know. 'Some kind of treasure hunt?'

'If only we knew,' Fitz said.

Jan showed her the page with the diagrams of the solar system on it.

'Dogma,' she read aloud. 'Paradigm change.'

'Are these two sets of drawings connected in any way?' Jan asked. 'And if so, how?'

'Is this some sort of brain-teaser?'

'You can say that again. For us, anyway.'

'Who drew these?'

'A . . . quant?' Jan said with a searching glance at Fitz, who nodded in return. 'He was working on something with a Nobel Prize winner.'

'A quantitative analyst. I see.'

This girl was beginning to unsettle Jan, but he nodded.

'Let's see what else this page can reveal,' Fitz said. 'We've barely started.'

He had the hang of it now. While they'd been chatting he'd shaded in half the page, revealing more closely spaced lines of tiny, scribbled handwriting.

'What a bloody mess!' Fitz cried. 'Will was just the kind of person keyboards were invented for.'

Jan did his best to decipher the scrawl.

'Completely illegible,' Kim mumbled.

Fitz had almost reached the bottom of the page before Jan recognized a word. *Picture*. Of course – the entire text was in English!

Fitz put the pencil down and inspected his work. 'OK, give me a few minutes to make sense of this chaos.'

'That I have to disguise myself to get in there at all is an insult,' muttered Jörn. '*And* it's against police regulations.'

He was dressed now in black tracksuit bottoms and a dark green T-shirt under a blue tracksuit top. They were walking towards the house as casually as they could. No one was paying them the slightest bit of attention.

'"Anyone who wears jogging pants has lost control of their life",' commented Maya with a broad grin. 'Karl Lagerfeld said that, even though he sells his own branded pairs. But they give you street cred – and you're going to need all you can get once we're inside.'

'What I need is a truckload of handcuffs. These total layabouts, taking over other people's property . . .'

'You can't blame them, seeing how expensive it is to rent.'

'Well, they should get off their arses and work.'

'Most of them do. Want to bet?'

'What work? Bed-hopping, studying, signing on?'

'Feel free to carry out a survey.'

'Like hell I will.'

'People are sick to the back teeth of everyone telling them

they've never had it so good when many workers have to claim benefits despite slaving away all week on low wages. They can't find a flat they can afford, their children's schools are crumbling and there aren't enough teachers. Public swimming pools are closing, and unless you have private health insurance you wait for months to see a doctor . . .'

'Not surprising when all the immigrants are—'

'Oh, don't give me that cra—'

'It's true though. They don't pay into the system but claim billions . . .'

Do I really have to spend all night with this guy?

'By that logic there's no reason to offer support to any German kids either. They don't pay anything into the system for fifteen to twenty-five years and yet they have access to healthcare, childcare, education and so much mo—'

'But their parents—'

'Many don't. Ultimately they receive more in tax relief, child allowance and other payments than they put in.'

'But still—'

'What?'

'Oh, there's no point discussing stuff like this with you.'

'Because I'm right?'

Jörn didn't rise to this bait and instead asked, 'So how do we get inside?'

They were thirty feet now from the front door of the squat. People were standing around outside chatting.

'We just go in like we're part of the scene.'

'I want to see this.'

'Watch and learn,' Maya said with a grin, 'and whatever you do, stay cool.'

'I'm always cool.'

A tall handsome guy in his mid-twenties was leaning against the doorjamb. His face twisted into a devilish grin that might have worked on women his own age but left Maya absolutely cold. 'Hey, I haven't seen you around here before, and trust me, I'd have noticed.'

Someone sure thinks he's God's gift to women.

He sized up Jörn. 'Nor this gym teacher here.'

Keep calm, Jörn.

'I'm Sören,' the man said. 'Who've you come to see?'

'Are you the doorman or something?'

'Nope. Just curious.'

Maybe he had some information.

'Jan and Fitzroy.'

'Fitz-what?'

'Fitzroy and Jan.'

'Never heard of them.'

'Well, you can't know everyone in here, can you?' said Maya, pushing past him with Jörn close behind.

In front of them the hallway split off to the left and right into two corridors of six to eight flats, with a staircase straight ahead. There were people everywhere, walking, propping up walls, talking and drinking.

Maya got her phone out. 'What's your number?'

Jörn gave it to her and fished out his own mobile. Maya called him.

'OK, you go left, I'll take right. We stay in touch, just in case. One of us keeps an eye on the stairs at all times, so we take turns searching the apartments.'

'That'll take for ever.'

'Stop whining and let's find them.'

33

'All right, all right,' Fitz murmured as he pored over the white hieroglyphics on the grey sheet of paper. 'OK.'

'What is it?' Jan asked urgently.

'I haven't finished yet,' Fitz objected.

'So what's it about? Any help?'

'Hmm.'

'Oh, come on!'

'I'm trying. This is a novel Will's written, or at least notes for a novel. A few times he's written "Illustration".' Fitz picked up the pencil, tore the shaded sheet from the pad and began to scribble on the blank page underneath.

He drew a square and divided it into four fields of equal size separated by something that looked to Jan like a road. In each field was a name – Ann, Bill, Carl and Dana – along with a few houses.

'What is it – a village?'

'Yep. Four farmers – two women and two men. Ann's and Carl's fields are to the west, on the flat land of the lower village. The farming conditions in their fields are identical. Bill's and Dana's fields are in the hillier area to the east of the upper village. Their circumstances are a bit different to those in the lower village. The conditions for growing grain are the same in Bill's and Dana's fields, but

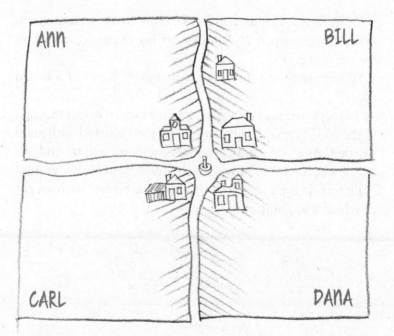

different to those on Ann and Carl's land. This is due to differences in water supply and climate and varying susceptibility to pest attacks.'

'Will's scribbles told you all that?' asked Jan.

'As I said, it's a collection of notes. Will describes the four farmers as follows: Ann is hard-working, organized and thrifty. Or as we are to understand: "If everyone farmed like her, everything would be fine."'

'A good housewife,' was Kim's comment.

'Exactly. The second farmer, Bill, is the competitive type. He always wants to be the best and tries to carve out an advantage for himself in any given situation. His motto is "If everyone takes care of themselves, then everyone's taken care of".'

'Nice,' Kim groaned.

'Naturally, Ann and Bill sow millions of seeds, but to make things easier, Will kicks off his example with Ann having one grain.'

'What are these?' Jan asked nervously. 'Rules of a board game?'

'No idea, because you didn't give me time to read it through to the end,' Fitz said. 'Anyway . . . in good soil and with good weather, Ann's one grain produces one ear of wheat. And one ear of wheat – to simplify matters – contains ten new grains.'

Fitz made a rapid sketch of a woman farmer with an ear of wheat and ten grains.

'The art world doesn't know what it's missing!' Jan teased him.

'I know. The aim is to keep the calculations simple, and we therefore assume that Ann doesn't eat any of her harvest herself nor does she sell any of her crop. The following year, therefore, she can plant ten grains instead of one.'

Fitz frowned as he applied himself to deciphering the rest of the scrawl. 'The second harvest is bad. A late frost kills three of the ten seedlings, pests eat another two and a further three succumb to the summer drought.'

'That leaves two ears,' said Kim. 'Twenty grains.'

'Picture, please,' said Jan. 'It'll help me figure it out.'

Fitz sketched a farmer, some dead plants and twenty grains.

3   2   3   2   20

'Her starting position for the third year is still better than it was in the first,' Fitz continued. 'She now has twenty grains instead of ten. And so it continues, year after year, each a little better or slightly worse than the others.'

'I just don't get where this is heading,' Jan muttered.

'Be patient, will you?' Kim said.

Jan blushed. He sat tight and hoped that Kim wouldn't notice his embarrassment.

'Carry on,' she told Fitz. 'Those look like more figures there . . .'

'Yep. Will assumes the following four-year growth rate for Ann's field: the first year, she turns one ear into two, which becomes six in the second year, followed by six again in the third year and twelve in the fourth.'

He wrote all of this down.

Baseline Ann	RESULTS			
1 Ear	2 Ears	6 Ears	6 Ears	12 Ears
Year	1	2	3	4

'Thus after four years Ann has twelve ears of wheat instead of her initial one,' Kim summarized.

'Over the same period, the wheat in Bill's fields to the east of the village develops differently,' Fitz continued. 'The first year he has four ears instead of one – much better than Ann – but in the second year he harvests only four, the same as his previous crop. However, in year three, those four become eight and in the fourth year that leaps to sixteen.'

Another drawing.

Baseline BILL	RESULTS			
🌾	🌾🌾🌾🌾	🌾🌾🌾🌾	🌾🌾🌾🌾🌾🌾🌾🌾	🌾🌾🌾🌾🌾🌾🌾🌾🌾🌾🌾🌾🌾🌾🌾🌾
1 Ear	4 Ears	4 Ears	8 Ears	16 Ears
Year	1	2	3	4

Jan clenched his fists in his pockets and reined in an urge to make a scathing remark. *What was the point of this numbers game?*

'So Bill managed to turn one ear of wheat into sixteen over four years,' said Fitz. 'In some years Ann had higher yields, in others Bill did. Add them together and we see that over four years the two of them harvested twenty-eight ears from an original base of two.'

'What now?' asked Jan. 'Do we have to do the same calculations for Carl and Dana too? We already know what the outcome will be.'

His nose almost touching the paper, Fitz ignored the snarky tone and said, 'Yes, but the figures are very different. Whereas Ann produced twelve ears of wheat after four years, Carl managed eighteen! On the other side of the village, Bill had sixteen ears at the end of four years. Well, Dana had eighteen too, meaning that Carl and Dana together produced thirty-six ears in the same length of time. Far more than Ann and Bill's combined crop!'

Fitz entered these figures into the drawing of the four fields.

4 YRS

Ann
12

BILL
16   28

18
CARL

18   36
DANA

'They must've had better fertilizer,' Jan interjected. 'Or pesticides. Or more productive seed. Or—'

'No, Will explicitly rules out such differences.'

'*Explicitly*,' Jan snorted.

'"All the conditions are identical." *All* of them. He was categorical.'

'All right, I get it.'

'So how does he explain Carl and Dana's higher productivity?' asked Kim.

'Good question,' said Fitz, pointing to the bottom of the sheet. 'The only thing here, at the end, is a brief dialogue between Bill and Dana.' He read it out.

'Bill: "How did you do it?"'

'Dana: "*Clever* farming. Remember how five years ago my harvest was terrible, while you had a very good year?"'

'Bill: "That's just the way it goes. There are good years and bad years."'

'Dana: "Back then I asked if you . . ."'

Fitz looked up and gazed innocently at Jan.

'The end.'

'What do you mean, the end?'

'Finished, all over. That's the end of the story.'

34

'That's it?' Jan asked drily.

'That's it,' said Fitz.

'What the fuck? Bloody hell – that's why we were almost beaten to a pulp, and took the risk of falling to our deaths from walls and rooftops? That's why we're on the run from the police? For some village fairy-tale bullshit? Bollocks! Fuck that! All for nothing.'

'Jan.' The word came to him as if through cotton wool. 'Jan!' Fitz, a blurred figure in front of his eyes, was shaking him by the shoulders. Only now did Jan realize that he'd leaped to his feet. Kim and two other people who'd just come into the room were staring at him in fascination and bemusement. He didn't care.

'Jan,' Fitz said again, 'we had to try. It's better to have a go than do nothing.'

Doesn't feel that way to me. 'That's exactly the attitude that got me into this shit to begin with! I should've kept cycling. I'd have been safely tucked up in bed by now if I had.'

'What are you talking about?' Kim asked. The furrowed brow didn't suit her.

'Forget it,' said Fitz. 'It's been a long day.' He slumped back on to his chair and stared absently into the distance.

Silence fell, and all of a sudden Jan's tiredness hit him.

The others in the room were glancing anxiously back and forth between Fitz and him, and when he met Kim's gaze, Jan bit his lip with embarrassment and sat down.

'I'm sorry,' he said.

'No need,' Fitz replied. 'It hit you before it hit me, that's all.' He flashed Jan a grin, one of his gambler's grins – sure of victory, or adept at making others believe it. It worked.

'All right then, but I repeat my question: what does it mean?' Jan asked.

'It's a kind of fable if you ask me,' Fitz said. 'With an economics theme, I guess, given Thompson's background. Will liked that kind of thing, and he was trying to illustrate something.' He laughed. 'Unfortunately the end is missing.'

'Who wrote this story of yours?' Kim asked. 'Why don't you just ask him or her?'

Fitz hesitated, and so did Jan.

'The author's dead,' Fitz said eventually.

'Oh,' Kim said, commiserating with the two friends. 'Was he a friend of yours?'

'Yes,' Fitz said.

'I'm so sorry.' She placed her hands on Jan's and Fitz's shoulders for a moment, sending a shockwave through Jan's body. A shock of pleasure – the first nice sensation that evening.

Maya was up on the third floor by now. She hadn't found either of the two men yet. The ground floor layout with passages leading off to the left and right of the central staircase was repeated on the upper storeys. Each hallway served several flats, some of which had no door, some a curtain and others a makeshift door. Maya suspected that the owner of the building must have removed any fittings that would have made it remotely habitable. She wondered how the squatters had managed to rig up power and water, as bulbs were casting light from the ceilings and the toilets seemed to be in working order, even if no one had given the ones she'd seen a serious clean recently.

She'd just finished checking the first flat on this particular floor when she came across an old acquaintance in the entrance to the next. Sören was leaning in the doorway, chatting up an attractive blonde. He hadn't wasted any time.

'So?' he asked. 'Find those people you were looking for?'

Maya ignored him and went past him into the rooms beyond. None of the people there paid any attention to her. She didn't spot Wutte or Peel in any of the three adjacent rooms. Most of the occupants had settled down to sleep on mats or in sleeping bags by now. Many had probably gathered under the glowing peace sign earlier that evening, gazing up in awe and excitement. Tomorrow they would be taking part in the big demo. For a second she envied these young people for their straightforwardness, their enthusiasm, their naivety.

'Not to be a socialist at twenty is proof of want of heart. To be one at thirty is proof of want of brain.' But what if you had both?

The hallways were less busy now too. As Maya left the apartment, she found Sören and the blonde still leaning against the wall. A young woman with ringlets and one with a striking black bob were passing by, but otherwise there was no one around.

'I'm out,' she said, casting an eye at Jörn lingering on the landing. 'Your turn to go in again.'

Jörn disappeared through the doorway. Maya took up a position outside the next flat. Three more on this floor. Lost in thought, she watched the two women vanish into the flat furthest away from her.

*

'This is Nida,' said Kim, introducing a tall woman with a snow-white complexion, dark glasses and a black bob. She was dressed in a hoodie, skinny jeans with ripped knees and the inevitable pair of Converse. 'Nida's an economist and I thought she might be able to help make sense of your story.'

A what? An economist? Seriously? How's she supposed to help? thought Jan. It was kind of Kim – how could she know that their real problem wasn't an economics puzzle, but a gang of killers as well as the police on their tail.

Nida nodded to them all, and Jan and Fitz briefly introduced themselves before Fitz explained the situation and showed her his drawings.

'Hmm,' was all Nida had to say in return.

'There you are!' came a cry from the doorway. It was Christo, with the guy in the hoodie from the IT hub.

Holding out a scrap of paper, the hoodie guy said, 'Here are Jeanne Dalli's mobile numbers. The first one's private, the other two are for work.'

'Thanks.'

'My pleasure,' the guy murmured, slipping away before Fitz could say anything else.

'Jan and Fitzroy, right?' Christo asked.

'Yep,' Fitz replied. The phone numbers had raised his spirits.

'A little bird told me that some chick and a bloke are walking around the place looking for two guys named Jan and Fitzroy.'

Jan felt a sick sensation in his gut.

'I thought no one could get in here,' Fitz retorted.

'Well, no one like those geezers out on the roof. These two look pretty normal though.'

'How did you find out anyway?'

'Internal comms,' Christo explained. 'Just because there's

a lot going on here doesn't mean we don't know *what's* going on.'

'What if they're with them?' Jan whispered to Fitz.

'A man and a woman?' Fitz said in a low voice. 'Sounds like those two from my hotel – the police.'

'How the hell do they know we're here?' Jan hissed, his cheek muscles twitching.

'The helicopter?' Fitz reminded him with a roll of his eyes.

'Are you in serious trouble?' Kim asked with more curiosity and amusement than concern.

'Do we puzzle champs look like we would be?' Fitz shot back.

'Where's the woman now?' Jan asked.

Christo peered out into the hallway and then said, 'Heading in this direction. About thirty feet away but closing fast.'

'They mustn't find us,' gasped Jan.

'There are fire escapes down into the courtyard,' Christo said, 'through the window in the next room . . .'

Jan was already on the move. He raced into a living room where five people were lounging on sofas, passing around a joint. Jan was fully focused on the window. There really was a fire escape ladder outside it. He pulled up the sash and looked out.

The remains of a fire escape ladder, more like.

Lit by the glow from various windows, Jan could make out its bent and rusting frame. The fire escape was already hanging a couple of feet out at this level, its attachments having been torn from the wall. One storey lower down, the distance was double that and further down the gap grew ever greater. Jan couldn't see the bottom of the ladder. Did this skeleton even reach the ground? He grabbed one of the struts. It shook and wobbled in the dark, screeching like an ancient windmill. Would the thing actually bear his weight?

'Jan!' Fitz was there, holding Jan back. 'If it is the police, maybe we should just put an end to all this. We can explain everything.'

'And what if it's the guy who wanted to haul me into the station?' Jan said, breaking free. He straddled the sill, groping for the rungs with the tip of his shoe.

Kim and Christo were standing in the kitchen doorway. A woman came into view behind them. The woman from Fitz's hotel.

FOURTH DECISION

'Finally, multicellular and complex organisms emerge. Life itself is a manifestation of this mathematical principle.'

Will Cantor

35

Maya quickly took stock of the scene in the kitchen. The young woman with the black bob whom Maya had seen out in the hallway. Table and chairs – empty, pushed back as if in a hurry. A couple of people standing in the doorway to the next room, one of them the woman who'd been with Black Bob earlier. The two of them staring wide-eyed back at her. As if she'd been expected.

They turned their attention back to the room beyond. Maya tried to get a glimpse of what was going on in there.

It was them! The gambler, definitely. And over by the window, with one leg in mid-air, was Jan Wutte!

Pressing her phone to her ear, Maya whispered, 'I've found them, Jörn! Last flat on the left.'

'Who are you?' asked the guy in the doorway. 'What do you want?'

'Oh, I'm sorry. I'm Maya, and you are?'

'Christo.'

'Are Jan and Fitzroy in there?'

Christo didn't reply.

'I just wanted a quick chat,' Maya said. She went up on her tiptoes and peeped over his shoulder. 'Ah, I can see them. Jan! Fitzroy! Have you got a minute?'

Unsure of what to do, Christo turned to look at the two men.

Fitzroy Peel came up behind Christo and said something quietly in his ear.

Christo's expression hardened. 'You're police?'

Damn, the rules of engagement had just changed! Before Maya could say anything, Christo asked, 'Do you have a search warrant?'

'Are you serious?' came a roar from behind them. Jörn. 'Are you taking the piss? You occupy this house illegally and then dare to deny us ac—'

'Jörn!' Maya exclaimed.

'—cess! Where are they? Let us through!'

'Are you a cop too?' Christo wanted to know.

Black Bob was now filming from her seat at the kitchen table. The girl with the ringlets was doing likewise as events unfolded around her. Figures appeared in the room behind Christo, their smartphones glowing.

'Jörn . . .' Maya said, trying to pacify her colleague. She gestured with her head to the mobiles and held him back as he attempted to shove past Christo. 'You're being filmed,' she hissed.

'Am I?' Jörn shouted. 'Well, I don't give a damn.'

'Jörn . . .' Maya pushed him away, but to no avail.

'Obstructing the police! You're accomplices to a homicide.'

'I didn't kill anyone,' Wutte shouted from the windowsill. 'In fact, I was the one who called emergency services. You're trying to frame me!'

'Typical,' one of the people on the couch said.

'I'll see you all in jail for aiding and abetting murder.'

He pushed Christo again, harder this time.

What an idiot! He's getting out of control.

'Jan Wutte!' Maya shouted. 'We only want to question you as a witness.'

'It doesn't sound like your colleague has the same idea,' cried a man who was filming proceedings with his phone.

'Let's see your credentials then,' said the young woman with the black bob.

Jörn stared at her in disbelief.

Maya grabbed his arm. 'Jörn!'

'I've had quite enough of this,' he seethed. 'I want everyone's ID.' He patted the pockets of his tracksuit top and then the bottoms.

Maya immediately realized that the moron had left his papers in his uniform. They couldn't afford to humiliate themselves like this. Maya pulled out her police ID card.

Jörn glossed over his inadequacy with added bluster. 'Papers, pronto. All of you!'

Maya shut her eyes and sighed. She hated working with imbeciles. Peel hadn't immediately run for the exit and Christo had seemed willing to talk . . . until Rambo Jörn barged in.

'You first,' Christo riposted. 'We've only seen your colleague's ID so far.'

Jörn was ready to go wild, but the sight of Maya's pursed lips defused any further outbursts. Her eyes roamed over Christo's shoulder and alighted on the open window.

'Where are Wutte and Peel?' she cried. 'And that girl too?' Miss Ringlets had vanished, and so had Black Bob.

Maya rushed over to the kitchen window. She could see the loose, rusty remains of a fire escape trembling out in the dark courtyard as two figures clambered down the swaying, squeaking metal frame.

Goodness, got suicidal urges, have they? They'd rather

climb down that death trap than speak to us? Mind you, after Jörn's performance ...

Or maybe they weren't as harmless as they made out ... There was a crash and several rungs broke off and bounced off the ladder before disappearing into the void with further loud clangs. Then the whole structure broke free.

'Oh my God!'

The vibrations ripped the ladder from under Jan's feet. He clung on, the rusty steel cutting into his palms, his legs dangling in mid-air. The screech of metal drowned out his cries. Pieces of iron rained down on them from above, ricocheting off the ladder against the wall of the house and plunging into the courtyard below. Lights came on in several windows. Fitz too had almost been thrown from the ladder and was clinging on with one arm, twisting this way and that, before he managed to grab hold of a rung with the other.

The fire escape's fall came to a juddering halt, almost loosening Jan's grip again until he caught hold at the last second. The structure had slipped about three feet down the wall. It was creaking, groaning, rocking and shaking.

We need to get off this thing!

The courtyard was lit down at ground level. The partial collapse of the fire escape had helped them because the bottom of the ladder was now less than ten feet above the concrete. Jan's descent was more about letting himself drop safely than actually climbing down. He reached the bottom of the ladder, lowered himself until he was clutching the last rung, glanced down and let go.

The landing was hard, even though he broke his fall with a half-somersault. Mentally he checked his body. Ankles, knees, wrists, lower arms, shoulders – all OK. He jumped up.

Fitz landed beside him, and Jan helped him to his feet.

'You maniac!' Fitz croaked.

'Let's get out of here before the whole thing comes crashing down on top of us!' Jan said, dragging his friend out of the courtyard and into the stairwell.

Kim was standing there, her hair wild and a savage look in her eyes. Nida was behind her.

'Come on,' called Kim. 'Those two cops will be here any moment.'

Bell was posted some twenty yards from the entrance of the house, with El roughly the same distance away to the right of it. Sam was waiting in the doorway opposite and Jack was waiting in the Range Rover in the street running parallel to the rear of the building.

It was past midnight.

The plainclothes policewoman and her ludicrously disguised partner were still in the building. Their appearance had added a fresh twist to the chase. It was too great a coincidence that they had turned up here after El's sighting of them at Peel's hotel – so the police were after them too. El could have done without the competition, but there was nothing he could do about that now.

He ground his teeth in frustration. The targets didn't have many options. Did they plan to sit tight and spend the night in there? They'd have to come out sometime, so he and his team needed to be ready for that moment.

They were all used to waiting. Guard duty at night in Afghanistan, Iraq or Sudan or anywhere else they'd conducted secret ops. This was a piece of cake compared with their time in the military.

There were still a few lights on inside the house.

'I think I can see them,' Jack said via the headset. 'Yep,

they're coming out of another house. The buildings must communicate. They're not alone. Four people in total.'

'Copy. We're on our way. Keep us posted.'

So they weren't going to sit tight after all. They might come to regret that decision.

36

Fitzroy sprinted alongside Kim towards Friedrichstrasse with the other two close behind. Occasional heavy drops of rain started to fall from the looming thunderclouds overhead.

'I hope we won't be sorry later about helping you like this,' Kim panted.

'You won't,' said Fitzroy. 'We haven't done anything, honest.' *Other than break into a hotel room, although technically we didn't even do that. We did, after all, have a key card.* 'I'll tell you another time. Where are we headed?'

'Follow me.'

Friedrichstrasse. Kim scanned the traffic. The street was still busy, with taxis making up much of the traffic at this hour. Jan peered nervously over his shoulder. There was no sign of the policewoman and her colleague. Kim flagged down a cab and looked back one last time before jumping inside.

Fitzroy suddenly froze. Three hulking dark figures were racing towards them from Reinhardtstrasse. They were definitely not police officers.

'Move it!' he shouted, leaping into the car. 'Fast as you can!'

'What is it?' Kim asked.

Fitzroy slammed the door behind them. 'I'll tell you later.' And to the driver, he said, 'Go, go, go!'

The three silhouettes stopped and stared at the receding taxi. A black SUV pulled up alongside them.

'Fu—' hissed Fitzroy, looking out of the back window. Jan had spotted them too.

Fitzroy waved two hundred-euro notes under the taxi driver's nose. 'I'll double this if you get rid of the black Range Rover back there.'

'What the h-hell?' Kim stammered.

'Get rid of it?' the driver asked. 'You mean, shake them off?'

'Yes.'

'Um, I've chased someone before, but shaking someone off . . .' He put his foot down.

'I want an explanation,' Kim demanded. 'Now.'

Fitzroy and Jan exchanged glances. Fitzroy nodded. *I've got this.*

'A friend of mine was murdered tonight,' he explained. 'Jan witnessed it, but, as you'll have gathered, the police suspect him of committing the crime.'

Kim stared at him open-mouthed. It was raining harder now, and the driver turned on the windscreen wipers.

'Sorry we've dragged you into this,' Jan muttered sheepishly.

'What about the guys behind us?' Kim snapped. 'They're not police officers, are they?'

Kim would freak out if he said any more, and they could do without that.

'Something else entirely,' Fitz said. 'I owe them money.'

'You guys are totally . . .' Kim cried.

The rain was pouring down now. The taxi driver swerved past a line of cars into the bus lane. The black Range Rover wasn't allowed to follow, but naturally it did and then found it even easier to close the gap.

'They're catching up!' said Fitzroy, struggling to keep calm.

'I can see that,' said the driver. 'Stick with me.' He accelerated through a green light. The Range Rover was right behind them now, its headlights spitting sparks from the ricocheting rain.

A flashing blue light and a howl of sirens. A police car screeched out of a gateway behind the SUV and pulled right up to their pursuers' bumper.

'Now the police,' groaned Jan. 'I'm done for.'

'Not if you didn't do anything . . .' Kim said, staring out of the back window along with the others. The SUV was lit up in the blue glare.

'You saw what the man was like,' Jan said. 'He doesn't care. He'd already made up his mind. I could really do without the hassle.'

'Sorted,' the driver announced cheerfully.

The Rover fell back and pulled over into a driveway. The patrol car stopped alongside it.

'They're not allowed to use the bus and taxi lane,' the cabbie explained. 'I knew the police were there. I saw them on my way into the centre. They were sitting there, waiting for someone like those guys.' He turned into a side street. 'Where exactly do you want to go?'

'Drive on a few blocks,' Fitzroy instructed him, 'and then stop at the next taxi rank.' He handed the driver the number of banknotes he'd promised.

Kim looked at Jan and raised an eyebrow.

Jan responded with shrug. 'He earns a decent wage.'

'Then he should give those gorillas their money back.'

Fitzroy grinned. This girl sure had the gift of repartee.

*

'Shit!' Maya cursed outside the squat. She was still peering along the street in both directions. 'They're gone.' She took a few steps one way, then a few paces the other. 'You were a true pro in there,' she barked at Jörn. Mentally checking that she hadn't left anything in his car, she added, 'Better no partner than someone like you. Go on home! Good night!'

'Oh, come on . . .'

She turned on her heel and without another glance at her partner marched off towards the hotel on to whose roof Wutte and Peel had climbed. Her jeans were already soaked from the rain.

The cabbie let them out at the next taxi rank. The downpour had subsided to a light drizzle by now.

'I'm going back to my gran's,' Kim said. 'I stay with her when I'm in Berlin. You can come with me if you need to think about your next move. You can hardly go home or head to a hotel at the moment.'

'Are you sure?' Jan asked, stunned.

'I can't really leave you at the mercy of that crazy cop.'

Jan ran his fingers distractedly through his hair. 'Well, yeah, that'd be . . . cool . . . Great.'

'Thanks,' said Fitz. They could look for a hotel, he thought, and ask one of the girls to show their ID, but it'd be better not to risk it.

'Are you coming too?' Kim asked Nida. 'After everything that's happened, I'd understand if—'

'Your brain-teaser . . .' Nida said. 'There's something about it. I'd like another look in peace and quiet this time, if that's OK.'

Kim shrugged her shoulders. 'It's fine with me and my gran.'

'The only thing is: how do I get back to Reinhardtstrasse afterwards?'

'Taxi,' Kim said, pointing to Fitz with a grin. 'He'll pay for it, and to get to my gran's too.'

Fitz grinned back at her. 'Fine by me.'

They hopped into another taxi, and Kim gave the address to the driver.

'Why are you so interested in that story anyway?' she asked.

'It's the last trace we have left of my friend who died,' Fitz explained. 'We were hoping it'd provide some clues.'

'About who killed him? A fable?'

'From the piece of paper. You were there. At first we had no idea what was written on it.'

'True,' she agreed, 'but now we do, and I don't see any clues.'

'Maybe they're hidden. There's a history to all this, but it's too complicated to tell it all right now. Maybe the end of the story will reveal a motive.'

'For murder?'

'Who knows?'

'A nice little challenge,' said Kim, turning to Nida. 'Do you have any idea what the outcome of the story might be?'

The rain was falling harder again.

'The classic solution would be game theory,' Nida said.

'This is no time for games!' Jan blurted out.

'It's only partly to do with games or even gambling,' Nida replied. 'Game theory deals with how decisions are made when several people are involved. It's used as a basis for strategizing in all kinds of decision-making processes and conflict situations – from business and societal change to social unrest and warfare.'

'So why's it called game theory?'

'Because it originated in games-related questions and is often still modelled using games. Mathematical models of it do exist though.'

'More bloody maths!'

'You might have heard of the prisoner's dilemma,' said Nida. 'That's the best-known example.'

Jan shook his head.

'Imagine two criminals are interrogated by the police. They're in a tricky position – the police can prove they committed robbery, but suspect them of involvement in armed robbery. If both of them stay silent, each serves two years in prison. If they confess to armed robbery, each gets a four-year jail sentence. But if one of them admits to robbery and the other says nothing, the one who confessed will serve only one year if he gives evidence against the other, whereas the second criminal will receive the maximum sentence of six years.'

'Can they communicate with each other?'

'That's a very good and important question. They're questioned separately and don't know what the other one has said.' She crossed her arms, sat back and grinned at the other three. 'What would you do?'

There was a short silence until Jan said, 'We'd be fucked.'

'Why?' asked Nida.

'If I spill the beans, I go to jail for only one year. That's the best outcome for me personally. Unfortunately, the other person's thinking the same thing, so we both talk. Meaning that both of us confess, and the police lock us both up for four years.'

'Correct,' said Nida. 'What would be the most rational strategy for the two of you?'

'To keep quiet,' he said. 'Then each of us will only go behind bars for two years for robbery.'

'Four years in total. In that case—'

'But it only works if the other person keeps his mouth shut too! If he talks, he can give evidence for the prosecution . . . while they put me away for six years!'

'It's a perfect illustration of how two individuals, each pursuing his own best interests, will not cooperate.'

'And land each other in the shit,' said Jan.

'The results are different if you repeat the game, however,' said Fitz.

'You know about this too?'

'A little bit.'

'You learn from your mistakes, so to speak,' Jan suggested.

'No,' said Nida, 'it's more like if you punish spoilsports, they'll keep to the rules next time. Robert Axelrod demonstrated it in the seventies. Tit-for-tat and similar strate—'

'OK, but how does that explain our farmer story then?' Jan interrupted impatiently. 'And more importantly, why do Carl and Dana have *more* after four years?'

37

They were *not* happy to see her back at Hotel Raal. A matter of discretion. Nothing had happened to any of their guests, and so they simply wanted to get back to their daily routine as soon as possible. And their night-time one too.

Five stars. Just a little bit fancier than the squat Maya had been in a few minutes ago. A manager showed her to Room 756. The men must have set off from here, he explained. Other hotel guests had caught sight of the men climbing along the ledge and up to the roof from the rooms opposite and called reception. The bathroom window had been open.

'Who was staying in this room?'

'A gentleman named Will Cantor. A US citizen, according to his passport.'

'Since when?'

'Since when is he a US citizen, or since when has he been our guest?'

Maya was too tired for lame jokes, which he could tell from her expression.

'Today.'

'How long did he book for?'

'Two nights.'

'The duration of the summit.'

She inspected the room, but found nothing of note. What

was striking, though, was what she didn't find. No laptop and no tablet, even though there were two cables plugged into sockets. No work documents either.

'Do you provide your guests with letter paper, notepads, pens or pencils?' she enquired.

'They're usually on the desk,' he said. 'Maybe the maids forgot to put them out.' He started hunting through the drawers.

'Perhaps you could check,' Maya said. 'The other guests you mentioned: are they still awake?'

'I don't think so.'

'How many people did they say they saw climbing?'

'One person mentioned two, but others said there were three.'

The bathroom window was open. Even peering out of it made Maya dizzy. Someone climbed out there? A gently sloping ledge about eight inches wide ran along the outside wall of the building level with the bathroom floor. The façade itself was clad with fake sandstone blocks, and the finger-wide gaps between them might have provided some kind of purchase to the climbers. To contemplate going out there you either had to be an excellent free climber or absolutely desperate.

The next stop on her tour was the roof terrace, where she interviewed the staff. The manager stuck close to her side. The few remaining guests were sheltering from the rain in the covered areas of the bar.

She ordered a White Lady and asked the barkeeper, 'How many of them were there?'

'Two men came over the railing,' he said. 'And four climbed on to the neighbouring roof. Two first, then another two. But I couldn't tell if the second lot were crack climbers too.'

'Security staff?' she asked the manager.

'Not ours. Maybe a guest's?'

'And they'd go into a stranger's room?'

'Maybe Mr Cantor brought his own bodyguards along.'

'Did he check in with any?'

'No, but that doesn't necessarily rule it out.'

Maya examined the spot where the men had apparently appeared from below. They must have fingers like geckos'.

It was long past midnight, and the bar was no longer as full as it must have been a few hours earlier. Maya got the manager to show her the sound system. She turned the music down and picked up the microphone.

'Good evening, ladies and gentlemen. This is the police. I'd like to talk to anyone who witnessed the incident about two hours ago. I need to know exactly what you saw. Maybe someone even filmed the event. You'll find me at the bar. Thank you for your attention.'

She turned the music up again.

They drew up outside a 1950s residential building on a dark street. It had stopped raining at last.

'Here we are,' announced the taxi driver.

Jan checked the surroundings for any suspicious activity before getting out of the car. He listened in briefly to the two women – student stuff. They were so caught up in their conversation that they simply got out and continued talking while Fitz settled up with the driver.

'Maybe Carl and Dana aren't competing but cooperating in some way?' said Kim.

'By helping the others out with grain if they had a bad harvest?' Nida guessed. 'Solidarity and altruism?'

'Redistribution from rich to poor,' Fitz corrected her. 'It's a nice idea, but it doesn't benefit them *both*, only the poor.'

'Says the guy with all the money . . .' Kim remarked scornfully.

'Who just paid for your taxi.'

'He's right,' Nida said. 'It's the idea underpinning the whole of classical economics. Economic systems seek a balance – equilibrium – which is generally taken to mean that you can't give to one person without taking away from another.'

'Although it's more often the other way around,' Kim said angrily. 'Redistribution from poor to rich, which is why inequality in terms of wealth just keeps on growing.'

Jan's attention was focused on the dimly lit street and the dark pavements. It was so late that there were no lights on in any of the surrounding buildings.

'A fairer distribution of wealth contributes to social harmony,' Kim exclaimed. 'And there are advantages to cooperation, collaboration, whatever you want to call it. There are countless examples . . .'

'Such as?' asked Fitz. 'Show us the maths.'

'I can't do the maths,' Kim admitted, growing incensed. 'But there are cooperatives and, um . . . You're the mathematician here.'

'That system was called communism and it failed.'

'I'm not talking about that!'

'Instead of wishful thinking and theoretical babble, I'd like mathematical models that can demonstrate and predict that your cooperative system will be more successful,' said Fitz.

'You can tell you're a physicist.'

'No such formulas exist,' Fitz continued. 'Amazing though it sounds, no one has actually found out yet how growth works. It's obvious that philosophers and sociologists have no idea, but nor do biologists.'

They reached the front door and Kim fished for her key.

'Thanks to capitalism, of course,' she scoffed. 'What else?'

'That's as much of an ideology as Marxism and all the others,' Nida interjected. 'Watch any of capitalism's most famous representatives in debates on YouTube – people like Hayek and Friedman. They mostly say "I believe". Nothing but assertions and pseudologic.'

'A capitalist smokescreen!' cried Kim before finally entering the house. 'I do have to agree with Fitz about one thing though.'

'Thanks!'

'None of your game theory exercises will solve the mystery of why Carl and Dana produce more than Ann and Bill in the first place.'

Let alone find our bloodthirsty pursuers, thought Jan. That, after all, was their real goal, not all this philosophizing. He looked back one last time before stepping into the building. The street was dark and deserted.

38

The lift gave her exclusive and direct access to Ted's suite. His door opened to reveal a loft-like space whose gigantic plate-glass windows offered Jeanne a panoramic view of the city.

It was shortly before midnight. Jeanne wanted to see how the next few minutes played out before deciding how the evening should end.

She cast an eye over the furnishings – expensive items in what was for her tastes an overly glitzy, bombastic style, designed with the overwhelming majority of suite-loving guests from the former Soviet states, Arab countries, China and Southeast Asia in mind. Perhaps even a few real estate, gambling and telecom billionaires from the United States and Latin America. African despots too, maybe. There were more than enough potential clients in the world.

'Aha,' said Ted behind her, picking up a fat, large-format envelope that was lying on an oversized sideboard, examining it briefly and putting it away in a drawer. He then turned his full attention to Jeanne. There were two three-piece suites arranged in different parts of the room. An ice bucket with a bottle of champagne cooling in it stood on one of the coffee tables. It was almost as if Ted had been counting on a guest before the night was out.

'Something to celebrate?' she asked.

'That *you're* here?' he replied with a smile. 'Can I get you something?'

'I'll have a glass of that,' she said.

With practised skill Ted opened the bottle without a loud pop and filled two glasses to halfway. He handed her one and raised his.

'Thank you for your delightful company this evening,' he said.

They both took a sip.

'Open the door to the terrace,' Ted ordered and the window slid aside as if by magic. Beyond lay a balcony that ran the entire width of the vast room. Dimmed strip lighting along the edges of the terrace provided just enough light to find one's way around. A cool evening breeze wafted gently indoors. The rain had cleansed and freshened the night air.

They stepped outside. The breeze played gently with Jeanne's hair and the gossamer fabric of her evening dress.

'You looked absolutely stunning tonight,' Ted said.

'Thank you.' Jeanne felt her cheeks turn red despite herself, but Ted wouldn't notice out here in the dark.

His eyes gazed into hers. Normally blue, they looked dark grey in this light. He was only a couple of inches taller than her, so he didn't have far to bend down. They were fully concentrated on each other, utterly absorbed.

If this was to work out, she'd have to avoid acting like a gold-digger or a potential trophy wife, but nor could she afford to be naive. The episode in the orangery earlier popped into her mind. She was no Cinderella. She smiled at Ted and his lips met hers.

39

Kim turned the key quietly in the lock, then slipped into the flat and switched on the light. Putting her finger to her lips she signalled to the others to enter and kicked off her shoes. As if to mock her care on entering, there was suddenly a huge clap of thunder outside.

Jan, Fitz and Nida followed Kim into the tiny hallway. She gestured at their shoes. My God, this was going to be a festival of fragrances – two pairs of Chucks and two pairs of feet whose owners had been chased for miles.

From the entrance a door led into a minuscule kitchen with a sideboard and wall units on the left, while the opposite wall, barely five feet away, was bare apart from a calendar with pictures of flowers. Under the window at the far end was a small table with two chairs. There was barely room for the four of them in the middle. Jan couldn't even see a washing machine.

Fitz left the room.

'I need to eat,' Kim said. 'Anyone else hungry?'

'I'd love something,' Jan said.

Kim put some spread from the fridge on a few slices of bread and filled four glasses with water from the tap. Fitz came back from the toilet.

'What now?' asked Kim. 'I won't be staying up for much longer. I've got an early start in the morning.'

'Same here,' Jan muttered, wolfing down his sandwich and draining his glass.

'So I needn't have bothered coming?' Nida said.

'I didn't mean that,' Kim said to appease her. 'After all our adventures, I need to come down first before I can even think about sleep. But make it snappy. Any ideas?'

Fitz fished the crumpled pieces of paper from his jacket pocket, smoothed them out and laid them on top of the stove.

'A variant of comparative advantage maybe?' offered Nida.

'I can't see it,' Fitz said. 'All the farmers produce the same goods.'

What are they talking about?

'Comparative advantage?' Kim asked.

Thanks, Kim. So I'm not the only dimwit here!

'It's the main argument in favour of international free trade.'

'I only know one argument in favour – free trade promotes prosperity,' Kim said. 'But where is that prosperity, eh? My pensioner gran hasn't seen it and nor have I. How about you?'

'Me neither,' Jan said.

'Exploitative capitalist doctrine,' Kim said.

'No, it's a simple calculation,' Nida replied, 'made by the British economist David Ricardo back in 1817. Take any two countries that produce specific goods. Ricardo's examples were England and Portugal, both of which produced cloth and wine.'

'English wine?' asked Kim. 'Gross!'

'I know,' said Nida. 'Different times. While we're on the subject, do you have anything else to drink?'

'Only water – either that or Gran's prized bargain rum.'

Nida pulled a face. 'We'll leave that for her. OK, let's update Ricardo and take China and the United States instead, with software and steel. China produces both of these goods at lower prices, and yet trade between the two countries makes sense if each focuses on the one it can manufacture more *efficiently*. Anyone got a pencil?'

She turned over one of Fitz's drawings and began sketching something on the back.

'Let's say nine programmers produce one hundred computer programs in China, whereas it takes ten programmers to do the same in the US. One Chinese programmer can therefore create 11.11 programs, while in the United States he – or she – creates ten. So the Chinese are more productive.'

She added the figures to her diagram.

CHINA	USA
9	10
Programmers	Programmers
⎯⎯	⎯⎯
11.11	10
Programs each	Programs each
↓	↓
100	100
Programs	Programs

'Eight Chinese steelworkers produce one hundred steel girders, whereas the same task requires twelve people in the United States. So a US steelworker produces one hundred divided by twelve, 8.33 girders, and a Chinese worker makes 12.5 – far more than the Yanks!

'Add together the production rates for the two countries and you get two hundred programs and two hundred steel girders.'

'Hey, slow down,' Kim cut in. 'I just need to digest that.'

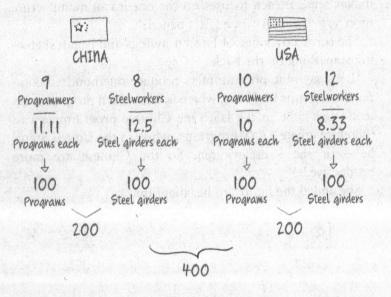

CHINA

9
Programmers

8
Steelworkers

USA

10
Programmers

12
Steelworkers

11.11
Programs each

12.5
Steel girders each

10
Programs each

8.33
Steel girders each

↓

100
Programs

↓

100
Steel girders

↓

100
Programs

↓

100
Steel girders

200

200

400

Jan had switched off long ago. Instead of concentrating on Nida's drawings, he was watching Kim. The way she brushed the hair away from her face, the little crease between her eyebrows as she studied Nida's sketches.

'What exactly is it that you just need to digest?' croaked a voice from the doorway.

'You don't eat enough!' said the old woman, who was no taller than Kim but took up most of the doorway. Her grey hair was sticking out from her head in all directions. She'd put on a threadbare dressing gown over her nightdress, and was wearing a pair of worn-out slippers.

'Who are all these people?'

'Friends of mine, Gran. Nida, Jan and Fitz.'

Grandma eyed them critically from top to toe. 'Do you and your friends realize what time it is? What are you doing?'

'Discussing something. You can go back to bed.'

'Not now I can't! Go into the living room. There's no room in here. Out! I need the loo as well.'

Kim signalled to the others that it was better to obey her grandmother, so they all moved to the living room. It wasn't much bigger than the kitchen and almost entirely occupied by a corner sofa that was at least thirty years old and a country-style coffee table. There was the inevitable painting of a roaring deer on the wall alongside a cartoonish picture of a boy with huge eyes peeing. A cheap wall clock and a plain cabinet containing piles of crockery and board games completed the furniture.

They sat on the couch and spread out their documents again. Nida was about to resume her explanations when Kim's grandma came back from the toilet.

'Budge up, I want to listen too.'

'No, Gran!' Kim exclaimed, but was silenced with a withering glance. Fitz offered the old lady his seat.

'Now that's what I call a gentleman.'

Fitz found a space on the floor.

'That's better. You may continue,' Gran said.

'Ladies and gentlemen,' announced Kim, 'meet my grand-mother, Anya.'

'Like the potato variety!' the old woman squawked.

Nida cleared her throat impatiently before continuing. 'OK, where were we? Ah, I know. China's productivity is greater in steelmaking than it is in software, which is why they specialize in the former. If the nine freed-up programmers—'

'Nine *unemployed* programmers, more like,' Kim butted in.

'—are as productive as the other steelworkers—'

'What utter codswallop!' Gran ranted. 'How are software programmers supposed to become steelworkers?'

Jan stifled a laugh.

'—then China can produce an additional 112.5 steel girders,' Nida soldiered on. 'Rather than one hundred programs and one hundred steel girders, China now produces 212.5 girders, which is more than the United States' and China's previous combined total. China sends part of its production output to the USA. That's trade.'

CHINA

9	8
Steelworkers	Steelworkers
12.5	12.5
Steel girders each	Steel girders each
↓	↓
112.5	100
Steel girders	Steel girders

212.5

'Who on earth wants steel girders made by computer programmers?' muttered Kim's grandmother.

Nida refused to be put off. 'As a result the United States churn out more software, and the twelve freed-up—'

'Unemployed . . .'

'—steelworkers can write one hundred and twenty programs.'

'Steelworkers writing software?' chirped the old lady. 'It just gets better and better!'

Don't laugh, Jan!

'This is a simplified model to illustrate the principle,' Nida said patiently. 'No one is claiming that steelworkers have to become software programmers overnight in the real world. In a modern economy offering a wide variety of professions, the steelworker could train to do a different job.'

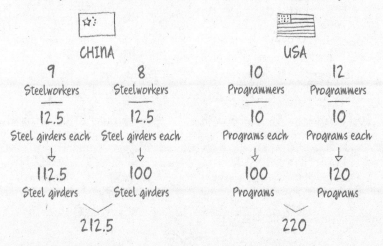

CHINA		USA	
9	8	10	12
Steelworkers	Steelworkers	Programmers	Programmers
12.5	12.5	10	10
Steel girders each	Steel girders each	Programs each	Programs each
↓	↓	↓	↓
112.5	100	100	120
Steel girders	Steel girders	Programs	Programs
212.5		220	

'When's he supposed to do that, after a forty-hour grind at the foundry, bringing up his children, looking after his parents and doing the shopping?' countered Gran.

'You're right, of course. Such changes take time, which is why the economist Karl Polanyi suggested slowing down the pace of processes of undirected change.'

'Clearly no one was listening,' hissed Gran.

'That still doesn't affect the basic advantages of comparative advantage,' Nida said with a sigh. 'Like I said, I've simplified things to make it easier to understand. The United States no longer produce one hundred programs and one hundred girders, but two hundred and twenty programs.

Which is also more than the USA and China put together originally. Again, part of this is now exported to China.'

'*If* the Chinese haven't copied the programs already . . .' Jan interjected.

Nida ignored him. 'Together the US and China have increased their production by twenty programs and twelve and a half girders, resulting in greater overall prosperity.

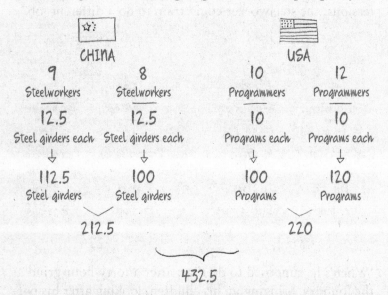

'Ruin this effect, for example by engaging in a trade war, and you reduce the standard of living on both sides.'

'Now all you have to do is find more customers for so many computer programs and steel girders,' Gran said scathingly. 'Personally, I can do without either.'

Jan had already noticed that Kim's eyes glinted when she got angry. How old was she? She was a student, so she might be his age or in her mid-twenties or anywhere in between. Was she as engaged and intense in everything she did as she was with the squat and in her fascination with this stupid farm story? Why was she listening so attentively, when he was really the one who needed to pay attention? His gaze shifted to Nida whose every word Kim was drinking in.

'As usual, it's far more complicated in practice,' Nida said. 'Already in the thirties and forties, economists like Ohlin, Stolper and Samuelson were highlighting the fact that globalization tended to make rich people in rich countries richer and poor people poorer. We've known that for decades! Incidentally, it can also have the opposite effect – make poor people in poor countries richer, as has been observed in countries like India and China in recent times. You can't blame comparative advantage if states don't distribute their increased wealth fairly.'

'My dad worked in the car industry,' Kim said. 'His job wasn't taken by Chinese workers; he was replaced by robots in Germany.' Taking Nida's pencil, she drew lines through the workers in both countries and added a robot arm instead.

'That's an important point,' Nida agreed. 'Nowadays even some of the programmers are starting to be replaced.' She took back the pencil and crossed out the programmers. 'Doctors and other highly qualified professionals too. Not by programmers or doctors in other countries, though – by artificial intelligence.' She drew a robot head next to the scratched-out programmers. 'Robots replace the workers, and now artificial intelligence's going to do the same in the academic world.'

40

El would have loved to crush the door handle in his fist. Instead he'd merely nodded understandingly and obediently to the police officers and thanked them politely when they returned Jack's registration documents and driving licence. And handed him a ticket.

The documents were no problem: they were perfect forgeries.

Had the taxi driver deliberately led them past the lurking police car? Probably. They had his registration number, but the gambler and the Samaritan weren't so stupid – they'd have got out somewhere and hailed another taxi to their final destination. If they had one.

El and his men had been driving aimlessly around the city for the past hour. As if their client possessed a sixth sense, he rang just as El was preparing to call him.

'Has the small matter been taken care of?' he asked without any introduction.

'There was a witness to the target's little accident,' El said. 'He managed to escape and then contacted a second person. We were able to follow the two of them to a squat, but we lost them shortly afterwards.'

There was a brief silence on the other end of the line.

'You messed up,' the client said. 'What do they know?'

'That it wasn't an accident. Later on they got into Will Cantor's hotel room.'

'What were they doing there?'

'We don't know.'

'Professionals?'

'No.'

'Just like you then . . . Do you know their identities?'

El controlled himself and reeled off the details.

'Finish the job,' said the client, 'or else you can forget the second payment. I'll be hearing from you.'

El ground his teeth. How was he to find two people in a city of three and a half million?

'I'm such an idiot!' spluttered Fitz.

Nida and Jan were startled. Fitz rummaged in his jacket pockets and held up the piece of paper triumphantly to Jan. 'Jeanne Dalli's numbers! I completely forgot in all the excitement.'

He took out his burner.

'It's the middle of the night,' Jan reminded him.

'She'll be organizing something or writing a report or a presentation. Or partying. Work hard, party hard – I know her kind, trust me. I used to be the same.'

Ringtone. If Jeanne Dalli was awake, she would see a withheld number. In the middle of the night. Fitzroy wouldn't have taken the call, and nor did Jeanne Dalli.

Please leave a message.

He didn't. Thanks to the computer whizzkids in the squat he still had two other numbers to try.

Fitzroy had worked with people like Jeanne Dalli – young, brilliantly educated go-getters in the finance industry. He knew how they arranged their lives; he knew how their minds worked. If a withheld number appeared on his second mobile so soon after someone had tried to reach him on his first, it would set him thinking. He would have given both numbers to very few people.

Please leave a message.

If Fitzroy had two work mobiles and one private number and someone tried to get hold of him successively on all three phones in the middle of the night Berlin time, late afternoon/early evening in the States, then there were very few possibilities indeed. Either one of a small handful of people he'd given all three numbers to was trying to reach him or – but Dalli was pretty unlikely to think of this possibility – her firm had a security problem.

Jeanne Dalli didn't seem to entertain either of these thoughts, or else she hadn't heard any of her three phones. There were very few possible explanations for that.

41

Jeanne sat up in shock. It was almost totally dark and, still half asleep, it only gradually dawned on her where she was. Beside her Ted's breathing was calm and regular. She was wearing one of his shirts as a nightdress. It had worked its way up her thighs as she slept. Her evening dress lay somewhere in the living room, as did her scattered underwear. They hadn't made it to the bedroom. Not the first time. The noise of the city seemed extremely remote as it filtered through the well-insulated windows. Jeanne could hear nothing in the dark room apart from Ted's breathing and the quiet beating of her own heart. The rumpled shirt rubbed against her back. She pulled it down and closed her eyes again, listening out one last time into the darkness and within her body. She drifted off to sleep again with a smile on her face.

42

'We're at a dead end.' Jan yawned and took another sip of rum.

Kim had fetched the bottle, and Fitz had laid a hundred-euro note on Gran's coffee table. 'Buy yourself another one with this.'

'Are you trying to turn me into an alcoholic?' Kim's grandmother had exclaimed. 'I can get ten for that!'

Jan's thoughts were elsewhere now. 'Was that true, what you said about the wealth distribution during the coin-toss game?' he asked Fitz.

'It's known as Pareto distribution after an Italian economist who lived from the mid-nineteenth to the early twentieth century. Most people have barely enough to live on, while the lucky few own virtually everything. It was true of most societies at that time and it's still true today.'

'We were tossing coins. The distribution during the game was random.'

'That's right.'

'But in real life a person's wealth doesn't depend on luck but on hard work, effort, skill and knowledge.'

'Oh, don't talk claptrap!' cried Gran. 'In real life, it all comes down to who your parents were and who you know.'

'What are you talking about?' Kim asked.

Fitz dug out a coin and gave a short summary of the game.

Kim took the coin from Fitz's fingers and flipped it absent-mindedly. 'That old chestnut,' she finally commented. 'The favourite myth peddled by our so-called "meritocracy" is that you're guaranteed success so long as you put in enough hard work and effort, pass all your exams and develop your skill set. Think about it though. Hard work, skill, effort and whatever qualifications you managed to achieve are themselves largely a matter of chance. We know that fifty per cent or more of a person's intelligence is genetically determined, and it's the same for so many other capabilities.' She flicked the coin and caught it again. 'It all comes down to luck. Then again, having the world's highest IQ won't get you very far if you're born as the child of subsistence farmers in today's South Sudan.'

'Or have a drunkard for a father who can neither read nor write,' muttered Gran.

Another flip of the coin.

'That's right. Your chances of surviving your first few years of life are slim enough, so your success also depends on what kind of family you were born into.' The metal disc spun through the air again and landed back on her hand. 'Unless your parents prize learning or higher education, you'll more than likely end up as a low-skilled, low-paid worker.'

'You can say that again,' Gran said quietly.

Another coin toss.

'Genes, family, social background, place and time – all random.' She caught the coin and slapped it on her wrist. Tails. 'Some people have lost before they're even born.'

Gran smiled bitterly to herself.

'You mean to say that success in life is a matter of pure chance?' asked Jan.

'Chance is at any rate a more important factor than we tend to assume and many successful people care to admit. So important, in fact, that one of the leading philosophers of our time, John Rawls, based his theory of justice on it. How would we shape society if we knew nothing about the position that the accident of birth would assign us within the social order?'

'And what conclusions did he come to?' asked Fitz before taking another swig of rum.

'He wrote an entire book about it called, obviously, *A Theory of Justice*. He and Bill Clinton often dined together.'

'Didn't help much, though, did it?' said Gran. She hauled herself up from the sofa and hobbled over to the cabinet, returning with one of the board games. Monopoly.

'Please, Gran, not now!' Kim objected.

'What you're describing is like Monopoly,' Gran said as she opened the box and set up the game. 'One player always cleans up in the end. It's the same distribution of wealth. If halfway intelligent people play on a regular basis, a different person generally wins each time.' She threw the dice, which skittered across the board. 'The important thing is that your roll of the dice gets you to one of the good properties fast. It's all about luck and chance.'

'Gran has a point,' Kim said, her eyes roaming around the tiny living room. 'In real life some people don't even have to buy up land and build houses because they already own the whole damn city.'

'They inherit a huge fortune, you mean,' said Nida.

'Without ever lifting a finger, while barely anyone else has a chance.'

'The cumulative effect of chance!' said Nida. 'Marx called it "accumulation" and blamed capitalism, but the phenomenon is far older than capitalism – it's been around for thousands of years. With it, wealth just keeps on growing.' She picked up one of the dice and rolled it over to Fitz.

'That's true,' Fitz said. 'The most recent examples are digital juggernauts like Amazon, Facebook, Google and co. They control the oil fields of our age – our data. They've amassed vast wealth at an even faster rate than the robber barons of nineteenth-century America.' Fitz spun the die in his fingers.

'That's why the Torah and the Bible prescribed a jubilee year long before modern capitalism existed,' Nida said. 'That's the root of our word "jubilee". Every forty-nine or fifty years, people were supposed to waive others' debts and free any slaves they owned.'

'The ancient Babylonians had a similar concept even earlier,' Fitz added. 'It was intended to restore a sense of balance to society.'

'But no one knows whether jubilees were actually implemented,' Nida said. 'Still, it was the first suggestion of how to control the accumulation dynamic.'

' "To those who have, more will be given",' said Gran. 'Jesus knew the score.'

'The Matthew effect,' Nida confirmed.

The die skidded from one side of the board to the other as the conversation skipped from subject to subject. Jan took his go.

'Money breeds money,' he said.

'Yep, the principle's reflected in lots of common sayings,' Nida said with a laugh.

Fitz blew on the die before rolling it. 'Even one of the great advocates of free markets, the economist Friedrich von Hayek, admitted that the workings of the market weren't fair.' He had rolled a two.

'You're a genius, Anya!' Nida said. 'Did you know that Monopoly was originally invented for this precise reason?'

'So you're fond of a little flutter too, are you?' Fitz asked with a grin.

'Only with play money,' Nida said, returning his smile. 'At the start of the twentieth century, the American short-hand typist Elizabeth Magie invented "The Landlord's Game". She believed in the ideas of a contemporary social reformer called Henry George, and wanted to show how unearned income from property ownership led to unequal wealth distribution.'

'Well, that would make for a very different game,' said Gran.

'Anyway, what's largely been forgotten is that Elizabeth Magie devised an additional dimension to the game – a form of the "Single Tax" on property Henry George had proposed. It completely changes the course of the game! Instead of one person winning, most players grow richer.'

Fitz was slumped on the sofa, but at this he sat up. 'What did you say?'

'It sounds a bit like what's going on with our farmers,' said Jan.

'I need to take a closer look at this,' Fitz muttered.

'But no one plays the alternative version now?' asked Jan.

'Nope,' said Nida. 'We only play the one dominated by luck, not reason.'

Kim threw the die and remarked pensively, 'A game with multiple winners isn't in tune with the zeitgeist.'

Why has the old lady stopped talking?

Gran's head had pitched forward on to her chest. Her wrinkly hands rested on the dressing gown under which the outline of her skinny thighs was visible.

'Gran? Gran?'

She woke up abruptly and gazed around in surprise. 'Who . . . what . . .?' She pulled herself together.

'Go back to bed, Gran,' Kim said, reaching out a hand to her grandmother and helping her to her feet.

Fitz yawned and stretched. 'I think it's time for all of us to get some rest now.'

The others agreed.

'I'll just tuck her in,' said Kim, 'and then I'll show you all where you can sleep.'

Gran wished them all a good night.

'Good night.'

They go so well together, Jan thought, watching them head for the door, the elderly lady shuffling along, Kim kind and supportive.

Back at the hotel Maya was trying her luck with headquarters one last time.

No, she couldn't have any reinforcements. Oskar, Jörn's partner, was also back on duty now.

No news yet from technical support or forensics, nor any information regarding the identity of the victims in the burnt-out car. No reports from the Golden Bar. No further sightings of Wutte or Peel.

Maya decided to walk for a bit and then hail the nearest cab.

The streets were quieter now. The cooler air announced the approach of autumn.

Her mobile buzzed. An email with the subject line 'Video'. Maya recognized the sender's name as that of one of the two eyewitnesses she'd talked to on the roof terrace.

Blurred, shaky footage. Loud music and people shouting. On the other side of a crowd of people two figures were running across the roof of the next building. Tall, dark shadows, too powerfully built to be Wutte and Peel – they must be the other guys – and then they were gone. Maya played the clip for a second time. The cameraman was too far away, the film too out of focus, too short. Not much to identify, but that might be due to her eyesight. It was two o'clock in the morning by now. She'd been on duty for eighteen hours straight after three hours' sleep. She'd had a few cocktails . . . and then a few more.

A lit-up yellow sign was coming towards her. She waved.

Maya slid into the back seat of the taxi and gave an address in the Friedrichshain area. She closed her eyes briefly and didn't notice herself falling asleep.

43

With a roar the jet lifted off into the blue-black early morning sky. Other planes, from a Learjet to a 747, were lined up behind it on the taxiway, their lights like a string of pearls.

Melanie Amado had taken up position on the viewing platform with her microphone. Gusts of wind ruffled her hair, and the noise of aircraft engines created a dramatic sound backdrop.

'Here in Berlin, a private jet belonging to a super-rich participant at the summit takes off every minute. Most of them arrived only yesterday. Rumour has it that some of them are flying directly to their doomsday resorts in New Zealand. Comments made by Italy's trade minister last night . . .'

Maurizio Trittone appeared in one half of the screen. 'We'd take care of Italian companies and employees if necessary, but a huge business like General Motors could not expect to gain any bailouts from us.'

Amado: '. . . immediately prompted speculation that the car manufacturer may be on the brink of bankruptcy, a claim dismissed by both the company itself and the US administration as completely unfounded. Asian markets nevertheless opened well down today, with losses concentrated in the automobile industry and its suppliers, especially since Trittone also stated that . . .'

Trittone: 'Italy will leave both the euro and the EU if . . .'

'Are they all out of their minds?' asked Jeanne. She dropped down next to Ted on the sofa in the dark living room and stared at the giant TV screen in front of which he was swiping and typing on his phone. He was wearing nothing but a pair of shorts, and she was still in his shirt.

'Come back to bed,' she said. *What time is it?* The TV said five a.m.

'The airwaves are ablaze,' he said.

Jeanne took her phones out of her bag. Someone had tried to call her during the night. 'Trittone must be aware of the reaction he's going to unleash.'

'Of course he knows.'

All three numbers. Jeanne had given all three to very few people. Caller identity withheld.

'I overheard him talking to George last night,' said Jeanne. 'It sounded to me as if George was promising Trittone money and lucrative positions in return for certain favours. Maybe a few media statements at opportune times?'

The caller hadn't left any message. It couldn't be that important. She opened her stock market app. Asia was a bloodbath. Markets in Europe and elsewhere would follow. If this went on, countless companies would enact swingeing cuts or go bust in the coming weeks, and millions would lose their jobs and no longer be able to pay off their loans and mortgages. And the anger would continue to build.

'It's a pleasure doing business with men like Maurizio.' Ted smiled to himself, his face bathed in the bluish light from the TV. 'And they come so cheap.'

'Did you . . .?'

Now he looked at her. 'What?'

'Do business with Maurizio?'

'I don't do business with people like Maurizio. That's what people like George are for.'

'George does a lot of work for you.'

'George doesn't work for me. He works for himself. Like all of us, he wants to earn money. If he solves problems for me, he earns a lot of money. The same goes for keeping the necessary official distance between me and the Maurizios of this world while he arranges and manages our mutual interest – making a shedload of money. I've no desire to know *how* he does it.'

'There's no need to explain the concept of plausible deniability to me.' *Does he think I'm stupid?* 'So did George solve "a problem" for you then?'

Ted laughed. 'No! Any other answer to your question would undermine plausible deniability, wouldn't it?'

She snuggled up to him. 'I'm neither a journalist nor a prosecutor.'

'You're still mighty nosey.'

'Shouldn't the man who shares my bed also share his thoughts?'

Ted's face turned serious, a hint of worry in his eyes. 'Have you ever thought that it might be for your protection too? If things take a turn for the worse, no one can accuse you of being involved in aspects of my business you know nothing about.'

Although she was initially touched by his concern, the feeling quickly gave way to annoyance. She simply didn't believe him.

'Look,' he said, twisting his screen to allow her to see. 'The share prices of GM and other car manufacturers are on the slide.'

So much for deniability. And his concern for her. It was good to have a glimpse of the foundations of a potential relationship with Ted. Had she seriously expected anything else?

'The same companies you shorted yesterday and whose shares would not be faring quite so badly today if it weren't for Trittone's statement . . .'

Fortunes will be made tonight. By betting on falling markets he was on course to make a small fortune. Small by his standards.

'A hunch that paid off,' said Ted. 'If George did indeed have a word with Trittone, then it was money well spent.'

'You can say that again. Did you bet against government bonds in Italy, Europe and emerging economies?' That smile again. 'And if the prices plunge to rock bottom, are you, Kemp Gellund and the others planning to ride to the rescue like knights in shining armour?'

'In a few countries,' he said. 'We can't save the whole world.'

Jeanne understood perfectly. 'So you wait until companies and states go bankrupt and then pick the choicest morsels from the carcasses of bust corporations and bad banks.'

Fortunes will be made tonight.

Huge fortunes, even by Ted's standards.

He sat up and gazed through the plate-glass window as the last stars faded into the first blue light of morning. Somewhere out there, the sun would soon come up.

'Markets rise and markets fall.'

'Taking businesses and millions of jobs with them.'

'I've never heard you express such sympathies before,' he said. 'There are ups and downs, as in the rest of life. After the cleansing storm comes the sunshine.'

'We haven't seen the worst of the storm yet,' said Jeanne, 'and it's going to be far worse than in 2008. Will you be jetting off to New Zealand too?'

Like many of his fellow billionaires, Ted had discreetly acquired New Zealand citizenship a few years ago and a large, closely guarded property there, complete with bunkers, an airstrip, several years' worth of provisions, round-the-clock security and all the other luxury trimmings required to sit out Armageddon. Their greatest worry was whether they'd be able to trust their staff during the apocalypse.

'Won't you be coming with me?' He laughed. 'That was a joke. I don't think it'll be necessary. Or only for a vacation.'

44

Fitzroy was having trouble opening his eyes. Jan was tossing and turning in his sleep on the other segment of the L-shaped sofa in Kim's grandmother's living room. The Monopoly board still lay on the coffee table with the empty bottle of rum beside it. The old lady was in her bedroom, while Kim and Nida had disappeared into the small room next to hers.

Fitzroy heaved his aching body upright. The thunderstorm in the night had swept away the clouds and the dazzling deep blue morning sky was visible through the treetops. Fitz rubbed his eyes and tiptoed into the windowless bathroom.

Ten minutes later he stood, showered and refreshed, in the kitchen, searching for an espresso machine. He found an old-fashioned filter funnel, filters and a pack of coffee and put some water on to boil. He went online with his phone to look up the latest news on Thompson and Will. It wasn't even six o'clock yet; he'd slept for maybe three hours. Thompson's death was now certain, even though the police had yet to provide official confirmation. There were no details about the identity of the second passenger as yet.

Next he called Singapore. It was almost noon there. When a woman's voice answered the phone, the only sound he could produce was an exhausted, surprised croak. He cleared his throat and tried again.

'My name's Ashton Cooper. I'm a reporter for *The Wall Street Journal*' – just then Nida crept past the kitchen door, looking like she'd slept under a hedge, reacted to what she had overheard with a bewildered glance and vanished into the bathroom opposite – 'and I'm calling for a statement on Herbert Thompson's death.'

'You can find a statement on the university website,' the woman responded slickly.

'It's a shame he won't be able to give his speech at the summit, but maybe the manuscript is available somewhere?'

'I know nothing about that. What was your name again?'

He wasn't so easily rattled. 'Ashton Cooper from *The Wall Street Journal*.'

'Please hold the line.' He heard the clatter of a keyboard in the background. 'I can't find any Ashton Cooper at *The Wall Street Journal*.'

'I work freelance,' he replied. 'We're not always listed.'

She hesitated a second before saying, 'I'll put you through to the Institute.'

The phone rang a few times before a second woman came on the line. Fitzroy repeated his request.

'I'm sorry, but I know nothing about it. Even if I did, I couldn't give you any information.'

'So you do have something?'

'No. Professor Thompson was here no more than a few days each month. He was only invited to give the speech a little over a week ago.'

'Do you happen to know what it was about?'

'Unfortunately not. He hasn't been to Singapore since he received the invitation.'

'But you do know that he was invited to speak?'

'It was in the Institute's newsletter.'

'Do you know who might have a copy of the text of the spee—'

'Listen, I know you're just doing your job, but I can't tell you any more than that. We genuinely don't have anything here. Goodbye.'

The line went dead.

He could believe her, or choose not to. Fitzroy watched the coffee drip into the jug.

Nida emerged from the bathroom dressed in jeans and a T-shirt, more awake now, and with her hair brushed.

'A reporter for *The Wall Street Journal*, eh?' she asked with a wry grin. 'I thought you used to be a banker and were now a gambler.'

'There are many facets to my personality.'

'Or you simply have multiple personality disorder. Is there enough coffee for me too?'

Ted had been on the phone for almost an hour. Jeanne could only guess at the subject of his conversations from the few snatches she overheard. Company assessments and risk analysis to be done by various teams at the Syllabus head office. Jeanne was fully involved in this frenzy of activity. For her colleagues it was late evening, but they were accustomed to working overtime. Living life in the fast lane.

Ted fielded calls from George and fellow billionaires, and rang investors, bankers and hedge fund managers to plan takeovers. They had to be prepared for things to move fast over the next few hours. The chairmen of gigantic corporations would make extravagant pitches for Ted to buy a stake. In actual fact, these gestures barely masked the reek of cold sweat, and their grandiose statements were in truth no more than a poorly disguised cry for help. Most of the appeals, however, were not for assistance for their company or their millions of employees but to safeguard the status of these top executives within the elite ranks of their peers. Central bankers and politicians would advance proposals, mindful that the man on the other side of the table was a potential employer.

The TV was tuned to Bloomberg, even though neither of them was watching it. Tokyo, Shanghai and Hong Kong had suspended trading several times already because most share prices had collapsed. Italian bonds had now attained junk status. If the Italian government didn't come to its senses fast enough, the country would be insolvent before the day was out, whether it remained in the Eurozone or not. Pensioners and civil servants wouldn't be paid, the elderly would either scavenge in dustbins or commit suicide, banks would crumble, bank accounts would be closed and capital controls introduced so that people would only be able to withdraw small sums of money while rising inflation destroyed their modest savings. The unemployment rate would rocket. The health system would fall apart, and relatives would have to supply food and medicine for patients, as in Greece or in a developing country. Other European countries and emerging economies would soon follow Italy into the abyss.

Ted hurled one of his phones on to the sofa.

'I need some exercise,' he shouted. 'I usually go jogging around this time.'

'So do I,' said Jeanne.

'Then let's go for a run together,' said Ted. 'I'll get changed and we can leave in ten minutes.'

He disappeared into the bedroom with its walk-in wardrobe. Jeanne slid into her evening dress, grabbed her underwear in one hand and her handbag in the other and was about to leave the room when she spotted a large envelope on the sideboard with the heads of some documents poking from the torn flap. This jogged her memory. Ted had picked up the envelope the previous evening as she arrived, and slipped it into a drawer.

Jeanne hesitated for a second before curiosity got the better of her. There was no sender's name or address on the parcel, which was heavy and about two inches thick. Ted didn't normally have hard copies of documents, with the possible exception of contracts. This must be a particularly large and detailed deal. She pulled the topmost paper a little further out of the envelope with her fingertips. It was a well-constructed flash card. The printed letters were at least half an inch in height and there were only six lines on the entire sheet.

'Ladies and gentlemen,' it began, followed by a series of titles including President, Excellency, Minister and other such honorifics that continued for the next two pages and ended with a greeting – 'Good evening'. Jeanne was not aware of Ted being scheduled to make a speech this evening or any of the following ones. He shunned public appearances other than to present a new business or annual results for an existing company.

She extracted a second flash card. 'For far too long we have trodden the path that has led us to where we find ourselves today. For too long I helped to chart this path and praised it, I argued vehemently for it and defended it, and for that I received many honours and plaudits, even the Nobel Prize. We . . .'

The Nobel Prize. Suddenly Jeanne realized what she was holding in her hands. But how on earth had Herbert Thompson's notes for his opening speech ended up in an envelope on the sideboard of Ted's hotel suite?

Frantically she pulled the other flash cards a few inches out of the package. Beneath the loose cards she found a stapled document comprising at least one hundred A4 pages.

'Wealth Economics' by Herbert Thompson and Will Cantor.

Will Cantor? She'd worked with someone called Will Cantor at Syllabus Invest until a few months ago. He'd asked her the odd question on economics and later claimed he was collaborating with a famous academic. Was it Thompson?

She speed-read the contents of the envelope until she came to a single sheet of a hotel's headed notepaper covered with tiny, almost illegible handwriting and a few scribbled diagrams. She tried to decipher the scrawl, but didn't get very far. Something about farmers.

She heard Ted on the phone again in his bedroom, but his voice was coming closer. Hurriedly she pushed the documents back in the envelope and replaced it exactly where she'd found it. She spun round to make it look as if she were just leaving the room.

'Still here?' remarked Ted, who was already in his running gear, phone in hand.

Jeanne held up her bra. 'I just couldn't find this anywhere,' she said, grinning. 'I hope I've got everything.'

She'd noticed his twitchy sideways glance at the envelope.

He came towards her, gave her a quick kiss and picked up the package. 'OK, see you in the lobby.'

Ted swung back a painting over the sideboard to reveal a safe.

'Oops, forgot my panties,' she said and went through to the bedroom.

Jeanne's presence didn't seem to bother Ted in the slightest. He entered the code, tossed the envelope into the safe, shut the door and pushed the picture back into position.

'Found them!' cried Jeanne. 'I'll be down in five minutes.'

45

Jan sat up with a start. He was being pursued by a pack of brutes clothed in black and they'd caught him!

Something had woken him. His body tensed immediately into panic mode. Nothing was familiar – the smell, the light, the air. His heart was racing and his pulse pounded at his temples. The aroma of fresh coffee reached his nostrils.

Fitz was there, sitting on his own half of the sofa. Jan felt dizzy and blinked his eyes a few times. Next to Fitz was Nida. Memories slowly came flooding back. Last night, followed at some stage by the black pit of sleep. Jan's pulse gradually settled. When had Nida come out of the little bedroom? Jan hadn't heard a thing.

She and Fitz were studying a piece of paper. How could they be awake already? Gamblers like Fitz had to be night owls, but Nida?

Jan knew he couldn't go back to sleep now. Next to the Monopoly board on the coffee table in front of them lay their notes and the hotel pad with the grey-shaded sheet on top. Two cups of coffee sat steaming beside them. Jan rubbed his face to wake himself up.

Fitz pointed to his cup without looking up. 'There's more in the kitchen.'

Jan inspected his bruises in the bathroom mirror. Ugly. Painful. But his face didn't look quite as bad as before. A few scratches that gave him a slightly raffish air. After showering he fetched himself a cup of coffee and went back into the living room. There wasn't a sound from either bedroom. Kim must still be fast asleep.

He went over to the window and peeked out from behind the thick curtain. The pavements were slick with last night's rain, gleaming amid the leaves and branches the storm had torn from the trees. There was no one about, no sign of the incredible hulks. Mind you, they weren't really going to stand out in the open, were they?

'You're completely nuts, mate,' he whispered. He'd have liked to discuss their next move with Fitz, but didn't want to mention the murders in front of Nida.

Fitz's only response was to take another swig of coffee and resume pondering the piece of paper.

'One cell, two cells, four cells, eight cells, lots of cells,' said Jan. 'It reminds me of that thing with the grains of rice on the chessboard.'

For the first time that morning, Fitz looked at him. 'That's not such a bad idea,' he murmured.

'What isn't?'

'The cells, the grains of rice. Both start with one unit, then two, then four, then eight. At every step they double. Exponential growth.'

Even Jan knew what that was. 'But why would that be similar to life?' he asked.

'Exponential rather than linear growth,' muttered Fitz. 'That might also be it. It's calculated differently.'

'Is every problem a calculation to you mathematicians?'

'For linear growth you keep *adding* the same constant. In the case of our cells, that'd be one cell *plus* one cell makes two. *Plus* another one makes three. But we've got four, so you have to *multiply*, in this case with a constant of two. It's like . . . Maybe I can explain it using the example of the farmers, and we might find out what it means.'

He picked up the second page of the farmers' fable.

'How interesting!' Jan said sarcastically. 'I'm hungry.'

'As always. Let's take Ann's story. In the second year she plants ten grains, but frost, pests and drought leave her with only two ears of wheat or twenty grains.'

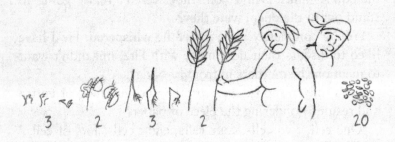

'I'm going to have to eat your imaginary grains!'

'So the ten original grains she sowed produce twenty. What was her growth rate?'

'I can't do maths when I've got low blood sugar.'

'She doubled her money,' said Fitz, picking up two sugar lumps from a saucer Jan hadn't spotted and dropping them into his coffee.

'No! I hate—'

'So her growth rate that year was two. Do the sums. Ten times two is twenty.'

'I refuse to do any sums.'

'OK, let's take a short break from Will's story.'

'For instance, to discuss what *we're* going to eat.'

For Jan, Fitz's passion for figures was as irritating as it was fascinating. He seldom met people who were quite so wrapped up in something – other than computer games, that was. Children were the same.

'Let's say that Ann has only a single ear of wheat left in the third year due to frost and drought.' Fitz didn't appear to have even heard him. 'Ten grains.'

Another little illustration. He was good at this.

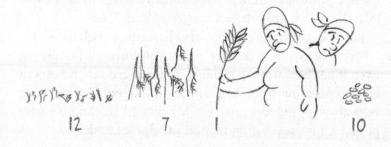

'So how much did her wealth grow this year?'

'Not at all. It shrunk. Like my stomach.'

'What was the growth rate? What do you multiply twenty grains by to get ten?'

'Even I can work that out. Half – or 0.5, if you prefer.'

'Hail the mathematical genius!'

'Politicians like to call that "negative growth",' said Nida.

'That's a piss-take,' snorted Jan. 'The way "redundancy" actually means "you're fired!".'

'And how do you work it out over the two years?' asked Fitz.

Jan's temper was at boiling point as he took the pencil – Fitz was behaving like his headmaster.

'Ten times two times 0.5 equals ten. There you go.'

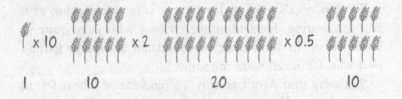

'See, you can do it! It's a gross simplification, of course, but it demonstrates the basic principle, which is that growth is itself a *multiplier* of what you already have. Most people mistakenly see growth as a matter of *addition*.'

Jan noticed that Nida was also listening closely now.

'We quickly see that's wrong if Ann loses all her plants. Even if her field were to produce a rate of growth, no ears of wheat can grow from no grains. A multiplication involving zero always produces zero. On her own, Ann can no longer produce any rate of growth, and she starves to death.'

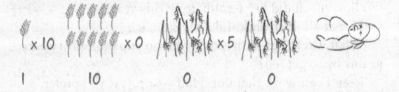

'As I'm about to!' Jan exclaimed.

'If one were – erroneously – to add something, Ann would suddenly have ten grains again. But where would they come from? They don't fall from heaven.'

'From the kitchen. Which is where I'm going right now,' said Jan, standing up.

'Or else Bill, Carl or Dana give her some,' suggested Nida.

'That would be additive growth, like winning the lottery.'

'Nice,' said Jan. 'I'd be quite happy with a slice of bread.'

Fitz and Nida followed him out of the room.

'So what I'm able to generate on my own depends on what I started with,' said Jan. 'That's logical, actually. But it's not so cool if I have nothing. It reminds me of what you told me about the time average, shares and compound interest. Is that multiplicative growth too?'

'Exactly! So you *did* understand!' Fitz said, as Nida disappeared into the bathroom.

Now that Nida was out of the way, however, he still had to answer Jan's burning question, 'Does multiplicative growth help us find Will's murderer?'

46

Fitzroy paid for the jam and rolls and said goodbye to the sales attendant in the bakery to which Kim had sent him. Back out in the street, he dialled one of Jeanne Dalli's numbers.

'Jeanne Dalli,' answered a woman's voice.

All of a sudden, the fresh morning air no longer seemed so cool. He'd only vaguely rehearsed what he was going to say.

'My name's Fitzroy Peel. I'm a friend of your former colleague, Will Cantor.' All he could hear on the other end of the line was the woman's fast breathing. On the treadmill, presumably, or in a park somewhere. 'Will's dead,' Fitzroy said to stop her hanging up.

'Will? Will's . . . I last saw him . . . How did you get hold of this number?'

'I wouldn't disturb you this early in the morning if it wasn't important,' he said. 'Will died in a car crash last night, here in Berlin.'

'Oh no!' she cried. 'But why are you calling me?'

'He said a few words before he died, including your name.'

'Oh my God. He's the second person I know who died in a car accident last night.'

Now it was Fitzroy's turn to be surprised – or to pretend to be.

'The second? Who was the other one?'

'Herbert Thompson, the Nobel Prize winner.'

Fitzroy could hear her breathing more clearly now. She didn't seem to have stopped running; she might even have quickened her pace. He decided to keep his knowledge about the connection between the two deaths to himself for the time being. It might come in handy later.

'I'm sorry to hear that,' he said. 'Did you know Thompson well?'

'Professionally, yes. We met a few times.'

'And when did you last see Will?'

'I'd no idea he was in town,' she said. 'How did *you* know?'

'We were due to meet, but he didn't show up.'

He turned into the road where Kim's grandmother lived, automatically checking for their pursuers of the night before, but there was no one in sight.

'You're British,' Jeanne said.

He confirmed this.

'And why did Will give my name?'

'That's precisely the question.'

'Does it still matter?'

'I think so, yes. It wasn't an accident. Will was murdered.'

Jeanne stumbled but caught herself and carried on jogging, more slowly now. *'Wealth Economics' by Herbert Thompson and Will Cantor.* Luckily, she was already sweating from running or her companions would have noticed her face turn red.

It must be a coincidence! Ted adapted his pace to hers, but Mitch almost ran into her from behind.

'What did you say?'

'It wasn't a car accident. It was made to look like one, and I want to find out why.'

'Why don't you go to the police?' Jeanne asked him.

Ted gave her a quizzical look.

'The police don't believe it,' Peel said.

'So why should I?'

'An as yet unidentified person burnt to death in the car alongside Herbert Thompson. That person—'

'Was Will?' Jeanne missed her footing again. She stopped, and Ted and Mitch reluctantly halted alongside her. 'Will Cantor?' *Hang on a second.* 'But if you'd told the police, they could've identified him by now.'

'It's more complicated than that,' the caller said. 'Anyway, the police probably know by now. It's only a matter of time before they issue a confirmation. However, they still don't believe it was murder.'

'Their official statement referred to an accident.'

'See.'

'I don't understand what I have to do with this. Why would Will mention me of all people? Did he say anything else?'

'He gave my name,' said the man, 'and the place the only witness could find me. Which he did.'

'You weren't even at the scene of this alleged murder?'

Ted's expression darkened at the M word. Jeanne glanced at him and shrugged.

'I never claimed I was,' the man replied.

'You said the police don't believe you.'

'I said the police don't believe *it*. "It" being that it was murder.'

'I don't know what to make of this conversation.'

'OK, I'll recap: before Will died he gave two names – mine and yours. I suspect it was a message to the two of us.'

Ted had turned away. He was on the phone again himself.

'I don't even know you,' said Jeanne.

'I don't know you either, which only makes things more interesting. What do we have in common?'

'Besides both knowing Will?'

'The last time I met Will, about nine months ago, he had a few questions related to gambling as well as about an investment strategy called the Kelly criterion. I was able to answer some of his questions, but not the ones relating to economics. He said it didn't matter because there were economists at Syllabus Invest, and he mentioned your name.'

Jeanne started to run again. Moving distracted her from this shocking news. Could this be true?

'That has to be eight months ago or even longer,' she said, recalling her meeting with Will.

'What did you talk about?' the caller asked. *What was his name again? Fitzroy Peel?* She could dimly remember Will referring to this man once. They'd studied or worked together or something. Was Peel a common English surname? Her mind went back to Ambrose the previous night.

'I got the impression he was flirting with me. Clumsily, like a nerd. Like the boys at my school used to say, "Shall we do our homework together?" You know the type.'

'What kind of homework did he want to do with you?'

'He wanted to know more about economic decision-making strategies and methods. He prattled on. I gave him a few tips about publications so he could read up on things like decision theory, game theory, heuristics and expected utility. His knowledge on those subjects was rudimentary, not surprising given his professional background.'

'That was all?'

'He tried a few more times. Updated me on his latest reading. He'd unearthed some scientific papers or something. He recommended I read them.'

Jeanne was overcome with guilt. Will had been a bit weird, but he was basically very nice, and interesting too. She hadn't taken him seriously, though, and now apparently he was dead, possibly murdered.

If the victim was Will, that was. Until the police had issued official confirmation, anyone who watched the news could claim the mysterious stranger was whoever they wanted him to be. Will Cantor, for example. The only passenger who'd been identified with any certainty so far was Thompson. His name reminded her of something else.

'I've just remembered something. A few months later, after I'd left Syllabus, I met Will again. He told me he was working on his project with someone "very senior".'

'You reckon that person might've been Thompson?'

'No idea.'

'You might remember other things that would help us. Can we meet?'

'I really don't have time . . .'

'Just for a few minutes – a quick breakfast perhaps. You can have a think in the shower beforehand.'

Jeanne didn't answer immediately, so Peel pressed home his point. 'Listen, if Will was murdered, then someone killed Herbert Thompson too. A Nobel laureate. Isn't that worth at least a few minutes of your time?'

Barely conscious of what she was doing, Jeanne continued to put one foot in front of the other. She could sense the asphalt through the soles of her running shoes, feel the cool air flooding her mouth and throat and then flooding back, warmer, in the other direction, her pulse a dull thud in her ears. The rhythmic motion helped her think and put her thoughts in order. *'Wealth Economics' by Herbert Thompson and Will Cantor.*

'Eight o'clock at The Estate hotel. One of the tables in the lobby will be reserved in my name. Make sure you're on time or I'll be gone.'

FIFTH DECISION

'At every level of hierarchy, entities appear that exploit the principle at the expense of others.'

Will Cantor

47

'Decision theory, game theory, heuristics,' Jan repeated after his first mouthful of bread and jam. 'Expected utility . . .'

The five of them were having breakfast at the coffee table in the living room.

'It's all gobbledegook to me. What do those words mean?'

'I've no idea why this is important to you, but as its name implies, decision theory studies individual decision-making,' Kim explained. 'On the other hand, game theory, which we discussed last night, is about group decisions. Put very simply, it looks at *how* people decide and how they *ought* to decide.'

'Pretty simple really,' her grandmother interrupted. 'You go for the best option.'

'Of course, Gran, but decision-making often involves uncertainties or unknown factors. Things like probability calculations come into play.'

'More calculations,' groaned Jan between bites. He was wolfing down his breakfast as if he hadn't eaten for days.

'Or you choose to do the right thing,' said Gran, sinking her teeth gleefully into a bread roll.

'That's one option,' said Kim. 'We often take shortcuts in our daily lives. If we're in a hurry, we reach for what are known as heuristics. A decision may not be perfect, but it's good enough for now.'

'Rule of thumb,' Jan said.

'Precisely. As my gran just suggested, heuristics also include moral rules. Either that or we plump for a decision, without thinking it over . . .'

'Gut instinct,' Jan said.

'Yes, there are all kinds of idioms. "Gut instinct" is the same as a reflex or intuition. It may work, but it can also go horribly wrong.'

'Always follow your gut,' Gran said, munching contentedly, 'especially if it's full of bread and jam.'

'It can be accurate in a familiar environment,' said Kim, 'but intuition is based on empirical knowledge. The intuitions of a city-dweller are of little use in the desert or the jungle – indeed, they might even be dangerous. And it's the same with the intuitions of someone from the rainforest in the city.'

'Oh, I'm sure they'd get by in the urban jungle,' Gran said.

'It's a very different type of jungle,' Kim answered patiently.

'I know that,' Gran said huffily.

'After all, instincts are quite an animal trait and so they can lead us badly astray in complex modern societies. Both instincts and intuitions tend to be a distraction when it comes to making the right decision. Finding out which psychological factors prevent you from making rational choices is another aspect of decision theory,' she said. 'They include prejudice and the famous confirmation bias.'

'What?' asked Jan. He enjoyed listening to Kim, even though she was a bit of a know-all.

'People believe they look at the facts and then make up their mind. Most of the time, though, it's the other way around – they look for information that confirms their opinion.'

'And if they can't find any, they make something up and call it "alternative facts",' Nida suggested.

'That's so true,' Kim said, laughing. 'And you tend to ignore any facts that don't reflect your views.'

'Or call them "fake news",' Fitz said. 'But I've got some real news for you. I'm meeting Jeanne Dalli in less than an hour at The Estate hotel. You should come along, Jan.'

'Where is The Estate?'

Fitz showed Jan on a map on his phone. 'Unter den Linden. It'd be best to take a taxi.'

'We need to head that way to get to the demo in Tiergarten,' Nida said. 'Can we hitch a ride?'

'What about me?' Gran asked.

'What about you?' Kim said.

'Now you listen to me – they want to make further cuts to my paltry pension, all to protect bonuses for bank executives,' Gran exclaimed, 'and I'm just not putting up with it any more!'

'Well, you're more than welcome to come along,' Kim said with a grin.

'That does sound very odd,' Ted panted when Jeanne had finished describing her conversation. He'd ended his own phone call and caught up with her. He signalled to his head of security to join them, and Mitch effortlessly closed the gap.

'Tell Mitch the whole story,' Ted said. He was obviously a practised runner, his breathing deep and regular. His forehead was glistening, but with no sign of sweat.

Jeanne gave Mitch a recap.

'Did this Peel say where he was?' asked Mitch.

'In Berlin.'

'I mean, where in Berlin?'

'I didn't ask.'

'Do you have the number he called from?'

Jeanne's phone was in the hip pocket of her leggings. She prised it out without breaking stride.

'Withheld,' she informed Mitch.

'What do you reckon?' asked Ted.

'Hard to say. Sounds pretty crazy to me. The official version is still that it was an accident. I don't believe there's any truth to this story, but we'd better look into it, just to be on the safe side.'

'Speaking of being on the safe side . . . Should I meet the guy?' asked Jeanne.

The two men exchanged glances.

'I've no objections,' Mitch said. 'The hotel lobby's secure. We've made sure of that, along with other teams of security personnel.'

'I think it's a good idea,' Ted said. 'Maybe they really do know something.'

'Shouldn't we call the police?' Jeanne asked.

'We can still do that afterwards if need be,' Mitch said.

They walked on for a while. Jeanne was thinking about Will when Mitch said, 'How would you feel if we listened in on your conversation?'

'You want to be there?'

'Not exactly,' Mitch said. 'We could attach a microphone to the underside of the table or somewhere near by. Or you unlock your mobile and let us install monitoring software.'

'No way!' Jeanne said with a surprised laugh, unsure if his suggestion had been serious or not.

'OK, the mike it is.'

'I don't know,' Jeanne said. 'I think I'd be uncomfortable.' A few more strides settled her thoughts. 'No, I'll go without.'

'As you wish. We'll hover in the background then.'

'We could agree on a signal,' Jeanne suggested, 'in case I need help or you need to call the police.'

'Good idea,' Ted said.

'If I put both hands to my ears, I need help. If I tap my nose twice, call the police.'

'Ears, help. Nose, police,' Mitch repeated. 'Got it.'

Jeanne forced the pace on their way back to the hotel.

'So you used to work with this guy Will Cantor at Syllabus?' asked Ted. 'What was he like?'

'A quant,' Jeanne said.

Ted nodded. 'A whizzkid.'

They said nothing further, saving their breath for the final sprint. The ground under their feet grew harder, and Jeanne switched off her brain to concentrate fully on her body.

48

All kinds of bells were clanging and chiming and clamouring for attention inside Maya's head. She screwed up her eyes more tightly in the hope of driving the din away.

But it wasn't in her head. The phone by her bed was ringing and buzzing, and the doorbell was jangling. She groped desperately for the device on the bedside table and held it closer so she could read the display. She didn't recognize the number. Who the hell was carrying on outside? What time was it? She struggled into an upright position, refused the call and crossed the flat in her pyjamas to answer the door.

'Who's there?' she shouted into the intercom.

'Morning! It's Jörn.'

His voice sounded so close. There was a loud knock on the door and only now did she realize that it was her own front doorbell rather than the one at the entrance to her building. A glance through the peephole confirmed her worst nightmare. Jörn was holding a bag up in front of his face, which was distorted by the fisheye glass.

'Let me in, I've brought breakfast!'

Is he nuts?

Maya slipped the chain into place and opened the door a fraction. 'What are you doing here?'

He had a bag and two paper cups of coffee.

'Breakfast.'

'That doesn't answer my question.'

'Köstritz sent me. There were some complaints after your performance at the hotel last night. My job is to keep you in check during our investigations.'

'You're supposed to keep *me* in check? During *our* investigations? Has Köstritz gone mad?'

This was unbelievable.

It felt as though a bulldozer were clearing a path through her brain. She shut her eyes. *The door.* It was no good. Maya took a deep breath, removed the chain and opened the door a little wider.

'Wait a minute before you come in and then go straight to the kitchen. Straight ahead, then right,' she said, disappearing into the bathroom.

The sight of her face in the mirror was pretty scary. Maya forced herself to have a cold shower and a few minutes later she went into the kitchen. Jörn had already set the small table. Maya didn't like the fact he'd had to rummage in her cupboards to do so and she trusted his unexpected peace offering even less.

On the small old TV, a newsreader was describing the events of the previous night. The demonstrations had passed off peacefully except in a few streets in Kreuzberg and around Bellevue. The demonstrators' glowing drone symbols and mass mobile compositions had taken place not only in Berlin but in many other cities around the globe. A statement by the Italian trade minister Maurizio Trittone had sent Asian stock markets into free fall that morning, and experts expected European exchanges to perform even worse.

This was followed by more bad news. Chinese warships

had sunk an Indonesian fishing trawler, prompting Indonesia, Japan and South Korea to place their armed forces at immediate readiness. Russia was making the most of these major crises to gather troops in the Baltic region and along its border with Ukraine. Saudi Arabia was publicly threatening to annexe Qatar, the unspoken objective of the almost bankrupt Saudi state, as a commentator explained, being to pilfer the coffers of the ultra-rich microstate. The world had gone bonkers. Luckily, Maya heard all of this as though through cotton wool.

'Not a word about our case,' Jörg noted.

'Not so bad, considering,' said Maya, sliding sullenly on to a chair. They could continue to fly under the radar.

'This job wasn't my idea,' said Jörn, 'so let's just make the best of it.'

Like yesterday evening?

Her mobile saved her from having to respond, by buzzing loudly in her pocket. It was Horst Becker, the head of the forensics unit.

'You're up early,' he said.

'Are you calling about the corpse in the burnt car?'

'You need to get here as quickly as you can to take a look.'

They all squeezed into the back of the large taxi. Jan had to sit in the direction of travel so he wouldn't get sick. Kim was sitting next to him. Her hair smelled freshly washed and he could feel her thigh against his.

'Nida,' Fitz asked the economist, 'could you please refresh my memory on expected utility?'

'Jan'll be delighted. More maths.'

Jan rolled his eyes.

'Too bad. Maths is part of life,' said Fitz.

'Not mine, thankfully,' Jan muttered.

'It's so strange,' Fitz said. 'Name me any other subject of which people are so proud to be ignorant.'

'Don't worry, I'll leave out the sums,' said Nida, interrupting his lament. 'It's too complicated. Expected utility is helpful with many decisions. Basically, it describes how useful a commodity or a service is to you. If a poor person receives a hundred euros, it means more to them than to a millionaire. Or put another way: the more money you have, the less utility you gain from each extra euro.'

'I'll let you know when I'm rich enough to judge,' Jan said.

'People who already have enough can tell you,' she countered.

'Of course. So I don't get it into my head to take some of theirs.'

'Scientists claim to have established that US citizens earning over 75,000 dollars per year derive virtually no additional happiness from each dollar over that amount,' Kim said.

'So why do millionaires always want more?' Gran chimed in.

'Good question,' Kim said.

'Because they want to keep increasing their utility,' said Nida. 'This theory suggests that, perversely, a few euros more doesn't cut it for them. They need a million or a billion more to feel any noticeable benefit.'

'And that's why they want to grow their wealth!' crowed the old lady. ' "Utility" is a euphemism to make them sound less greedy.'

'Not everyone's the same, though,' Nida said. 'In theory, every person has his or her own expected utility. Some people are willing to take greater risks to gain something, others less so.'

'What rubbish!' Gran cried. 'Some people simply find it easier to take risks because they start out with more in the first place. They don't need to stake everything they own. People with less have to be more cautious.'

'Like Ann the farmer,' Jan said, thinking out loud. 'She can't afford to lose everything.'

'What's he on about?'

'What type of decisions does expected utility help with?' asked Jan.

'How to invest your money, for one thing. Your bank will ask if you're willing to take risks in the hope of a higher return, or if you're risk-averse and prepared to accept a lower yield.'

'But I go to the bank so *they* can tell me how best to grow my money. Anyway, I don't have any. So do you have a more relevant example of the utility of this utility hypothesis?' asked Jan.

'There's the question of whether you ought to work more to earn more,' Nida replied patiently, 'and if the additional money you earn from working harder makes you so much happier that your extra efforts feel worthwhile.'

'I can't work enough to earn that kind of money,' Jan objected. 'That's not the way people get rich, as you've already demonstrated. Chance, multiplicative growth, Monopoly. "To those who have, more will be given" ... Your expected utility is of no use whatsoever when it comes to the question of how I even get to an income of 75,000 dollars per year.'

'The concept helps businesses set their prices,' Nida said. 'The more of something there is, the lower its so-called marginal utility. If a hundred people bid for one bread roll, the price of that bun goes up. If there are a hundred buns, the price of each bun falls.'

'Sorry, but there's a huge flaw in that theory,' Jan

countered angrily. 'We're short of ten thousand nurses in Germany. I'm the equivalent of one bun for a hundred people, and still my pay is shit. On the other hand, every position is taken on the board of every company, suggesting there's no labour shortage, and yet those people earn a fortune. Explain that to me with your marginal utility.'

'You're a right communist in the making, aren't you!' Kim said, giggling.

'It's the only option when you're faced with stupid explanations.'

They were approaching Potsdamer Platz by now. There was more traffic, and various streets were cordoned off.

'This is the turn-off for The Estate. Anyone going to the demo will have to get out here,' said the driver, 'and continue on foot.'

'OK, we'll get out then,' Kim said.

The car stopped. Kim and Nida gave Jan and Fitz a hug – all too brief in Jan's opinion – and Gran shook hands with them both.

Kim waved her mobile. 'You've got our numbers, so let us know when you're done. I want to know the end of this crazy tale. See you later!'

See you later!

The driver took a big detour eastwards in the direction of Unter den Linden. 'I'll have to go this way to avoid getting snarled up in all the roadblocks.'

On arrival at the boulevard, he turned again towards the Brandenburg Gate. This was the section they'd sprinted along last night. They passed the small huddle of protestors by the bank, who had moved and were now standing around the entrance. Jan noticed that many of the people didn't look like demonstrators at all and some were even wearing suits.

'What's going on over there?' he asked.

'By the bank, you mean?' the driver said. 'It's not the only one. I've seen queues outside quite a few branches today already. People want to get their hands on their money. Probably scared they won't be able to withdraw it soon following the news this morning – look what happened in Greece and Cyprus a few years back. Or they're afraid the bank might run out of reserves.'

'A run on the banks?' Fitz asked in astonishment. He chuckled, even though it was no laughing matter. 'Yesterday they were against the banks, and now the banking hours are too short.'

The driver slowed down. 'That's The Estate up ahead.'

49

There was absolutely nothing sculptural about the wrecked car in the cold neon light of the hangar. It lay there like a corpse, with technicians crawling around it like maggots in search of conclusive information. Dotted around the wreck on the floor were countless transparent bags filled with splinters and other parts. Maya spotted more bags and tools arranged on two long trestle tables at the side of the hangar. She approached to within a couple of feet of the cold grey skeleton. Jörn stuck by her side like a limpet.

'Impressive set-up,' she said.

'A Nobel Prize winner may have died in that vehicle,' said Horst Becker, head of the forensics unit.

'That's not been confirmed yet,' Maya replied. She'd already paid a visit to the colleague who was responsible for identifying the victims. 'I'd love to have this many people working alongside me out in the field.'

'That's precisely why you don't,' Horst said without looking up. 'Because they're all here working in the shadows, and you're out there in the light.'

'So has your work in the shadows produced any results?'

'We know a whole heap of nothing.'

'That's the kind of pronouncement only a philosopher

could make and seem wise. Coming from a policeman it sounds pretty stupid.'

Horst stood up and towered over Maya. 'We haven't been able to identify yet what caused the fire,' he explained. In a few strides he reached one of the scattered bags. 'Some of the shards of glass are from the car, others from bottles.'

'Molotov cocktails, do you think?' Jörn asked.

'Impossible to say because the glass caught fire. The pieces outside the burnt zone were normal rubbish left by litterbugs well before the accident.'

'Fingerprints? Traces of DNA?'

'We did a sweep. No identifiable fingerprints, and as you know DNA takes a while.'

Horst stopped beside an isolated bag containing a jagged black item about the size of a geometry set square. 'Now, this is interesting,' he said, picking it up and carrying it over to the wreck. He held it up next to a heavily damaged part of the car that must once have been the bumper. It fitted perfectly. 'Fragments splintered off the bumper during the crash,' he explained. A photo showing the place where the scrap had been found had been stapled to the side of the bag. 'Unlike the other splinters, this one was outside the fire zone.' Carefully he removed the skewed triangle from its wrapping. One of the points had a fine crust on it.

'Blood?' Maya asked.

'Yep. Analysis is already underway on several samples.'

'How did it get there? It can't be from the passengers.' She turned to Jörn. 'Didn't Jan Wutte claim he'd stabbed a sharp object he'd found into the hand of one of the alleged assassins?'

'He claimed many things.'

'Still, this blood might just support his story,' said Horst.
Jörn turned away resentfully.

El had calibrated his sleep so finely that he was wide awake
when the first signal arrived via his earpiece. He'd reclined
the Range Rover's passenger seat. Jack was lounging behind
the wheel. The virtual assistant on his phone announced the
caller. It was the client.

'Hello.'

'Do you have Wutte and Peel?'

'Not yet.'

'You're in luck. We've learned that they'll be at The Estate
hotel at eight o'clock this morning. In the lobby.'

'Where are they now?'

'We don't know.'

'OK.'

End of conversation.

El woke Jack while simultaneously searching for The
Estate on his maps app. Unter den Linden, not far from
Pariser Platz and the Brandenburg Gate. He gave Jack an
update and showed him the map.

'We don't know what direction they're coming from,' Jack
said, 'and there are too many entrances to secure them all.'

'We'll watch the main ones,' El said.

'We won't be able to operate close to the hotel.'

'At least we'll have them in our sights again.'

'It'll take us around half an hour to get to The Estate in
this traffic,' Jack said. 'We need to get moving.'

He called Sam and Bell back in the car.

50

The Estate was an imposing building that had the appearance of an ancient castle, but in fact was nothing more than a reinforced concrete block in disguise. Chest-high steel barricades and a barrier blocked the sweeping drive to deter unwanted guests. Patrons had to get out of their cars at this point and proceed through airport-style security gates.

Maybe Fitz should've agreed on a different meeting point, Jan thought as he waited in line, his throat tight. He watched as the two people in front of him had their bags X-rayed and were asked to walk through a portal. No ID checks, but this didn't calm Jan's nerves. Ahead of him, Fitz emptied his pockets, passed through the scanner and gathered his belongings as Jan followed him through the gate. Then they were inside.

At the entrance stood three men in gold-embroidered tailcoats and top hats. Two of them were black, like in an old Hollywood film. Was that still appropriate? Politically correct? They took the revolving door so that none of the lackeys had to open the swing doors next to it.

The environment they encountered inside was very similar to that within Will Cantor's hotel, if not even more opulent. It wasn't as if all the men were walking around in bespoke suits exactly – Jan couldn't have told the difference, and in any case some of them were dressed like him and Fitz. The guests here were just different somehow. They moved differently. They behaved differently too, with a naturalness and self-confidence that presumably only the appropriate upbringing – or exceptional success – could bestow. They had pedigree. For Jan they were all simply rich, which meant that according to Kim's study they should be gloriously happy, although they didn't all look it.

Some of them might be less well off than others. Jan pictured it this way: if you have a million and are surrounded by poor people, you feel rich; but if you're surrounded by billionaires, having only a million makes you feel like a total failure. He guessed Kim and Nida probably had a few mathematical formulas up their sleeves to explain it.

On the other hand, these people were all human. However much dosh they had, they could still get sick or catch a fatal disease. They aged, and might be trapped in an unhappy marriage or be hopelessly in love with the wrong person. Did anyone ever consider those possibilities?

Jan was usually very self-assured, but he felt uncomfortable in these surroundings. He reflected on Kim's words. He'd grown up in a different world to these people. Here, his instincts might prove to be his downfall.

Fitz, on the other hand, was in his element. He immediately strode over to a woman behind a table with a 'Concierge' sign on it. She smiled at them, studiously ignoring their appearance.

'Ms Jeanne Dalli is expecting us,' Fitz announced.

The woman cast a glance at the screen in front of her and pointed to the right-hand side of the lobby, where tables of some dark, exotic-looking wood and curving armchairs upholstered in blue velvet stood between marble columns.

Before the concierge could say 'Your table is over there,' Jan had spotted the woman whose photos he'd seen online.

'Not fair' was the first phrase that occurred to him. His mind went back to the conversations of the past few hours. An accident of birth had placed a silver spoon in the mouth of this creature. She looked like a model from the pages of a magazine. He knew she was incredibly intelligent and successful. She had probably already earned many times over his total expected lifetime income. She worked with one of the richest men in the world and rubbed shoulders with the others. It was not fair.

She was wearing a suit consisting of a brightly coloured jacket and a tight skirt cut just above the knee. He was nearly knocked sideways by Jeanne Dalli's gorgeous smile when she greeted them. *Thank you, cruel world!*

No sooner had they sat down than one of the waiters in a white jacket and black bowtie hurried over to their table. Jeanne ordered still water, Fitzroy Peel tea and the kid – introducing him, Fitz had simply said, 'This is Jan' – a coffee.

'Fitzroy Peel,' she said to the lanky Brit with the shaved head. The only thing he had in common with the ageing diplomat of the previous evening, aside from self-assurance bordering on arrogance, was his height. 'I met a man called Ambrose Peel last night. A British diplomat. You—'

'My father,' Peel said, interrupting her. 'I should've guessed he'd be here. Did he behave himself?' he asked facetiously.

'Like a true gentleman,' Jeanne replied, surprised that Pell should lay bare a family conflict quite so blithely, but Peel's tone of voice suggested he didn't wish to discuss the matter any further. 'But you wanted to talk to me about

Will.' She glanced at her small and very expensive watch, adding, 'I can give you ten minutes before I need to leave for the summit.'

'That's fine,' Peel said. 'To cut to the chase: I knew Will from our studies and from our first jobs together at Goldman Sachs. We saw each other occasionally after that, the last time being about nine months ago. Last night our young friend Jan here witnessed Herbert Thompson, Will Cantor and the driver of their limousine being burned alive in their car by a hit squad after their car crashed. Before he died, Will apparently mentioned my name and yours. That's how Jan managed to trace me to a bar. The hit squad attacked us there and then tried again later at Will's hotel, where Jan and I had been searching for clues. All we found, however, were a few notes that didn't help us much. That was the short version.'

Are you pulling my leg? Am I really supposed to believe this story? Her facial expression must have betrayed her thoughts.

'I wouldn't have believed a word I'm saying either,' Peel said. A restless depth to his eyes, the little dimples around his mouth: very much his father's son.

'I told you all I have to say over the phone,' Jeanne said hesitantly. 'I couldn't recall anything else about my conversations with Will. He did initially ask me about the Kelly criterion, but Kelly really isn't compatible with modern economic theory. He was written off back in the sixties.'

'That's strange,' Fitzroy said. 'I use Kelly every day with great success to count poker and blackjack cards. You mean I'm earning my living with a theory that economic science says doesn't work?'

Jeanne gave an involuntary and bitter laugh. 'You sound like Will sometimes did. I can tell you were friends.'

'Great minds think alike,' Fitzroy said nostalgically. He shrugged. 'But my job is to earn money, not challenge economic theories.'

'That was clearly the task Will had set himself. He apparently read a great deal on the subject, uncovered scientific papers by some mathematician or physicist or other, and raised various abstruse ideas with me. One of the Bernoullis was apparently wrong . . .'

'Family of major eighteenth-century mathematicians and physicists,' Peel whispered to the German kid. He was clearly capable of following their conversation in English. 'Which particular Bernoulli,' he asked Jeanne, 'and on what subject?'

'Daniel,' she said. 'On expected utility, one of the pillars of micro-economic theory. According to Will, or to the papers he cited, our calculations have been faulty for almost four hundred years. As I said, I thought it was just a clumsy attempt at flirting with me.'

'It may well have been that too. Getting on with women wasn't Will's greatest talent. You don't know anything about his acquaintance with Thompson?'

She shook her head, but her thoughts drifted to the manuscript in Ted's safe. She intended to remain wary of this stranger for now.

Peel laid out several sheets of paper in front of her. Diagrams with text. It looked like a simple village. Wheat, a woman.

'Can you make sense of these?'

'What are they?'

'Will's notes,' Peel said, 'edited by me.'

Jeanne skim-read the first page. *Picture four farmers.* Her cheeks grew hot. She'd read about farmers a few hours earlier on a scribbled sheet of paper in Ted's suite.

'Do you have the original?' she asked, barely managing to stay calm.

Peel hesitated before producing another sheet of paper from his inside pocket. White writing on a grey shaded background. There was a little drawing in the top corner.

'This is the imprint of the original, which must have been written on the sheet above it,' Peel said.

Jeanne immediately recognized the sketch of the little balls. She took a sip of water to buy herself some time. 'Thanks,' she said, pushing the sheet aside. 'Why don't you give me a quick précis of this funny little story?'

51

Maya leaned against the outside wall of the technical lab, closed her eyes and tried to wish her headache away. In vain. She dug a cigarette out of her handbag, offered one to Jörn, who declined, and lit hers. That was better.

Her phone rang in the bottom of her bag. Headquarters.

'Paritta.'

'We've received a call from The Estate hotel. They think they've seen the two men you're hunting.'

Maya immediately stood to attention. Because of Thompson's importance, they'd forwarded the wanted notice to all the summit hotels. You never knew.

'At The Estate?' *That super-luxury place? Unlikely.* 'When?'

'A few minutes ago.'

'And where are they now?'

'At the hotel.'

'At the hotel? What are they doing?'

'Drinking coffee.'

'What?! I'm on my way.'

52

El was able to follow the conversation via his earphone, albeit with quite a lot of static. Footage from a CCTV camera was relayed to the screen of his smartphone. Judging by the angle, the camera must be somewhere near him on the lobby mezzanine. Peel was telling a story about farmers and their fields to the woman whose name the client hadn't told him. As Peel talked, he pointed to a number of diagrams he'd spread out on the table in front of him.

El had selected a position on the mezzanine from which he needed to crane his neck to see the table in real life rather than simply on his phone. If he sat where he was, the group down below wouldn't be able to see him.

His eyes once more drifted away from the screen briefly in search of the camera. Nowadays the things were so tiny it was hard to spot them if they'd been installed with a modicum of skill. He hadn't mounted them himself; his client had provided him with a live stream and the accompanying sound via his mobile. He had no idea how they'd done it. A tiny bug under the table? Maybe they'd hacked the lady's phone, although El couldn't see it anywhere. The sound quality was too good for a hacked mobile in a handbag.

The woman studied the papers again.

His client's tinny-sounding voice asked, 'What's that?'

'I can't see,' El said. 'Can we zoom in?'

'Not close enough.'

The woman laid the documents back on the table and looked across at Fitzroy Peel. 'So?' she asked. 'What comes next?'

'We've weighed up all the possibilities,' Fitz said after he'd finished relating the farmers' fable, 'but we still can't figure it out.'

'Nor can I,' Jeanne said, checking her watch. The meeting had lasted longer than scheduled. 'I wouldn't know how to go about it either.'

She had a hunch, though, and it was getting stronger and stronger. She'd not felt this uneasy since she was small.

'I have to go,' she said, wrangling with her conscience. For years her job had forced her to make quick, tough decisions, but this was a whole different kettle of fish. The potential consequences . . .

No, she couldn't afford to look round right now. She was losing her cool and she hated it. *Keep calm!*

Mitch and two of his men were watching to see if she touched her ears or her nose. She took another sip of water.

Disappointed, Fitzroy tucked the sheets outlining the farmers' fable back in his pocket. How had he ever thought this woman or this stupid fable might help them? It was nothing but a wild goose chase. He blamed it on last night's crazy events and lack of sleep. It was over. He would return to his hotel, shower, sleep, call the police – in whatever order – and await subsequent developments. He'd done all he could for Will, and sooner or later the police would realize that Jan was innocent too.

What was wrong with the kid? Jan's face was as ashen as the sheets of paper the three of them had been poring over. His eyes roamed wildly around the room until they locked on to Fitzroy's face with the desperation of a drowning man.

'Don't look up,' he breathed. 'One of the men from the Golden Bar and Will's hotel is standing at the back of the lobby. He's watching us.'

Fitzroy was sitting with his back to the lobby and thus, if Jan was right, to one of the hitmen.

Ignore the elephant in the room. Don't look round at the man who almost murdered you.

Fitzroy summoned all his powers of self-control to repress his desire to run.

Jeanne picked up on their peculiar behaviour. 'What is it?' she asked, as she prepared to take her leave of them, her body half turned away.

Fitzroy stood up and whispered to her, 'Don't do anything that'll attract attention. Jan says one of Will's murderers is here.'

He could tell from the stiffness of her body language that she too was struggling not to look.

'Who?' she said. 'Where is he?'

Jan had also got to his feet.

'Where?' Fitzroy asked him.

'Next to the last column, right at the back,' he whispered.

53

Jeanne's head was about to burst from the mixture of sounds in the lobby – people talking, suitcases being rolled along the floor, phones ringing, the clatter of crockery and the rustle of clothing and newspapers. Her body felt numb. The kid was imagining things, surely?

'How did he find us?' Jan asked. The panic in his voice made his English falter even more. 'How did he know we were here?' He stared at Jeanne. 'Who knew about our meeting?'

Jeanne bit back her indignation. 'You cannot be serious!' she hissed.

'I don't believe this is an accident,' Jan said. 'Did you tell anyone we were meeting here?'

'That's an absurd allegation,' she said frostily as her mind whirred. Who had she told? Ted and Mitch. She'd never seen the man before. He wasn't a member of Ted's security detail. 'I've never seen that guy in my life before.'

'That's not what I asked,' Jan said. 'I had only one question.'

'OK, everyone stay calm,' Peel said. 'I'm going to check him out.'

He turned round and moved his head back and forth as if searching for a waiter. When one spotted him, Peel beckoned discreetly with his hand and the man hurried over to them.

'The bill, please,' Peel said.

The man walked away again.

Peel turned back to Jeanne.

'Jan's right,' he told her. Beads of sweat were gathering on his brow. 'I recognize him all right. He tried twice to kill us last night, but we were able to shake him off. How come he's back on our trail?'

We were able to shake him off.

She wrestled with herself for a second. 'I told Ted Holden about your suspicion,' she confessed, 'and his head of security, Mitch McConnell, too. Herbert Thompson was his adviser and a close acquaintance after all, and Will Cantor was his employee.'

'Anyone else?'

Jeanne objected to Jan's tone of voice. Like an inquisitor. She'd had enough. 'No,' she snapped.

'Then there are only two possibilities,' Peel suggested. 'The first is coincidence, but that's highly unlikely. The second is that someone informed the hit squad, and that can only have been you, Ted Holden or his head of security.'

'Are you mad? This has nothing to do with me! This has nothing to do with *us*.'

If only she didn't have that nagging doubt at the back of her mind. On the other hand, Thompson had advised Ted, and Will had worked for him. Maybe they gave him the manuscript or sent it to him.

One of her phones rang in her bag.

It was Ted. 'We need to get going,' he announced. 'I'm down in the car park already. Are you coming?'

She glanced at Fitzroy and Jan and out of the corner of her eye at the killer. Next she looked for Mitch and the other two. They were nowhere in sight. She sat down again and put her hand to her shoe.

'You go ahead,' she said. 'I've broken a strap on one of my shoes. I'll have to go back to my room and change it. My whole outfit too, of course, so it matches the shoes, you know how it is . . . I'll take a taxi there.'

'OK, fine. How was your conversation?' he asked.

'A waste of time.'

'I thought it would be. I'll see you later then.'

'What are they doing?' El heard his client say via his earpiece.

'Saying goodbye, shaking hands. The woman's leaving.'

'Which way?'

'Towards the lifts, I think.'

'And the other two?'

'Standing around, waiting.'

'What are they talking about?'

'I'm listening to your stream,' said El, 'and I can't hear a thing. They must be too far away from the mike, and there's too much background noise.'

'Where's the woman now?'

'Just getting into the lift.'

El could see on his phone display that Wutte and Peel were still hovering next to their table. Finally the waiter came back and handed them the bill. Peel exchanged a few words with him and settled up. El could see his lips move but all he heard were the sounds of the lobby – the rattle of cups and the hum of conversation.

'OK,' the client said. 'You've got them covered then?'

The waiter walked away, but this time over to the reception desk rather than back to the restaurant at the other end of the lobby. The Samaritan and the gambler sat down again, watching the waiter in silence.

'They're not leaving yet,' El reported, 'but we're ready for them when they do.'

'No change to the instructions, but don't try anything in the hotel. Is that clear?' the client said. 'Wait till they're outside when they're a good distance away.'

'Copy that,' El said.

'No more mistakes or you'll suffer the consequences. Let me know when it's done.'

El clenched his jaw. *Or you'll suffer the consequences.* The man was threatening him, but if he thought he could scare El, he could think again. All he'd done was make him angry.

Downstairs, Wutte and Peel were sitting there as if they were just regular guests waiting for another coffee, looking around mutely as though they were bored.

Jack's muted voice in El's ear: 'Five hotel staff coming my way. One looks like a manager, the others like security.'

'And they're heading straight for you?' El asked in alarm.

'I can't tell . . . yes.'

'Get out of here!'

'Too late.'

Via his headset El vaguely picked up a new voice.

'Good morning, sir. My name's Kreuzer, I'm the hotel manager. A guest has reported seeing you fiddling with a gun. May I ask you—'

Damn! El jumped up and made his way as inconspicuously as possible to the stairs while the unseen man said, 'There's a bulge at the back of your belt. May we?'

Jack was now visible from the mezzanine, and El could see he was surrounded by four security guards, their hands discreetly but noticeably on the handles of their own weapons. A quick glance at his phone confirmed that Wutte and Peel were still at their table. Jack was cornered. He lifted the back of his jacket to reveal the holster fastened to the back of his belt.

'I can carry gun,' Jack explained to the manager and his men in broken German. 'Bodyguard. Not only one here, right?'

'Our house policy is that you register any weapon with us,' the manager explained. 'I would therefore request that you do so at reception.'

'Very strange,' said Jack, 'but if you want.'

He glanced over at El, who was standing at the top of the stairs. El mouthed the word 'leave', signalling with a sideways nod that Jack should walk out of the hotel without undergoing a check. El would have to keep an eye on the gambler and the Samaritan on his own for a while. They were still at their table.

Flanked by the security guards, Jack made as if to go to reception but then walked straight towards the exit.

'Stop!' the manager shouted. 'Where are you going?'

The guards walked helplessly alongside Jack, not daring to obstruct him.

Sissies!

'If I not welcome, I go,' Jack replied.

The manager hurried after him. 'I asked you to—'

'I will tell client,' Jack said. 'Important man. Not come your hotel again.'

He'd made it outside. The manager and his team lingered in the doorway, watching him go, but El couldn't hear what they were saying to each other.

El checked his phone. Wutte and Peel's table was deserted.

'Seventh floor,' Jan panted. 'By foot.'

They'd climbed two storeys so far. Their footsteps echoed up the bare stairwell. It seemed pretty unlikely that anyone ever took the stairs, Jan thought, other than if the fire alarm went off.

'You're young. You're meant to be fit,' Fitz said, overtaking him.

'Not after last night,' Jan groaned.

The door to the stairs was at the very back of the lobby. Jan and Fitz had checked no one was following them on their way there. Where there was one killer, his mates were bound to be close by. One or two inside the hotel, Fitz had guessed, and the others at the exits, in the underground car park, maybe even someone among the hotel staff. Once they'd reached the stairs, they tried to make as little noise as possible so they could hear if anyone opened or closed a door or started after them.

Fourth floor. Carry on.

Somewhere up above them a door opened. Footsteps.

Jan froze. Fitz looked back at him from a few steps up. They tiptoed back down to the fourth floor where Jan inched open the plain door on to the hallway and peered out. He gestured to Fitz to follow him.

They found themselves at the end of a long hallway with dark brown wooden flooring and dark blue walls interrupted at regular intervals by doorways. There wasn't a soul in sight.

His ears pricked, Jan waited a second. The footsteps on the stairs drew closer, nonchalant, not in the least bothered about being quiet, wary or secretive. Whoever it was even whistled a little tune to himself. Jan waited until the whistling and the steps had gone by and faded into the distance before glancing at Fitz and opening the door again. They slithered through the gap into the stairwell.

'Right, you've had your little breather,' Fitz whispered, pushing past him and taking the stairs two at a time.

On the seventh floor, an electronic lock similar to those on the doors to each room blocked their access to the hallway. This was the VIP floor. Jan pulled out the card Jeanne Dalli had slipped into his hand as they'd said goodbye. The door opened with a soft click on to a similar hallway to the one on the fourth floor, although here the walls were painted dark green.

Fitz speeded up, hurrying past wooden doors stained to match the floorboards. Jan scurried after him, casting regular glances over his shoulder to check no one had followed them through the door.

They stopped outside Junior Suite 723.

'What if this is a trap,' Jan asked, 'and someone's in there, waiting for us?'

54

Jeanne was busy typing numbers into the door of the safe that she'd noted while she was supposed to be looking for her panties, and hoping they were correct.

The heavy metal door swung open with a soft click. The envelope was in the middle one of the three compartments. Jeanne took it out and closed the safe using the same combination of digits, then took the VIP lift down two floors and walked to her room. She knocked.

There was no answer.

She knocked again. Nothing.

'Peel? It's me, Jeanne Dalli,' she whispered. 'I've got the envelope. Let me in.'

'We're here.' Peel and the kid were standing behind her.

'Jesus, you gave me a shock!' she hissed. 'What the hell are you doing?'

Fitz put the key card to the lock to open the door. 'A mere precaution,' he said.

He entered the junior suite like a stalking tiger – quickly, quietly and carefully. Jeanne followed him across the living room-cum-study into the bathroom and the bedroom while the kid waited outside.

'You can come in now,' Peel called to him once he'd inspected the suite.

Jeanne placed the envelope on the desk.

'Something important in there?'

'I think there are Herbert Thompson's notes for his speech last night, and the paper Thompson and Will wrote together.'

In one quick movement Fitzroy drew out the contents of the envelope and spread out the two piles of paper in front of him. The first consisted of small flash cards with large writing on them.

'Look like notes for a speech, don't they?'

The second was a pile of closely typed A4 sheets, held together with staples. The title on the cover was '*Wealth Economics' by Herbert Thompson and Will Cantor.*

'The manuscript.'

The third item was a single page of completely illegible, tiny handwriting.

'I only had time to glance through it,' said Jeanne, 'and decipher a few words at the beginning.'

'Holy sh—' whispered Fitzroy. He delved into his trouser pocket for the grey, shaded sheet with the white scrawl on it and laid it alongside the single page from the envelope. 'Yin and yang,' he declared.

'Will only arrived yesterday,' Fitz said. 'That's what he wrote in an email to confirm our meeting. He scribbled the notes on a hotel notepad, meaning he can only have done it after checking in. Soon afterwards, he and Herbert Thompson set off for the speech, so they probably took the notes with them.'

A thought kept flashing into Jan's mind. These loose sheets reminded him of something . . .

'Or else he put it in an envelope along with the notes for his speech and the manuscript and sent it to his employer,' Jeanne suggested.

Her complexion's gone a whole two shades lighter than before, thought Jan.

'We can check that out if necessary,' Fitz said. While Jeanne leafed through the notes for the speech, Fitz typed a number into his mobile and waited.

'Yes, hello, I'm calling from The Estate hotel on Unter den Linden. I've been waiting since yesterday for a package from Will Cantor, a guest at your hotel. Room 756. Did he leave you an envelope to post yesterday?'

Jan could hardly hear the person on the other end of the line. He or she probably said something like, 'One moment, please. I'll just check.'

He flicked through the manuscript. A whole load of text. Diagrams, graphs, formulas. The subject was economics – even he could see that straight off, but the rest was beyond him. The final pages were filled with small print: names, titles of articles and books, page numbers and dates. References, he realized.

'OK, thank you,' said Fitz, putting his phone away. 'There was nothing sent by Will from the hotel yesterday.'

'There are more than enough courier services in this city,' Jeanne said without looking up. She was shifting the cards from one pile to another at a speed that would have allowed her to skim-read them at best. She held her phone some distance above them, but she wasn't taking photos, she was filming. The last two cards then she put her phone in her bag and, without even looking, quickly rearranged the cards in their original order.

'Would you entrust a sensitive assignment like this to a courier or to someone from your hotel?' Fitz asked.

Jeanne had finished. She sat up straight. Her expression was colder than before and her face even paler. 'My hotel.'

'Exactly. Anyone would.'

Jan would probably have delivered it himself. His bruise was itching, and he ran his fingers over it. All of a sudden, he knew where he'd seen the papers before.

Inside the upside-down car. Anvil Chin grabbing the open briefcase and then the smell of petrol and hands trying to drag him into the fire . . .

Even flashing lights and the siren were of no use once they got to within two hundred yards of The Estate. The road was packed with crowds of people on their way to the demonstration.

Jörn cut the engine where they were, and Maya jumped out of the car to walk the remaining distance. They didn't really walk, though; they shoved their way through the masses and sometimes allowed themselves to be carried along by the crowd. They had to go through a security barrier outside the hotel. With a perfunctory glance at Jörn's uniform, the female security guard waved them through.

At the sight of Maya's police ID, the woman at reception rang through to the hotel manager. While she was waiting, Maya surveyed the part of the lobby she could see from the reception desk. People were trooping past on their way to breakfast, heading back from a jog or cheerily setting off in light summer clothing to explore the city, while men and women in suits were leaving to attend the summit.

'Inspector,' said a middle-aged man in a suit, addressing her from the side. Bavarian or Austrian from his accent. 'I'm Edwin Kreuzer, the hotel manager.' He was accompanied by a slightly younger man with a sculpted hairstyle and shoulders too broad for his jacket. 'This is one of my security managers.'

'Where are the two men?' asked Maya.

'They left a couple of minutes ago.'

'You wouldn't happen to know where they were going?' Maya groaned.

'No, I'm sorry.'

'But they didn't just march in here and order coffee. What were they doing here?'

'They had an appointment.'

'With whom?'

Kreuzer shifted uneasily from one foot to the other. 'I can't say.'

'Can't or won't?' The man was a poor liar.

'You know who it was,' Maya said. 'One of your guests.'

The manager squirmed.

'I'm sure you realize that we don't put out wanted notices willy-nilly. I could arrest you for obstructing a police investigation.'

Kreuzer considered this threat.

'I've no time for playing games,' Maya snapped. 'I need to know who met these men and where they went!'

To judge by his appearance, the hotel manager had aspirations to be an industrialist or an investment banker perhaps, although neither his gelled-back hair nor the quality of his suit fitted the bill.

'How am I supposed to know?' he said insolently.

'Who did they meet?'

'I'm sorry,' Kreuzer said, 'but I'm not permitted to disclose that information unless you have a search warrant. We have many distinguished guests, for whom privacy is very important.'

'Maya,' Jörn butted in, 'if the hotel manager says he can't—'

'I must warn you that there are two murder suspects on the loose in your hotel,' Maya said, brushing his objections aside. She'd long since given up listening to her chaperone.

'What are you going to say to your distinguished guests when they're suddenly stretched out stone cold on the floor, eh? Now, who did the two men meet? Where did they go? Do you have CCTV cameras here in the lobby?'

Kreuzer pursed his lips, but he couldn't hold her gaze. 'This is going to get me in big trouble,' he said.

55

Fitz took the manuscript from Jan's hands and began to leaf through it. Jeanne sat alongside him, reading it at the same time. They skipped quickly through the list of contents.

There were at least seventy chapters.

'They've really opened a Pandora's box here,' Jeanne said.

'You can say that again,' said Fitz, moving on to the abstract. The short summary at the beginning of the paper was pleasantly accessible, and Jeanne had read the majority of it within a couple of minutes.

'Wow,' Fitz murmured.

This was quite something. Thompson and Will were really sticking their necks out. They'd obviously based their work on studies by physicists at an institute called the London Mathematical Laboratory, who claimed to have discovered a glaring error in the calculations on which the whole of modern economic theory had relied for three hundred and fifty years.

'Is this really possible?' Fitz asked, pointing to the relevant passage.

'I've no idea,' admitted Jeanne.

The London-based researchers had produced fundamental mathematical models in a number of fields, which Thompson and Will had then developed into a detailed theory, accompanied by preliminary political recommendations. A policy brief in other words.

'This would obviously have made them a fair few enemies,' muttered Fitz when he'd read the abstract. 'Not least among Thompson's previous supporters like Ted Holden.' He gave Jeanne a sideways glance.

'Tell me what it's about,' said Jan.

'It's about everything,' Jeanne said, more to herself than to the other two. 'Our idea of who we are. Proper decision-making. How we organize society. Sensible wealth distribution. Selfishness. Business management. Conflict resolution . . .'

'If Thompson and Will are right, this is going to shake prevailing concepts of society and economics to the core,' Fitz added. 'Good old Thompson was evidently out to prove his revolutionary credentials one last time.'

Jeanne flicked through a few pages until she came to an illustration of a line dividing into many more lines. A form of tree. *Decision models and expected utility.* She skimmed through the accompanying text as did Fitzroy until he asked, 'Do you economists really make calculations in this way?'

'If I remember correctly, we do,' Jeanne answered. She was desperate to put the papers back and head to the conference, but her curiosity was too great. She gave herself a few more minutes. 'The maths in this part is over my head. Can you make anything of it?'

'It's crystal clear to me,' Fitz said.

'Not to me, it isn't,' Jan said in heavily accented English. Jeanne had almost forgotten him.

'It's about modelling the way people make decisions,' Fitz explained. 'We've already discussed expected utility today. Economists will work out mathematically almost every possible outcome of a decision and calculate the average – or, in more developed theories, not averages of outcomes but averages of probabilities or even derivatives of probabilities. It's pretty complex.'

'It sounds like it. So if I work out the average of every possible outcome, is it the same as in your coin-toss game yesterday evening? The ensemble average?'

What on earth are they talking about? thought Jeanne.

'Exactly. Of course, it's completely absurd. It's as if you were standing at a crossroads and could take all the different paths at once, or an average of the paths, whatever that might look like. It's clearly impossible,' Fitz said with a disbelieving shake of his head, 'which is why I just asked Jeanne if economists really do calculate in that way. The other decision model, the one Thompson and Will were using, assumes that people optimize their decision-making via the time average.'

'Ah, we talked about that,' Jan said. 'You choose a path, then choose again at the next crossroads, and so forth.'

'You've got it. Life is a long series of decisions you can only make on the basis of previous ones you've taken.'

Visibly proud to have understood, Jan tried again. 'And the time average can produce a completely different result from the ensemble average . . . I get it.'

Fitz turned to Jeanne. 'Do you see? The maths seems logical to me.'

'In which case, they may be right,' said Jeanne, who in the meantime had turned to a different page with a picture of the Leaning Tower of Pisa. 'Thompson and Will claim that the dominant economic models are like the Leaning Tower of Pisa, which sank while it was still being built due to poor foundations. Subsequently, the architects tried to correct the slant by making the upper storeys straighter. They quite literally piled error upon error in an attempt to rectify the faulty base. As a result the tower is both leaning *and* crooked.'

'Thompson and Will believe that expected utility and equilibrium have had a similar effect on economics,' Fitz said.

'It's not that dramatic where a single tower is concerned,' Jeanne said, 'but it's a massive deal for the pillars of modern economics as well as many political theories.' She looked up. 'And just like that Thompson and Will have demolished great swathes of current economic theory. In essence they've torn down the leaning tower and started building a whole new version.'

'It was about time,' Jan said. 'That old tower was useless, in any case. It wasn't able to predict the recent crises nor prevent growing inequality.'

'It's going to make a lot of people unhappy,' said Jeanne. 'Classical economists are a very orthodox bunch. Many trust their holy scriptures and the words of their forefathers in the same way creationists believe in the Bible.'

'Unhappy enough to murder Thompson and Cantor?' asked Jan.

'Not the economists, no,' Fitz said pensively, 'but maybe people who gain the most from the current circumstances, and whose models Thompson and Cantor claim they can disprove mathematically.'

'Jeanne Dalli,' the young man at reception replied after briefly consulting his computer. 'She reserved a table.'

'She's a guest?'

The man shot a glance at Kreuzer, who nodded. 'Yes.'

'Is she here? Look up when she last used her key card.'

A glance at Kreuzer. A nod.

'A few minutes ago,' the man said. 'Three times. First, the one for Ted Holden's suite upstairs, then her own to enter the VIP suite area from the stairwell . . .'

'Hold on a second. She has two cards?'

'Yes,' the man answered after again checking with Kreuzer. 'One for the hotel's royal suite. Mr Holden himself has the master card, but several of his staff received additional cards. Ms Dalli's card opened the suite about twenty minutes ago. Three minutes later, the card for her own room opened the door leading from the stairwell into the VIP suite area.'

'You have a separate area for—'

'Suites with private access,' Kreuzer explained. 'It's very popular with extended Arab families, for example. Ted Holden booked it for the duration of the summit.'

'And two minutes later she entered her own junior suite,' the receptionist concluded.

'Why did she take the stairs?' asked Maya. 'Is the lift out of order?'

'No, it's working,' Kreuzer said.

'Give me her room number,' Maya demanded. 'I want to

meet this lady if she's still there.' Turning to the manager, she added, 'You're coming with me. What about cameras?'

'In the entrance, the lobby and the lifts,' Kreuzer said through gritted teeth.

'Get your people to check the footage for the last half hour and find out where the two men went. OK, let's go.'

56

'Interesting,' Fitz mumbled, who'd read on. 'This model negates various forms of bias. Probability neglect, irrational loss aversion, hyperbolic discounting . . .'

'Bias?' Jan asked with irritation in his voice. 'Guys, is this really getting us anywhere?'

'Prejudice, irrational behaviour,' Fitz continued. 'Probability neglect, for example—'

'Who comes up with all these terms?'

'It's when the probability of a major disaster is infinitesimal, but people pay more attention to it than to more common minor accidents.'

'Because they're looking for thrills?'

'Nope. The common explanation is that people are poor judges of probability, which means they're irrational,' Fitz continued, unperturbed. 'If you calculate the ensemble average as you would in a normal decision model, a fatal risk – a plane crash, say – is just one of many. So we should actually give them less weight than to other more frequent risks such as everyday mishaps, from burning your finger on the stove to having your wallet stolen. With the time average, however, you're never allowed to hit zero.

'Think of our farmer. If she reaches zero, she starves because it's impossible to recover on her own. So it's natural and by no means irrational to pay attention to the greater risks, even if a fatal accident hardly ever happens.'

'Because I'll never recover if it does,' Jan said. 'A plane crash will kill me, whereas a small burn heals in a couple of days.'

'Look here,' said Jeanne, pointing to the chapter's introduction.

Apply a false model of rationality and various rational actions appear 'irrational', 'biased' or 'emotional'.

'This is all hugely exciting, no doubt,' Jan said impatiently. He was still shaken at the thought that the killers had tracked them to the hotel, even if they had managed to lose one of the bruisers for now. Anyone this doggedly on their tail would keep on catching up with them. And if they found out where he and Fitz were right now, they'd be trapped in Jeanne's room. 'Could we please finally figure out if any of this is linked to the murders?' he insisted.

Fitz just kept turning the pages and paused on a sheet featuring a number of complicated-looking graphs and formulas.

'Here it is,' he said. 'This is what Will was trying to explain in the farmers' fable. And I know why . . . Wow, this is so cool!'

'The cops are here,' El warned his team quietly via his headset. 'The two officers we saw yesterday outside Fitzroy Peel's hotel.'

Now Jack had been forced to leave the hotel, El was the only member of his squad left inside the building. Jack had taken up a position opposite The Estate, while the others were watching the remaining exits. There'd been no sign of Wutte and Peel so they must be inside still.

The plainclothes policewoman took the lift, while the officer in uniform waited down in the lobby.

El received an incoming call via his earpiece. It was their client.

'Change of plan,' the voice said. 'Gather your men and be on standby in the underground car park.'

The car park?

'Copy that.'

Call ended.

Jan was gazing at Jeanne's hair and over her shoulder at her ear and cheekbones as she stared at the pages of formulas.

'Sorry, I don't understand this either,' she said.

Either? *What did she mean – like him?*

'This shows why Will was so interested in Kelly's work,' Fitz explained, studying the calculations and lines of texts in between the diagrams. 'The stuff we all know about was just the tip of an iceberg that economists in the sixties, who were against the whole idea in the first place, didn't even know was there. Will and Thompson based this paper on studies by physicists and mathematicians at the London Mathematical Laboratory. Kelly's criterion is just one variation on the ergodic hypothesis advanced by the famous Austrian physicist Ludwig Boltzmann in the 1870s and further developed by Gibbs and Maxwell.'

'This is the physicist in him speaking,' Jeanne whispered to Jan. Yet again, the young German was so intrigued by Fitz's passion for his subject that he almost forgot his own fear.

'Ergodic?' he asked. 'Wasn't that the thing with the different averages in the coin-toss game?'

'That's right. Ergodicity.' Fitz looked up in surprise, as if he hadn't realized Jan was still there. 'You've got a good memory. Actually, it was non-ergodic. Yet the principle doesn't simply help to optimize processes, as in Kelly's wagers,' he muttered, absorbed in the manuscript again. 'It opens up a whole new field of economic theory. The London Mathematical Laboratory wrote a paper called "The Evolutionary Advantage of Cooperation", which Thompson and Will have elaborated further. I'll explain it to you in a second using the farmers' fable.'

He took photos of the pages with his phone before grabbing the hotel notepad from the desk.

'What they've provided here is *mathematical proof* of an absolutely fundamental principle. That principle is something many people have assumed – even intuitively *known* – for millennia, but until now there was no mathematical evidence demonstrating the advantage of cooperation over non-cooperation . . . or competition, the free market, whatever you want to call it. But you need to have studied physics or maths for quite a while to understand these formulas. Will wrote the farmers' fable to explain the principle to non-specialists.'

He took out his original diagrams and laid them on the desk.

'Fitz,' cried Jan to shake him out of his bubble.

'Fitzroy.'

'Shouldn't we be doing this later?'

'Why?' Fitz asked with studied nonchalance. 'We're quite safe here. Who on earth would suspect we're in the room of Jeanne Dalli?' His fingers tapped the diagrams. 'This here is the most important thing right now. For me, anyway.'

'Fitzroy has piqued my curiosity,' Jeanne said to back him up. 'I want to know too.'

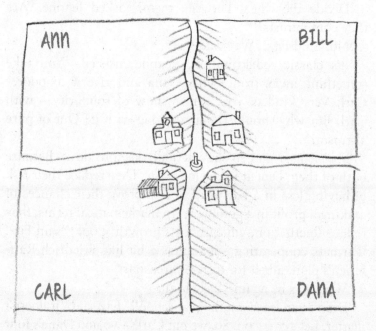

'Anyway,' said Fitz, resuming his story, 'we have Ann, Carl, Bill and Dana. Each of them starts off with one ear of wheat. In year one, Ann and Carl each turn one ear into two in the west of the village. In the east Bill and Dana each grow four from the one they started with.'

Year	Ann	Carl	Dana	Bill
	0	0	0	0
1	× 2	× 2	× 4	× 4
	∞	∞	∞∞	∞∞

'Together, Carl and Dana produced six ears of wheat. If they pool their resources and divide the grains equally . . .'

'Divide the wheat between them?' asked Jeanne. 'Are they communists?'

'No,' said Fitz. 'Wait and see.'

'It's classic redistribution,' Jeanne insisted. 'You take something away from richer Dana and give it to poorer Carl. Very kind of you, a nice show of solidarity – with Carl. But why should Dana go along with it? Out of pure altruism?'

'She's smart and so she's actually keen to do it. Because both of them benefit in the long run. They reduce their risk of having less in a bad year, and improve their chances of making a profit in a good year. In mathematical terms, they reduce fluctuation, which boosts growth. Look!' said Fitz. 'Farmers cooperating – it sounds a bit like Friedrich Raiffeisen's plan, albeit for different reasons.'

'Who was he again?' asked Jan.

'Didn't you learn anything at school?' Fitz said. 'It doesn't matter. Let's carry on. So, we put Carl's two and Dana's four ears of wheat from the first year together, which makes six. If they share them equally, each of them receives three.'

Year	Ann	Carl	Dana	Bill
	0	0	0	0
1	× 2	× 2	× 4	× 4
	00	00 ⟍ ⟋ 0000		0000
		00000		
		000 ⟋ ⟍ 000		

'The following year, Ann and Carl harvest three times what they sowed in the west of the village. So Ann produces

302

six ears from her two. Carl, however, had more seed at the start of this fertile year – three ears – and this triples to nine.' Fitz pencilled in the sums. 'So he's already out-produced Ann, who didn't cooperate.'

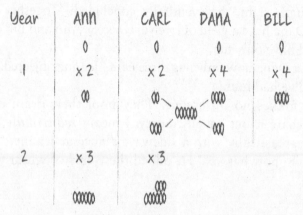

He continued his drawing. 'In the east, on the other hand, Bill and Dana have had a bad year, harvesting only as much as they sowed, a growth factor of one.'

Year	ANN	CARL	DANA	BILL
	0	0	0	0
1	× 2	× 2	× 4	× 4
	00	00	000	0000
		000	00	
2	× 3	× 3	× 1	× 1
	00000	00000	00	0000

'Bill's four ears of wheat yield four, and Dana's three produce another three.'

'Hang on a sec!' said Jan. 'Not so fast. I need another look at this.' His eyes moved slowly over the diagrams, checking all the sums, from the original ears of wheat to the pooling, dividing up and growth of the second year.

'That's right,' he eventually concluded. 'Together Carl and Dana have a yield of twelve, whereas Ann and Bill combined have only ten.'

'But Dana now only has three ears,' Jeanne objected. 'She could've had four.'

'It makes no difference. They pool their grain again and share it out equally. Sorry, I meant *redistribute*,' Fitz said sarcastically with a sideways glance at Jeanne. 'Each of them now has six.' He added these ears of wheat to his table.

Year	Ann	Carl	Dana	Bill
	0	0	0	0
1	×2	×2	×4	×4
2	×3	×3	×1	×1

'So Dana has more than the three she started the year with, and more than the four Bill produced in the same period of time.'

Jan tried to keep up. He stared at the drawings, checking all the maths. He was stunned.

Jeanne seemed shocked too. 'This is . . . Let's carry on,' she said excitedly.

Year	Ann	Carl	Dana	Bill
	0	0	0	0
1	× 2	× 2	× 4	× 4
2	× 3	× 3	× 1	× 1
3	× 1	× 1	× 2	× 2
4	× 2	× 2	× 2	× 2

Fitz was now writing and drawing at the same lightning speed as he'd calculated and jotted down the points in the pub the previous night. 'Every year they put their crop together and share out the pooled amount equally.'

'After the third year, Carl and Dana both have nine ears,' Jeanne noted. 'Which is more than Ann's six and Bill's eight that same year.'

'So after four years Carl and Dana each have eighteen ears, which is what Will's fable said at the beginning,' Fitz said, completing the calculation. 'That's it. It's true.'

They stared at the piece of paper.

'Amazing,' said Jeanne. 'Even without increasing their individual annual growth rates, by cooperating they still manage to improve their overall growth. And they also harvest more than Ann and Bill.'

'Great,' said Jan, 'but what now?'

'First we have to let the implications sink in,' Jeanne said quietly. 'Conventional economic doctrine maintains that growth and greater prosperity are the result of each of us ramping up our individual efforts, or thanks to new technologies increasing productivity, population growth or capital accumulation.'

'Capital *what*?' Jan asked before signalling that he didn't wish to hear.

'The farmers' fable shows that a better distribution of resources and profits boosts overall growth with the same level of effort and without the need for new technologies or other conventional factors.'

'Or that we can achieve the same as Ann and Bill but with less hard graft,' said Fitz.

'Economists have always suspected there was a connection between wealth distribution and growth,' Jeanne said, 'and this is the maths underpinning that link.'

None of them said anything. They were all doing the sums again.

'Now I understand why someone was so desperate to kill Will and Thompson,' Jeanne murmured. 'This changes everything.'

57

Waiting for the lift, Maya stared impatiently at the floor indicator. One of the express elevators to the VIP suite area was on its way down to meet them in the lobby. It seemed to be taking an age. Jörn was waiting outside the normal lifts just in case Jeanne Dalli, Jan Wutte or Fitzroy Peel should appear, or hotel security discovered anything from the CCTV footage.

'So who is Ted Holden?' Maya asked the hotel manager in a low voice.

'An American investor,' the man replied even more quietly. 'A multi-billionaire before he's even turned fifty.'

'And Jeanne Dalli?'

'One of his team. They booked the royal suite and eleven junior suites and rooms.'

So there are people who'll book an entire ultra-luxury floor of a five-star hotel! Maya took secret pleasure in being a thorn in the side of the elite. Maybe Köstritz was right to have her chaperoned, although he could have chosen someone better than Jörn.

At long last the lift reached the ground floor.

58

'What exactly does it change?' asked Jan.

'Where do I start?' Jeanne said. 'As I said: it changes everything. It shakes the founding principles of modern society to the core. It's revolutionary.'

Jan would never have expected such hyperbole from this woman.

'For one thing, it offers mathematical proof of the advantage of cooperation over non-cooperation or competition,' Fitz repeated in a more sober tone of voice.

'Didn't that proof exist already?' Jan asked innocently.

'If it did, would people keep repeating that competition is the best path to growth and prosperity?'

'But people do say the whole is greater than the sum of its parts.'

'That's only a saying,' muttered Fitz, patting the manuscript. '*This* is the mathematical proof.'

'Not that again!' Jan exclaimed.

'Western democratic societies are based on the idea of Ann and Bill,' Jeanne explained. She sounded as enthusiastic as Fitz now. All her reservations seemed to have been swept away. 'Every person looks out for themselves, as far as they are able. Only when someone is incapable of doing so do others help out – or not. People only work together when it's the only way to get something done. If I can't cope, my family or friends step in. If they can't solve the problem, the council tries; if the council can't deal with it on its own, the regional government coordinates the response, and if the region can't do it, the state takes over. Above this, in Europe, is the EU, and on a global level there's the UN. They either take over or they don't. It's what's known as the principle of subsidiarity.'

'You two and your fancy words,' Jan complained.

'This principle has become the basic attitude underpinning our social system,' Jeanne continued. 'It determines what we do and how.'

'In a nutshell: everyone for themselves, unless . . .' Fitz said.

Jeanne pointed to his sketches. 'The formula developed by the London Mathematical Laboratory and this example here show that it'd be better for our social system if we adopted exactly the opposite approach: everyone together, unless . . .'

'Unless what?'

'Thompson and Cantor study this question in more detail.' Fitz flicked frantically through the manuscript. 'Well, it's obvious really – unless someone doesn't want to participate. After all, cooperation is voluntary. Or unless someone tries to rip people off and cheat: freeloaders. Or contributes less, for example, by "optimizing" or evading tax. Or even developing advantageous tax models for certain people.'

'For the rich,' said Jan.

The three of them gazed silently at Fitz's sketches.

'The dominant economic paradigm of equilibrium suddenly looks very, very outdated,' Jeanne mused.

'We talked about that last night,' said Jan. Even he found Jeanne's excitement infectious. 'You can't give someone something without taking it away from someone else.'

'In simple terms, yes, but this paper proves the opposite,' said Jeanne. 'In the final analysis, pooling and sharing is better for everyone than Ann and Bill's selfish behaviour. No pursuit of equilibrium, just constant dynamics.'

'A paradigm shift,' said Jan. 'That's the phrase Will uses in his notes. The diagrams of the universe. The move from viewing the Earth as the centre of the solar system to understanding that in fact it's the Sun.'

'That's exactly what Will meant. This work heralds an entire paradigm shift in our view of humankind and how our society operates.'

While Jeanne was explaining, Fitz had produced another quick sketch showing Carl and Dana's cooperation bonus more clearly.

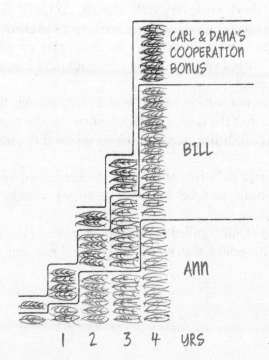

'And the beautiful thing about it,' said Fitz, 'is that Carl and Dana don't really need to work any harder to achieve this better outcome.'

'Not really?' said Jan. 'Not at all.'

'Just a little,' Fitz corrected him. 'They need to arrange the sharing of their crop and also ensure they're both in it for the long-term.'

'There are transaction costs,' Jeanne explained, 'especially when you get more than four farmers, just as there are in complex societies and nation states and in the global economy.'

'Humans have established institutions and roles,' said Fitz, 'to take care of issues of distribution: markets, politics, managers in companies.'

'They don't work very well, though, do they?' Jan countered. 'Somehow it's those very distributors – bankers, traders, managers – who always get the most ears of wheat, or money, instead of the farmers who could use it to produce more grain.'

'You're not wrong there,' said Fitz, grinning, 'but that doesn't affect the fundamental advantage of the principle of cooperation. It just needs to be organized differently from no—'

He stared in horror at the door. Someone had knocked.

Jan's heart skipped a beat. The killers wouldn't give a polite knock . . .

'Jeanne Dalli!' called a woman's voice from the hallway. 'This is the police. Can we talk to you for a moment, please?'

SIXTH DECISION

'Under certain circumstances the principle allows
even small entities to destroy complex structures.'

Will Cantor

59

Maya knocked again.

'Are you in there, Ms Dalli?' she repeated.

'Just a second,' came the reply from inside.

Maya heard a clatter of high heels approaching. The door was opened by a woman in her late twenties who looked like a model. Her suit was visibly expensive, and Maya caught the delicate scent of a costly perfume.

'The police?' Jeanne Dalli asked in English with a trace of irritation. 'How can I be of help?'

'I apologize most sincerely, Ms Dalli,' the manager blurted out at once, 'but the police—'

'We were informed that you met two men we're looking for a short time ago in the lobby,' Maya interrupted. 'Fitzroy Peel and Jan Wutte.'

'I . . . yes, I did,' she replied, surprised. 'Why are you looking for them?'

'We'd like to know why you met them and if you know where they are now.'

'Well, OK, come in,' said Dalli, stepping to one side. Something about her demeanour told Maya that this woman was made of sterner stuff than her good looks suggested.

It was a junior suite with a bedroom and a living room-cum-study. Virtually the same size as Maya's entire flat. A blazer and two blouses were spread out on the bed, and the doors to the wardrobe stood open. Otherwise the suite was extremely neat and tidy, showing barely any sign of occupation. The full-length plate-glass windows gave a view over the hotel's sweeping gardens.

'I need to leave for the summit soon,' Dalli said. 'May I offer you a drink?'

'No thanks,' said Maya. 'This won't take long.'

There was no need to beat around the bush with this woman.

'Peel and Wutte,' said Jeanne Dalli. 'I had a coffee in the lobby with them. Peel contacted me this morning because he wanted to talk about a mutual acquaintance.'

'About what?'

'Conversations I'd had with this old acquaintance. Months ago. About professional matters,' she said dismissively. 'Nothing very interesting. Finance and economics.'

She peered at her expensive watch, but Maya refused to be distracted.

'Finance and economics,' Maya repeated. 'Fascinating. You weren't by any chance talking about Herbert Thompson?'

Maya had surprised her. Or maybe not.

'The Nobel Prize winner who may have died last night?'

'*May* have?'

'Have the police officially confirmed his death then?'

'No.'

'Why would we have been talking about him?'

'An innocent question.'

Jeanne Dalli shot another glance at her watch.

'What does Wutte have to do with a mutual acquaintance of yours and Peel's?' asked Maya. Something about this woman got under her skin. She was too smooth, too professional, too well prepared. Then again, maybe a multi-billionaire's assistant had to be.

'I didn't ask, and he didn't say anything, as far as I can remember. Maybe he simply tagged along with Peel?'

'All right. So who was this mutual acquaintance?'

'A man named Will Cantor.'

The man whose room Peel and Wutte had broken into last night. Maya knew that if you were going to lie, you should stick as closely as possible to the truth, and Jeanne Dalli seemed to know that too.

'Will Cantor is, or was, in Berlin too,' Maya said. 'Did you know that?'

'Not until Peel told me. I haven't seen Will for months.'

'Do you know where the two of them are now?'

'I haven't a clue. I left the lobby before they did. Why are you are in such a hurry to find them?'

Perhaps she needed to shake this woman out of her complacency. 'They're suspected of murder.'

Jeanne Dalli's face betrayed a flicker of emotion. 'Murder! Whose murder?'

Maya decided to try her luck. 'Herbert Thompson's.'

'I thought it was an accident.'

'That's what the media are reporting,' said Maya.

'But if those two had anything to do with it,' Jeanne Dalli said, 'they surely wouldn't be walking into a five-star hotel in the city centre in broad daylight?'

This woman had an answer to everything. Maya's enquiries were getting her nowhere for now. She handed Jeanne Dalli her card. 'Thank you for your time. Do please give me a call if you think of anything else, find out anything new or hear from those two men.'

*

'I'm not doing that again,' Jeanne hissed after waiting a couple of minutes with her ear pressed to the door. Jan and Fitz were standing in the bathroom doorway. Fitz had the stack of papers tucked under his arm.

'Thanks,' he said for the second time.

'I should've handed you and the documents over and told her everything,' she said.

'And where would that have got you?' Fitz replied. 'Nowhere. We can only claim that the papers came from Ted Holden's safe, we can't prove it. We have even less evidence that Will's notes were in there – and they're the only link.'

'*Potential* link,' Jeanne corrected him. 'I've had enough. I've got to go, but first I've got to return the documents to Ted's safe or he'll smell a rat.'

'But—'

'No buts.' She removed Fitz's own drawings from the sheaf of paper and put the rest back into the envelope. 'I was supposed to be at the summit ages ago. Ted will be wondering where I've got to.'

'He'll be wondering a lot more than that when this study's published.'

'I'm leaving now,' she said, extending her free hand towards Fitz. 'The key card to my room, please.' Fitz gave it to her. 'Wait ten minutes before you leave just in case someone's still out there.'

At long last! Jan couldn't wait to get out of this room.

'What will you do?' Fitz asked as she turned to go.

Without turning round or breaking stride, she said with a shrug, 'I've no idea.'

Maya and Jörn followed the manager past the reception desk and into the back office where two men were sitting in front of banks of monitors. Each man was keeping an eye on two rows of ten screens arranged in a slight arc.

'Did you find anything?' Kreuzer asked.

'There they are,' said the younger of the two, pointing to the screen directly in front of him. 'In the lobby having coffee with Ms Dalli.'

He fast-forwarded the footage and the three people shifted around on their chairs, stood up, called a waiter, chatted and said goodbye. Wutte and Peel stayed where they were, paid, had another brief exchange with the waiter and got to their feet.

'They go to the back of the lobby,' the security guard explained, playing the relevant footage, 'and disappear into the stairwell.'

'Damn!' said Maya. 'Do you have cameras there too?'

'No.'

'What about in the hallway leading to Jeanne Dalli's room?'

'Only in the standard lifts. Beyond that, our guests have complete privacy.'

'There's far less surveillance in the VIP area,' Kreuzer added. 'Privacy for special guests begins in the express elevators.'

'You have special elevators up to the suites?' Jörn asked in disbelief.

'We need to go back up to Jeanne Dalli's room,' said Maya, 'and also check Ted Holden's suite.'

'Why?' Kreuzer asked in alarm.

'Because Dalli went there too, and Wutte and Peel may be in there right now.'

'Our orders are to keep a low profile,' Jörn reminded her.

'Like you did at the squat yesterday? Come on, let's go,' she said to Kreuzer.

'I can't simply let you into our luxury suites!' the manager protested.

'Oh, but you have no problem with potential murderers being there?' Maya retorted.

'Do you want to see the other guy too?' one of the security guards interrupted her.

What was he talking about?

'What other guy?' Maya asked.

60

Jeanne returned the envelope to exactly the same position in the safe as she'd found it. She still didn't know quite what to make of what she'd read. How had Ted got hold of Thompson and Will's manuscript? Thompson was a long-standing adviser to the billionaire; some would even describe them as friends. Why shouldn't he have given the documents to Ted? It was the scribbled and crumpled sheet of paper, whose imprint Fitzroy and Jan claimed to have found in Will's hotel room, that really puzzled her. Fitzroy's question was a good one. How had Ted come by it, especially in conjunction with a manuscript and notes for a speech by two men who had died the previous evening? Murdered, if Fitzroy and Jan were to be believed.

However, the two of them had as little evidence for their story as they did for the rest of the affair. There might be some other explanation.

The handwritten note was the only new element. In the manuscript, Fitzroy had located the passage that might be the basis for the vivid parable of the farmers. There might be a link between the authors of the two texts. Maybe the scrawl really was from Will's hand, but who knew how it had come into Fitz and Jan's possession in the first place? Will was an old friend of Fitz's. Maybe they hadn't merely planned to meet but had actually done so. Maybe Fitzroy had paid a visit to Will in his room and caught sight of the paper by chance, realized how revolutionary it was and been desperate to find the original? Now he'd invented some story about killers and Ted's involvement in murder in order to get his hands on the documents. She had no idea what to believe. All these thoughts were running through her mind as she hurried towards the express elevator. Still ruminating, she pressed the button next to the lift door, which slid open without a sound.

'Hi, Jeanne,' the man in the lift said softly.

Jeanne's face turned red. 'What are you doing here?'

He put his finger to his lips. *Shush. Be quiet.*

61

'What do we do now?' Jan asked.

Fitz studied his drawings. 'We wait a few more minutes,' he said, 'like Jeanne told us to.' He went back to reading. 'This particular example also refutes the notorious statement by our equally notorious British prime minister, Margaret Thatcher,' Fitz said. ' "There is no such thing as society." '

'I want out of here,' said Jan. 'It doesn't interest me right now.'

'It should, though,' Fitz replied absently, reaching for his pencil. 'How wrong Thatcher was!'

This was unbelievable! This idiot could live in his mathematical world if he liked, but Jan needed to grapple with reality. He caught sight of a mobile on the sofa.

'Jeanne forgot her phone,' he said.

Fitz didn't answer. He simply drew a bracket around Carl + Dana's Cooperation Bonus and wrote one word. *Society.*

'This is society, right here! The extra prosperity created by working together, which is only possible thanks to cooperation, thanks to society.'

'Then maybe the two of us should start working together,' Jan barked. 'So what do we do now?'

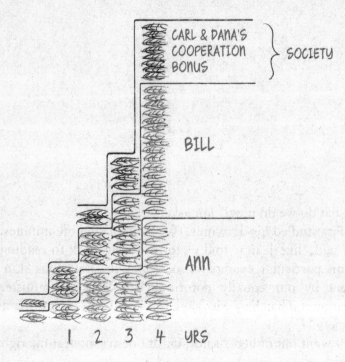

'We've been working together since yesterday evening,' said Fitz, 'and pretty well too, I'd say. Look what we've managed to uncover.'

'You really do have a screw loose, you know. Are those formulas the only thing that you can think about? That policewoman was searching for us on suspicion of murder! And—'

'Oh, give me a break. She was only trying to unsettle Jeanne. This here . . . this is big news!' He took a photo of the diagrams and typed a message. 'I'm sending all this to Nida and Kim. *They'll* be interested.'

You mean, you're interested in Nida, more like.

'It gets even more paradoxical,' Fitz exclaimed. 'Modern

economics assumes that human beings are pure profit maximizers – *Homo economicus*. That—'

'Fitz!'

'Fitzroy, if you please. That implies that humans will do anything to bolster their own advantage. Capitalism is driven by self-interest. By greed.'

'I'm not driven by greed, just by my own self-interest not to end up in police custody!' cried Jan.

'So you're greedy for freedom,' said Fitz.

'And what about those maniacs out there looking for us? I bet they're not sitting around, twiddling their thumbs.'

'No one suspects we're here. We're safe,' said Fitz, staring at his drawing. 'In Will's example, Ann and Bill are driven by greed. They think only of themselves. But that's not what people are really like – or at least not only. People are altruistic, selfless, compassionate. They help others . . .'

'Just like our black-clad killer friends,' Jan joked.

'The farmers' fable shows that greed should motivate people to pool and share their resources,' Fitz declared. ' "Greed is good." Greed is right. Remember *Wall Street*, the cult eighties film?'

'You old fogey,' Jan said. 'That was long before my time.'

'This wasn't quite what Gordon Gekko had in mind.' Fitz burst out laughing, then folded up the documents and stuffed them into his pocket. 'If you want to achieve something that lasts, then you can't afford to cheat people and try to rob them of all they have. If you're really greedy, you need to give people something. Solidarity, altruism and charity are not romantic ideals. In actual fact, unsentimental, rational mathematics proves that in the long run they're the best bet for everyone.'

'The best bet for us right now would be to get out of here.'

'Put your hands behind your head and relax. Don't move.'

Jan felt as if his blood had turned to molten lava. Standing halfway between them and the door was a large, athletic man in a dark suit and tie with sharply defined features, a grade-one buzz cut and a very discreet earpiece. He had a pistol in his right hand, and Jan was staring down the barrel. In the other hand, at the same height, he was holding a mobile phone.

He was a more civilized version of the men who'd been chasing them since yesterday evening, and out in the hallway were two more like him.

Oh shit, shit and double shit!!!

62

Fitz had dropped the phone and put his hands behind his head. Jan followed his example. The two other suits entered the room, also brandishing guns, and surrounded them.

'Don't even think about trying anything stupid,' said their leader. 'We're now going to cuff you and turn you over to the police.'

The two men grabbed Jan's wrists and twisted them expertly behind his back.

At least they're not the hit squad!

'Why?' Fitz asked. 'We haven't done anything.'

'Tell him about your cooperation theory,' Jan taunted him. 'Maybe it'll persuade him to be nice to us.' Under his breath he hissed, 'Why didn't you listen to me? We could've been long gone. Safe, my arse.'

He felt a hard, narrow band being ratcheted tighter until it cut into his skin.

'Leave me alone!' Jan shouted. 'Hel—' he tried to yell, but his cry subsided into a whimper as the man grabbed him between the legs and squeezed so hard that it sent a sickening jolt up through his groin and stomach and into his throat. He retched and almost threw up. The man squeezed hard for a second time, sending another wave of sheer agony surging through Jan's body.

'Don't. Try. Anything. Stupid,' the bastard repeated. Doubled up in pain, Jan nodded, although his head was nearly bursting.

The men pulled tight a second strip of plastic around Jan's wrists. 'Cable ties,' the leader said. 'Unbreakable.'

By now they had also grabbed hold of Fitz.

'We're part of Mr Holden's security team. We've caught you breaking and entering and we'll hold on to you until we can hand you over to the police. Come with us!'

'We didn't break—'

'So where's the card you used to open the door?'

'It's . . .' Jan began.

Damn! Jeanne had asked for it back before she left. He was still reeling from the searing pain in his groin.

The men shoved them towards the exit, where two more guards were waiting.

'Good!' said Fitz. 'Because the police will have their work cut out investigating how the notes for Herbert Thompson's speech and a manuscript on exciting new social, political and economic concepts by Herbert Thompson and a second author came to be in Ted Holden's safe. Only a few hours after both men died in an alleged accident too. Concepts that may not all be to Ted Holden's liking.'

Jan dimly heard this whole declaration through the buzzing in his ears, but now fear was mingling with the piercing discomfort in his nether regions.

'You'll have plenty of time to explain all of that, I'm sure, though I doubt the police will be very interested in political or economic theories. Especially as the police – even if they did wish or were authorized to search the safe – would find nothing there.'

'In that case, they can look elsewhere. On Thompson's and Cantor's computers, in their notebooks . . .'

'Don't get your hopes up about telling the police any tall tales. You don't have a shred of proof.'

Fitz and Jan exchanged glances. Jan guessed from Fitz's expression that his friend was wondering the same thing as he was. *Where's Jeanne?*

63

'What's going on here?'

On the screen Kreuzer and four members of his staff could be seen talking to a guy in dark clothing. A mountain of a man, clean shaven, with shades.

'Looks like a security guard,' said Jörn.

'That's what he said he was,' Kreuzer replied. 'Wutte and Peel told the waiter they'd seen him fiddling with a gun, so we were forced to check.'

The speeded-up footage showed the group swarming towards the entrance, and the black-clad bear of a man leaving the building.

'He didn't show any ID, acted all offended and left.'

'You let him go?' asked Jörn.

'He hadn't done anything,' the manager said.

'And? Was he carrying a weapon?'

'A pistol. With the safety catch on, in a holster on his belt.'

'So he may have been someone's bodyguard,' Jörn said.

'We can deal with this later,' Maya said. 'But first we need to go to Holden's suite and back to Dalli's.'

'I can't allow—'

'I can also come back with a search warrant and a SWAT team,' Maya interrupted Kreuzer gently. 'How would your prestigious guests like *that*?'

Jörn was about to say something, but Maya warned him off with a glare. He was as useless as a guard dog as he was as a mediator.

The hotel manager stared at her aghast. 'We can't just . . .'

'I repeat: a SWAT team.'

'How will we explain . . . ?'

'You'll think of something.'

'Come with us,' Holden's guard ordered, his gun digging into Fitzroy's ribs. 'And I don't want to hear a squeak out of you!'

'Where to?' he asked. 'I thought you were handing us over to the police.'

'We will.' The two henchmen dragged them along the corridor, while their leader stayed behind and made a phone call. Fitzroy couldn't hear what he was saying.

'Why aren't we waiting here?' Fitzroy asked. There was something fishy about this.

The lift was waiting for them with open doors. The two men bundled Fitzroy and Jan inside and then squeezed in themselves. The lift was designed for ten persons, but the guards were tall and powerfully built, so space was at a premium.

No one said a word. Jan leaned against the wall, his face still white from the lingering after-effects of his bruised groin. Fitzroy stared at the floor indicator over their heads. 2 – 1 – G. The lift passed the ground floor where reception and the exit were located, and continued its journey down into the underworld.

'The police are waiting in the car park?' Fitzroy said, alarm in his voice.

'Would you rather be escorted out through the lobby in your present state?' the leader asked.

The lift stopped moving and the doors opened.

Jeanne was waiting outside.

'I'll need copies of the footage of the two men,' said Maya on the way up, 'and of that weird security guy too.'

'Can we at least handle that part via the official channels?' the manager asked coolly. They'd left Jörn behind in the CCTV room just in case.

They reached the suite area. Holden's door was shut.

Kreuzer pressed a button at the side of the door. 'Room service,' he said into an invisible microphone. He waited a moment, leaned forward and pressed again. 'Room service!'

'There's no one there,' Maya said impatiently. 'Go ahead and open up.'

As if by magic, the double doors slid apart.

'Very swish,' she said drily.

The Tiergarten park, the Brandenburg Gate and the entire Berlin skyline were laid out at her feet on the other side of the living room's panoramic floor-to-ceiling window. The Tiergarten was already black with crowds of people. At least three helicopters were patrolling the sky, and the sound of rotor blades and police sirens was audible even through this top-of-the-range soundproof glass.

Maya heard a hum punctuated by ripping noises off to her right. She hurried across the impressively sized room to a glass door, beyond which lay a large office in which a young man in a dark suit was feeding a pile of documents into a noisy machine. Only now did he notice her presence, and Maya produced her police identity card before he could react.

'Police!' she shouted.

The man hesitated and then relaxed. 'I didn't hear you,' he apologized, pointing at the machine.

Maya recognized the headset in his ear, the lean physique

and athletic posture, the tell-tale bulge where his jacket concealed a waist holster. Security. She put her card away.

The man tore a few sheets off a stack of stapled papers lying on top of an envelope beside the shredder. Maya could make out some printed text and something that looked like mathematical formulas and statistical diagrams.

'Is there anyone else here?'

'The others are at the summit,' the man explained, continuing his noisy work.

Maya cast a quick glance through the glass doors of the adjoining meeting room. No one there.

'Sorry for the disturbance,' Kreuzer said.

'No problem. You're only doing your job,' the man answered, feeding the next sheaf of paper into the shredder.

Jörn watched one of the two operators in The Estate's video-monitoring room rewind at speed through the scenes of the past few hours. They showed the black-clad guest scurrying backwards from the entrance to be surrounded by Kreuzer and the other three staff members, then the manager and his colleagues disappeared off screen and the man stood there for a long time until he too disappeared out of shot. The time code indicated that he'd waited there for over half an hour.

The operator searched for the preceding footage from the relevant cameras. The man could be seen entering via the front doors, looking around and then taking up his position.

The operator ran through the first sequence once more.

'Who was the man waiting for?' Jörn asked rhetorically. 'Or who was he watching?'

The operator paused the video, started it and stopped it again. The bruiser in dark clothing seemed to be talking quietly to himself, or maybe into his earpiece. Then he focused on something and stared unwaveringly in the same direction for several minutes.

'What's he looking at?' asked Jörn.

'Maybe the table where Ms Dalli was having coffee with those two men?' guessed the operator. 'The direction's right in any case.'

'What happened there?' his colleague asked from his seat in front of his own bank of monitors.

Jörn and the operator turned towards him and saw what he meant. Two screens had gone blank.

'Where's that?' asked the operator next to Jörn.

'Outside the VIP car park,' said his colleague, tapping on several different keys to no effect.

'Well,' said the man next to Jörn, 'the system's been working so well for so long, I guess something had to give at some point.'

'I'll wait a bit,' his colleague said. 'It's bound to be back up soon.' He reached for his phone. 'I'll call the valet downstairs to let him know.'

64

'Oh shit!' Jan groaned when he saw Jeanne. 'I should've known it was a trap.'

Jeanne didn't say a word. She was standing on the red carpet leading to the lifts, studying the newcomers with her arms behind her back. In spite of their critical situation, Jan couldn't help noticing how this position showed off her striking figure to even greater advantage.

'Keep your mouth shut,' the security chief snapped.

Hands shoved Fitzroy hard in the back, propelling him out of the elevator and past Jeanne with Jan at his side. The exit into the car park was very plush.

Fitzroy looked back over his shoulder. Beyond their captors, who were the same height as him, he could make out Jeanne's smaller frame flanked by her companions.

'Eyes straight ahead,' the security chief said, underlining his order with a violent blow to Fitz's ear. Beside him Jan was venting a stream of unintelligible curses.

They reached a peculiar glass enclosure that reminded Fitzroy of the diner on the corner in Edward Hopper's *Nighthawks* painting. In front of it was a vehicle lane and a parking space separated from the rest of the car park by a wall. Leading to it were another few yards of red carpet, lined with pots containing head-high palm trees like sad presidential guards in a banana republic. Next to the large glasshouse was a smaller one furnished with a desk, a phone and a computer. It was probably for the valet, but was currently unoccupied. This must be the VIP pick-up point.

There was no police car parked at the end of the red carpet. Instead, two black Mercedes SUVs were waiting there.

'Where are the police?' Fitzroy asked, panicking.

'We'll drive you there,' the man explained.

Fitzroy braced himself against the two men pushing him along. 'No way!'

'You're going anyway,' said the man.

'No, we won't,' said Fitzroy, leaning back with all his weight and using the full leverage of his height. This made no impression on his guards, who shoved him against the glass door, which slid silently aside. Where was the valet?

'Screaming won't help you either,' said the security chief when he saw Fitzroy filling his lungs to shout. 'No one can hear you down here. And besides . . .' He grabbed hold of Fitzroy's groin and squeezed slightly as a warning.

Fitzroy looked around frantically. Weren't there any surveillance cameras watching everything and transmitting it to the people in charge of hotel security?

The two henchmen threw open the rear doors of the SUVs, but were startled by the sudden roar of an engine and a squeal of tyres. For a second the headlights of the fast-approaching vehicle bathed the scene in dazzling light, blinding them all. For what seemed like an age, all Fitzroy could see were dancing dots of light in the darkness.

Even before the four-wheel drive had drawn up alongside,

shadowy figures leaped out, shouting, 'On the ground! Don't touch your weapons!' as they trained semi-automatics on Holden's security detail. 'Get down!'

The men in suits outnumbered their assailants, but their pistols were in the wrong place – stuck in their shoulder holsters. They were well trained but not willing to die, so they did as they were told. Fitzroy sank on to one knee. Having his hands shackled behind his back made any other position difficult or painful.

'Not you!' one of the shadows ordered.

Fitzroy's eyes were getting used to the half-darkness again. Five bull-necked figures in black balaclavas, cargo trousers and shirts were standing in front of him. Fitzroy thought he recognized their silhouettes. He felt sick to the pit of his stomach.

'Not you either!' they yelled at Jeanne, who was still standing where she'd been when Fitzroy and Jan stepped out of the lift.

'Hands behind your backs!' This was directed at the prostrate security guards.

'You three, in the car!' one man instructed Fitzroy, Jan and Jeanne, jabbing them in the ribs with the muzzle of his assault rifle by way of encouragement. Jeanne let out a shriek, to which he responded by yelling 'Shut up!' and dealing her an even more violent blow to the side. Jeanne groaned but managed to stifle another howl as she writhed in pain. Fitzroy saw why her hands were still behind her back: they were bound just like his and Jan's.

In a flash the other masked men had disabled the sprawling security men with cable ties.

At least we're not the only ones.

'Get in the boot!' snarled the man who'd herded them with his gun towards the black Range Rover.

'It's too small,' Jan said.

'Shut up and get inside!'

'We won't all fit.' A crashing blow with the rifle butt to Jan's head put an end to his objections. He toppled into the boot and lay there unconscious.

'Anyone else?' the man roared.

In the meantime the other four men had finished dealing with Holden's security team. One of them lifted Jan's legs in, while the others grabbed Fitzroy and Jeanne by the arm and thrust them into the boot alongside him. They shoved and manhandled them into position and closed two flaps over their heads, blocking out the light, then slammed the tailgate shut.

It was dark and muggy in their tiny prison cell. Fitzroy could neither move nor draw breath. He heard four doors slam and the car started up.

'Jan,' hissed Fitzroy. 'Jan! Are you OK?'

'Help!' Jeanne croaked behind him. 'I can hardly breathe.'

'Good,' said a voice from the front. 'Then hopefully you'll keep your mouth shut.'

Fitzroy heard her gasping for air. He was doing the same.

'We're suffocating back here!' he shouted.

'You're done for one way or the other,' said the voice. 'To be honest, you'd be better off dying now than later.'

Now Fitzroy could hear Jeanne breathing as if she were kicking for the line in a two-hundred-metre sprint. She was hyperventilating.

'Put your mouth against a soft surface,' he whispered to her. 'My clothing, for example. Breathe through the fabric.'

Her breathing was muffled now, but it didn't slow down. The Range Rover stopped, probably at the exit barrier. Jeanne's breathing grew quieter, then slower and calmer.

The vehicle drove off again.
'You all right now?' Fitzroy asked softly.
There was no answer.
'Jeanne?'
The boot was silent.

65

'Are you in there, Ms Dalli?' Maya knocked on the door of Junior Suite 723 for a second time.

No answer.

'Ms Dalli? OK, open it,' she said to Kreuzer.

'I don't understand why you need to go in there again,' he complained.

'Wutte and Peel vanished into the stairwell from the lobby. A few minutes later, Ms Dalli's card was used to open the door from the stairwell into the exclusive suite area. Dalli may have slipped the two men her key card during their conversation.'

'And why would she do that?'

'I'd like to ask her that very question.'

'But she may also have come down from the floor above, where she'd accessed Mr Holden's suite only minutes earlier with her extra card.'

'She came down the stairs in her high heels?' Maya said sarcastically, adding with an exaggerate groan, 'Men!' and then instructing Kreuzer once again to open the door. He reluctantly obeyed.

The suite was empty. Maya checked all the rooms, searching for traces of any recent visits. She found nothing.

She ignored the manager's triumphant expression as they left the suite.

'Call your CCTV team. Dalli was planning to go to the summit. Has she left the hotel?'

Kreuzer had abandoned his resistance. He phoned and waited for an answer as they headed towards the lift.

'Not through the lobby,' he eventually reported.

'Via the car park? Do you have cameras down there?'

'Only outside the VIP area,' Kreuzer said, rolling his eyes as if explaining something very simple to a dim-witted child.

'I'd like to see it,' Maya said.

'We've had a short blackout.'

'You what?'

'Jan?'

Jan heard someone breathe his name into his ear. It was dark, and he was lying on his side, cramped and curled up, his hands tied behind his back and hemmed in on all sides, jolted and deafened by the sound of an engine. He was hot, he felt sick, he couldn't breathe. His pulse was pounding memory back into his skull like a jackhammer.

'Jan?'

'Yes?' he wheezed.

'Thank God!' He could feel Fitz's breath close to his ear. He could feel the whole length of Fitz's body pressing against his back. They must be lying in the spooning position. 'Keep quiet.'

Jan had no idea why it was so dark. Fitz's whispering was almost inaudible over the hum of the engine. No one could really have heard him apart from Jan.

'What's going on? Where are we?'

'Inside that bloody black Range Rover.'

The jackhammer in Jan's head sent its twin down to torture his entrails.

'Where's Jeanne?'

'Behind me.'

The bruises from the previous day added their torment to the aches in his head and his stomach.

'Where are they taking us?'

'I've no idea, but I don't want to go there.'

Oh fuck! Don't puke now.

In action movies the heroes always learned from the most terrible situations the really useful stuff they'd need when they made their bid for freedom later in the film. Since yesterday evening he'd learned a whole load of new things about averages, expected utility, economics, mathematics, decision-making and cooperation, but what use were they to him now? None!

'We have only one hope,' hissed Fitz.

Maya didn't wait for Kreuzer when the doors of the lift finally opened on the car park level. She stepped out on to the red carpet and followed it along the corridor.

It led her through to a waiting room clearly meant to resemble the lounge of some small and exotic airport. Despite the designer trimmings, it was somewhat overly baroque and pretentious. On the other side of the glass wall, another short red carpet led through palm trees to a pick-up point. The parking space was empty, as was the lounge.

Kreuzer caught up with her and surveyed the scene. 'Where's the valet?' he wondered aloud.

'What *is* a valet?'

'The member of staff who brings your car or takes it away.'

A man in a white jacket was walking towards them on the narrow pavement that ran alongside the vehicle lane to the end of the red carpet.

Maya rushed over to him. 'Where were you?' she asked.

'Taking a car away,' he said.

'When?'

'About ten minutes ago,' he said. 'I had to drive it down to the lowest level.'

Maya calculated. That was about the length of time it had taken her to travel up to the suite, search it and come back down again. Long enough for someone to leave the car park unnoticed.

'We need to go back to the video suite,' she told Kreuzer.

'That won't help you much,' the valet said, waving his phone. 'Security called to say they had a blackout down here.'

'I know. Just now?'

The car in whose boot they were imprisoned kept slowing down and accelerating again without ever reaching any great speed. Occasionally it would stop. City traffic.

Jan could feel Fitz's body glued to his, shoulder to collarbone, back to chest and tummy, backside to groin, back of legs to thighs and shins. The cable ties were biting into his wrists and his hands were swollen from lack of blood, his fingertips already numb. He tested whether he was able to move them back and forth. His hands must be touching Fitz's belly, maybe even lower.

'In all that kerfuffle back there they forgot to confiscate my mobile,' whispered Fitz. 'And you must still have yours.'

Jan could indeed feel the slim rectangle in his back pocket.

'Get it out,' Fitz said quietly.

'Very funny.'

'Try.'

Jan fumbled in his pocket and eventually managed to extract the phone. He mustn't let go of it now. In fact, they were almost lying on top of each other, so there was little chance it would slip between them and end up on the floor. He knew the next bit would be the hardest though.

'You need to push it up as far as possible towards my face so I can speak into it,' Fitz said as quietly as he could. 'And before that, you need to dial the number.'

'Which number?'

'Emergency services, you idiot.'

Luckily, the burner was an old model with proper buttons. Jan began to work his bound hands up between his back and Fitz's chest. For the first half of the way it was sufficient to flex his elbows, but then he had to move his shoulders. Not a particularly pleasant sensation. Fitz's chest was a good prop, but still. The higher he levered his hands up behind his back, the more it felt as if his shoulders were about to pop out of their sockets. As if his headache, the pains in his lower belly and the bruises all over his body weren't bad enough!

'I can't get it any higher,' he groaned. The phone must now be somewhere between Fitz's chest and neck. Not high enough. He could talk into it, but he wouldn't understand what the operator said.

'We have to try,' Fitz whispered. 'The second button from the top on the far left is one. The fifth button from the top in the middle is zero. Press one twice and zero once.'

Jan's numb fingertips groped their way across the small bulges.

1 – 1 – 0.

Let's hope this works.

He waited and heard nothing.

'I don't bloody believe it,' Fitz muttered.

'What?'

'Busy,' said Fitz. 'The emergency number is busy!'

'Fucking summit!'

66

'Play it back, please,' Maya said.

The screen reproduced the camera's view of the section of the underground car park outside the VIP lounge. First, a black limousine drew up and a man got out. Suit and tie: a businessman. He handed the keys to the valet, who'd rushed out, and went into the lounge. The valet drove the car away and out of shot, exactly as he'd said. Immediately afterwards, the footage stopped and the monitor went black.

'Very strange,' Maya said.

'It certainly is,' said the operator. He played the video again, frame by frame. 'Did someone sneak up in the camera's blind spot and cover it?'

He played the footage recorded by the other blacked-out camera. 'No, probably not,' he said, 'but I can't be completely sure.'

'Do these cameras often break down?'

'Only very rarely.'

'What an amazing coincidence,' she said.

He ran the recording until the cameras came back on.

'The blackout only lasted about ten minutes,' the operator said.

'Show me the other footage from the car park over the

346

same period,' Maya said. 'The images of the VIP entrance and exit first.'

The man played the footage on the next screen along in his bank of monitors. A black Range Rover arrived, bypassed the barrier and drove into the normal car park. Next came the limo the valet was taking down to the lower deck. Directly afterwards, two Mercedes SUVs entered the VIP area, followed three minutes later by a black Range Rover.

'The same one as before,' Maya said. 'Look at the number plate.'

This time it stopped at the barrier to the VIP car park. An arm reached out of the driver's window and typed in a code that raised the barrier. The car started up again and disappeared into the VIP area. It passed the camera four minutes later on its way out.

After a few more minutes, the Mercedes SUVs took the same route. As with the Range Rover, their tinted windows made it impossible to identify the vehicles' occupants.

'Were they hotel guests?' asked Maya.

The operator entered the number plate into the system. 'They didn't check in here.'

'Could they be accompanying one of your guests without being registered at The Estate or be staying elsewhere?'

'Maybe.'

A minute later, both cameras simultaneously started recording again.

'I don't believe in coincidences this great,' said Maya. She pulled out her mobile and pressed speed dial. 'I need the owners of three vehicles, please.'

'Still busy,' Fitzroy whispered.

'You've got to be joking,' Jan groaned. Fitzroy couldn't

hear a sound from the front of the car. Their five kidnappers weren't particularly chatty, which meant that Fitzroy and Jan had to talk even more quietly.

The vehicle negotiated a fairly bumpy stretch of road, jolting Fitzroy this way and that. He prayed that the mobile wouldn't slip from Jan's grasp.

'Let's try something else,' he mumbled and told Jan which combination of numbers to dial. He could feel Jan's fingers against his chest. They'd see if the phone was close enough to his ear to hear the voices on the other end of the line.

Jan's hand stopped moving. The dialling tone, far away. The car slowed down. Where were they going?

Fitzroy heard a muffled voice answer the phone.

'Hi, this is Kim. Who—'

'Hello, Kim? Can you hear me? It's Fitzroy,' he whispered.

'Fitzroy, is that you?'

He had to speak quietly. He had only one go at this. 'Yes. Listen closely. Jan, Jeanne and I are trapped in the boot of a black Range Rover.' He gave Kim its number plate.

Thank you, dear God or my genes or whoever's responsible, that my memory for numbers is so good!

'Are you kidding me?'

'Take down this number plate and call the police. Tell them they need to pass it on to the officers investigating the deaths of Herbert Thompson and Will Cantor. We've been kidnapped by their murderers.' He repeated the vehicle's registration.

'You want me to cooperate with the police?'

'For hell's sake, yes!'

'Will who?'

'Cantor. Did you get the number?'

'What the fuck are you doing?' a voice yelled over Fitzroy's head. Someone tore open the flaps, and light flooded into the boot.

Jan covered Fitzroy's chest and stomach with his hands, and at the same time he let out a loud yelp and attempted to sit up. 'I'm suffocating in here!'

Fitzroy felt the mobile slip down his thighs and tumble to the floor.

'Shut up!' the man roared, shoving Jan's head back down into the boot. The kid had just enough time to note that the car had stopped at a junction before a large hand in a dark grey glove closed the flaps again.

67

'You're kidding me,' Maya said into her mobile. 'Play me the phone call again.'

Her colleague at police headquarters ran the recording again.

A woman's voice: '110, what can we—'

A second woman's voice, higher pitched and younger: 'I've been told to give a message to the investigators in the Herbert Thompson and Will Cantor case.'

Will Cantor. His name hasn't been made public yet.

'Fitzroy Peel, Jan Wutte and Jeanne Dalli claim they've been kidnapped by the men who murdered Herbert Thompson and Will Cantor. They're in a black Range Rover.' She gave the vehicle's number plate.

Maya felt as if she'd been punched in the stomach. She put her hand over the microphone and whispered urgently, 'Get me the number plate of that Range Rover!' to the operator studying his screen while she listened to the emergency call.

First voice: 'Your name?'

Second voice: 'I know you're recording this call. I've given you all the information you need, now get on and do your job.'

Click.

The monitor showed a picture of the back of the Range Rover. The number plate was identical to the one the woman had taken down.

'Launch a manhunt!' Maya shouted into the phone. 'You've got the vehicle number, so go!'

'Maya,' said her colleague on the other end of the line, 'it just sounded like a prank call. I thought I'd better play it safe and call—'

'It may not be a prank,' Maya said coolly. 'They know information that's not yet in the public domain. They must realize that, which is why they told us. It's a signal. I told you to launch a manhunt. Tell the entire force to look out for that Range Rover and stop it getting away.'

There was a crackle and a man's voice came on the line. Deputy Superintendent Köstritz. What was he doing there? Maya shot Jörn a dirty look. Had he snitched on her for how she'd behaved at the hotel?

'Do you know what we've got on our hands, Paritta?' he barked into the phone. 'At least a million protesters have swamped the city. Every single one of your colleagues is on duty protecting the summit!'

'Their primary duty is to protect our own citizens,' Maya countered. 'Herbert Thompson was scheduled to make one of the opening speeches.' She had to play hardball with Köstritz. 'Who knows what his killers are planning next?'

'You mean—'

'Run the number plate through the system at least. That's not too much to ask, is it?'

More crackling.

'OK,' sighed the woman, who was now back on the line.

Maya imagined Köstritz standing next to her, listening to the speakerphone with smoke coming out of his ears. 'If you think . . .'

'I don't think anything – I'm telling you. Get a move on! And find out who made that call while you're about it.'

68

Jochen Fürst was hating this assignment. He'd been dispatched to Berlin from Bavaria especially for the summit, along with tens of thousands of colleagues from other parts of the country. Towns and villages throughout the republic had been left with only skeleton staff, all because a handful of politicians and billionaires felt like playing geopolitics and a few other people fancied demonstrating.

Jochen would have loved to confront them. He'd have beaten those pathetic revolutionary songs and moronic slogans right out of their heads. Special units had even been called in from other countries. Mitte was where it was going to go down, where the action was.

In fact, the action was everywhere bar where he was right now. He, five Bavarian colleagues and two Berliners were, for inexplicable reasons, hanging around on Kantstrasse near the showground in the former western half of the city. There was nothing happening on the dual carriageway divided by a green central reservation. Even the traffic seemed to have opted for a different route, with only the occasional car to liven things up.

He couldn't understand why they were there. Orders. Apparently, groups of demonstrators might lose their way and end up out here. How? According to the latest reports, the demonstrators were at least four miles away.

The police officers swapped anecdotes of previous assignments and boasted about their alleged feats of heroism and womanizing. There were no women present, as was only right.

The crackle of static or of an imminent announcement came over the radio.

'Come in, GKP 27.'

These stupid summit codenames. Theirs was GKP 27. Their commander, a tough guy with a crew cut, answered.

'A search is on for a black Range Rover.' The control at headquarters gave its number plate. 'Traffic cameras have picked it up heading your way on Kantstrasse, still about three hundred yards from you.'

Their commander repeated the information and requested further instruction.

'Stop the vehicle. Check all papers.'

Three hundred yards – less by now. A few small cars and light lorries passed them, then a black SUV appeared in the distance.

The police driver turned on the flashing blue light and steered the van a few yards from their parking space into the middle of the road so that it was perpendicular to the oncoming vehicle and blocking most of both lanes. Jochen and the others jumped out and took up positions. Four of them walked towards the Range Rover on either side of the road and had passed the SUV before it had even stopped.

The Range Rover came to a juddering halt before the barricade. Jochen could make out five heavily built men in dark grey clothing inside, all with close-cropped hair and wraparound shades. Security guards, probably. None of them moved. The driver kept his hands in full view on the steering wheel, but the Bavarian placed his hand on the handle of his pistol just in case.

Their commander walked up to the driver's door. The window slid open silently, and the driver looked at him and asked with a friendly smile, 'What's up, mate?'

El sized up the situation at a glance. Four officers in front, four behind. Seven of them had their hands on their weapons, one was walking back along the carriageway to warn approaching traffic. The street ahead was blocked. Between them and the two opposite lanes lay a central reservation with small trees planted along it, although that didn't represent an insurmountable challenge for the Range Rover. A small car was closing on them from behind, and the police officer stopped it thirty feet away with an outstretched hand. There was another vehicle behind that one. The traffic on the other side of the central green strip was flowing freely into the city centre.

'What can we do for you?' Jack asked the police officer, looking down at him through the open window of the car.

'ID and car registration documents, please,' the man said, peering at the covered boot space behind Sam, Rob and Bell, who were sitting on the back seat.

Jack handed him the papers, while the police officer kept a close eye on the others as they rummaged in their trouser and shirt pockets for their ID cards. El collected the cards and passed them over to Jack, who offered them to the police commander. The man was still examining the registration documents for the car, but he accepted the ID cards and walked around to the front of the vehicle to check the licence plate. He came back, studied El's papers and then glanced up at El.

'This is you?'

'Yep.'

Same procedure with all the others.

'Get out of the car, please,' the police officer asked.

This was a critical moment. Jack could still throw the car into reverse, step on the accelerator and drive off over the central reservation, while the rest of them drew their weapons and used them if need be. They'd discussed the necessary signal when they saw the police van, its blue lights flashing, blocking the road ahead.

The question was: how far would they get? And what would they do with their passengers? Their mission was to do away with them, but, just as with Thompson and Cantor the night before, they were to make it look like an accident. They didn't want to attract any more attention, and that had just become a lot more complicated.

If in doubt, their orders were to abort the mission.

If they got out of the car, their chances of escaping were nil. And if the police got it into their minds to search the car . . . How come they'd decided to stop the Range Rover in any case?

The boot was quiet. Had their guests twigged?

The papers the policeman was holding were of course fakes, the identities borrowed, but sooner or later the police would find their faces in their database and match them to the right profiles. By that time, El and the others could be long gone.

El coughed twice. That was the signal.

The car suddenly started to reverse in Jochen's direction. A squeal of rubber, a streak of black on the asphalt. The man at the wheel was staring intently at the rear-view mirror. The Range Rover picked up speed, sped over the kerb of the central reservation and slalomed between two trees towards

Jochen and the opposite carriageway. He was the last man able to stop them.

His response was immediate. He sprinted on to the grassy strip and aimed his gun at the car, which was trying desperately to maintain a straight course on the cambered central reservation. A few of his colleagues ran on to the other side of the road where they stopped the traffic and levelled their weapons at the fugitives, but they couldn't risk shooting – the chances of hitting a bystander or a colleague were simply too high.

Jochen was faced with the same choice. Should he let the men get away? The car was heading towards him at speed, its engine wailing. He aimed at the right-hand rear wheel and pulled the trigger.

Bang.

Bangbangbang.

Shit, he'd missed! The car sped past him. He spun round and tried again. The car was getting further and further away. He'd failed.

All of a sudden, the Range Rover started to career across the two lanes without losing speed. The driver regained control of the vehicle and put his foot to the floor again. An arm appeared from the front passenger's window and took aim at the other police officers by the van. Jochen couldn't tell if the guy was actually shooting, but he dived for cover behind a parked car anyway. Why had no one warned them that these guys were dangerous? He turned and took fresh aim, joined now by other policemen firing volleys of bullets at the SUV.

There was a colossal din in the distance as the Range Rover scraped past waiting cars in the left-hand lane and smashed into parked vehicles on the right. Screaming passengers from the waiting cars leaped out on to the road in panic or ducked down into the footwells. The windscreen shattered on the Range Rover and the car swerved from side to side before ramming rear first into a parked car. It twisted on its own axis, causing the tailgate to fly open, and kept on spinning until its front bumper crashed into a SUV. The tyres screeched and smoked as the driver sought to break free, but this time he was trapped by splintered metal. Jochen peered down the barrel of his pistol at the Range Rover as it came to a standstill at an angle to them.

69

Jeanne was almost hurled out of the boot when the tailgate burst open. Her feet were dangling in mid-air, but now they touched the asphalt, and she used all her strength to lever herself upright. Jumping out, she ducked behind the nearest car and stayed in cover there. All around her people were screaming, individual figures ran across the pavement doubled over and took shelter in doorways, cars pulled up wherever they happened to be on the street, and there was an atmosphere of complete chaos in which no one paid attention to anyone else, intent only on saving their own skin. Fitz had followed her lead, but Jan was still writhing around in the boot of the Range Rover before he eventually found his footing and, catching sight of them, dashed over to where they crouched, his hair a tousled mess.

Jeanne spotted the fleeing hitmen away to her right. One of them spun round and fired at them, although the bullet was probably meant for the police.

At least eighty yards away to Jeanne's left, a posse of policemen were huddled low behind parked and stopped cars. Their guns were trained on the Range Rover and they were all yelling at one another, then suddenly started shooting.

The rear of the SUV was facing diagonally away from

them and was close to the line of parked cars, so there was no way they could have seen Jan, Fitz and Jeanne. Bullets thudded into the bodywork of the Range Rover as well as nearby cars.

While the other killers were making good their escape, one of them turned and fired off several shots in return as he ran before catching up with the others.

'Are they all out of their minds?' Jan cried. 'They're going to hit someone!'

It was some time before a shouted order brought the gun battle to an end.

'For hell's sake, stop shooting!' Jeanne heard a police officer roar in the distance.

'Keep down,' Fitz hissed. 'They'll have no idea who we are if we stand up now, and I don't fancy getting my head blown off by a trigger-happy Rambo.'

The cable ties were slicing into Jeanne's wrists. 'Yeah, not to mention we'll be in trouble if they order us to put our hands up,' she joked.

The policemen shouted something, but none of them moved.

'What now?' Jeanne asked.

'Let's get out of here,' said Jan.

In the chaos, no one had noticed the three figures squatting between two cars. Keeping low, Jan darted into a doorway.

'Wait there!' hissed Fitz, following him, with Jeanne hot on his heels. 'Maybe it's all a big misunderstanding.'

'Yeah, one that might have killed us,' Jan said.

'Where are you going?' called Fitzroy as Jan scurried from one doorway to the next, away from the police. Jeanne could hear sirens in the distance. Stunned bystanders couldn't figure out where to look or to hide.

'We should join forces with the police,' Fitz hissed, but this didn't stop him running after Jan.

'The police just riddled that Range Rover with bullets,' Jan argued, 'and we could've still been inside. I'm not staying here another second.'

He did have a point, Jeanne thought, as much as she could think amid the wreckage and the screaming. Everything seemed to be happening all at the same time – a total mess no one would be later capable of describing with any accuracy.

'There's no way I'm trusting the police after this,' Jan continued. 'What if it wasn't our call that triggered the police intervention? Holden's security team must've raised the alarm immediately after the attack in the car park. Maybe the police are after those killers for kidnapping people, but they still want us for burglary.' He quickened his pace. 'Whichever way, I'm not sticking around to find out.'

A few of Jochen's colleagues were standing in the middle of the road, while others were sheltering along the verges behind waiting cars whose panic-stricken occupants were cowering on the floor. At first sight the line of vehicles looked as deserted as in a scene from a zombie apocalypse movie.

The Bavarian lagged a little behind the first police officers to reach the empty Range Rover. They gave it a quick once-over, but by this time the men in dark clothing were mere specks in the distance; they were surprisingly fast for their size and build. These were no ordinary security guards, drawn from a pool of the great unemployed, ageing rockers and gym bunnies. Ex-military, he reckoned – professionally trained and seriously tough.

He glanced inside the Range Rover. The broken glass of the shattered windscreen lay in a sea of shards on the front seats and floor. The tailgate window was scattered all over the boot. All five doors including the tailgate were open. There were two bullet holes in the roof, and one in the C-pillar. He couldn't spot any others at the moment, but they could do a closer inspection later.

He looked back at their own van. One policeman was on the radio and another was walking along the line of traffic, checking for collateral damage. They'd get an earful for engaging in a shoot-out among innocent bystanders. Jochen had started it, and he was damned if he wasn't going to end it. He'd seen all he needed to here. He set off after the fugitives.

El was running along the empty carriageway, his four comrades keeping pace alongside him. He could feel his restless night in his bones, but had no concerns regarding his fitness. He glanced over his shoulder. Six police officers were pursuing them at varying distances and speeds. Two of them had fairly big beer bellies to haul around so they'd soon give up. Which left four against five. He assessed the situation. They were coming to a crossroads.

'Crossroads,' he panted into his headset. 'Sam and Rob, go left, Jack and Bell straight ahead and I'll take a right. Split up as soon as possible.'

The policemen weren't gaining on them. The two overweight men were already slackening their pace. El turned right. The street ahead was lined with shops and offices. There were quite a few pedestrians on the pavements and a moderate amount of traffic on the road. The police wouldn't dare fire their guns along here.

El shoved his way through the crowd, but his pumping

elbows barely registered the impact as he barged people aside. Another glance over his shoulder. There was only one policeman on his tail now, and he was a good twenty yards back. Even after a bad night's sleep, El was still fit enough to toy with the man and eventually outrun him. He wasn't planning to do that though. He didn't know how much stamina the man had and how many reinforcements, if any, he might be able to call upon at key moments. He couldn't afford to take any chances.

This whole job had been a disaster. It never rains but it pours . . .

'Stop!' his pursuer shouted. 'Police!'

Bystanders looked round in surprise, but made way for El rather than attempting to block his path. El slackened his pace even further. The policeman closed the gap.

'Stay right where you are!' The officer was only eight yards behind him now.

Suddenly El stopped dead, spun round and charged the man. They collided before the officer could react, and El felled him with a punch to the temple. A second blow knocked the man out cold. Screaming passers-by took to their heels, while he disarmed the man and quickly bound his hands and feet with two cable ties. The whole operation had taken no more than five seconds. He leaped to his feet and ran back to the junction he'd crossed moments earlier.

In the other two streets he could see police officers chasing his team members into the distance. The whole area was gridlocked, and honking horns filled the air in the road where the Range Rover had crashed. He could see the black SUV about a hundred yards away and the flashing lights of the police van beyond it. He was aware the bystanders would be watching him and might already have alerted the police.

El ran back towards the scene of the shoot-out and slipped into the nearest doorway from which he could survey the scene. None of the eyewitnesses to his attack on the policeman appeared to have followed him.

Time for a change of outfit. He removed his shirt, flipped it inside out to display the orange side and put it back on again, this time leaving it hanging outside his trousers rather than tucking it in. The team's reversible clothing was designed for precisely this kind of situation. From the hip pocket of his cargo trousers he pulled a mint-green baseball cap with coloured piping along the edges and emblazoned with the logo of a well-known brand. All that remained of the former security man were the grey trousers. An old trick. If you don't want to stand out, do something that makes you stand out, as no one will imagine you're hiding in broad daylight.

Thus camouflaged, he ventured across the street and planted himself in another doorway that gave him a better view of the Range Rover. He couldn't stay here for ever, but maybe he'd catch a glimpse of the three passengers in the boot the police had strafed so ruthlessly.

70

'The men slipped through the net and are on the run,' the field commander told Maya over the phone. 'We're dealing with it.'

'Slipped through the net?' Maya asked incredulously. 'How is that even possible?' She'd just left The Estate and was wondering where to head next.

'First by car, and then on foot. No one warned us they were armed.'

'No one warned you?' Maya had informed control all right, so why hadn't their colleagues passed on the message? 'What happened to the people they'd supposedly abducted?'

'What do you mean?'

'The vehicle was apparently carrying three kidnapped passengers. Did you find or free anyone?'

'No, I didn't see a soul. My men advanced as far as the vehicle and then pursued the fugitives. I'll take a closer look, but as far as I can tell from here, the car's empty.'

'How many fugitives were there?'

'Five, according to first reports. All of them wearing dark grey or black clothing.'

Maya heard him address a second person but couldn't make out another word until the man came back on the line.

'I'm standing next to the Range Rover now with a

colleague who's been taking care of the bystanders. The car, including the boot, is empty.'

Maya suppressed her urge to swear. 'Can you see two men and a woman nearby? One of the men is pretty tall, and the woman's very attractive.'

'There are a few people standing around,' the policeman said, 'but none fitting that precise description.'

Maya let out a long silent scream.

'Running away will only make us seem more suspicious,' said Fitzroy. 'And having our hands tied definitely will.' He'd begun to run the cable ties up and down the sharp edge of a metal plate. They were huddled with their backs to the wooden door of a building about two hundred yards from the wrecked car. 'We should let the police do their job. The hotel must have CCTV footage of our abduction.'

'At least our kidnappers seem to be gone for now,' said Jeanne. 'So you think they were the same men who murdered Thompson and Will?'

'Yeah,' said Fitzroy. 'Ha, done it!' He rubbed the spots on his freed wrists where the cable ties had gouged out dark red furrows.

'Can you do mine?' begged Jeanne.

'Just a second.' Fitzroy went over to the kerb and returned with a jagged piece of glass, then set about slicing through Jeanne's shackles.

'Holden's security detail never intended to take us to the police,' Jan said.

'You've got to be kidding!' cried Jeanne. 'Anyway, if Ted really was behind this, why were we kidnapped by a different crew?'

'Maybe because someone else got wind of the speech and the manuscript?'

'That sounds absurd to me. Oh, thanks.'

While Jeanne was rubbing her wounds, Fitzroy attacked the cable ties around Jan's wrists and realized that the kid was still clutching the mobile.

'You managed to grab the burner in the midst of all that chaos?' he said with some admiration.

'I thought it might come in handy.'

'I expect you're going to lose your job,' Fitzroy said to Jeanne as he hacked away at Jan's bindings.

'Not only that,' she mumbled. 'One thing's clear though. We've got to find out who gave the orders to the men in the Range Rover.'

'Oh, not that again,' groaned Fitzroy. 'The last time I got sucked into something like this, I missed a lucrative poker game, had to sprint across a roof sixty feet up—'

'Fifty feet,' Jan corrected him.

'Oh yeah, those ten feet would've made a massive difference if we'd fallen off. Carry on if you like, but count me out.'

'There's no way the police are going to listen to us after the things we got up to last night,' Jan insisted. 'They'll clap us in jail until the demos are over. They won't have time to deal with us beforehand.'

Fitzroy paused.

'Get on with it,' Jan demanded crossly, holding up his bound hands, 'and focus instead on to how to find those guys. All we've got is a number plate.'

'We have to go back to the hotel,' Jeanne said, relieving Fitz of the shard of glass so she could finish off his work.

'Oh, I'm sure they'll be delighted to give you the information,' Fitzroy scoffed. 'I bet Mitch is waiting there with the next set of cable ties. Along with those police inspectors investigating how we were kidnapped, not to mention how we managed to break into Will's room and all the rest of it.'

'Got a better idea?' she shot back, marching off. Jan stalked after her, nursing his swollen wrists.

'Sam, Rob, Bell, Jack,' El whispered into his headset. 'How are things your end?'

'I've lost mine,' Rob said.

'Ditto,' Jack replied, breathing heavily.

'Mine gave up,' Bell reported.

El was concentrating on the vehicle in front. He was a few cars behind the taxi that Fitz, Jan and Jeanne had flagged down a couple of blocks away from the accident. Luckily, El had managed to hail one too.

'Good. I shook mine off too and I'm back on the trail of our targets. They're in a taxi heading for the centre. I'm following them in another taxi. Make your way into the city and I'll give you a precise location as soon as I've got one. How about you, Sam?'

El waited for an answer. The driver stuck religiously to his instructions to keep a safe distance behind the other cab. The dense traffic and large number of other taxis made this a fairly straightforward task.

'Let me hear you, Sam.'

Jörn had to make a detour to avoid the demonstrations, blockades and traffic jams. Flashing lights on and siren blaring, he raced through the streets of Berlin towards Checkpoint Charlie, from where he swung west to give a wide berth to Potsdamer Platz and the Tiergarten.

The colleague who'd just reported from the empty Range Rover radioed them again. 'We've got one,' he said breathlessly.

'One what?' asked Maya.

'One of the occupants of the Range Rover.'

The first good news she'd had since this whole bloody case began.

'Who is it?'

'He's not carrying any papers, but he does have a pistol.'

'Are you and your team OK?'

'One man injured, but not critically.'

'That's bad news, but also good. I'm on my way. Where are you exactly?'

71

'OK, we do as we agreed,' said Jeanne as she got out of the
taxi in front of the hotel. She could hear a faint noise like
thunder in the distance, even though the demonstration was
half a mile away. Hundreds of thousands of voices, mingled
with music, like ocean waves breaking on a beach. It was
broken only by the buzz of a helicopter circling overhead.

Fitzroy and Jan melted into the crowd on the pavement,
while Jeanne passed through the security checks outside the
entrance to the hotel. She wasn't made to wait and the
guards didn't ask her any questions.

There was no way she could carry out her plan in her current state, so she hurried to the lift and took it to the seventh
floor. Stepping out, she checked the hallway. There was no
one in sight.

Glancing in the mirror, she looked as though she'd been
dragged through a hedge backwards. She slipped out of her
suit and blouse, went into the bathroom, quickly washed her
face with a damp towel and put on some perfume, a fresh
blouse and a different suit. A couple of strokes of the comb
would have to do. Her job had taught her to be extremely fast
and efficient in specific situations, one of which was freshen-
ing up. She opened the safe, took a few banknotes from the
envelope of cash she kept there and grabbed the phone she'd

left on the sofa. It wasn't the one she'd used to photograph Thompson's notes for his speech, unfortunately.

Less than ten minutes after entering her suite, she was striding across the foyer towards reception. Giving her name and room number to one of the young women behind the desk, she announced, 'I'd like to speak to the hotel manager, please.'

The woman gave her an uncertain smile before picking up the phone. Jeanne paid close attention to what was said. If she got the slightest impression that the police were searching for her, she'd leave the hotel immediately. Obviously, there was no way she could know whether the hotel and the police had agreed on some innocuous code word, but she had to risk it.

'There's a guest who'd like to speak to you,' the receptionist said into the phone. That certainly sounded harmless enough.

The young woman hung up, smiled at Jeanne again and said, 'I hope you don't mind waiting. Herr Kreuzer will be with you in a minute or two.'

'I can't believe I'm doing this,' Fitzroy muttered. They were walking down the sloping entrance ramp into the underground car park at the back of the building. They passed a long line of cars, most of them expensive, before a left-hand bend offered them the choice of following the ramp into the regular car park or continuing straight ahead to a barrier blocking access to the VIP area. Opting for the latter, they stopped at the barrier and peered around a corner at the unattended glass-walled lounge at the end of the palm-lined red carpet.

'There's no one there,' Fitzroy said in a whisper.

'An hour ago, several security guards were overpowered and tied up and we were kidnapped, and the police have already wrapped up their forensic investigation and questioning?' said Jan.

'Maybe they never even started.'

'Well, it's all down to us then,' said Jan, squeezing around the end of the barrier.

'I've no idea what you're talking about,' the manager said. 'You're saying there was a holdup in our car park?'

He'd stepped out from behind reception and ushered her towards one of the large pillars in the lobby where he listened to her with his head bowed meekly like a priest.

'Just over an hour ago,' Jeanne confirmed. 'You have security cameras down there – I saw the warning signs everywhere. Your staff must have witnessed it.'

'I can't comment, unfortunately,' said the man, who'd introduced himself as Edwin Kreuzer. 'And even if it happened to be true, I could only discuss it with the police.'

'If it happened to be true? So you don't have any video?'

'No comment.'

The man was visibly agitated. Jeanne knew his kind – a subservient employee and yes-man who hated nothing more than attracting attention.

'*I* was one of the people attacked. *Me* – one of your guests!' Anyone could make this claim, of course, especially if there was genuinely no footage of the incident.

'T-that, um . . .' stammered Kreuzer before hastily regaining his composure. 'Have you reported it to the police?'

'Should I infer from that that the police have not yet been to investigate?'

'I haven't seen anyone doing the forensics or questioning witnesses,' the valet explained with a frown. 'Herr Kreuzer did bring this one plainclothes policewoman down here, and she asked me where I'd been after taking a car down to the bottom level.'

'A woman, you say?' asked Fitzroy, pressing another twenty-euro note into the valet's palm. 'What kind of woman?'

'No idea,' the valet said with a shrug. 'She was with the manager. Must've been about an hour ago.'

'So you weren't here the whole time then?'

'Most of the time I was, sometimes not.'

'What did the woman look like?' Jan asked. Another twenty euros from Fitz.

'Um, pretty normal. Short, sporty. Mid-forties. Ponytail.'

Fitz could hazard a guess as to the identity of this mystery woman.

'Nothing,' said Jeanne. 'There's nothing in the CCTV footage and some of the cameras were down.' They'd met up again in a dark doorway near the hotel.

'Fantastic security arrangements,' Fitzroy said. 'The valet also claims he saw nothing. The police did pay the hotel a visit though. Just that one policewoman, mind.'

'Either they're all in cahoots,' said Jan, 'or someone deliberately lured the valet away and manipulated the videos to make sure there were no witnesses.'

'That would take a heap of organization,' Fitzroy objected, 'and wouldn't probably be that easy to pull off.'

'Got a better explanation?'

'And even if it were true,' said Jeanne, 'how were Mitch and his men able to free themselves quickly enough that neither the valet nor the policewoman came across them?' She shook her head as she pondered this question.

'Maybe they weren't really overpowered after all?' Jan suggested.

'It's no use,' she muttered, pulling herself up to her full height. 'There's no other way.'

'What are you planning to do?'

'Sort out a particular relationship,' she said.

Jeanne Dalli strode away. El and Bell, who'd joined him in the meantime, watched her go from the other side of the street. The traffic was moving slowly now, with parts of the road as well as the pavements full of people streaming towards the demonstration.

The Samaritan and the gambler remained behind, deep in conversation.

'Stick with her,' El ordered.

Bell followed the woman, who was heading for the Brandenburg Gate. To the conference, or maybe to the demo? Probably not the latter, by his reckoning.

The gambler was making a phone call. He and the Samaritan joined the crowd marching in the direction of the demonstration, although the kid kept glancing nervously over his shoulder.

Quite right, kid, thought El, keeping some distance away from them and ducking behind the other marchers. *I have a job to do and I'm going to do it.*

Her colleagues in uniform had cordoned off the section of the Windscheidstrasse with red-and-white tape, and tailbacks were already forming on both sides. A few cars were doing U-turns and heading back the way they'd come on the other carriageway in search of an alternative route along side streets.

Four police officers were gathered around a bundle of clothes on the pavement. An emergency doctor and a paramedic were attending to two policemen a little way off.

The man who had been arrested was lying on his front with his hands cuffed behind his back. Even in this helpless position he looked dangerous. He was wearing dark grey cargo trousers and a purple paisley shirt stretched taut by enough ripped muscles for three men. *Honestly, some people's taste in fashion.*

'Sit him up,' she asked her colleagues.

They grabbed hold of the man's upper arms and hauled him into a sitting position. He looked as if he ate kittens for breakfast.

'He won't say a word,' said the colleague she'd talked to on the phone. His name was Tibor.

The constrained man briefly assessed Maya through narrowed eyes in his meaty face, then returned to staring through the legs of his guards with a bored look. His body, attitude and gaze were not those of a run-of-the-mill bodybuilder. This man had served in the forces, probably special services. There'd be no hope of making him talk if he'd set his mind against it.

'No ID,' said Tibor, holding up two plastic bags with their contents. 'A pistol and a mobile phone with an earpiece. A burner, I reckon. We're in the process of running his fingerprints and doing facial recognition.'

Maya gestured to him to hand over the mobile. An old-fashioned pre-smartphone model. She'd had one ten years ago. She tested the 'on' button and the display lit up. No passcode. Overconfident, or unprofessional. She fiddled around with it until she found the list of outgoing calls. The man had dialled only one number.

She rang headquarters. 'I need the owner of the mobile with the following number, please,' she said before reading it out, digit by digit. 'Plus where the phone is now, if at all possible, and I need it fast – very fast. It's linked to the

Thompson investigation.' To Tibor, she said, 'I'll hang on to this for the time being. And what about the Range Rover?'

'Just around the corner.'

There were more traffic jams caused by another cordoned-off section of road. Her mobile buzzed in her pocket. She didn't recognize the number.

'Hello, Paritta.'

'This is Edwin Kreuzer at The Estate. I thought you'd be interested to hear that Jan Wutte and Fitzroy Peel were just at the hotel.'

Maya held her breath for a second before releasing the air from her lungs very slowly. 'What do you mean, *were*?' She could have throttled the man over the phone.

'The video operators told me as soon as they spotted the two of them down in the car park, but they'd disappeared again by the time I got there with security.'

'Any idea where they went?'

'No, we don't have any cameras outside. You'll have to ask your colleagues. Speaking of cameras, Ms Dalli asked to see me around the same time and claimed she'd been assaulted and kidnapped, also in our car park. She wanted to see the CCTV footage from down there. The same footage you watched after inspecting her suite.'

Maya tried hard not to groan out loud. 'And I bet she's left too now . . .'

'She left the hotel a few minutes ago.'

'Why only call me now?'

'I have plenty of other things on my hands,' he said defensively. 'You're a full-time troubleshooter as a hotel manager.'

Try my job some time!

'I don't expect you know where Ms Dalli was heading next?'

'I'm sorry, no.'

'Do your CCTV cameras cover the area outside the front doors of the hotel?'

'Only the part with the drive and the hotel taxi rank nearest to the entrance. That's on private property.'

72

Helicopters thrummed overhead. Next to the Branden-burg Gate, following the line which had once divided East and West Berlin, an impenetrable row of police officers stood helmet to helmet, shoulder to shoulder and shield to shield, to keep the crowd away from the conference area around Pariser Platz.

Not far from the police cordon, a rock band was playing on the trailer beds of two giant lorries that had been parked side by side to make a stage. From time to time the music even drowned out the roar of helicopter engines.

'*El pueblo unido* . . .' they sang.

'*Jamás será vencido!*' hundreds of thousands of voices replied in unison. Many people were reading the words on their phones.

Fitzroy recognized it as the chorus of the Chilean resist-ance's chant from the seventies, although he didn't know this rock version with its smatterings of Russian and the slightly altered lyrics.

They were still about two hundred yards from the stage and just passing between the Holocaust Memorial to the right and the Tiergarten to the left. At first he could see only an arm waving to him between raised fists. Fitzroy had retrieved the burner from Jan and was still holding it up to his ear, but he waved back. They burrowed their way through the dancing, singing masses – was this a demo or a party? – to Kim and Nida.

'Look at this!' Kim shouted. They were standing near the front of the demo at the edge of a smaller platform dotted with laptops, computers, megaphones, microphones and technical gear. Fitzroy caught sight of the Argentinian woman from the previous night. Amistad.

'We won't be able to identify the number plate until after the demo,' Kim said. 'Only a very few specialists can do that kind of search.'

'It's pretty urgent!' Jan yelled.

'Did someone really kidnap you?' Nida shouted.

'Yeah,' Fitzroy replied, 'but we escaped.'

'Thank God nothing happened to you. Did the police catch them?'

'No idea.'

'That's why we need the information about the number plate as quickly as possible,' said Jan. 'It'll be too late after the demo.'

'Where's your gran?' Fitz asked Kim.

'With some friends of hers. Old trade unionists.'

Amistad had spotted them and was beckoning to them. Nida and Kim guided Fitzroy and Jan to the platform.

'Are you the ones who read Thompson's manuscript?' Amistad asked. 'The photos of those few pages and your scribbled notes were fascinating. Have you got the rest?'

'Unfortunately not.'

'Why?'

'It's a long story.'

The band wound up their show with one final drumroll and then trooped off the stage at the foot of the Brandenburg Gate to the applause of hundreds of thousands of people.

'Listen,' Jan began, but Amistad got there before him.

'That's a pity, although the acknowledgements to the photos have led us to a number of other interesting articles. Some of my team are currently looking into them.'

'*Docteur!*' she cried suddenly, grabbing a man who was standing near by on the platform. A lanky bearded guy with a long plait, twinkling eyes and a jacket over his T-shirt, he reminded Jan of the Spanish Podemos leader.

'These are the people,' was her only introduction. 'And this is Marius or rather Mari-yoos. He's French.'

'You've really landed a scoop with your farmers' fable and the photos,' Marius cried, sitting down so that his legs dangled over the edge of the platform. 'We've already come up with a little software program that enables us to try out some fun experiments. Look at this.'

Marius held out his mobile to show them a colour version of Fitz's sketch of the village with a matrix underneath it. 'You can use this to set a range of starting quantities of wheat for each of the four farmers, various annual growth rates and different rates of distribution. The individual fortunes of the four farmers vary accordingly, and you can play it out over forty years. It's a simplified representation of how a society can generate and distribute wealth. That was the idea, right?'

'I guess so,' Fitzroy said. '*One* of the ideas.' Someone had drawn very swiftly the correct conclusions from a mere handful of images. Smart people, and fast workers too. This whole thing seemed much better organized than your average demonstration.

Fitzroy tested Marius's game by typing and swiping. It was fun.

'Growth, growth, growth!' Kim burst out after listening to their talk. 'I can't stand that word any longer. We consume and consume as if we had three planets at our disposal, and still you talk about growth. There are limits to any kind of growth.'

'Hear, hear,' said Nida, pointing to the screen of her phone. The various newsfeeds all reported panic on the stock exchanges and statements from worried CEOs and politicians. 'Anyway, it looks more like we're in for a massive crash than for continued growth.'

'But it'll just start all over again regardless,' Kim complained. 'Cycles of boom and bust.'

'Oh, Kim,' Marius sighed. 'Two hundred years ago, good old Malthus thought demographic growth would plunge humanity into misery. That never happened because he underestimated technological and social progress.'

'So you believe we can simply carry on as before?' Kim sneered. 'Plundering our planet without a second thought? Oh, might I have forgotten to mention that we only have this one?'

'That's not what I'm saying,' Marius replied. 'I'm saying we'll come up with solutions.'

'What about the climate crisis?' Kim snorted.

Up on the stage, a woman at the mic was announcing the next band.

'Maybe this could be a solution,' Fitz said, intervening. 'The studies by the London Mathematical Laboratory show that there are different ways of channelling individual and overall growth. There's a whole passage in Thompson and Cantor's paper that explains how it can be achieved. No growth in the overall economy, while individual prosperity continues to rise.'

'That's like squaring the circle,' Kim exclaimed.

'No, it's not,' said Fitzroy, 'it's maths.'

'That's why we need to see the manuscript,' said Marius.

'Someone over there might well have it,' said Fitz, nodding towards Pariser Platz. 'Not that they'd want to see it published.'

'Someone at the summit? Now there's a surprise.'

'Yep.'

'You think you can really get somewhere in there?'

'We need to ask someone a few questions.'

'It might just be possible, but you'll need to get a move on.'

Jeanne reached the security checkpoint in Hannah-Arendt-Strasse. By now almost all the participants were listening to the first speeches at the opening ceremony.

She stepped forward to the makeshift counter behind which a welcoming committee of a dozen young people in dark suits were waiting by their computers. Off to one side were ten metal gates guarded by heavily armed police officers in bulletproof vests and helmets. This was one of eight official entrances.

Jeanne presented her badge to a young woman. 'Jeanne Dalli,' she said. 'My name's on the list of participants.'

The woman studied the plastic badge and then the screen in front of her. She frowned. 'I'm sorry, but your access has been cancelled.'

'Cancelled?' said Jeanne. 'Why?'

She wasn't going to ring Ted to sort this out, but how about George? On second thoughts, it was probably better not to contact anyone close to Ted right now.

'It doesn't say here,' the woman answered, giving Jeanne a sceptical look. It might be time to leave before the woman thought of reporting her to the police.

'Arrive a few minutes late and . . .' She grabbed her badge. 'In that case . . .' She turned on her heel and walked quickly away but with her head held high. There was a burning sensation in the pit of her stomach.

Jan and Fitz hurried breathlessly after Amistad. Yet more jogging after such a trying night and testing morning. What next?

Amistad had led them on a long detour out of the mass of demonstrators and around the back of Pariser Platz. There were police blocks set up on Mauerstrasse and Behrenstrasse. Long barricades consisting of steel barriers, tank traps, police and military vehicles, water cannons and whole squads of riot police. There was probably a sniper on every roof. Jan felt queasy. In this area there was only the occasional wandering demonstrator to be seen.

'Can the ideas of a Nobel Prize winner and a few others really bring the world back from the brink?' Jan asked Fitz. 'Stop the crash and end mass unemployment and war?' He was wondering if this caper was worth taking yet more mad risks for.

'Not this time, I don't think,' Fitz answered, 'or only partially. But maybe some of those things in the long run.'

In the long run I'll be dead, thought Jan. He could still duck out of this if he chose to.

A few guards were standing around looking bored at a security checkpoint with two metal gates. A handful of people were queuing to be frisked and let inside.

'It's this one,' said Amistad. 'This checkpoint is for staff and helpers only.' She looked around as if searching for something. Someone waved to her from a group of people in waiters' uniforms on the other side of the street. Some of them were wearing small rucksacks.

'There they are.'

Fitz dug his hand into the pocket of his jeans and pulled out his mobile.

'Jeanne,' he said, staring at the display in surprise. He answered the phone as they walked over to the group of five people in their black-and-white uniforms. Jan couldn't hear what Jeanne said, only Fitz's answers.

'That's funny, we're just trying to do the same.'

'. . .'

'Oh.'

'. . .'

'Where are you?'

'. . .'

'Let me try something.' He lowered the phone and turned towards Amistad. 'I know this sounds cheeky, but is there any way we could smuggle in another person? She's almost more important than we are.'

Amistad looked annoyed and frowned.

'She has a better grasp of the subject,' Fitz explained, 'and she knows the guy we want to question very well indeed.'

Amistad had a quick think and glanced at her watch. 'How soon can she get here?'

'Five minutes.'

'She's got five minutes,' said Amistad, 'then we're gone.'

73

The Range Rover was wedged between two half-demolished cars with its doors and tailgate wide open. The front seats were strewn with splinters of glass, while more fragments lay everywhere on the surrounding road surface.

Patrol cars had sealed off the area, with two police officers left guarding the crash site – the crime scene – while others patrolled the perimeter to keep onlookers out and witnesses in.

There were a number of bullet holes in the rear as well as the front of the Range Rover.

'You went and shot the thing to bits?' asked Maya, taking stock of the scene. 'With so many people around?'

'It's certainly nothing to brag about,' Tibor admitted. 'There's bound to be an inquiry.'

'It's a miracle no one was hurt,' said Jörn, showing more compassion than Maya would have credited him with.

'And you're sure there was no one in the back?' she asked.

'Well, we didn't see anyone,' said Tibor, 'but the impact flung the tailgate open and it took us ten minutes to get control of the situation and the vehicle. You can see the position it's in. Someone could well have escaped during that time.'

She examined the boot without touching anything.

'Forensics are on their way,' Tibor informed her.

Her mobile buzzed. A text from headquarters. With pictures. Maya was shocked. The images had been recorded a few minutes earlier by a surveillance camera overlooking one of the security checkpoints outside the conference centre where the opening ceremony of the summit had begun an hour ago.

Maya called back immediately. 'Did she get in?'

'She was turned away,' her colleague at headquarters explained, 'even though she was on the guest list. Her security clearance was cancelled and so was her pass.'

'Why?'

'We don't know yet.'

Maya put her phone away. 'Thanks,' she said to Tibor, grabbing Jörn's arm. 'We're off!'

The Samaritan and the gambler were standing with the person from the demo and the bunch of penguins near a small security checkpoint a block away from the American and British embassies and the Hotel Adlon. El was keeping watch from the shadow of a building across the street. He could barely hear the voice in his earpiece due to the noise from the demonstration and a helicopter hovering overhead.

'She's running east,' Bell panted.

Towards us?!

She appeared about two hundred yards behind the group he had his eye on. About three hundred yards away, the sound of the demo ratcheted up a notch. El could hear a rising wave of oohs and aahs from the crowd, culminating in cheers and applause.

El's eyes darted back and forth between the sprinting woman and the demonstration.

The cause of all the excitement was a host of tiny dots rising higher and higher over the heads of the crowd. More and more of them climbed into the air – soon there would be hundreds of them, thousands. They coalesced into a cloud like a flock of starlings over a field, producing an ever-shifting series of new and fascinating patterns.

El identified the dots as a multitude of miniature drones. *The same show as last night, but this time without the lights.*

The spectacle was also visible to the guards at the security checkpoints and to the cluster around the Samaritan and the gambler. The only person not gazing into the sky was Dalli, who was racing single-mindedly towards them, had almost reached them in fact.

More recently launched drones joined the others as if part of a larger whole. The wild surges and movements constantly changed the shape of the cloud, and before El could figure out how it had been done, the drones had formed another gigantic peace sign over Pariser Platz. Everyone in the area had thrown back their head and was gazing up into the sky. El caught himself succumbing to the same temptation as everyone else, and when he looked over at the Samaritan, Peel, Dalli and the others again, they were gone.

He caught sight of them at the security checkpoint. Most of the guards were still watching the air show over the conference centre, and only one bothered to verify the waiters' papers, giving their rucksacks a cursory check before casually waving them through.

More and more drones took flight, weaving slogans in various languages around, through and within the peace symbol in a procession of beautiful choreography, intertwining with it, breaking off again and merging into new forms.

The security guard was letting the gambler into the summit compound! El instructed his phone to dial the client's number.

Dalli was inside now too.

Ringtone. The drama overhead was so absorbing that the other guards were completely oblivious to their overworked colleague and only threw him an occasional glance.

El's client answered his phone.

Only the Samaritan and two penguins were still queuing. El would eat his hat if they really were conference staff.

SEVENTH DECISION

'Knowledge of the mathematical principle
makes it easier to identify and address
undesirable developments.'

Will Cantor

74

Fitz and Jeanne had passed through the checkpoint ahead of Jan. The security guard paid no attention to the papers they held up. It was all a show for the cameras, Amistad had explained – the guard was one of theirs. They'd infiltrated him into the system long ago, along with two other members of the six-person team. No one seemed to give a damn. Nonetheless, Jan's heart was in his mouth and his knees had turned to jelly. Now was his last opportunity to turn back and forget the whole thing. He was far more eager to prove his innocence than to track down the manuscript and reveal its contents.

Jan could only see the backs of the other security guards because their eyes were trained on the drone ballet overhead. It was quite a sight, he had to admit, even the second time around. Eye-catching pictures for the international media.

'Papers, please,' the guard asked.

Jan's heart almost jumped out of his mouth and tears welled in his eyes. Hundreds of heavily armed soldiers. All those armoured vehicles over there. His decision was made, and there was no going back without attracting attention and putting the others in danger. He showed the man his ID. The man squinted at him and Jan gave an awkward smile in return. The man waved him through.

With adrenaline still coursing through Jan's veins, he and the others moved quickly away from the checkpoint along Behrenstrasse to where it met Wilhelmstrasse. On reaching the crossroads, they came upon more barricades. To the right, towards the British embassy, Wilhelmstrasse was in complete lockdown. One hundred and fifty yards straight ahead, barricades, vehicles and police officers obscured their view of the Jewish memorial and the Tiergarten. Between the blockades and the park a double security cordon surrounded the American embassy.

Their gait was determined rather than anxious as they walked along the back of Hotel Adlon and past the Academy of Arts towards the barricades in front of the American embassy. Beneath their helmets, the soldiers' fierce expressions made them feel as if a company of snipers held them in their crosshairs.

A few smokers were taking a cigarette break under the portico of the last house before the barricade. Jeanne, Fitzroy and the others entered this house via a ramp leading down into the underground car park, and from there they continued along a succession of concrete tunnels. Serving staff were busy pushing trolleys piled high with crates of bottles and boxes of catering, talking via headsets as they hurried past or leaning against walls for a quick rest. Jan was reminded of computer games in which players had to build up a civilization until the screen teemed with hundreds of bustling figures.

No one paid the slightest attention to the newcomers despite Jan's feeling that their clothing – not to mention his bruised and battered face – must surely mark them out as intruders.

Amistad instructed them to follow one of the black-and-white waiters, and they climbed a few flights of stairs up into the conference centre where staff were now clad in white clothing, chef's hats and headscarves. Steam, the clatter of crockery, a hum of voices, barked orders, and a whole potpourri of aromas.

Their guide led them purposefully through the hurly-burly into another corridor with waiters and waitresses rushing with loaded trays in one direction and empty ones in the other.

Amistad stopped at the next door and peered out. It was a different world beyond. Red carpet, elegant wood panelling and, between them and the far wall, room-length tables with white tablecloths and flower arrangements. This was where the tray-bearers were unloading their delicacies. Dotted around the room were small round bar tables covered with long tablecloths and small vases of flowers that added a dash of conviviality to the busy scene.

A pair of double doors in the far wall hid the buffet from the guests. It was approaching noon, and in a couple of hours they would open and hundreds of hungry summit participants would pour through the gap.

'This is the foyer before the conference room,' Amistad explained. 'We're all on our own from here on,' she said. 'Good luck!'

She took another peek, beckoned to her companions and one by one they slipped out into the room. Scattered around the foyer, delegates to the summit who had allowed themselves a little time out from the speeches or simply weren't interested were chatting around bar tables. Large screens relayed the events inside the conference room with subtitles but no sound. Amistad and her team melted effortlessly into the crowd.

Jan, Fitz and Jeanne hadn't exchanged a word all this time. 'I'd like to speak to Ted first,' said Jeanne.

'We'll keep out of the way then,' said Fitz.

We?

Jeanne turned around and was about to step out into the foyer when Jan grabbed her shoulder and jerked her back into hiding. A tall, athletic, short-haired man in a suit had just appeared through a door at the back of the lobby, followed by a second guy. Jan had seen them both before – a few hours ago in Jeanne's suite.

Fitzroy pushed Jeanne to one side and they flattened themselves against the wall to let the serving staff come and go.

'What are they doing here?' he asked quietly.

'Guarding Ted,' Jeanne replied. 'He always has several of them around, even in high-security areas like here.'

'High-security!' Fitzroy scoffed. 'They let us in, didn't they?'

'Are they allowed to carry guns in here?' Jan asked.

'No,' said Jeanne.

'Thank God for small mercies.'

'How come those guys choose this very moment to appear and head straight towards us?' Fitzroy hissed as he peered out through the gap.

Jan watched the two men exchange a few words. One man stayed in the lobby, while the other set off up the broad stairway to the first floor.

'We won't make it past him,' he said.

'Overtake the bastard,' Maya yelled. This was a little unfair, because Jörn was speeding, lights flashing and siren howling, towards the conference centre like a racing driver, and a good one at that. He was fast but he was in complete control. They were somewhere south of the Tiergarten, and the traffic was getting worse.

'What do you want me to do?' his voice in her ear asked pointedly.

'You? You need to pass on the faces and names to the police at the conference sites. And tell them to watch out – some of those guys are highly dangerous.'

'Terrorists?'

'Probably not.'

'What then?'

'If only I knew. They need to look for those men and arrest any of them that they find – all of them.'

'Evacuate the place?'

'God, no! Let's keep this quiet.'

They were still half a mile from the conference centre. There was a swarm of something in the air, but it wasn't birds.

We want our share, it said in huge letters.

Not again.

'Cool.'

'What did you say?'

'Oh, nothing. Just do as I told you.'

'I'm on my way,' said the voice in El's ear. He saw a tall man in a suit advancing towards the security checkpoint from inside the enclosure. The drones were still dancing over the building, and the strains of a classic soul track being sung by hundreds of thousands of people drifted over from the demonstration outside.

R-E-S-P-E-C-T

El crossed the street to the checkpoint. It was only now that one of the security guards took any notice of him.

'This one is with me,' said the man who'd come to meet him. He showed his ID and a second badge – probably his security pass – to the guard. 'Let him in.'

El presented his ID. The security guard checked his

name against his list. Rattled, he looked uncertainly back and forth between the man in the suit and El. His colleagues still seemed more interested in the drone extravaganza in the sky.

'But he's not on our—'

'So what?' Mr Suit snapped at him. 'As you can see, I came from this side. *Inside*. I have a security pass and this man is with me, so he's covered.' The man in the suit waved his pass under the guard's nose. 'Do I need to have a word with your manager? Are you looking for trouble?'

'Let him through,' said one of his distracted colleagues. 'He's obviously security like us.'

The tight-lipped guard waved El into the compound.

Mr Suit greeted him with a questioning look. 'So where did they go?' he asked.

El walked along Behrenstrasse to the car park entrance behind Hotel Adlon into which the Samaritan and the gambler had vanished.

'I've had enough of hanging around,' said Jan. 'I'm going to go out and distract that guy.'

All around them, obliging waiters were gradually loading the buffet and bar tables with canapés, plates, napkins and glasses.

'He can't really do me any harm. He won't call the police. The hotel staff didn't, and even if he does . . . Jeanne will confirm we didn't break in.'

'How about the suspected murder?' Fitzroy pointed out.

'I didn't murder them. The police must know that by now, and if they don't, what was it Thompson and Cantor's story and paper taught us? Trust and cooperation.'

'Precisely,' said Fitzroy. 'And now they're both dead.'

'See you later,' said Jan. He slid through the gap in the

door and made his way stealthily towards the stairwell. Fitzroy hadn't credited the kid with such guts. He watched the guy in the suit near the opposite wall.

Jan was about halfway across the room before the man spotted him. He said a few words – into his headset, probably. At first he simply watched Jan, but then he sparked into life and started to move.

The kid reached the stairs. The other man followed him at an easy, inconspicuous pace.

Jeanne was desperate to get going, but Fitzroy held her back.

The man in the suit glanced over his shoulder, but then switched his attention back to Jan, who'd now disappeared from view.

Jeanne and Fitzroy darted out of the lobby and took cover behind a cluster of people around the nearest bar table just before the guy in the suit looked around again from the bottom of the stairs. Spying nothing suspicious, he continued up the steps. Fitzroy made it to the conference room doors and eased them open. He slipped inside.

'Oh sh—!' he cursed.

75

Jeanne wasn't the least bit surprised. She and Fitzroy had entered the hall through one of the side doors. Her eyes swept over the room. Beneath a vast glass dome, around three hundred people were crammed on lines of chairs or around tables, their attention focused on the speaker, who looked tiny behind his lectern on the enormous stage. His face, however, was plastered across a giant wall of monitors stretching the entire width of the podium, ensuring that the crowd could see every wrinkle and change of expression.

Most of the guests were dressed in Western suits or traditional costumes from a variety of cultures. On the tables in front of them lay an array of briefcases, papers, glowing laptops and tablets. Many of them were wearing headphones connected by cables to their desks. Everyone looked extremely serious. The seating was arranged in eight blocks of six rows each. The front four blocks had tables, the back four only chairs, but with wide aisles in between to allow people to reach their seats. Raised platforms around three sides of the hall were packed with hundreds of journalists and their camera teams from around the world.

Most of the guests were listening attentively, but in the dimly lit hall Jeanne also spotted a number of people trying to catch a glimpse of the swarm of drones through the glass dome or staring at their smartphones or tablets. She could make out several screens near by playing a live stream of the demonstration, cut with footage of the dancing drones. Further delegates were watching other news, sending texts or even playing games on their devices. To Jeanne, the scurrying fingers on the touchscreens resembled insects lured and deluded by the light into crashing into windows again and again in a desperate bid for freedom.

Occasionally, a member of the audience would leave his or her seat or return to it. Jeanne had attended many of these events in the past. Someone always needed to go to the toilet or make an urgent phone call.

'Stay here,' she whispered to Fitzroy. She strode away along the nearest aisle to the centre of the hall, then turned towards the podium and walked past the front ten rows. There were so many VIPs present that the organizers had allocated fixed seat numbers to many of them. She espied Ted in the fourth row, four seats along. The seat next to his was empty.

El and Mr Suit zigzagged between groups of catering staff and along supply tunnels in the underbelly of the conference centre. Every now and then, narrow or wider corridors branched off to the side, but El and the other man followed the main flow of workers.

In a large room, dozens of chefs were bent over long tables, applying the finishing touches to a selection of hors d'oeuvres. A couple of shrimps here, a sprinkling of caviar there.

Mr Suit began to speak, and El realized after the first couple of words that they weren't addressed to him.

'OK,' the man concluded and turned to look at El. 'Our

orders are to concentrate on two individuals first,' he said. 'Jan Wutte and Fitzroy Peel.'

The revolving blue light cleared Maya's path through the vehicle checkpoint on Unter den Linden. The cloud of drones looked even more impressive from close up, more threatening too, although she had trouble figuring out what it was supposed to represent from down here, as the performance was designed to be viewed from afar.

Jörn turned off the blue lights and swung round to the front of the building. He pulled up outside the main entrance with a screech of tyres. They jumped out of the car and ran up the red carpet to a pair of large glass doors.

Maya suddenly remembered having read somewhere that thousands of people had been hired to work at the summit's three locations near Pariser Platz. She showed her police ID to the people on the welcome desk as she hurried past, but Jörn's uniform was really all the explanation the guards required. They found themselves in an atrium occupying several floors at the front of the building. A vast screen was broadcasting proceedings inside the hall live. Hundreds of people in rows upon rows of seats were listening to a man on the podium.

Her phone rang. It was headquarters.

'Yes?'

'You're actually inside the summit compound?' she heard Köstritz say in horrified tones.

'Yep, luckily for us,' she said, 'but there's a lot on my plate right now, so if there's no vital message for me . . .'

'No, there is,' he said. 'Carry on like the last few days and you'll get it in the neck.'

'Was that all?'

'No!' Köstritz shouted.

A crackle on the line. The familiar voice of the colleague she'd talked to several times already that morning. 'I've got two bits of news for you. Which do you want first?'

'Two good ones.'

'Depends on your perspective.'

'Quit philosophizing and just give it to me straight.'

There was room enough behind the chairs for Jeanne to reach her seat. Ted was checking the news on the mobile on his lap. The short distance along the row felt like a mile.

It was only a few hours ago she'd been a successful and attractive young woman enjoying a burgeoning relationship with a self-made billionaire. Life as a fairy-tale princess seemed to stretch out before her, at least for a couple of years or even one or two decades. She wasn't naive enough not to know that the Teds of this world tended to swap their wives for younger versions sooner or later, while the cars, planes and works of art they collected got older and more classic.

Her mind kept drifting, probably so she didn't have to consider the predictable consequences of the past few hours. She continued to hope that Ted would have some plausible explanation for the envelope in his safe and for Mitch's actions, but she sensed deep down that her hopes would be dashed and she'd have to decide what path to follow next. Whatever her decision, it would be a new path, and Jeanne didn't have the faintest idea where it might lead.

She sat down beside Ted as though she'd just returned from the restroom. He looked up with irritation and recognized her. 'Jeanne, where have you been all this time? I was worried,' he said quietly. 'I tried contacting you several times.'

She put her phone down on the table in front of him and pulled up her call history. 'Not on this phone you didn't.'

'You have others.'

This was just his style. Did he genuinely know nothing? On whose orders would Mitch have acted otherwise?

'What was it about Herbert Thompson and Will Cantor's ideas that bothered you the most?' she asked him point-blank. 'The consequences for finance companies like Syllabus Invest? The publicity it gave to scientific articles pointing out that the very richest individuals in the United States, like you, have been raking in the country's GDP since the eighties?' A man in front of them shifted angrily in his seat. Jeanne ignored him. 'Is it only the money, or is it ideological? Because they've refuted economists' and politicians' blind faith in markets and competition? Not with abstract theories, but by simple maths. Or—'

'What are you talking about?' Ted whispered. He stood up, but stooped so as not to obscure the view of those behind him. He gestured for her to go ahead of him. 'Let's discuss this further outside.'

Caught by surprise, she allowed him to guide her along the row.

Maya put her mobile away and walked over to the welcome desk where a group of security guards was waiting for her. She turned to a short man with a protruding belly and a uniform that was too big for him.

'Follow me, all of you.'

'But we—'

'And get your boss down here too.'

'What the heck!' hissed Ted. 'Yes, I was aware of Thompson's speech and their paper. You haven't recognized the scale of this thing. Even Thompson and Cantor are only scratching the surface. Thompson's ideas are valid, of course, but they're from the last century. He was still thinking in analogue terms, in old categories like classical economics, capitalism and money. A completely new world is dawning.' There was an unfamiliar tinge of excitement to his voice. Words were pouring out of his mouth faster and more haphazardly than usual. 'Why do I need markets, competition and money to determine a price if prices are no longer a signal, just a reflection of data? If unimaginable volumes of data provide faster and more accurate information about people's needs and how to satisfy them? And if all I need is the data and the relevant algorithms to compare and allocate goods and services as efficiently as possible to consumer demand? In short, to coordinate and organize society!'

'All *you* need, as one of the collectors and owners of this modern-day capital. What about the rest of the world?'

They crept past someone who shushed them aggressively.

'Thompson and Cantor's model – or to be more precise, the work of the London laboratory – lays the foundations for a whole new understanding and reconfiguration of wealth distribution,' Jeanne declared. 'But it all depends on who does the reconfiguring.'

'We live in a knowledge-based society,' said Ted, propelling her along the row. His hunched posture seemed less and less like a sign of consideration for the other guests and more and more like a big cat on the prowl, maybe even a predator with its back to the wall. 'Data is knowledge, and knowledge has always been power – and that will only increase in the future.'

'That's your problem right there. The more knowledge is shared, the more it thrives, but sharing your knowledge also means sharing your power.'

'It's the same with money, land, real estate, shares and

other forms of capital, and always has been,' Ted reminded her. He shrugged, but it wasn't enough to relax him.

'Shh!'

All right! They'd almost reached the exit now.

'And yet Thompson, Will and the scientists whose studies they cite show that cooperation is better for all of us in the long run,' Jeanne said.

'Except for me. You still don't get it. Distribution has never been about wealth. It's about power.' He'd pulled his head so far into his shoulders that he looked like a bull ready to charge. 'Herb and Cantor demonstrated very elegantly that there are essentially two mechanisms at play. On the one hand, there are the multiplicative, exponential dynamics of chance or luck, which keep heaping riches on a lucky few and don't strive for distribution above everything else. It's true – once you have money, it sticks to you like glue.'

'And as one of the lucky few, you can nudge those dynamics in your own favour, as we saw last night,' Jeanne remarked. 'But on the other hand, as demonstrated by the people in London and also by Thompson and Will, there are the dynamics of cooperation, pooling and sharing, which produce even greater growth. That was true of multicellular organisms over single-cell organisms, but that was during the evolutionary process of blind trial and error. We humans, however, are the very first living beings who are capable of *deliberately* channelling these dynamics so they yield more and bring about progress for all.'

'I can see you read it thoroughly,' said Ted. Again he shrugged his shoulders, but this time he did relax. He seemed to have accepted the situation, and that made Jeanne wary.

'Those in our society who distribute have always been

the most powerful,' she said. 'They determine who benefits from the fruits of those dynamics. They determine who has the luck – or at least whatever luck can be determined.'

'You're a woman of such beauty and intelligence,' said Ted. 'I can see why I find you so attractive. Yes, new technologies such as artificial intelligence, potentially along with blockchains and other approaches still to be invented, will greatly reduce the costs of distribution and also generate huge profits. Whoever controls them will hold power in the society of the future and define how wealth is distributed. You could be one of those people.'

'Why not let everyone share the wealth?'

'We've already dealt with that,' he said, furrowing his brow in pretend disappointment. 'Because they'll also then share the power.'

'And you don't want to share it.'

'Why would I? That was the one thing Herb and Cantor didn't understand. You don't give people arguments; you give them a *feeling* that *resembles* an argument. Something they already feel themselves: perceived discrimination, repression, not being taken seriously, moral superiority, and so forth. They'll totally fall for it. Even if you're a billionaire and you've – to use your wonderful expression – been raking in those same people's money for decades.'

'It'll be a remotely controlled surveillance state!'

'No – *society*. There's no need for the state – or only at best as decor. As it is already, to some extent. But people don't notice. They go along with it. Of course, they sense that fulfilling their desires doesn't always work quite as well as it might in these circumstances. It leaves them with a vague sense of dissatisfaction, but that's easy to channel and always has been. Tell them foreigners are to blame. Tell them it's the fault of the state. Tell them it's the fault of the

EU. Give them a feeling that resembles an argument, and they'll believe you all right.'

'My question is still: how did you get your hands on Thompson and Will's documents.'

'The real question is what kind of society you want to live in – mine or a different one?' He studied her through narrowed eyes. 'Although I've a feeling I already know the answer.'

A tall figure appeared out of nowhere in front of her. Mitch.

He smiled at her. 'Jeanne,' he said, slipping his arm through hers.

76

'They don't want to . . .' said the face on the wall of monitors. Fitzroy was all ears as far as the speech was concerned,
but his eyes were trained on Jeanne and the stooped man
following her along the rows of tables in the half-darkness.
Then there was the man who'd just slid his arm under hers –
the security guard from Jeanne's suite earlier.

'What . . . what should . . .' the loudspeakers blasted.

A murmur went around the hall. Some members of the
audience rose to their feet so they could get a better view.
Jeanne and the men on either side of her also stopped and
stared at the podium.

A mighty roar went up over the Brandenburg Gate as Amistad and her fellow campaigners stormed the stage in the
conference centre. The speaker raged at them as they
unfurled a banner. Kim was following the operation in real
time on her mobile and on the screen behind the outdoor
music platform, where the current speaker had broken off
her address. The demo app was broadcasting the events live.
The screens showed Amistad approaching the microphone,
from which the speaker retreated fearfully as if Amistad
were surrounded by an invisible force field. The banks of
monitors in the conference hall switched from a close-up of

Amistad's face to footage of the demo, showing a whole sea of people out in the Tiergarten.

'How cool is this?' cried Kim, nudging Nida with her elbow. 'They've done it!'

The demonstrators' IT team had hacked into the computer system set up for the summit and were broadcasting images of the demonstration to the conference participants.

Amistad raised her right fist and shouted, 'Peace, freedom and justice!' She repeated this slogan, and this time countless other protesters joined in. A chorus of voices whose volume further intoxicated the crowd and echoed throughout the city.

But then Amistad lowered her fist and pointed to the audience inside the centre.

'OK, here they come,' cried Amistad.

Fitz had a good view of the turmoil from his position at the side of the hall. A dozen men were marching towards the stage along the aisles where everyone was on their feet, chattering excitedly; some were hurling outraged comments at the podium, many were holding their cameras over their heads to film what was happening. The next moment, figures were clambering up the sides of the stage.

All of this agitation jerked Jeanne's companions out of their shocked torpor, and they pushed her forwards through the commotion. Her resistance to the two men's hold of her was barely perceptible, but Fitzroy could spot it well enough. It was amazing how quickly you could get to know someone in an extreme situation, and they'd experienced more than enough jeopardy over the past few hours. He stepped away from the wall beside the exit and set off towards them.

'But,' Amistad declared hurriedly before the first security guards could reach her, 'I would just like to express my enormous regret that we didn't get to hear Herbert Thompson's speech today . . . because he was murdered last night.'

We told you that in confidence, Jan cursed under his breath as he watched the monitor he had lingered in front of in the lobby.

The whispering in the hall grew louder, and guests around Jan gasped in surprise. For a moment time seemed to stand still.

The first guards reached the protesters who'd unfurled the banner on the stage and tried to wrest it from their grasp.

'I have it from a reliable source that he was going to present some truly fascinating ideas,' Amistad continued.

Jan wasn't the only one with his eyes glued to the screen. Other curious participants at the conference taking a break from the hall had joined him. He felt relatively safe for the moment, but nevertheless kept half an eye out for his pursuer. He was obviously well hidden: Jan couldn't see him anywhere.

'Thompson's ideas might help solve many of the problems you've come here to discuss.'

The screen showed the security guards grabbing Amistad by her arms and legs and trying to pull her away from the lectern. Meanwhile, one of the people holding the banner fell over, the fabric crumpled into a heap and a second campaigner was overpowered.

'Herbert Thompson can't make that speech now because he was murdered.' She didn't struggle against her assailants, simply clung to the stand as they tugged her until her legs were virtually horizontal in the air. 'A handful of people in the audience today did, however, read that unpublished speech.'

Jan's stomach began to churn. One of the security officials had managed to prise Amistad's right hand away from the lectern. Another pulled her head back from the microphone by her hair.

'They're familiar with Thompson's ideas. They could fill us in with the details!' Amistad's left hand was now beginning to slip from its grasp. 'Jeanne? Fitz? Jan? One of you? Ted Holden?'

This last name sent a fresh shock wave around the hall.

Is she crazy? Why drag us into this? Jan glanced around nervously. No one here recognized him or knew that Amistad was referring to him.

Up on stage the security men were dragging her away from the lectern as she yelled to the audience, her head thrown back, 'Do you want to hear Thompson's secret theory?!' Without the benefit of amplification, her words were now audible only in the front rows.

'I do!' someone in the audience shouted in jest.

'Get out of here!' bellowed another voice.

'Why not?' someone else cried. As far as Jan could tell, this request was not meant sarcastically, although it was lost amid the general cacophony.

'Let the woman speak!' said a third person.

'Clear off!'

And then suddenly a woman's voice came over the loudspeakers loud and clear. 'I think I'd like to hear this.'

77

There was a sudden pause in the clamour that had gripped the hall. Fitzroy, who'd almost reached Jeanne, Holden and Mitch, recognized the woman standing at the lectern, her face projected on to the gigantic wall of monitors behind her. He'd seen her twice the previous day – once outside his hotel yesterday evening with another policeman, and a second time during their escape from the squat later the same evening. Now she was up there on the stage, flanked by security personnel in suits or uniforms.

'I'm Maya Paritta from the homicide and serious crime squad,' she said, holding up her police ID card so that everyone saw it magnified to poster size on the screens behind her. 'There may be some truth in what the lady said about Herbert Thompson.'

With all eyes fixed on the stage, Mitch shoved Jeanne's slender frame towards the exit. Jeanne resisted, but she stood no chance against the much stronger man. After his name was mentioned, Ted had made straight for the exit.

'Jeanne Dalli?' the police inspector called out. 'Fitzroy Peel? Jan Wutte? Are any of you here?'

She'd tracked Fitzroy to his hotel and it was no surprise that she'd come across Jan's name in the course of her investigations, but how did she know about Jeanne? From Kim's call during their abduction? From a completely different case? Fitzroy tried to calculate the implications. Was this good news for them, or bad?

Mitch tightened his grip on Jeanne's arm when the police officer repeated the three names. 'Jeanne Dalli? Fitzroy Peel? Jan Wutte? We know what happened.'

This woman had told her at the hotel that Peel and the kid were wanted for murder, and now she was calling them up on to the stage?

Mitch gave her a final shove to get her moving again. A few yards ahead of them she spotted Fitzroy in the half-darkness.

'Over here!' he yelled. 'We're right here!'

Jeanne braced herself with all her might against Mitch's attempts to push her out of the hall, just as Fitzroy blocked their path.

'I'm here too!' she cried. This was her chance to escape Mitch and Ted. 'This is Jeanne Dalli speaking. Over here!'

Heads turned in her direction. Eyes swivelled towards her corner of the hall.

'We're over here!' Fitzroy shouted.

Caught in the full beam of the audience's gaze, Mitch loosened his grip on her arm, and Jeanne took her chance to break free. In a flash Fitzroy stepped between her and the head of Holden's security team, and the two of them launched themselves towards the podium. Ted and Mitch set off after them in hot pursuit, but quickly aborted their plan and slunk away into the shadows.

The police inspector welcomed Jeanne and Fitzroy up on to the stage. Amistad and her team were still surrounded by a swarm of security guards but each of them was upright now rather than flat on the floor with a man's knee in the small of their back.

'We've met before,' the policewoman said in English out of range of the microphone. 'I've done my bit, now tell them what you know, and we'll discuss everything else later.' She made no move to arrest Jeanne or Fitz.

'Me?' Jeanne said in disbelief, almost loud enough for the microphone to pick up.

The previous speaker had reappeared on stage, and he and several other white-haired gentlemen protested at the interruption, but the police inspector silenced them with a raised hand.

'You or Peel. Your choice.'

Jeanne cast her eyes over the hall. The spotlights were so dazzling that she could only sense the presence of so many illustrious guests, hear their excited chatter and their exhortations to clear the stage at last and get on with the scheduled programme, while a few dissenting voices shouted, 'No, we want to hear what Thompson . . .'

'Let them go,' Fitz said to the police inspector, pointing to Amistad and her team.

The police officer hesitated, exchanged a few words with Amistad and a glance with Fitz and then instructed the security guards to do as he'd requested. Reluctantly they released their grip, and the protesters twisted free and waited to see what would happen next.

Without another word the policewoman stepped back and invited the demonstrators to do the same. Amistad was allowed to stay where she was.

Jeanne stared out through the blinding lights at the dark hall packed with expectant senior politicians and business leaders from all over the world. They were waiting to see if the young lady up on stage would dare say something.

Jeanne stepped up to the microphone.

*

Fitzroy kept to the background. He wondered what Jeanne would do. Try to make Thompson's speech on his behalf? She hadn't read it in detail. Did she have a photographic memory perhaps, or was she going to give an off-the-cuff explanation of what she'd gleaned and understood? During her education and career she must have learned how to make improvised presentations in front of large gatherings. She was sharp as a tack and brave with it, but it was still a big ask to address this audience without any preparation or script.

Jeanne pulled her shoulders back, adjusted the microphone and looked out at the audience.

'Ladies and gentlemen, my name is Jeanne Dalli. I currently work for a hedge fund and before that I worked on Wall Street. This morning I was lucky enough to get the chance to read some of Herbert Thompson's speech. And so did' – gesturing behind her with one hand – 'Fitzroy Peel, who also used to be an investment banker and who's now . . . Oh well, it doesn't matter.'

Just leave me out of this, will you?

She looked round, smiled and nodded to him to step forward. Fitzroy hesitated, but then a voice in the audience cried, 'Izzy?'

It was a nickname only his family used. This nasal voice, slightly cracked with age, was one of the first he'd ever known but it had been several months since he'd last heard it. Jeanne had mentioned the man it belonged to and he was obviously out there in the audience, but its tone now was tinged with incredulity, horror and expectation. Fitzroy could interpret every shade of the man's moods from his voice, and felt a sudden simultaneous rush of profound affection and intense resistance, as if he were still the same small boy he once had been.

Fitz took a deep breath and took up a position a couple of steps behind Jeanne.

The people watching the monitor near Jan were chatting excitedly among themselves, and a few peeled off down the stairs leading back into the hall. Jan saw Fitz unfold a crumpled piece of paper behind Jeanne's back and pull out his mobile as she began to speak.

'Our decisions shape our lives and they shape the lives of others. They shape the world itself, which is why' – here she smiled – 'it is of *decisive* importance to know precisely the basis on which people make decisions. Herbert Thompson and Will Cantor . . .'

Jan glanced over his shoulder, looking for his pursuer, but he still couldn't see him. Not only had the police inspector left Fitz in peace, she'd invited him to join her on stage and was even letting him speak. She'd called all three of them up there. She wouldn't have done that if he were still a suspect. It was all over!

Jan turned away from the screen and galloped down the stairs two at a time.

El and the man in the suit who'd picked him up at the security checkpoint walked through the arcade outside one of the conference halls. The sound of excited voices issued from the open doors. People standing around bar tables out in the corridors were staring with rapt attention at screens that were obviously broadcasting the events taking place in the hall to those outside. Many delegates were jostling to enter, while some were leaving in disgust. Two individuals were addressing the audience from behind a small lectern on a large stage, and the various monitors showed their faces in close-up.

The woman. The gambler. Only the Samaritan was missing.

'Using these decision models, we develop conscious and unconscious strategies for every area of our lives: relationships, social systems, asset growth, economic concepts, strategies for escalating or avoiding social unrest of the kind we're increasingly seeing, even peace negotiations such as those you need to conduct here . . .'

The man in the suit beside El put his hand to his earpiece and listened. He turned to El.

'Your mission is terminated,' he said curtly, and walked away towards the hall without another word.

El needed no further explanation. Their mission had been an unmitigated failure, and the client had dropped them. They could forget the second instalment of their fee. They were on their own, and there was even a possibility the client would throw them under the bus to make sure the investigators had their culprits and left everyone else in peace.

El still didn't know who their client was, although the operation in the hotel car park had thrown up some clues from which he could potentially work backwards and identify him. Who were the men who'd handed over the three hostages in that staged kidnapping? El had made a mental note of the car's number plate. Where had the men come from? Where had they gone afterwards? And who was the woman? He had no time to ponder these questions right now though.

'Jack, Bell, Rob?'

Within seconds the three of them had reported back, and in the meantime his eyes roamed around the room, over all these people in their suits living the high life.

'Code Stealth,' was all he said. First step: make themselves scarce.

Should he retrace his steps or head up the stairs over there and leave via the front entrance? But when El spotted that bloody face, he realized he had one last matter to take care of.

78

Jan overtook everyone else on his way down to the main conference hall. The arcades were now significantly busier than before. Clusters of people had gathered around the monitors, on which Fitz was presenting a hastily sketched Leaning Tower of Pisa. Jan slalomed his way to the nearest entrance, where a small queue of other interested men and women had formed. He perched on his tiptoes to see over their heads into the hall. There was no point in pushing. He went with the flow.

Fitz's powerful and eloquent voice issued from the loud-speakers. '. . . built on false decision models will necessarily produce bad outcomes . . .'

Thank God I'm not up there on stage.

The annoying person behind him in the queue pressed his knuckles into Jan's back. 'Keep quiet!' a harsh voice hissed in his ear. A vice-like hand seized his left upper arm and yanked him around. Jan struggled, but the blunt pressure on his back became a stabbing pain. 'That's a knife,' the voice whispered in English, 'and I won't hesitate to use it. Now come with me.'

Jan submitted to his captor for now. Who was he? The man's voice was coming from behind Jan's head, so he must be fairly tall. His hands were like shovels, and the bulldozer-like force propelling him forwards could only belong to a bodybuilder. A furtive glance at his abductor's shoes and trousers confirmed his worst fears.

It was Anvil Chin or one of his mates. How had he got in here? How had he found Jan again? Was nowhere in this world safe, not even among heads of state and captains of industry with all their security precautions? Jan suddenly felt all hope drain from him, and let himself be steered away from the hall. Only occasionally did a passer-by glance at the unusual duo before quickly turning back to the monitors.

He could hear Jeanne speaking, but couldn't at all take in what she was saying. He'd seen these men murder someone in cold blood. Jan believed the guy when he said he wouldn't hesitate to plunge a knife into his back. If security had let him, Fitz and Jeanne into the summit, then why not this madman and his knife as well? One tiny glimmer of hope crept out of the deep, dark hole inside him. *I'm still alive! Don't make any move that might get you killed.*

Resistance might get him killed. Now. Then again, not resisting might also get him killed.

Repeated prodding drove him into the foyer, which was far emptier.

There might be a few more chances between now and later. Decisions with no certain outcome. Again.

Maya would have loved to listen to Dalli and Peel, but she had more important things on her mind. It did indeed come down to one's perspective as to whether the news from headquarters was good or bad, but it also depended on the next few minutes.

The first piece of information came from forensics. The blood on the bodywork of Thompson's crashed limousine had come up trumps. The DNA sample belonged to a suspected serial murderer who was the subject of an international arrest warrant. The man had a number of aliases but only one face. The forensics crew had sent her a photo that sent a shiver down Maya's spine. She knew the guy all right.

The second bit of news was about the phone number she'd asked her colleagues to trace. They'd pinpointed the device – the owner must be in the building. Her colleagues had enabled Maya's mobile to live-stream the geolocation process. The mobile she was looking for was very close by.

She tried to get her bearings by comparing the diagram on her display with the layout of the conference centre. A flashing green dot at the edge of the main hall gave her own approximate location to within ten feet. The pulsating red dot was moving slowly away from her. If she was reading the map properly, the person was currently three rooms away, but in which direction? These apps drove her up the wall.

She looked up at Jeanne one last time – 'So I'd like to tell you a short story. Once upon a time there were two farmers called Ann and Bill. They . . .' – before rushing out of the room, her eyes glued to her phone display. The direction was correct. Having crossed the lobby with the bar tables dotted around it, she entered a relatively empty buffet room with a glass wall along one side. No one there seemed particularly interested in the food because they were all staring at the monitors broadcasting the scenes in the main hall. Other screens were playing footage from outside, where the demonstrators were still swaying, their banners like the sails of small ships out at sea.

There must be an exit leading in the opposite direction somewhere.

*

Jan's attacker was being a little careless with his sharp weapon. The killer had laid his tree trunk of a right arm around Jan's shoulder as if they were close friends. In his left he hid the knife out of sight under his victim's left armpit, constantly probing with its tip for a spot between two ribs through which he could dig the blade straight into Jan's chest and heart. He slit the skin in several places, looking for the right angle. To Jan it was like a dental operation without an anaesthetic and he felt warm blood soaking into his T-shirt. He gritted his teeth to avoid making a sound. He didn't want to experience the steel sliding into his side. Every fibre of his being was tense with panic.

'You've been a right pain in the arse,' the man hissed in Jan's ear. 'I'm not leaving any witnesses alive.'

He shoved him roughly through the room where busy staff were preparing the catering. Jan had no idea how to escape from his vice-like grip. The surrounding workers must have thought the two men were best mates. They would soon be entering one of the access tunnels with any number of dark alcoves and corners where anything might happen.

The door was open. Twenty yards ahead, a single figure was walking in the same direction as they were. There was no one coming towards them. Jan's stomach was rioting, and his knees were wobbly with fright.

The man maintained his headlock. Jan reared up, but the muscular arm resisted with a casual jerk while a lancing pain bored into the skin over Jan's ribcage.

'Don't,' the man murmured. 'It'll only make things worse.' He drew Jan behind a pillar.

Don't make any move that might get you killed.

But the only thing that'd get him killed now was not making a move.

He clenched his left fist, concentrated for a second, twisted his body as far from the man as possible and swung his bent arm upwards, dealing an almighty blow to his assailant's nose. The man let out a loud grunt, but he instinctively tightened his right arm yet further around Jan's neck like a python.

Jan was amazed to feel the blade plunge into the left-hand side of his chest with minimal resistance, like a knife slicing through steak. It scraped his ribs before Jan, with courage born of despair, made one last desperate attempt to throw off this giant of a man.

79

As Maya entered the catering area with two men from event security, the two figures were just exiting on the far side. The colossus had Jan Wutte in his power. It might look at first sight as if the two of them were good pals, but Maya knew instinctively what was going on: the enormous thug must be pressing some kind of concealed weapon into Jan Wutte's side. She couldn't even begin to imagine how the man could have got into the summit complex without security clearance, let alone armed. It was even less conceivable that he had a gun. Maybe he'd strapped a knife to his body made of some special material that the security gates couldn't pick up?

Maya started to run as soon as the two men stepped through the doorway. She reached the beginning of the corridor and caught sight of two silhouettes wrestling with each other under a dim neon tube, half concealed by a pillar. She drew her gun as she sprinted towards them.

'Police! Hands up! Let go of each other!'

Something glinted between the two bodies and Maya didn't hesitate. She fired.

The man toppled over on to his back, his gigantic, lifeless body sprawling on the floor like a dead walrus, still cradling Jan Wutte's head in his arms like a lover.

Maya felt for the artery in the lad's neck, but she couldn't be sure. In the sudden rush of adrenaline, she might have touched the wrong place and it could simply have been her fingertips brushing against one another.

Meanwhile, the two security guards who had followed in her wake checked the motionless assailant for signs of life. 'There's a pulse,' one of them said.

Maya pulled up Jan Wutte's hoodie as best she could and ripped his T-shirt. Blood was oozing from a nasty gash between his ribs. She rolled a section of his top into a ball and pressed it tightly on to the wound.

Blood was pooling beneath the body of the man she'd shot. She'd fired three bullets and hit the target with all three, but she didn't know exactly where.

'Turn him over,' she instructed the security guards. 'Handcuff him just in case, then tend to his wounds.'

As the men did their best to heave the heavy body on to its front, they were joined by three more guards, along with two paramedics and a doctor.

Maya searched the hulk's pockets, but all she came up with was a simple phone – the same model the police had found on the guy arrested near the Range Rover. Together, the five guards heaved him on to his stomach while the doctor was treating Jan Wutte. With the injured men now in capable hands, Maya knew she was of no further use here.

She checked the confiscated phone. With her eyes on the screen she walked along the tunnel back towards the summit. One of *Homo sapiens digitalis*'s newest achievements: an ability to walk while staring at a phone without bumping into lampposts or other people.

This phone wasn't locked either. She ran her eye over the call history. On numerous occasions the owner had rung four numbers at the same time. Probably a sort of conference call. Maya recognized one of them – the number of the other guy from the crash scene. The four numbers filled most of the list, with only one other appearing at regular intervals.

She used her own mobile to call headquarters. 'I need you to locate four more phones. As fast as you can. Any delay and we're in trouble.'

'We shouldn't actually need mathematical proof to know that working together, cooperation, solidarity, fraternity, altruism, mutual support, peace – call it what you like – has always advanced the cause of humanity and resulted in greater prosperity for all,' Fitz explained, 'than competition, conflict, division, exclusion, partition, barriers and isolation. Since many people obviously need evidence, however . . . here it is in black and white for anyone who understands the world through numbers.' Here he grinned. 'Like me, for example.'

Fitz held his mobile with the illustrations of the farmers' fable closer to the lens of one of the cameramen circling around the stage. The shot filled the giant screen behind him.

'In colour too,' Jeanne joked. 'The advantage of cooperation as a principle is not restricted to our four hypothetical farmers. Instead of Ann, Bill, Carl and Dana, think of any personal relationship you like, replace the farmers in the story with left-wing and right-wing, up and down, town and country, young and old, natives and foreigners, Amsterdam, Beijing, Chicago and Dar es Salaam. Or Indonesia, Burundi, the USA, Mexico, Chile, China, Nigeria, Russia, Laos and Denmark. Choose any country, any continent . . .'

'Anyone who supports "America First", "*la préférence nationale*", "*prima la nostra gente*" or any other form of discrimination is like Ann and Bill,' said Fitzroy. He picked up the crumpled sheet with the diagram of Carl and Dana's cooperation bonus. Once it too had been projected on to the wall behind them, he suddenly tore off the strip of paper at the top bearing those words.

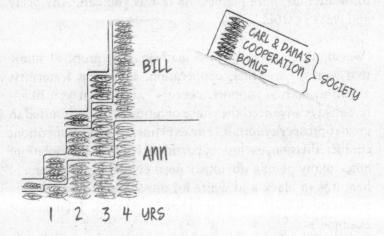

'They're depriving themselves and their loved ones of the additional prosperity that the Carls and Danas of this world produce by cooperating. Instead of benefitting their families and friends, they're doing the very opposite!'

He held up the torn-off slip of paper to the camera as a reminder and paused to allow the thought to sink into the minds of the audience.

Jeanne took over again, as if they'd been performing this double act all their lives. 'Substitute generations for years and you'll understand how important strong and stable institutions are for upholding the principle over the generations. Replace the years with fractions of a second and you have the strategies of the finance industry and realize what a decisive role time plays in economics.'

Her eyes had now grown accustomed to the blinding

spotlights and she took a little time to gaze out over the heads of the audience before continuing. 'Any company that enjoys lasting success, just like every successful society and any thriving country, ultimately operates according to the principle that resources should be shared in a way that generates the optimum level of growth for all. Sooner or later, businesses and states that promote competition and conflict over cooperation always fail, or only profit by impoverishing the overwhelming majority. In a globalized world, this obviously applies on a global scale.'

'Think of football,' Fitzroy cried. 'Football or any other team sport for that matter. Again and again we see managers buy a set of fantastically expensive players, but they don't win because these superstars play for themselves rather than as a team. That's what we love about team sports – the fact that a tight-knit group of good players who complement and give their all for one another can beat a non-team of arrogant individualists, however supremely talented.'

'If the world is like a football team of puffed-up egotists, then this team – and therefore every single one of its players – will be beaten by climate change, hunger, poverty, violence and other adversaries. If they play as a team, on the other hand, they'll create lasting prospects for all,' Jeanne Dalli explained, holding up two halves of a torn piece of paper that she had taken from Fitzroy Peel, just as Maya entered the hall.

Maya had opted for the side entrance closest to the stage at the front and remained standing near it. She had a good view from here. The hall was packed. The vast majority of the audience were on their feet, and some were filming or taking photos. A giant image of a mobile phone display was projected on to the screen behind Jeanne Dalli, showing a strange diagram of a village and ears of wheat and, below it, a table containing a string of numbers.

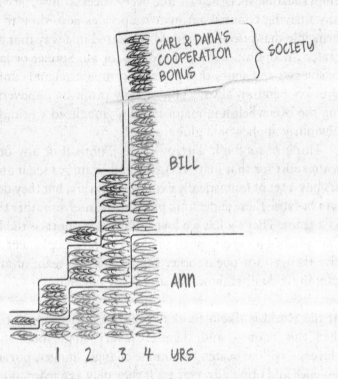

Maya rang headquarters.

'How are you getting on with locating those numbers? I need them now.'

'We're on it. We've received two this very second. One of the four is in Mitte, another at the far end of Unter den Linden.'

'Send someone to arrest the owners of the numbers.'

'Maya, you know—'

'That there are a few madmen out there who've been taking pot-shots at police officers! Do I need to remind you of that?'

'No,' he replied, his tail firmly between his legs.

'Thank you. How about the remaining two numbers?'

'We've only got approximate fixes on them so far. The third is close to Potsdamer Platz, and the other is somewhere near you.'

'Near me?' A few audience members looked round at her, so Maya lowered her voice. 'Where?'

'At Pariser Platz,' the man on the end of the line said laconically. 'Maybe even *inside* the summit building. I'll call you when we have the exact location.'

Quickly, please! 'Thanks.'

She just needed to hold her nerve.

80

'That farmer story is communist,' cried someone in the audience. 'If I have to hand over my entire crop . . .'

'That's not what we're saying,' Fitzroy answered calmly. Another idiot who either didn't think or associated anything that didn't match his worldview with his favourite ideological bogeymen, be it communists, left-wing activists, 'do-gooders', fascists, Nazis, liberals . . .

'The farmers' fable merely illustrates the *principle* of cooperation. The example of Carl and Dana pooling and sharing everything is an extreme scenario to keep the maths simple. In real life, people pool things proportionately . . .'

'Just like state taxation and social security systems,' called someone else.

'Yeah, exactly!' the first heckler scoffed. 'Punishing decent, hard-working people with taxes and stuffing it up shirkers' backsides!'

'Not at all!' cried the other man. 'The two authors have just proved mathematically that properly devised taxation and redistribution schemes *boost* growth, just as I've always said.'

Fitzroy squinted into the half-darkness in search of the speaker and spied him in the second row. The man had leaped to his feet and was gesticulating alternately at the podium and the giant screens. He'd been one of the first super-rich individuals to commit to the Giving Pledge, an initiative set up by Microsoft founder Bill Gates and legendary investor Warren Buffett, in the promise of donating the majority of their fortunes to charitable causes. Support from an unlikely source indeed . . .

Without further ado Fitzroy held up to the camera the ripped sheet of paper without the part showing the 'cooperation bonus'.

'Look at this. And I repeat: Ann and Bill work with virtually no taxation, social security and public health care.'

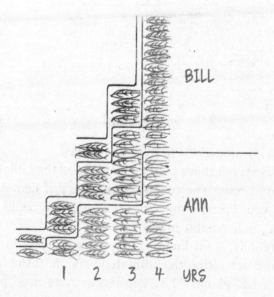

He then added the torn-off piece of paper with Carl and Dana's cooperation bonus to the picture. 'Carl and Dana do pay taxes, into a social security fund and public health care – and benefit from them.'

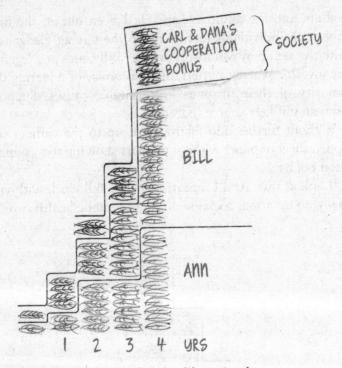

'That's ridiculous!' the first heckler griped.

'I'm sorry, but that's mathematics,' cried the billionaire in the second row. 'The two of them have just demonstrated that to you. Pretty simple maths too, as we could all see. Ironclad, indisputable maths.'

'Absolutely,' said Fitzroy, removing the piece of paper again and activating the animated version of the farmers' fable on his phone. 'The key words here are "properly devised".'

'Precisely!' roared the first heckler.

'You're right of course that this form of cooperation – pooling and sharing resources – is not always to everyone's advantage. It depends on how much people put in and how much they get out.'

'Yeah, some people put everything in, and others get everything out.'

'True,' Fitz said. 'The London-based mathematicians who inspired Thompson and Cantor's study showed mathematically – and not simply empirically – that there's been a steady redistribution of wealth from the poor to the rich in the United States since at least the 1980s. The poor pay in, and the rich take out. No doubt it's the same in many other countries.'

'This is an outrage!'

'I think so too,' Fitzroy said, unperturbed. 'Since Thompson and Cantor define pooling and sharing in general as cooperation, they call this particular form "negative cooperation".'

'Like "negative growth",' Amistad piped up from the background.

'The London Mathematical Laboratory's calculations also provide some preliminary indications of the relevant rates of taxation at which unfair wealth distribution would tail off or decrease.'

'Those could be a one or two per cent annual wealth tax,' Jeanne said, taking over, 'or inheritance taxes of forty per cent or more. It immediately becomes clear that anyone who decries income and inheritance tax and many other taxes as "anti-growth" or "unfair", either doesn't know what they're talking about or is a bare-faced liar. The opposite is true: if properly devised, they actually promote growth. Special tax breaks for the rich are *demonstrably* a long-term impediment to growth.'

'I've been saying that for years!' shouted the super-rich man in the second row.

'It would be the same as if one of the farmers paid in less because he'd done well for a few years,' Fitzroy continued.

'Trickle-down has never made sense, but this offers mathematical proof of *why* it doesn't work.' He ignored the muttering this caused. 'Thompson and Cantor had analysed the question in greater detail.'

Fitzroy had already sufficiently irritated the first heckler and probably enraged him, but the wonderful thing about this new theory was that he could present a different facet that would be more to the man's taste.

'Here, though,' he announced to his critic, 'is the bit you'll like. Communism, the great planner, the great leveller! What happens when everyone is equal? The farmers' fable provides a wonderful illustration. Ann and Carl have the same growth rates and are therefore economically equal, as are Bill and Dana. Oh, to hell with it – I'll show you.'

He held up his phone to the camera and typed something.

'Just to remind ourselves: Ann and Carl are from the same side of the village and enjoy the same rate of growth. What happens if Carl chooses not to cooperate with Dana but with Ann, his economic equal? That'd be similar to communism.'

Fitzroy tapped and swiped until the fully calculated example popped up on the screen.

'*Et voilà!* Ann and Carl make exactly the same profit from cooperating as if they'd worked alone, and since more complex systems also involve some transfer costs, cooperating with one's equals may even be loss-making. In this case, it's true that you're better off working on your own.'

'The same is true of the other great levellers,' Jeanne added, 'from so-called "dominant cultures" right through to fascists dreaming of a homogeneous "pure race". Diversity is key,

Year	Ann	CARL	Ann	CARL
	0	0	0	0
1	×2	×2	×2	×2
	∞	∞	∞ ⟍ ⟋ ∞	
			∞ ⟋ ⟍ ∞	
2	×3	×3	×3	×3
	∞∞∞	∞∞∞	∞∞∞ ⟍ ∞∞∞ ⟋	∞∞∞
			∞∞∞ ⟋ ∞∞∞ ⟍	∞∞∞
3	×1	×1	×1	×1
	∞∞∞	∞∞∞	∞∞∞ ⟍ ∞∞∞ ⟋	∞∞∞
			∞∞∞ ⟋ ∞∞∞ ⟍	∞∞∞
4	×2	×2	×2	×2
	∞∞∞	∞∞∞	∞∞∞	∞∞∞

and all it takes to bring different people together is a willingness to cooperate.'

Kim didn't know whether to look at her mobile or at the demo. Was the man on the screen really the quirky Englishman who'd slept on her gran's sofa? Fitz was just bringing the slip of paper with the cooperation bonus into shot so the audience could compare the two examples. And why hadn't Jan responded to the policewoman's call to join the others on the stage?

Along with hundreds of thousands of protesters in Berlin and millions of people worldwide, she'd watched the operation by Amistad and her team live on her phone. Just getting through security and unfurling the banner had been a massive triumph, but no one could have imagined the impact of this speech. Were they aware they were addressing a global audience?

'Levelling *kills* cooperation!' said the woman standing on the podium next to Fitz. Kim didn't like the look of her – a career chick, she thought – but she did like what she was saying. 'It *thrives* on diversity, variety and the freedom to do things differently. On conventional people *and* oddballs. Only freedom creates the diversity that makes cooperation the logical path. The English language draws a clear distinction between two different concepts. Cooperation can't thrive on the *freedom* of the lone wolf who does and takes what he wants, but on *liberty* – the freedom of people in their social relations, the liberty of all citizens in free countries to be free together, so long as their freedom doesn't impinge on the rights of others.'

'In turn, diversity benefits from cooperation,' Fitz continued. 'Which just goes to show that it's logical for those who produce more at one moment to give to those in difficulty, and in turn receive a little when they themselves hit a rough patch. It's an insurance policy for the future. This principle doesn't make everyone equal: it creates lasting *equal opportunities* for people who are different. In doing so, it allows every man and every woman, every girl and every boy, the whole of society, to fulfil their potential. One woman can therefore receive more, another man less, each according to their own contribution and abilities. There are incentives and rewards – as long as they cooperate!'

'So you see, it has nothing to do with communism,' said the woman. 'Quite the opposite: it's the smartest, most profitable form of capitalism. Capitalism is a fabulous thing.'

What?!?! Kim had been spot on – the woman was a career chick.

'The thing is, we've always misunderstood it, or it was wrongly explained to us. Yes, capitalism is driven by self-interest and selfishness and greed, but as the farmer example goes to show, our greatest self-interest lies in bearing other people's interests in mind! We should work together out of selfishness! Share out of greed!'

Work together out of selfishness? Share out of greed? Shocked, Kim looked around and saw similar surprise etched on other people's faces too.

'It may sound paradoxical,' this woman Jeanne went on, 'but acting in other people's interests is actually in our *own* best interest. Jesus recognized that two thousand years ago: "Love your neighbour as yourself." '

OK, Kim could live with that. She nudged Nida. 'Sounds familiar, eh?'

'This isn't about the common good for the sake of the common good, you see,' the woman cried, 'but for the sake of the *individual*.'

'These aren't mere ideologies, vague theories or woolly castles in the air, unable to justify their claims,' Fitz explained on the screen and via the app. 'Anyone can see this is simple mathematics. Calculable and predictable.'

'A society needs of course to ensure that everyone sticks to the principle,' Jeanne continued, 'meaning not only receiving when they're down but also contributing when things are going better. Cooperation is voluntary, but it's based on reciprocity. It needs to discourage free riders and tax dodgers who don't pay their fair share, or at least not let them multiply and overwhelm the majority. Think of Madoff, the greatest fraudster in history, although parasites like him do at least have one advantage: they reveal loopholes in the system that can then be fixed. So how does it work, I hear you say?'

Kim for one was desperate to find out.

81

'There are plenty of related models in game theory, psychology, sociology and biology,' said Jeanne, amazing even herself by the fervour in her voice. It probably helped that the spotlights were so bright she couldn't properly see the audience. It definitely helped that Ted had so disappointed her. Also, Fitz was a delightful co-speaker ... 'Think of Robert Axelrod's work, although Thompson and Cantor made some preliminary and necessary alterations to his theories because Axelrod often uses the problematic concept of expected utility. In complex modern societies, this requires strong and reliable institutions. They can be public, private, technological, whatever ... but they must exist. And they must run successfully.'

No one in the hall said a word. Jeanne gazed out into the silhouettes in the darkness. They needed a little time to do the maths and think it through. That wasn't a problem. Even the heckler had fallen silent.

Maya stared at the wall of screens in puzzlement. She checked the sums again. She'd only caught part of the story, but luckily she'd always been good at maths and these were simple calculations.

'So the crucial question,' an audience member shouted,

'is who decides how much each person should contribute and how much everyone should receive?'

'Obviously, figures can't tell the whole story,' said Fitzroy Peel, 'not even in a world as mapped out and as fully digitized as our own – and thank God for that! We all depend on one another in so many ways, and our interdependencies are far too complex for anyone to fully understand. What we do understand now, though, is *that* the principle works and *how* it works!'

'And wherever things can be quantified,' Jeanne Dalli added, 'it's a powerful tool for stimulating more sustainable, more responsible, more stable and more future-proof business management, to—'

'Liberties on the one hand, redistribution on the other,' a woman in the audience said. 'Sounds like the traditional welfare state. A mixture of markets and state intervention.'

'A little bit, yes,' Jeanne replied, 'although naturally it will have an effect on the markets. The historical example that Thompson and Cantor cite as being closest to their idea is the Western economic miracle of the fifties to seventies, when international trade recovered after the protectionism of the world wars and interwar years. It was a period when institutions – states, primarily – made at least a partial effort to ensure that the wealth everyone had helped to create was fairly distributed. We tend to forget that the highest tax band in a country like the US was over ninety per cent. That's right – over ninety per cent! Taxes used to be higher, not lower. Those were the "good old days" when democracies kept their promise of greater prosperity for all and were therefore popular.'

'But it wasn't the great surge in economic growth that

created the trickle-down effect that made everyone upwardly mobile,' said Peel. 'It was the other way around! It was *because* everyone had enough money to power the economic miracle that the boom was possible in the first place.

'Thompson and Cantor don't rely on flimsy terms such as welfare and solidarity but on cold, predictable mathematics, and are able to show – as one can see from the farmers' fable – how prosperity grows faster *with* the correct measures than without them.

'If correctly implemented, "redistribution", as it's often called, isn't merely altruistic, nice and compassionate; it is quite simply the best deal for everyone, as well as a formula for prosperity and peace. That's why Thompson and Cantor call it not the wel*fare* state but the well-*being* state. With globalization, it's clear that the idea would have to be implemented on a global scale.'

Maya glanced again at her phone. *When am I going to get confirmation of the exact location of the last remaining phone the assailant made calls to?*

'Thompson and Cantor's ideas are based on many empirical data sets and scientific papers showing how the distribution rates of overall wealth – again in the United States, for example – shifted in favour of the rich in the 1980s, at the same time that economic growth was shrinking and shrinking and trust in our democracies began to dwindle.'

'You can read up on all of this. Ted Holden' – here Jeanne scanned the audience – 'has the manuscript, but he's refusing to release it.'

Heads turned.

Maya jumped as her mobile vibrated in her hand.

'We've got it,' said her colleague at headquarters. 'I've logged you on to the live tracker.'

The flashing green dot on the animated map on her touchscreen indicated that she was in the bottom right-hand corner of the conference hall. She'd deliberately chosen this position near the podium to have a good overview of the room.

A pulsating red dot appeared. In the hall. On her side of the room, at the end of a row somewhere near the middle.

Maya fished the phone they'd confiscated from the injured man out of her pocket as she advanced stealthily towards the red dot. She stuck close to the wall, against which a few people were leaning as they listened to the speech.

Her green dot was closing on the red one. The person could only be a matter of yards away now, near a side entrance with a particularly dense throng of delegates. Maya could barely make their faces out in the dim light. Most seemed to be listening attentively, but some were typing and swiping on their phones.

She selected the number in the call history. Put her thumb on the green phone icon. Peered towards where the owner of the phone must be. Compared the position with the flashing red dot. Dialled.

She raised the phone to her ear.

There was a ringtone.

No one near her reacted.

Still the same ringtone.

Maya's eyes darted back and forth over the heads of the crowd. Either the person was unable to hear the incoming call or they were refusing to pick up.

The ringtone continued.

Her gaze settled on a man with a very precise parting a

dozen feet away, who she hadn't spotted until now. She took a step to one side to study his face.

George Lamarck raised the phone to his ear and hissed, 'What do you want? Your work is done here.' He looked up to find the inspector staring at him, a phone in one hand, another held to her ear.

82

'It all sounds fine in theory, but people just aren't like that,' objected a white-haired man in a suit. 'Humans are inherently selfish . . .'

'Of course they are,' a younger tieless man in designer glasses shouted back vigorously. 'If you ask someone in the street for directions, they'll tell you and be happy with a "thank you". When a group of boys get stuck in a cave in Thailand, rescuers from all over the world come together to fight for their survival. After an earthquake or a flood, people from every corner of the globe rush to help. The urge to help others is ingrained within each and every one of us.'

'As long as humans exist there'll be competition and domination and a social hierarchy!' another guest yelled at a woman in a suit, who responded with equal vim.

'I wouldn't be so sure. It depends on how they're organized.'

'So where do you think competition comes from?' a tall man in spectacles without frames challenged a group of young people. 'Why does it even exist?'

'Maybe we're competing to cooperate?' someone suggested.

'Or competition creates and sustains the difference and diversity that encourage cooperation?' a young woman proposed.

'Competition won't become obsolete,' offered another young man, 'but it will take on a new role – no longer as the dominant paradigm or the goal, but purely as a means to an end . . .'

'Humanity and altruism are the best deal for everyone?' a woman cried indignantly. 'I'm not going to let my emotions be reduced to a simple equation and then be co-opted by capitalism, what's more!'

One elderly gentleman said to another, 'A hardcore, growth-obsessed capitalist like you must absolutely love this idea!'

'I do admit,' said the other man, 'that I find it hard to argue with the maths.'

'It's amazing that no one's done this before. It's so simple too.'

'This demolishes the whole traditional left–right, progressive versus conservative battle lines,' announced a corpulent man in glasses to a woman who towered over him. 'It has something for everyone.'

'But it also demolishes cherished beliefs held on all sides,' the woman replied. 'For instance, this policy of reciprocal cooperation doesn't argue for unconditional welfare. We're entitled to expect something in return from those who wish to receive, if they're able . . .'

'That cooperation – or social – bonus feeds into the reserves for those who are genuinely in need, but also finances long-term projects such as experimentation, research and development, art and culture,' Jan heard another voice explaining. 'It creates some headroom to deal with the quirks of fate.'

Jeanne and Fitz's speech was still making waves as Jan hobbled through the crowd to the stage, supported by a paramedic. A broad white bandage around his chest was peeping through his torn T-shirt.

'We'll be able to completely rethink our business management models,' said a tall man with sharp features to a very similar-looking colleague who had a slightly fuller head of hair.

'We'll have to. Leadership skills too,' the second man said pensively.

Jan could see Fitz's shaven head in the midst of a group of people on stage. There was no sign of Jeanne or the policewoman though.

'That's all well and good, but how do I apply this to my day-to-day business?' a waspish managerial type said to a well-groomed lady who looked more like a scientist than a diplomat.

'That's not so very hard,' she answered. 'Many of us have always known or felt this is right, as the great religions and philosophers have taught us: "Give and it will be given unto you." Don't chase every cent. Back people who have ideas. Help the needy. Practise a bit of redistribution in your normal life – don't divide up dinner bills, for example. Tip fast-food staff. Overpay your cleaner.' *Or your carer*, thought Jan. 'And above all, stop counting everything you spend and on what!'

Fitz caught sight of Jan, struggled free from his cluster of fans and walked towards him with arms outspread. Spotting the state his friend was in, he asked in a worried tone, 'What have you gone and done now?'

'Played decoy for some killers again while you were bathing in the limelight. Someone has to do the heavy lifting.'

Jan now also located Jeanne in front of the first rows of seats below the podium, surrounded by dozens of delegates who were questioning her, gesticulating and chatting among themselves. News teams were desperately pointing cameras and waving booms, trying to grab a picture or catch a statement.

Fitz lifted Jan's top a little. A thick compression bandage under Jan's left armpit bulged where it held a dressing in place.

'The doctor said I was lucky the blade glanced off my ribs,' Jan said. 'If it hadn't . . . I have to go to the hospital for a check-up and some stitches.'

'You do indeed,' confirmed a woman's voice behind him. The inspector was gazing at him anxiously.

'Thanks again,' Jan said to her, pointing to his wound.

'I should be thanking you,' she replied. 'We should be thanking you.'

'Did you get them?'

'One's still on the run, but my colleagues will catch him eventually.'

'Jan!' came a cry from the group in front of the podium. Jeanne pushed through the people around her and climbed up to Jan and Fitzroy.

'What happened?' she gasped, catching sight of the bandage.

'Nothing much,' he answered. 'They've caught the men.'

'That was a fine speech,' the police investigator said to Jeanne. 'What I heard of it, in any case.'

'It wasn't our own work. We were simply repeating more or less what we'd read.'

'Oh, it contains most of the Londoners' main research,' said Fitz and laughed. 'You got pretty emotional for a former hedge fund manager and assistant to a billionaire.'

'That wasn't necessarily related to the subject matter,' Jeanne muttered darkly.

Jan's eyes wandered out over the audience, all of whom were engaged in heated debate, and then back to Jeanne. 'I only caught parts of your speech, but you seemed to do a pretty good job up here, you and . . .' – turning to Fitz – 'Fitzroy.'

'You can call me Fitz,' Fitzroy said.

A white-haired, suited man of about Fitz's height and build appeared behind him and patted him on the shoulder.

'I'll say he did a good job!' the man announced. He grabbed Jeanne's hand and gave it an air kiss. 'No wonder, with a partner of this calibre.'

Fitz rolled his eyes. 'Jan, this is my father. Dad, this is the guy who got us into this whole mess.' He grinned at Jan.

'So who was behind the whole thing?' asked Jan. 'Holden?'

The police inspector pulled a face suggesting only relative satisfaction. 'We traced the killers' calls to one of Ted Holden's lobbyists, George Lamarck, but he denies having anything to do with it. His disavowal won't do him much good. It remains to be seen whether we can ever prove the orders came from your billionaire.'

'But we found Herbert Thompson's notes for his speech and the manuscript written by Thompson and Cantor in a safe in his suite!' Jeanne exclaimed.

'Along with a sketch Will Cantor drew in his hotel room only a few hours before he died,' Fitz added.

'It won't be easy to arrange a warrant to search Mr Holden's suite,' the inspector said. 'He's a rich and powerful man.'

Jeanne glanced around. 'Where *is* Ted? Did you arrest him too?'

'Insufficient evidence,' the inspector confessed.

'Then he's probably already on his way to his plane and then to New Zealand.'

'We don't have much chance of stopping him.'

'There might be a way,' Jeanne said. 'He started initiating illegal business activities and share transactions yesterday evening. Potential grounds for preventing him from leaving the country at the very least.'

'Not my field,' the policewoman said, 'but if you can give me more details, I'll pass them on to the relevant colleagues.'

'You can count on me.'

'I'm just happy the whole thing's over at last,' Jan groaned.

Fitz looked out over the excited audience again and at the wall of monitors screening images of the hundreds of thousands of demonstrators outside. 'I'm wondering if this is actually just the start . . .'

The Scent of Soil

Dana surveyed the fresh furrows with satisfaction. The first birds had settled on the tilled land and were pecking hungrily at the soil.

'You were right. Over twice as fast,' the blacksmith said at her side. He'd helped Dana with this test.

It had been no more than the germ of an idea in Dana's head at first, but she'd ended up taking the blacksmith into her confidence. Although initially sceptical, he'd mulled it over and come up with a few suggestions. They'd run various trials over the winter when there was less work in the fields.

Dana's plan and the blacksmith's craftsmanship had eventually forged the tool, and now the two of them gazed proudly at the plough.

The fact that they could plough twice as much land in the same amount of time meant either half the toil or double the crop. Twice as much as Carl or the other farmers who'd joined them over time.

Dana began to count.

Afterword and Acknowledgements

I developed the farmers' fable on the basis of research by Ole Peters' group at the London Mathematical Laboratory (lml.org.uk) so that their work would be accessible to non-experts like myself. The ramifications of this research for individuals, politics and the economy are so far-reaching that I've only been able to touch on a few of them in this book. The papers published by this group (and ones written by other participants, including the Nobel Prize winners Murray Gell-Mann and Ken Arrow, who were partners and mentors) lay the groundwork for further development into practical applications, but this work is only just getting going.

If you would like to take a closer look at this research and the mathematics that underpins it, a good place to start is lml.org.uk/research/economics.

A fully interactive version of the farmers' fable is available also at farmersfable.org.

I would like to thank Ole Peters and Alexander Adamou for their patience and for the time they've taken to communicate and discuss their work with me. Non-mathematicians and non-physicists like myself will gather from reading their papers why it took a while for the ideas to click into place in my head.

I'd also like to thank David Sarac for the image of the Leaning Tower of Pisa, which we came up with during a joint session in London, and also for facilitating the online version of the farmers' fable (the fable was in itself a fine example of cooperation, involving an author, entrepreneurs, programmers and designers in England, France, Austria, Australia and Canada).

Much of this book is fictional, including most of the characters. I took some liberties in terms of the locations in Berlin. The crisis scenario I've sketched out could take a different form – a whole variety of factors could potentially trigger a chain of reactions and sweep through our political and economic systems.

What are very much applied in the real world, however, are the established socio-political and economic concepts I present, including the subsidiarity principle, equilibrium, expected utility hypotheses, comparative advantage, decision theory and game theory.

Naturally, the theories and findings of many other scientists, philosophers, politicians and other public figures have fed into this book. Their names would take up several pages, so I wish simply to acknowledge their overall contribution here.

I'd like to thank the team at Blanvalet/Transworld and everyone at Gaeb literary agency. Without you a book like this would not have been possible.

But my extra special thanks go to you, my dear reader, for daring to enrol in this adventure. If you liked the book and think others might too, then do please pass on your recommendation.

Marc Elsberg
Vienna, July 2020

marcelsberg.com

Q&A with Marc Elsberg

What do you see as the biggest threat to our society?
Growing factions within societies and the global community. They make the conciliation necessary to fight major
threats like COVID-19, the looming climate catastrophe and
conflict management increasingly difficult, if not impossible.

***Greed* is about unleashed capitalism. How can a topic like
this be made into a thriller?**
Every topic can be turned into a thriller. I think the truly
ground-breaking point here is the scientific solution I am
able to present. Some might do that in a non-fiction book. I
wrap it up into a thriller.

What inspired you to write this novel?
The development of the world's societies during the last decades, on one hand. On the other hand, the ground-breaking
work of a few scientists – physicists and mathematicians – at
the London Mathematical Laboratory. They are shaking the
foundations of our political and economic paradigms, and
show the underlying mechanisms of a constructive solution.

***Greed* is fiction. Could it become reality?**
The events in *Greed* mirror real life even more now than

when I wrote it, as I anticipated. Even before COVID-19 struck, these events were a reality in many places. Worldwide conflicts had been on the rise, internationally and nationally. Just think of the US–Chinese trade war, Brexit, or popular uprisings such as Occupy, Podemos in Spain, the Umbrella movement in Hong Kong and the Yellow Vest movement in France. And now, due to the coronavirus, we face the worst economic crisis in decades – exactly the scenario in *Greed*.

In what way is *Greed* a global novel?
The concepts presented offer a new perspective on dealing with some of the world's most important challenges. They concern everyone on this planet.